JAN — — 2017

DEAD COLD BREW

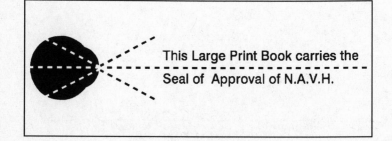

This Large Print Book carries the
Seal of Approval of N.A.V.H.

A COFFEEHOUSE MYSTERY

DEAD COLD BREW

CLEO COYLE

THORNDIKE PRESS
A part of Gale, Cengage Learning

GALE
CENGAGE Learning®

Farmington Hills, Mich • San Francisco • New York • Waterville, Maine
Meriden, Conn • Mason, Ohio • Chicago

GALE
CENGAGE Learning

LIBRARY OF CONGRESS CATALOGING-IN-PUBLICATION DATA

Names: Coyle, Cleo, author.
Title: Dead cold brew / Cleo Coyle.
Description: Large print edition. | Waterville, Maine : Thorndike Press, 2017. |
    Series: A coffeehouse mystery | Series: Thorndike Press large print mystery
Identifiers: LCCN 2016046409| ISBN 9781410494429 (hardback) | ISBN 141049442X
    (hardcover)
Subjects: LCSH: Cosi, Clare (Fictitious character)—Fiction. | Women
    detectives—Fiction. | Murder—Investigation—Fiction. | Coffeehouses—Fiction. |
    Large type books. | BISAC: FICTION / Mystery & Detective / General. | GSAFD:
    Mystery fiction.
Classification: LCC PS3603.O94 D415 2017b | DDC 813/.6—dc23
LC record available at https://lccn.loc.gov/2016046409

Published in 2017 by arrangement with The Berkley Publishing Group, an imprint of Penguin Publishing Group, a division of Penguin Random House LLC

Printed in Mexico
1 2 3 4 5 6 7 21 20 19 18 17

I believe cats to be spirits come to earth. A cat, I am sure, could walk on a cloud without coming through.

— Jules Verne

This book is dedicated to the memory of Nemo, Punkin, and "Little Dick" Grayson, three New York strays who lifted our earthly spirits — and now walk among the clouds.

ACKNOWLEDGMENTS

Dead Cold Brew is the sixteenth entry in our Coffeehouse Mysteries. As our longtime readers know, I have written every one with my very talented spouse, Marc Cerasini. I couldn't ask for a better partner — in writing or in life.

Both Marc and I have been long intrigued by the stunning fate of Italy's SS *Andrea Doria*. Though the mystery in these pages is fictional, the shipwreck was all too real, and we are grateful to the sources that provided details of that tragic history, including *Life* magazine (August 6, 1956).

For further reading on the subject, our suggestions include: Alvin Moscow's *Collision Course,* perhaps the best all-round history; Richard Goldstein's *Desperate Hours,* which tells the story through the testimonies of survivors and eyewitnesses; and Kevin F. McMurray's *Deep Descent,* which focuses on attempts by scuba divers to explore the sunken hulk, despite the perils.

A few of New York City's many "secret places" were also important to this tale.

The real-life model for Gus Campana's jewelry shop and backhouse is located at 93 Perry Street. You can view photos of the property at Nick Carr's website *Scouting New York:* scoutingny.com/the-secret -courtyard-on-perry-street.

Author H. P. Lovecraft used this very Perry Street address in a 1926 short story "He," which you can read in *The Call of Cthulhu and Other Weird Stories* by H. P. Lovecraft (Penguin 20th Century Classics, 1999).

Our second secret place is found inside the 21 Club, a New York City institution with a history that stretches back to the dark days of the Volstead Act. Today you can *legally* partake of a cocktail at this historic speakeasy — as long as you're of drinking age, of course! And its kitchen continues to serve one of the most famous menus in the city. Learn more at: 21club.com

To learn about more secret New York places mentioned in our book, drop by our website: coffeehousemystery.com.

For coffee inspiration in this entry in the series, we thank the New York–based coffee company Joe and its flagship store in Greenwich Village (joe-newyork.com) as well as Intelligentsia Coffee of Chicago, LA, and NYC (intelligentsiacoffee.com), and Big Island Coffee Roasters of Hawaii (bigis landcoffeeroasters.com).

Our interaction with New York's Finest is always nothing but the finest, and we thank them for providing answers to our questions, and risking their blue lives every day. Do bear in mind that this is a work of amateur sleuth fiction, and the rules occasionally get bent — or witness "corrected," as Sergeant Emmanuel Franco might say.

A continued caffeinated round of applause goes to everyone at our publisher who helped put this book into your hands. Special thanks to Kate Seaver, our editor, whose valuable suggestions made our story stronger. Cheers also go out to assistant editor Katherine Pelz for keeping us on track; to senior production editor Stacy Edwards and copyeditor Marianne Aguiar for their kind diligence. We also sincerely thank our designers Rita Frangie and Kristin del Rosario, as well as Roxanne Jones in publicity for their hard work.

Another salute goes to artist Cathy Gendron for her unique and striking covers.

To John Talbot, our longtime agent, we

send heartfelt appreciation for the treasure of his support and professionalism.

Last but far from least, special thanks to everyone whom we could not mention by name, including friends, family, and so many of you who read our books and send us notes via e-mail, our website's message board, and on social media. Your encouragement keeps us going, and we cannot thank you enough for that.

Our virtual coffeehouse is always open. Marc and I invite you to join our Coffeehouse community at coffeehousemystery .com where you will find recipes, coffee picks, and a link to stay in touch by signing up for our newsletter.

— Cleo Coyle,
New York City

Drown your troubles in coffee.

— Unknown

People who drink to drown their sorrow should be told that sorrow knows how to swim.

— Ann Landers

PROLOGUE

11:10 PM, July 25, 1956
Off the coast of Nantucket

He was red-faced again, too much wine at dinner.

In the ship's dining room Angelica Campana watched her husband drink, all smiles — until the gallant ship's officer complimented her dress, her hair, made her laugh.

That's when the storm clouds returned, forming in Gustavo's dark, cold gaze. Their tablemates failed to notice. Nor did they question her husband's thirst for more Primitivo. They saw only the fine fabric of his suit, the oily smoothness of his flattery. But Angelica saw the portents. And she knew what was coming.

Alone in their cabin, she resisted; she always did. He would laugh at her feeble defense, then at her tears as he would belittle her, force himself on her.

The brat of a boy had grown into a conceited man, spinning righteous reasons for his "punishments," reasons she believed, until the light of love, *real* love, had shown her another truth —

There was nothing wrong with her. He was the twisted one, taking pleasure from her pain.

As a backward teenage bride, orphaned in the terrible war, she believed she'd found a savior. For too long she had endured his filthy accusations and stinging slaps, even prayed to God for forgiveness . . . and then her own death. Until her baby came. After that, she prayed for strength. Not an end to life, but a chance to make a new one for herself and her little Perla.

In time, he grew bored with her and took a mistress. The beatings stopped and life improved — until these last few months, when the storms returned.

That night, aboard the elegant *Andrea Doria,* in the depths of the fateful fog, she prayed her hardest, even as his fat fingers strangled her slender wrist, even as his free hand rose high to administer his brutal "correction" for her "whorish flirtations" —

But the blow never came. A screech of rending metal froze his arm, and then a terrible impact flung husband and wife against the steel bulkhead.

The awful crash ended the man's curses,

14

but not his contempt. When she groped for help, he shoved her away.

A moment before, she feared the horrible names he called her would be heard by the others in first class. Now only the gushing roar of water and cries of terrified souls filled the ship's corridors.

Amid the screams and chaos, she heard a woman shout —

"La nave sta affondando!" The ship is sinking!

Cold sea water gushed under their stateroom door as the ship tilted so severely she feared it would capsize. Instead, the mighty ocean liner rocked like a toy in a baby's tub before settling on one side. The earsplitting noises of the shipwreck quieted, too, and that's when she heard her little pearl —

"Mamma! Mamma!"

Despite the rising water and sloping floor, Angelica reached the bathroom door. Her husband had shoved the child inside and wedged a chair against the knob. Now the chair was gone, but the knob was jammed. Whatever crippled the ship had warped the door, trapping her four-year-old in a tiny room filling with water.

Angelica begged Gustavo to help.

But his focus remained on the dresser, his fat hands ripping open the top drawer with the same possessive greed he'd used to rip her gown.

The jewel! That's all he cares about. Not the beauty of the diamond or its rich history, but only for the fortune it will bring him in America.

Pig eyes, bright as polished jet, glanced her way as he thrust the silk bag under his lapel. Again she pleaded for help, but his weak chin lifted in smug superiority as his hand moved to a vest pocket.

When they first boarded the ship, he'd pulled out his jeweler's tools and fiddled with the stateroom door. Like their bedroom in Italy, he wanted the option of locking her in. Now he held the room's key, and she knew why.

He means to lock us in! Me and my little girl!

At dinner she'd watched him flirting with that young American, heard him boast about his family's jewelry business, his plan to help them start anew in New York — as he wished to start anew, a *free* man in a New World.

The shipwreck had given him an easy way to end the burden of his "harlot" wife and troublesome daughter.

"No!" Angelica cried. "I won't let you!"

She always thought herself weak and helpless. Now a power rose in her that she could not explain. Like a rocket ignited, she flew across the room, years of abuse propelling her petite form into his thick body.

Shocked by the attack, his feet slipped out from under him.

"Mamma! Mamma!"

The baby's cries sent her over the edge. Protective ferocity drove her now, an instinct so primitive, it blocked all senses. She even failed to hear or see the two men who burst in on a rescue mission.

The men gawked at the young Italian beauty in the shredded evening gown, her body draped over a heavyset, middle-aged man. Unsure what she was doing, they focused instead on the little girl's cries behind a warped door.

The pair waded across the room. The first man, a strong, young Italian with a head of thick, dark hair, kicked in the door and snatched up the child. Turning to her parents, he finally realized what was taking place.

The young beauty straddling her husband was not giving him aid. She was holding his head *down.*

The men exchanged glances, but — for very different reasons — neither interfered.

In the ruined stateroom of the sinking ship, two silent witnesses watched Angelica

Campana drown her husband in the rising waters of the dark, cold deep.

ONE

Sixty years later . . .

A pelting rain transformed the Village Blend's French windows into tiny, wood-framed waterfalls. I pulled my sweater tight against the autumn chill and considered the predawn clouds.

Sure, the weather was lousy, and it was the first day of another long workweek, but (all due respect to the Carpenters) I utterly refused to let rainy days or Mondays get *me* down.

Why should they? I was back home in New York, once again managing my beloved Greenwich Village coffeehouse and living in the same city as the man I loved. Everything felt so right, what could possibly go wrong — other than my opening team calling in late?

Hey, an easy enough problem to handle.

Switching tunes, I swayed across the restored plank floor to the "Rhythm of the

Rain." Humming the old Cascades hit, I pulled upside-down chairs from the café tabletops, setting things right as I went.

Next I calibrated the espresso machine, restocked our dairy products, and accepted the pastry delivery. I was about to kindle a blaze in the brick hearth to dispel the dampness when my phone buzzed.

"Madame? I'm surprised you're awake. It's only —"

"Six fifteen AM. I'm well aware of the time, dear."

"Is everything all right?"

"That's the question I have for you."

"Excuse me?"

"Something's not right with Matteo."

I almost laughed. "And you just figured that out?"

"Don't crack wise at this hour, Clare. Withstanding wit takes at least *two* pots of coffee, and I'm only on my first."

"That's not wit. It's crankiness. I haven't had *any* coffee yet."

"Then you have my sympathy, but not my surrender."

"What makes you think there's a problem with our intrepid coffee hunter?"

"I'm his mother. I can sense these things. Didn't you — with Joy?"

"Plenty. But mostly in her teen years . . ."

20

Which made me reconsider my employer's concern, given my ex-husband's penchant for acting like an overgrown adolescent (seeking thrills and shunning consequences).

"Okay, you got me. How can I help?"

"If you wouldn't mind using that snooping sense of yours to fact find for me, I'd appreciate it."

How could I say no? Matteo Allegro and I were no longer partners in marriage, but thanks to his mother, we were now coupled in business.

Not that it happened overnight.

After Matt and I split, I spent ten years in the quiet suburbs of New Jersey, raising my young daughter through grade school and high school, Girl Scouts and girlfriends, broken toys and broken hearts — until she headed back to the city on her own, a confident young woman, ready for Manhattan's crowded streets and one of the country's best culinary schools.

I'd hardly had time to mourn my empty nest before Matt's mother called with a generous arrangement. She hired me back into the Allegro family firm, not only as a manager and master roaster, but also as a partner and heir.

Now my ex-husband and I had good

reasons to put the past behind us. Not just for ourselves, but for Joy, because it was our deepest wish to leave this thriving coffee business as a legacy to our daughter.

Once again, the Village Blend was the center of my life, along with its diverse blend of customers — from young hipsters to senior hippies; aspiring actors to investment bankers; NYU students to nearly every badge working the Sixth Precinct of the NYPD.

We all depended on Matt to source the best coffees in the world. So if he had a problem, it had the potential to hurt our entire business.

"I'll see what I can find out, Madame. I promise."

"Good."

I stifled a yawn.

"You sound tired. Are you getting enough sleep?"

"That community board meeting last night went on forever, and the official from Sanitation refused to move the Dumpsters from that vacant building down the block. He says the property is private and it's the owner's responsibility, but the owner halted renovations and left the country. Now partying kids are using the Dumpsters to boost themselves onto the fire escape and up to the roof. The police can't waste officers babysitting a Dumpster 24/7. But the city *should* do something before someone gets hurt . . ."

Madame listened until I was tired of hearing myself vent. She then reminded me that bureaucracies were like bus routes: "Wait a little while and a better driver will come along . . ."

Shifting subjects, her voice suddenly dropped an octave — a tone I only heard when she felt grave concern.

"Clare . . . have you seen the newspapers this morning?"

"No. I just came down to open when you called."

"Well, when you do, I'm here for you."

"You're there for me? Why? What's in the papers?"

When she demurred on saying anything more (except a hasty good-bye), I gritted my teeth and gazed longingly at the espresso machine. A double wouldn't be enough. I could tell already —

This was going to be a triple-shot day.

Two

Fifteen minutes later, my ex-husband buzzed for entry.

Matt was drenched and shivering from the chilly downpour, an irony considering his tropical tan and the designer sunglasses dangling from his T-shirt's neckline.

I opened the door with one hand while closing my mouth around a buttermilk-tender sample of our new Farmhouse Apple Cake Muffins, my own recipe with the baker's addition of Cinnamon-Vanilla Glaze. (The perfect kiss of spice and sweetness; the very description I'd used for Matt's smooches, once upon a time. If not for his compulsive need to spread them around the globe — the kisses, not the glaze — we still might be husband and wife.)

"Your mother and I were just talking about you," I informed him while licking my fingers clean.

"And this is news? Now are you going to

let me in or let me drown?"

I stepped aside, and he moved through the doorway, dripping Niagara.

"I thought you were still in Costa Rica for the harvest."

"I was, and I'm going back. Urgent business forced me to take a red-eye from Juan Santamaria to JFK . . ."

As he spoke, he shrugged out of his hooded Windbreaker and hand-combed his disheveled, dark hair. That's when I smelled something far less appealing than apples and cinnamon.

"Well *that* explains it."

"Explains what?"

"Why you're so . . . shall we say *pungent*? You're suffering from jet lag."

"I've been back for two days."

"Is there a plumbing problem at *Casa* Breanne?" (That seemed doubtful. Matt's fashionable wife ran her personal life with the same zealous efficiency as she ran her fashionable magazine.) "The Queen of *Trend* usually keeps you pampered with the latest fancy soap and designer cologne."

Matt sniffed his shirt and frowned. "I'll shower at the health club later."

"I'd suggest *sooner*. Unless the hot new trend is *eau de* body odor."

"Very funny. Now thank me. I brought

over your consignment in the van."

"From the warehouse? Why were you in Red Hook at the crack of dawn?"

"I told you I had business to take care of. And so do you." He draped his sopping Windbreaker over a chair near the now-crackling fireplace and waved me over to the coffee bar. "Sit. And brace yourself for another reason to thank me, because I have news. *Big* news."

I resisted the temptation to roll my eyes. The last time Matt had "big news" it involved his honorary judgeship at a Panamanian beauty contest.

While Matt pulled us fresh shots, I checked my watch. "Will you please get on with it? My morning baristas are late, I still have to mop up that ocean you dripped, and we open in twenty minutes —"

"I know that. Who do you think managed this place while you were playing footsie with the flatfoot in DC?"

"You now have *ten seconds* to tell me —"

"Okay!" He slid my espresso across the bar. "Drink up and *listen*. The Village Blend has been asked to create an exclusive signature coffee blend for a brand-new luxury cruise liner."

I blinked. "You're right. That is huge."

"It's huger than huge . . ." He took the

26

stool next to mine, dark eyes gleaming. "Think of it, Clare. A luxury cruise liner carrying thousands of passengers every year, all of them drinking our coffee. Think of what it will do for our brand. All we need to do is come up with an affordable version of your Billionaire Blend . . ."

Creating the world's finest (and most expensive) coffee blend had thrust this century-old business into an international spotlight, so I shouldn't have been all that surprised at this chance to supply a luxury cruise liner. In terms of volume, however, that rarefied "Billionaire" roast was a Lilliputian part of our bottom line, available to a select group of elite clientele, only a few times a year.

Matt was clearly proposing a broader opportunity. I could already imagine contented travelers sipping an exclusive Village Blend espresso while gazing out at the Atlantic — or was it the Pacific?

"When and where will this ship sail?"

"There's a shakedown cruise next week, she goes from New York to Nova Scotia and back, staff only to work out the kinks. Then she tests passengers on short hops before embarking on ports of call in the Med and United Arab Emirates, where the real money is."

"I'll need some inspiration for this blend. What's the ship called?"

"The *Andrea Doria.*"

I stared at my ex long enough to comprehend his reply. Then I punched him.

"Ouch!" He rubbed his arm. "What was that for?!"

"I'm barely awake. We're about to open. And you waste my time with a stupid joke?"

"It's no joke!"

I blinked at the man, wondering when he'd switched from caffeine to crack. "You want me to come up with a boffo coffee blend to serve on a ship sitting two hundred feet below the Atlantic?"

"Clare, are you nuts?"

"Me?" I clamped my hands on his muscular shoulders. "The *Andrea Doria* hasn't carried passengers since before we were born. She was struck on her way to New York and sank to the bottom of the ocean!"

THREE

With the patience of a professor explaining thermodynamics to a chimpanzee, Matt informed me that he was *not* talking about the sunken flagship of the Italia Line.

"This will be a brand-new *replica* of the *Andrea Doria.* Get it now?"

"A replica?" I sat back, appalled. "Why rebuild a sunken ship? That's bad luck!"

"Oh, please. That's your nonna talking. Don't be so Old World."

"Excuse me, but I'll take Old World charm over New World smarm any day."

"Fine, then create the coffee as a matter of honor. The original *Andrea Doria* was the pride of Italy."

"That's your argument? The same come-on as every restaurant in Esquilino. '*Prego, prego.* Our pasta is the pride of Italy!'"

"You can't compare the tourist traps of Rome to the *Andrea Doria*! That ship was a jewel on the ocean. Gourmet food. Top-notch service. Celebrity passengers, even royalty. Her decks were decorated with original art and sculpture, all of it lost when she went down. She was a beauty that deserves resurrection — and a loaded investor decided to do just that."

Matt waved his smartphone. "I want you to see something."

A few taps, and we were watching a prospectus documentary with a smooth storyteller talking up his dream come true, a new, ultramodern *Andrea Doria* that closely resembled the original — but with Wi-Fi, spa, fitness facilities, and other amenities today's travelers expected.

"Who is this narrator?"

"That's Victor Fontana, head of the consortium that built the ship. He's some kind of investor with a playboy reputation in Europe. You'll meet him soon, but we've already made an impression. Fontana is one of our regular Billionaire Blend customers — it's how we got this opportunity."

Matt froze the screen. "That's him."

Dressed with casual elegance, Victor Fontana's impressive appearance matched his reputation. Fortyish with an aquiline nose and direct chin, the man projected relaxed confidence and sharp intelligence, an attractive combination I'd seen often, in my recent brushes with the upper echelons of high tech.

Intense purpose shined in his aquamarine eyes, an aggressive energy nicely softened by boyish, Harry Potter glasses, shaggy brown "surfer" hair, and a crookedly enthusiastic grin.

"Fontana announced this plan last July," Matt continued. "He timed the replica's launch to coincide with the sixtieth anniversary of the original *Andrea Doria*'s sinking. They're a few months behind schedule, but the superstructure of the new ship is finally completed. Now she's outfitted, and he's preparing to unveil her to the world."

"I don't know . . . It still feels wrong."

"This is a lucrative opportunity. Once in a lifetime. Are you going to let superstition drive your business decisions?"

"Don't put it like that."

"It *is* like that. You can use logic or cast runes and visit a palm reader. Which is it going to be?"

I hated to admit it, but I was out of arguments. No matter what I thought of the project, it was a tempting offer. Someone was going to supply the coffee to that ship. Why not the Village Blend?

At my reluctant thumbs-up, Matt clapped

his hands. "Good decision!"

"Not so fast." I grabbed his damp tee as he tried to dash away. "I still have questions. For starters, if this is a true replica, the ship's galley may be re-creating the original menus. What kind of coffee did the *Andrea Doria* serve?"

Matt sat back down. "As far as I know, the surviving menu lists 'Italian and American coffees.' "

"That's it? No other details?"

He shrugged.

"Then I'll have to do research."

"We don't have time for that! Look, it's a *luxury* cruise liner, filled with sophisticated travelers who know quality when they taste it. Just create a versatile, premium blend that brews up rich, sweet espressos, magnificently complex cups of French press, and a smooth, clean cold brew."

"And while I'm at it, I'll cure the common cold and compose a thesis on the meaning of life."

"It's a tall order, I admit. But you have two weeks."

"Two weeks?!"

"Or we forfeit to the other roasters."

"Other roasters?!"

"Did I forget to mention this is a competition? There are five roasters in all, four of them European. We're the only Americans invited to participate, so it's double the honor."

"Oh, Matt, you made this sound like a sure thing."

"It is a sure thing. All you have to do is come up with an *Andrea Doria* blend that will blow those investors away, present it to the judges, and we're in."

"I don't know . . ."

"You can do it. Come on. Remember, I went along with that whole Billionaire Blend project, despite the fact that it took up too much of my time and failed to deliver nearly as much profit as we'd hoped. Now I'm asking you to come through for me. I need the revenue. *We* need the revenue."

Matt didn't have to sell me on that. Salaries were up, along with inflation and taxes. And I hadn't forgotten Madame's belief that her son was in trouble. If it was financial trouble (my assumption from this exchange), how could I say no?

"Okay," I replied. "But I *insist* on doing some research."

Matt thought a moment and nodded. "Why don't you talk to my godfather, Gustavo Campana?"

"Gus? The jeweler?"

"Gus was on that final crossing. He survived the *Andrea Doria* shipwreck . . ."

Everyone in New York had heard of the Campana family's jewelry business. They were renowned for creating highly original pieces for an exclusive clientele — musicians, actors, the superrich.

Despite all the celebrity attention, Gus was a down-to-earth artisan who remained dedicated to quality craftsmanship. I'd spoken with the charming elderly man dozens of times, but never had a clue he'd survived an epic sea disaster.

"Did Gus ever tell you about the sinking?" I asked.

"He never said a word. It was Mother who let me in on that secret. He and his late wife, Angelica, survived, along with their daughter Perla — but she was little more than a baby at the time."

"If Gus never mentioned his experience to you, why would he talk to me?"

"I'll tell you what . . . Tomorrow we'll visit him together. I'm sure he'll open up — especially if you bring a box of those cannoli cupcakes you baked for Mother's last birthday party. Gus took home a half-dozen leftovers."

"It's worth a try. I've bribed harder cases than Gus with my goodies."

"Your goodies?" With a teasing smile, Matt leaned over the V-neck of my sweater. "You know that's a perfect setup for a wisecrack."

"Are you angling for another punch?"

"Not unless it's foreplay."

I pushed him away.

"Okay, I'm going . . ." He moved to grab his Windbreaker. "Just don't be disappointed if Gus doesn't remember the *Doria*'s coffee. When your ship is sinking, you've got bigger concerns than fine dining."

"I get it."

"Good. I'll see you —" His words stopped short when he noticed the folded newspaper in his jacket pocket. "Oh, yeah, almost forget. How's your flatfoot boyfriend? I don't smell his drugstore buy-it-by-the-gallon aftershave, so I'm guessing he's not around this morning."

"If you're referring to Mike Quinn, he's on an overnight stakeout. I'll be seeing him sometime today."

"He's okay then?"

That question surprised me. Although Matt had gained a grudging respect for Quinn over time, it struck me as odd that he'd ask after the man's health, and I said so.

"My concern is for you, Clare. I know you

35

have feelings for that Boy Scout, so I figured you'd be tied up in knots over this."

"Over what?"

Matt pulled out the damp New York tabloid and showed me the front page. The picture was a target, its bull's-eye an NYPD shield haloed by an explosion of lurid red ink.

The headline was even more disturbing . . .

OPEN SEASON ON THE NYPD:
4 COPS SHOT IN 3 DAYS!

FOUR

Matt handed me the paper. "Have they arrested anyone connected to the shootings? The article doesn't have many details. What did Quinn tell you?"

When I didn't reply he studied my expression.

"You didn't know, did you?"

"No. Your mother tried to warn me, but with my morning team late, I haven't had time to run to a newsstand or read the papers."

"Well, you might want to read this one." He slipped on his still-wet jacket and shivered. "I'm off for that shower — the one at the health club, not the one that nearly drowned me. See you tomorrow."

"Tomorrow?" I echoed, staring at the headline. "What's tomorrow?"

"We're going to see Gus, *remember*?"

"Oh. Right!"

"And don't forget those cannoli cupcakes.

I wouldn't mind eating one or two or four myself."

As soon as Matt pushed through the front door, I opened the paper and began to read — until I was interrupted by the arrival of my (late) morning shift.

"Hey, boss. On break already to read the paper? Wow, the perks of management never end."

Esther Best (shortened by a forefather from Bestovasky) unwound her black spiderweb lace shawl. The commando overcoat came off next, to reveal zaftig hips and a short-sleeved *Poetry Slam* tee that displayed her literary tribute tattoos. With a rare smile on my goth barista's fetching face, I let her barb pass without comment.

Nancy Kelly, my youngest barista, staggered in behind Esther. Her Midwest farm girl cheerfulness was absent today, her wheat-colored braids coming loose, her eyes puffy and red.

"Coffee," she croaked. "Nancy needs coffee *bad.*"

"Tired?" I asked.

"We didn't get much sleep, which is why we're late, by the way." She paused to glare at Esther. "My *roommate* was up all hours, listening to a creepy guy with a creepier voice recite really creepy poetry."

"That was Allen Ginsberg," Esther said, examining her nails. "I always listen to Ginsberg's poetry when I'm feeling down."

"Why? To push you over the edge? And you call that *yacketayakking* poetry? Ugh. After work, I'm buying earplugs. That demented maniac gave me nightmares."

"That's the idea. I get my best poems from nightmares."

"Okay, enough!" I declared. "I need one of you to fill the pastry case and the other to unroll the rain mat at the front door."

"But the storm is over, boss. Look outside. The sun is shining."

"Fine, forget the mat. Just make sure all the rain that *our* Matt tracked in is mopped up. Flip a coin on the chores and get going. We open in eight minutes."

Still bickering — but quietly now — my Odd Couple got to work. I opened the paper, only to be interrupted again, by another staff member, my longtime assistant manager, Tucker Burton.

"What are you doing here, Tuck? You're ten hours early."

"Only for this job . . ." He frowned down at Matt's puddles before dodging Esther on a mission with her mop. "I have another gig starting in two hours, and I need some strong java mojo to pump me up."

"What's the other job? Theatrical, I assume?"

He headed for the espresso machine. "I'm holding auditions all day."

"Another public service announcement?" Esther asked. "What is it this time? The dangers of salt? Sugar? Breathing?"

"I've been hired to direct a charity show at Irving Plaza. A superhero extravaganza for kids with cancer."

"So what's it going to be, a chorus line for men in tights?"

Tuck waved his hand. "A musical revue will hardly do. These kids have seen all the movies. They expect epic fight scenes, and that's what I'm going to give them."

"Rubber sets and breakaway furniture?"

"Precisely."

"How exciting," Nancy gushed from behind the pastry case. "Will the dark and brooding Batman be there? And the hunky Superman?"

"Both capes will be fluttering," Tuck assured her. "And we'll have that hot new dynamic duo Panther Man and Cub. I've also got to find an Iron Man, a Thor, and a square-jawed Captain America."

Nancy sidled up to him. "You know, I wouldn't mind helping you find a really hot Superman. Someone a Lois Lane like me could swoon over."

Tuck tossed his floppy mop. "This is Greenwich Village, sugar. Finding a Superman is easy. What I need is an *actor.*"

"One who also happens to fill out the tights?" Esther cracked.

Tuck shot back his espresso. "That wouldn't hurt, either."

Nancy's second offer to join the Great Superman Search was interrupted by the bell over our front door.

"Are you serving?" asked a desperate-looking young woman with a bulging NYU backpack. "My first law school class starts in thirty minutes, and I need coffee *badly.*"

"You've come to the right mountaintop, oh, Decaffeinated One!" Esther intoned. "And props for using the grammatically correct *badly.*"

"That means, *come right in,*" I told the law student. As I flipped our CLOSED sign to OPEN, she headed inside. That's when I spied a familiar face.

"Hey, Clare, how's it going?"

The jovial tenor belonged to Detective Finbar "Sully" Sullivan, twenty-two-year veteran of the NYPD and right-hand man to the decorated narcotics detective who'd won my heart.

As Sully entered, I gave him a hug and

41

saw the man himself approach our door, Detective Lieutenant Michael Ryan Francis Quinn, the respected head of the department's famous OD Squad.

Quinn's commanding presence filled the coffeehouse the way his broad-shouldered silhouette filled the sunlit door, the way his courage and caring filled my life.

"Hi, Clare."

"Hi, Mike."

His NYPD jacket was rumpled from the all-nighter, and the dark sand of his five-o'clock shadow stubbled the hard line of his jaw. But despite his lack of sleep, there was no sign of fatigue in the blue of his switchblade eyes, or the sweet-sly smile he offered me.

"I'd give you a kiss," I told him, "but I'd rather your mouth start moving for another reason."

Quinn's smile all but vanished when I unfolded the newspaper still clutched in my hand.

" 'Open Season on the NYPD,' " I read aloud. " '*Four* Cops Shot in *Three* Days.' And not *one* word from you. So come in, please. Because I want answers, and I want them now."

FIVE

"Easy, Cosi. Don't overreact —"

"Overreact? To what? The fact that you're a member of a subset being actively hunted and gunned down? Or that you kept it from me?"

Quinn raised his hands in mock surrender. "The press is blowing a couple of random events out of proportion to sell papers, that's all."

"That's not all —"

"True, but Sully and I just spent twelve long hours arresting and flipping a street dealer who just gave us the means to nail the most notorious suppliers of synthetic drugs in the five boroughs. Can't we have a little coffee and kindness before we start explaining why you shouldn't worry?"

I was no less desperate for answers on the shootings, but Quinn got me on that one.

I directed them to the espresso bar, tied on my apron, and soon the two were drinking up steaming cups of my new City Sunrise blend and chowing down on a mountain of fresh-baked muffins.

"Okay . . ." I rested my elbows on the counter. "Start explaining why I shouldn't worry about these shootings."

Sully couldn't do much explaining with half a Snickerdoodle Muffin in his mouth. Swiping crumbs off his NYPD jacket, he pointed to Quinn, who told me —

"The first incident happened during a vertical patrol in Brooklyn. That's a routine sweep of a building's stairwell. A rookie housing cop stumbled into the middle of an armed robbery. Cop wounded, suspect caught. Happens a few times a year."

"I see. Next?"

Now Quinn's mouth was stuffed with a Maple-Glazed Oatmeal Muffin, so Sully took over —

"Shooting number two was a traffic cop, Clare. She was writing parking tickets in Queens when —"

"She took a bullet in the shoulder. But she's fine." Quinn forcefully jumped in, mouth still full. "Treated and released."

It was quick, but I saw Sully and Quinn exchange a grim glance.

"What was that look?" I challenged.

"What look?" Quinn asked.

"Don't play with me. Who shot that poor woman?"

"It's right there in your paper." Quinn tapped the tabloid. "No one was apprehended, but the blame was put on an ongoing gang feud in the neighborhood."

"Then what about shootings three and four?" I asked. "I scanned the article, but there's very little beyond the fact that two cops were shot last night."

Both detectives went suspiciously silent. Quinn looked cool as a cuke. But Sully was starting to sweat. Before I could press them, Sully's smartphone buzzed —

"It's Fran, phoning from her mother's place in Rochester." Looking relieved, he glanced at Quinn. "I'll just take this outside . . ."

He also took our seasonal Pecan Pie Muffin (a beautifully caramelized cross between a mini pecan pie and a breakfast muffin). "See you soon, Clare!"

"Give your wife my best," I called to him. "And let her know I finally typed up that Baileys Chocolate Chip Cookie recipe. I'll e-mail it tonight."

"Thanks for her — and me." Sully winked, waving the muffin. "I could have eaten that whole plate myself last Sunday!"

As he headed out the door, Quinn threw

me a half smile. "I think he did eat the whole plate, didn't he?"

"Half the plate. You ate the other half."

"Speaking of second helpings. I'd love a refill," Quinn said, holding out his cup. "And maybe one of those cute little Pumpkin Pie Muffins?"

I delivered both. "Now where were we?"

"On the Baileys Irish Cream Cookies?"

"On the third and fourth *shootings.*"

Quinn made a show of shrugging. "Those two incidents happened last night. I haven't been officially briefed on the details."

"*Officially* briefed? But you've heard all about it *unofficially,* haven't you?" His expression appeared unreadable — to the general public. Not to me. "What are you hiding, Michael Quinn? What don't you want me to know?"

"Take easy, Cosi, or I'll charge you with harassment."

"Don't joke about this!"

"Look, sweetheart, there are thirty-five thousand cops in this city. Even if one of them got shot every single day, the odds of anyone you know getting hurt are miniscule. You'd probably have a better chance at winning the New York Lottery —"

A sharp crack interrupted him, loud and unmistakable. A gunshot.

46

We both froze as the blast echoed off the buildings along Hudson, followed by frightened cries and stampeding feet.

Finally, a shocked silence descended, broken only by a woman's hysterical plea —

"Oh, God! Someone call 911. A policeman's been shot!"

Six

"Stay inside, Clare!" Quinn shouted as he flew out the front door.

I ignored the command. If someone was hurt, I wanted to help, so I pushed through right behind him — and stopped dead.

After a chilly morning in a shuttered coffeehouse, I was blinded by the dazzling poststorm sunshine. Before my eyes could adjust, a powerful tug yanked me to the sidewalk.

"You should have stayed inside." Quinn's tone was not gentle.

I blinked away stars, to focus on the very large gun in his hands.

Quinn was down on one knee, crouched inside the Village Blend's recessed doorway. I was tucked behind him, squashed against the door.

"What do you see?"

Quinn didn't answer. He was too busy calling out a string of police codes into his smartphone. So I peeked above the broad shoulder of my human shield, at the scene on the street.

At first I saw only pedestrians, cowering behind parked cars, a trash can, even a mailbox.

Vehicular traffic flowed rush-hour normal along all four lanes of Hudson. But on the side street next to the Village Blend, a delivery van blocked traffic. The driver's side door hung open, and the driver himself was taking cover in a doorway, just like me.

In front of that van, a figure in an NYPD jacket was sprawled on the pavement. I could see red pooling around him.

"It's Sully," Quinn hissed, his white-knuckle grip tightening on his weapon.

Oh, God . . . I tried to rise higher for a better view, but Quinn dragged me down.

"The sniper is still out there." His hard gaze remained on the high windows and rooftops around us.

"Sully's hurt. He's bleeding," I rasped. "We have to do something!"

"I've called for backup, Clare, paramedics and SWAT. And if the shooter gives his position away, I'll take him out."

I could hear a siren. Police? An ambulance? Whatever it was, it seemed very far away.

Then someone cried out, and we instantly saw the reason: a young woman in a rose pink jogging suit was exiting a building. Eyes fixed on her smartphone, earphones muting the shouted warnings, she blithely walked into the line of fire. Even worse, when the jogger finally noticed the bleeding cop lying in the street, she froze like a mouse at last spotting the cobra.

"She's going to get killed —"

Quinn instinctively moved out of the doorway, and a bullet immediately shattered our front window frame beside his head. As he threw himself backward again, splinters peppered us both.

The shot snapped the jogger out of her paralysis. The young woman turned and ran back to her building at a speed that would do any Olympian proud.

An easy target, I thought, *so why didn't the sniper pull the trigger?*

I flashed on the newspaper headline, and knew the answer.

Because this shooter's one and only goal is to target cops!

I glanced at Sully. The man hadn't budged, but there was more blood pooling on the concrete.

That's when I made the decision. Praying I'd jumped to the right conclusion, I told

Mike —

"Don't move. *You're* the target. Not me."
Then I ran into the street.

SEVEN

A bone-chilling wind gusted in off the Hudson River, just a few blocks away. I wore no coat, only my slacks, a thin sweater, and an apron for warmth.

But that wasn't why I was shivering.

With every step I anticipated the thunderclap of the rifle, and the punch and burn of a bullet ripping through me. My spine tingled. I felt a bull's-eye on the back of my neck. Time slowed to a crawl, but I kept going.

I heard Quinn calling after me — okay, he was *yelling* at me like crazy — but it wasn't the most opportune time to debate my actions.

Meanwhile, the sirens seemed no closer, their advance slowed by rush-hour traffic, now at a complete stop along Hudson.

Finally, I dropped to the glacial concrete beside Sully's still form. His back was turned, so I shook his shoulder and called his name.

No response.

Quinn tried again to move out of cover —
and another shot dinged the Village Blend's
redbrick facade.

"Stay down!" I shouted. "I told you, the
sniper's only shooting at police!"

"And you know that . . . *for sure?*"

There was a shockingly calm irony in
Quinn's reply that shouldn't have surprised
me, given the countless firefights he'd been
in. But then he was the one who'd told
me —

*"Cool, clear thinking is what gets you
through. Emotion is what gets you killed . . ."*

I clung to that advice. Using Quinn as my
example, I beat down the rising panic as
another shot rang out. This one sounded
different and also much closer and easier to
pinpoint!

It had come from the rooftop *directly
across* from the Village Blend. The shot
failed to hit anyone (thank goodness), and
Quinn quickly returned fire, giving me
cover.

With no better target in plain sight, I realized the shooter might be trying to finish
off Sully, so before I administered first aid,
I decided to drag him behind the delivery
van. But when I turned him over, I changed

my mind.

Sully's gaze was unfocused, his eyelids fluttering, his pale flesh cold as the morning air.

My hands came away sticky with blood, and I soon found a ghastly hole above Sully's left elbow. I compressed the wound, but blood continued to gush around my fingers. If the flow was not stopped, Sully could bleed to death before the ambulance came.

As I untied my Village Blend apron and tugged it off, a creeping chill transferred from the pavement right up my spine. I quickly tore up the blue fabric, circled the strips around Sully's wound, and wound the apron strings around his arm, several inches above the injury.

When I pulled my instant tourniquet tight, Sully groaned.

"Hang in there, Sully! Help is coming . . ."

And, thank God, some was already here. Within a few seconds, I'd managed to slow the scarlet tide to a trickle.

Holding the tourniquet in place, I searched the rooftop directly across the street from the Village Blend but saw no one. Another *bang* came from there, and Quinn fired several times, appearing to scare the shooter back.

Now I scanned the entire area, looking for any others in need of help. That's when I noticed something moving on a nearby roof. It was that vacant building, the one I'd complained about at the community board meeting.

Kids had been using the Dumpsters to boost themselves onto the fire escape and up to the roof. But I doubted any partying was going on at this hour of the morning.

Something black and flowing fluttered into view and then disappeared again.

I shouted at Quinn, asking if he could see the building. The Village Blend sat on a corner, and the abandoned building was partway down the cross street we shared — it would be hard for Quinn to see from his vantage. But he wasn't paying attention to my pointing. He was on his smartphone again, his eyes on the rooftop directly across from the coffeehouse, where the loud *bang*s had gone off. Then his attention moved to the sky.

Why the sky?

Suddenly, my ears were battered as an NYPD helicopter swept over the building where we'd last heard shots fired. It flew so low the churning blades shook power lines and rattled windows and doors. Downdrafts battered the few pedestrians who remained.

Still tending Sully, I blinked against the maelstrom.

Men in SWAT team jackets hung out of the helicopter doors, searching the rooftop for the hidden sniper.

I jumped when a gentle hand touched my shoulder. Then I saw the pair of tense paramedics, here to treat Sully, and I felt a rush of relief.

The man and woman bent low to speak to me. I saw their lips move, but the hovering machines annihilated all sounds. It didn't matter. I understood and relinquished the tourniquet, so the paramedics could begin their (please, God!) lifesaving work.

Shivering, I got back on my feet and immediately spied officers in bulletproof vests, storming the building across the street. I shouted to them, trying to get their attention. But the noise was fierce, communication impossible.

Certain I'd spotted a second shooter that no one else had, I ran along the cross street, toward the empty building, confident Mike Quinn would see me and follow.

EIGHT

As I drew closer to the vacant structure, I heard the crash of breaking glass from somewhere above.

The building's windows were boarded up, the front door padlocked. An empty beer bottle plunged from the top of a rusting fire escape on the side of the building. As the glass shattered on two large Dumpsters, I saw a black object above, fluttering in the wind.

A flag? No! It was a *cape,* flapping behind a muscular, black-clothed figure on the top rung of the fire stairs. I quickly took cover behind a parked car, watching as the figure swung out on a rope and deftly rappelled down the pitted red facade, landing with a hollow clang on one of the Dumpsters before somehow releasing the rope and yanking it down after him.

That's when I saw the long rifle slung over one shoulder.

I turned my head, looking for Quinn, but he hadn't followed me. No one had. I was alone, about thirty yards from the shooter.

If I run for the police, I'll lose him.

As the only eyewitness, I refused to miss this chance to ID the perp. I felt for my mobile phone and silently cursed. I'd left it behind the espresso bar!

Standing as quietly and still as I could, I took mental pictures of the sniper as he leaped off the Dumpster and ran toward the river.

Okay. I have a basic description and a direction. I have to get back to Mike!

"Where the hell were you, Clare?"

Quinn's voice was barely audible over the sirens wailing at the crime scene. "I looked around and you were gone!"

"I saw a second shooter! I saw him!"

Quinn realized I was shivering and gasping for breath after my sprint back to the Village Blend. He took off his jacket, turned it inside out, and draped it around me, with NYPD markings hidden (just in case).

"There was no *second* shooter," Quinn said. "According to SWAT, the roof across from your coffeehouse was rigged with pyrotechnics, and —"

"Then I saw your sniper!"

Quinn lifted his smartphone again. "What did he look like? Tell me quickly. We'll drop a dragnet —"

"I only got a glimpse, but I saw the rifle and watched him run toward the Hudson River."

"Good, excellent, what was he wearing? What did he look like? Build, race, scars, features? Give me something to give to our search parties."

Uniformed cops were gathering around me now, waiting impatiently for a description.

"He looked like Panther Man!" I cried.

Quinn stared. "Who?"

"The comic book superhero?" asked one of the younger officers. "Are you joking?"

"No! He had the cape, the mask, the build, the trick rappelling rope. I saw him plain as pudding."

"Panther Man?"

At my wild-eyed nod, Quinn glanced at the other cops, most of whom were looking at me as if I'd been shot — *in the head.*

NINE

"But if you really saw someone dressed as Panther Man —"

"There's no *really* about it, Mike. That's what I saw . . ."

We were in a police car, siren blaring. Quinn's hard blue eyes never left the road. *Good thing, too. I didn't think it was possible to race through Manhattan at this speed, not during morning rush.*

I was sharing the front seat with him, and glad about it since one of my last trips in a cop car was a backseat perp ride to an interrogation room. (The view was much better up here.) Cars swerved, buses and taxis stopped dead, and pedestrians scrambled out of the way to give us room as we barreled east to the hospital.

"In the last sixty minutes, an army of officers found nothing, Clare. We dropped the dragnet and found no one dressed as Panther Man; no evidence of a discarded costume; no mask; no rope; no rifle. We searched the riverbank and every boat in the area. We searched buildings within the perimeter. We questioned pedestrians, frisked suspects in street clothes who fit the Panther Man build. How do you explain it?"

"I can't."

"Trauma can play tricks on the mind. Do you think you could have imagined —"

"I *know* what I saw. I'm not crazy!"

"Where are you getting *crazy*? I didn't say *crazy*. I only meant that stress can alter perceptions . . ."

Despite the seat belt, a sharp turn threw me against the passenger's door.

"I can't believe you don't believe me!"

"I didn't say that, either!"

We were shouting over the siren's wail — *How do cops think with all this noise?!* — but even I had to admit that the louder I talked, the crazier my claim sounded.

"What about surveillance cameras?" I asked.

"Detectives reviewing the area's traffic cameras saw nothing that could help —"

"But those are limited views, aren't they? The shooter could have found his way down an alley and into a building's subbasement, maybe through a hidden trapdoor —"

"Like Panther Man's Cat Cave?"

"He could have climbed a fence and hid in a private garden —"

"Up a tree, maybe?"

"Enough with the cop cracks! Your army of blue eyeballs isn't infallible. What about St. Luke's walled garden? Or the Chumley courtyard? There are secret places and tiny hideaways all over the West Village!"

"And our eyeballs aren't done looking yet. They're working to get hold of any private security camera feeds in the area and view them for clues. In the meantime, you're the only *eyewitness,* and you're going to have to provide us with more."

"I'll be happy to draw you a picture. Get me a pad and pen, and I'll —"

"No. A picture is a good idea. But you're not drawing it yourself."

"I know how to draw, Mike. I went to art school."

"Police sketch artists do more than draw. They're trained interrogators, like any other detective. Besides, we need to make it official. I'll request that an NYPD sketch artist meet us at the hospital."

"Fine," I said, adding a big nod in case he couldn't hear me.

Two minutes later Quinn wrapped up a conversation with the Sixth Precinct commander, and we arrived at the hospital. Inside, I had to sprint to keep up as he pushed his way across the crowded lobby and up to the admissions desk.

"I'm looking for a gunshot victim," Quinn said. "Sully Sullivan, NYPD."

The woman behind the desk raised an eyebrow. "Sully, you say?"

"*Finbar* Sullivan," I corrected, laying my hand over Mike's white-knuckle fist. "The ambulance picked him up about an hour ago. Can you tell me his condition?"

"Mr. Sullivan is in the Trauma and Shock Unit. I'm sorry, but I don't have any more information that I can —"

Quinn was off again. He didn't ask for directions, because he didn't need them. As head of the OD Squad, he'd been here often enough.

At the Trauma and Shock Unit, I beat Mike out of the elevator and to the nurse's desk.

"Excuse me, can you help me find a shooting victim?" I asked in rapid-fire New Yorkese. "Finbar Sullivan is his name, and I was told he was in this unit."

The woman in white closed the file she'd been reading and gave me a hard, bureaucratic stare.

"You're Mrs. Sullivan?"

"No, I, uh —"

"Mrs. Sullivan is visiting her family in Rochester," Mike explained. "Fran has been notified and is on her way back to the city."

The nurse shifted her eyes to Quinn. "And you are?"

"I'm Detective Sullivan's CO — commanding officer." He flashed his badge.

"And I'm Sully's friend," I said, jumping in.

"Friendship has no legal status, Ms. —"

"Cosi. Clare Cosi. I treated Sully until the ambulance arrived. Now I need to know if he's okay —"

"I can't give you any further information. You'll have to get it through the family."

"But his spouse isn't here —"

The nurse ignored my pleas and focused on Quinn. "And you, Officer —"

"Quinn. *Detective* Quinn."

"Well, *Detective,* if you're here on official police business, you may speak with the attending physician. But you'll have to wait here at the desk."

Then the nurse locked eyes with me. "There's a break room down the hall. I suggest you wait for the detective there."

TEN

Fifteen minutes later, feeling helpless and useless, I was pacing the hospital break room with the nurse's words still echoing in my ears.

"Friendship has no legal status . . ."

She wasn't wrong, and I didn't blame her. But, like a badly aimed bullet, the statement continued to ricochet inside me, hurting me for reasons I didn't want to face.

When the sketch artist finally arrived, I was grateful for something new to focus on besides my fears and worries.

All right, I thought, *here's something concrete to do. A way to help!*

Not that Sergeant Barry Sitko was similarly motivated — at least not outwardly. The sergeant looked more like an absent-minded academic than most law enforcement officers I'd encountered.

For starters, he wore lenses so thick I couldn't understand how he'd passed the

Police Academy vision exam. He'd totally forgotten to shave — for several days, apparently — and his graying hair hadn't seen a comb since he'd tumbled out of bed. Sitko's shield was buffed and shiny, but his blue uniform was rumpled and lightly dusted with powdered sugar, no doubt from a donut he'd grabbed on the way to our meeting.

As he introduced himself, he set a chair mere inches in front of me, and set down his backpack. When he took a seat, he produced a computer tablet.

"First, I need to know if you got a good look at the suspect's face. Could you determine sex, age, and race?"

"I was crouched behind a parked car to stay hidden, and I didn't glimpse him long, but I could tell the shooter was well-built with muscular arms, lean legs, and a strong-looking chest. He moved quickly and gracefully — like a cat. As for his face, he was wearing a mask."

"Then I needn't have dragged this along." Sitko set aside the tablet. "And I don't have to ask my next question, either."

"What's that?"

"If the person resembled someone famous, a celebrity, an actor, a sports figure, or a rock star."

"He did resemble someone famous. I recognized him instantly. It was Panther Man." When a lengthy pause ensued, I took a breath. "I know. You think I'm crazy, right?"

Sitko shook his head. "If anyone's crazy, it's the person running around dressed as the Caped Cat and shooting police officers."

"So you believe me. This isn't a waste of time?"

"It's the exact opposite, Ms. Cosi."

Sitko reached into the bag and pulled out an old-fashioned sketchbook and some pencils. "Why don't we draw a picture together. You tell me everything you remember from when you spotted this person until they fled the scene. I'll put pencil to paper and come up with a portrait . . ."

Ten minutes later, we both stared at the results.

"Yeah," Sitko said. "That's Panther Man. Too bad you didn't see his face. We could have narrowed it down to Adam West, Michael Keaton, Matt Affleck, that Aussie bloke, or any of the other actors who'd played the role over the past forty years."

"*Ben*. It's Ben Affleck."

"Your Panther Man looked like Ben Affleck?"

"No, I told you. I never saw his face. And

making fun of me won't help us find the shooter any faster."

"I wasn't making fun. If this person is a maniac, he likely has some kind of obsession with aspects of Panther Man, the same way the Colorado movie theater shooter immersed himself in the Batman universe before portraying himself as one of its characters."

The sergeant sat back in his chair. "You know it's possible that you didn't see Panther Man, either. What if you misinterpreted what you witnessed?"

He ripped his first sketch out of the pad and tossed it into the shallow wastepaper basket. Then he gripped the pencil. "We'll start again. First, let's talk about this cape business —"

"I saw a dark cape."

"Was it ribbed, like Panther Man's?"

"No, now that you mention it."

"It looked cheap?"

"The material did seem a bit flimsy . . . by the way it fluttered —" I paused, suddenly remembering Matt's drenched state when he first arrived at the Village Blend. "It rained this morning. A real downpour."

Sitko nodded. "And?"

"And, well . . . I suppose, in theory, what I could have seen was some kind of rain cape or poncho, even a garbage bag the shooter wrapped around himself to keep dry."

Sergeant Sitko nodded enthusiastically, and then frowned. "Now what about those ears?"

"He really was wearing a Panther Man mask, Sergeant."

"Then I'd say that fellow who poses as the Caped Cat in Times Square had better have a good alibi."

He began sketching again. The next portrait he showed me was still not right. "You moved the pointy ears down, to where human ears normally are —"

"I actually drew noise suppressors. These devices are used in conjunction with the type of high-powered rifle you saw over the perp's shoulder."

"That makes rational sense. But that's not what I saw. The long, pointed ears were sticking up, like a cat's, out of the *top* of his head."

Sitko sketched again, and showed me the result.

"That's him."

Quinn entered just then, and I forgot everything else.

"Mike! How's Sully?"

"Stable, but he hasn't regained consciousness. The doctor is hopeful, but he lost a lot of blood, so . . ."

I took a shaky breath. "Poor Fran."

"Her plane just landed at LaGuardia. A police escort is rushing her here."

Quinn faced the other man. "So, Barry, how did she do?"

"Great."

"He's being kind," I said. "I wasn't any help at all."

"On the contrary. You were enormous help. Because of you, we know the shooter's location, where we can look for forensic evidence. We know the shooter has the build of a strong man with lean legs, muscular arms, and a built-up chest, and we know he's athletic enough to rappel down a rope from the top of a building." Sitko paused, then shrugged. "And we know he was wearing a Panther Man mask."

He showed Quinn the sketch and they both shook their heads.

"If the press gets wind of this, we're in for a citywide circus." Quinn frowned at the door. "Reporters are already swarming outside. They know a sketch artist was consulted. With the police commissioner arriving any minute, I think it's best if I get you both out of here."

Eleven

"Have you seen this?" my ex-husband asked the next day.

"Seen what?"

He dropped one of the morning papers onto the coffee bar.

COPS HUNT PANTHER MAN
Witness Claims Village Sniper
Is Comic Book Superhero

I sighed. "None of the newspapers tell the whole story."

Matt leaned one elbow on the marble countertop. "Why am I not surprised that you're privy to the whole story? Maybe because you're part of it?"

He opened the paper to page two.

"This blurry smartphone snapshot of the 'Good Samaritan' giving aid to the fallen cop — with our coffeehouse in the background — looks an awful lot like you."

"No comment."

So far this morning had gone a lot smoother than yesterday's. No predawn storm. No frigid wind off the river. No stinky ex-husband. And no sniper shooting policemen in front of my coffeehouse.

It was a groomed and pleasantly scented Matteo Allegro who delivered the paper, and I was feeling calm, cool, and collected, until someone yelled —

"Open fire?!"

The alarming cry from barista Esther Best turned a few heads. And I nearly dived under the counter — until I realized her reference was culinary.

Esther and her roommate, Nancy, were having a discussion about Nancy's attempt to barbecue last evening's dinner on the landing of their East Village fire escape.

I was about to dress down Esther for her unfiltered cry (the day after a cop shooting!) when one of the customers sitting at our crowded coffee bar jumped in to say —

"Hey, I've cooked over an open fire many times. You can control the smoke, if you know what you're doing."

"Well, please give Nancy some tips," Esther begged. "She nearly suffocated our neighbors. Smoke alarms were beeping

72

faster than the heart monitors in Bellevue's cardiac ward."

"But I miss the taste of grilled food," Nancy whined. "That's the worst thing about living in the city. No cookouts."

"Why can't you just go to Chinatown and order ribs?"

"It's not the same," Nancy insisted.

As our helpful customer agreed with her, I remembered her from the morning before. This was the same coffee-needy student who'd impressed Esther with her proper grammar. And she wasn't just any student, she was an NYU *law* student — which was probably why she jumped to Nancy's defense.

"Your roommate's making a good point," she told Esther. "There's nothing quite like a steak you grill yourself. Chicken's great, too, and *boerewors* —"

"*Boer* what?" Esther blurted.

"*Boerewors,*" Matt repeated to the group. "Beef sausage."

"That's right!" the young woman said, tossing back her auburn hair before shooting a flirty smile Matt's way.

I shot something Matt's way, too, a silent warning not to flirt with the customers, especially ones so young.

With a shrug, he explained. "I ate *boere-*

wors in South Africa. They're very good. Lots of coriander."

"Where I come from, people cook outside all year," the young woman went on. "Some don't even have kitchens, just cooking pits."

"Sorry," said Esther, "but cooking *is* the pits when you have to beg your neighbors not to call 911!"

The law student, who introduced herself as Carla, went on to give some good grilling tips to Nancy and Esther — including what to use (lighter fluid, charcoal) and what *not* to use.

"You hear that?" Esther said, poking Nancy's shoulder. "Listen to Carla. I never again want to see you start a grill with old newspapers — unless you're planning to smoke signal a hookup with a Native American in Jersey City!"

Just then, the bell over our door signaled a new round of customers, and my battling baristas got back to work. I exhaled with relief as the comforting sounds of orders being called and milk being frothed resumed.

"Come with me," I told Matt, and led him into our back pantry, where he helped me box my Cannoli Cream Cupcakes — while sampling two in a row. As he licked sweet mascarpone frosting from his lips and made annoyingly orgasmic sounds, I admitted the real story behind today's headlines. As usual, he didn't bother dialing back the sarcasm.

"So? Are you going to tell me what happened after you spotted the Caped Cat?"

"Panther Man ran off toward the river and disappeared."

"Disappeared? Then I'm sure he must have had an accomplice, Clare."

"Why do you say that? Is there something I missed?"

"Elementary, my dear. Panther Man never goes anywhere without Cub, the Boy Marvel."

If I wasn't afraid of jostling my perfectly frosted cupcakes, I would have elbowed him. "I felt terrible. That front-page picture of Panther Man repeated online thousands of times was drawn from *my* description."

"So? What's wrong with that?"

I filled Matt in on my meeting with Sergeant Sitko at the hospital.

"A reporter recognized Sitko coming out of the waiting room. She knew he was a police sketch artist. She snuck into the room after we left and found the sketch he'd tossed into the wastebasket."

"What's your boyfriend's take on all this?"

"I haven't seen Mike since we left the

hospital yesterday. But we talked on the phone and he's been texting me with updates. Sully is doing fine, thank heaven; he regained consciousness overnight and is recuperating with his wife and children by his side — but that's the only good news. It seems Mike is in trouble with his superiors, and poor Sergeant Sitko may be fired off the force."

"Why?"

"Because that sketch I helped create should never have leaked to the press. Certainly not that way. The NYPD brass felt blindsided. Instead of a somber press conference with the police commissioner and mayor controlling the story, they get headlines screaming about a Panther Man shooter. Now everyone in the city — and most of the country — is making men-in-tights jokes instead of focusing on the seriousness of the crime. It's just like Mike predicted, a media circus!"

I tied closed the bakery box, snapping the string with an angry yank.

"Take it easy, Clare. It'll blow over."

"Sure it will — and the force of the storm will leave bodies behind."

With a furious exhale, I retied my loose ponytail.

"I listened to the mayor's weekly radio

show this morning. It was cut short after three crank callers in a row made stupid superhero cracks. After the show was over, the mayor chewed out the police commissioner, and Quinn and Sitko were called to One Police Plaza. That's where they are now, no doubt for a bureaucratic lashing of epic proportions — or a suspension. Or both."

Matt tilted his head. "There *is* a silver lining. On my way in, Tucker told me you had a big spike in business: Panther Man fans were lining up for coffee and selfies all morning."

"And it's made me feel even worse. We're as good as profiting from Sully's pain. I'm beginning to regret telling anybody what I saw."

"Don't get your Spanx in a bunch. You saw what you saw, and you did your civic duty reporting it. Anyway, you got lucky."

"Lucky?"

"The newspapers have only identified you as 'witness.' Knock wood it stays that way."

"Knock wood? Look who's being 'Old World' superstitious now."

With a grunt, he checked his watch. "Okay, enough chitchat. Time to bribe my godfather with our coffee — and your cupcakes."

TWELVE

As we walked up Hudson Street, I checked my phone about five times before Matt told me to *"turn it off already"* and put it away.

"I'll put it away, but I am *not* turning it off . . ."

A block later, a piercing ambulance siren made me jump like a frightened rabbit — and pull out my phone again.

"Clare —"

"I'm just worried about Mike."

"I know, but look . . ." My ex stopped me. "Making yourself a nervous wreck won't help him or you. Try to put it out of your mind . . ."

A block later, my hand itching to check the phone again, I asked instead how Matt's wife was doing. The fashion-forward Breanne Summour, editor of *Trend* magazine, was always planning some spectacular event, meeting with some flashy celebrity, or flying off to an exciting locale.

I hoped a story about his wife's fabulous life would distract me, but Matt shut down the topic with disturbing speed. When I tried to ask what was wrong, he cut me off again —

"Let's talk about something more productive — the *Andrea Doria* blend. Remember, the new ship will be cruising temperate zones, so the blend needs to be cold brew friendly."

"So you said. About a hundred times."

"Well, my godfather consumes cold brew the way Southerners guzzle sweet tea. We should ask Gus what he likes about it."

"What's not to like? When it's made right, it passes the lips like a wake-up kiss: cool, smooth, sweet, and beautiful."

"Nice, Clare. You should use that in the competition presentation. The judges will eat it up — or more like drink it up."

"Whatever they consume from us, let's hope they love it."

We turned onto Perry Street, a one-way lane lined with tall trees and brick-and-stone town houses built before the Civil War. These four-story structures also predated the building codes of the 1860s, which was why the home of the Campana family jewelers was so impressive.

The pristine white town house stood out

like an untouched dove in a forest of brown and red. Its wooden shutters were also white, along with the window boxes filled with lilies of the valley, their tiny white blossoms the perfect shape for the Campana family name — which meant *bell* in Italian.

A white brick arch extended from one side of Gus's building, bending over a small alleyway. This little cobblestoned corridor was guarded by a stout door of ornate wrought iron.

We moved beyond that locked black gate to the front of the white building. The only signage was a small gold plaque with the words *House of Campana* written inside a stylized bell. Two small windows with thick unbreakable glass displayed pieces of jewelry designed in the distinctive Campana style.

Like the bricks of this historic Village house, the windowless door to the storefront was white. And like every exclusive jeweler in Manhattan, that door was locked.

I spied a pair of security cameras aimed at our faces and smiled for them both.

We were buzzed in, and hardly stepped through the door before being greeted by an attractive young blonde wearing a baby blue minidress and shiny Louboutins with heels so high and platforms so big, the petite girl looked like she was wearing her mother's shoes.

"I'm Matt Allegro, Gus's godson. I'd like to see my godfather —"

Two angry voices drowned out the rest of Matt's words. A man and a woman were loudly arguing, somewhere out of sight.

With a quick glance at my ex-husband, I knew we were thinking the same thing: the couple's identity might be a mystery, but their argument sounded awfully familiar.

"Why have you come back?" the woman's voice railed. "Are you so bored with bed-hopping that you decided to visit your long-suffering wife?"

The male reply was cool and confident. "The other women meant nothing, you know that . . ."

The deep voice betrayed an intriguing accent — one that I couldn't quite identify. But boy did I recognize the adoringly seductive tone.

"Your jealousy is clouding your vision, my precious gem. *You* are my wife, the woman I gave my heart to in marriage, and I have always been faithful, because *my heart* belongs only to you."

"Yet you're so generous with everything else!"

THIRTEEN

Matt and I pretended not to eavesdrop. But it wasn't easy. The showroom was partitioned into sections, and the unseen couple continued to squabble beyond one of those thin walls.

"Well, you've got some nerve turning up now," the woman said. "We're in the middle of finalizing our aquatic collection . . ."

Despite the continued warm cajoling of her husband, the wife's tone remained as frosty as this section of the showroom's design.

The setup displayed breathtaking pieces of Campana jewelry on glass sculpted to look like frozen ocean waves and ice-bound waterfalls. There were flowing necklaces of pearl and aquamarine; "wave" bracelets of platinum and sapphires; and drop earrings of white and blue diamonds.

Of course I wanted it all — and could afford exactly none.

The salesgirl hovered nervously, sharing an uncomfortable smile. "I'm sorry, did you say you were Gus's godson?"

Matt nodded, repeated his request to see him, and she scampered off to phone the famous jeweler.

The next few seconds were filled with hope and dread. Hope that the feuding couple would discretely end their discussion. Dread that they would walk around the corner and realize two strangers had heard every "private" word they'd said.

Hope failed. After a beat, the man said —

"Enough. Please, my gem, I did not come to upset you. I came to see Gustavo."

"Why? What are you peddling now? Blood diamonds? Smuggled Russian amber? Pilfered European heirlooms? Contraband jade from Myanmar?"

"I have something far more valuable — information. News that Gus will surely want to hear."

"I doubt my father would be interested in anything you have to say."

"Darling Sophia, I have always said that you are wrong more times than you are right, and you are very wrong about this."

Matt groaned softly, and not because of the insult.

We both believed we'd been eavesdropping on an anonymous couple. Now we understood that the woman so bitterly arguing with her husband was the perpetually globe-trotting "Sophia" — as in Sophia Campana, Gus's younger daughter.

I'd met Sophia years ago, when I was married to Matt. But with our divorce and all her traveling, I hadn't seen her in years, and I'd certainly never met the Swedish gemstone dealer she had married overseas. Now Sophia was speaking again, but in a quieter tone.

"Hunter, you know Dad won't see you. He's done with you. If you give me the message I'll *consider* passing it on."

"You must do more than consider, given what I have learned," he replied with earnest concern. "For his own sake — and yours, my love, and your family — you had better pass *this* on."

"Just give me the message!"

"Tell Gustavo that I met a man in Rome. A very old man. A man who was aboard that sinking ship with him, your mother, and your elder sister. This man —"

"Good news!" The nervous salesgirl announced her return loudly enough to silence the feuding couple. (*And just when the conversation was heating up!*)

"Mr. Campana would love to see you, Mr.

Allegro. He'll meet you in the courtyard. Go back outside and through the white arch —"

"I know the way," Matt said.

She nodded. "I'll buzz the gate's lock for you."

Matt couldn't escape that display room fast enough.

I, on the other hand, dragged my low boot heels, hoping to hear more of the argument. But that chance was already blown, and the young salesgirl on designer stilts stared hard at me until I followed Matt back out to the sidewalk.

FOURTEEN

"Well, that was interesting," I said, taking a much-needed breath of cool autumn air.

"Poor Sophia." Matt shook his head. "I haven't seen her in years, but I remember her as such a sweet kid. It sounds like she married a complete jackass."

"Hum," I said.

"Hum?" he echoed. "What's that supposed to mean? You and I had rough patches, but we never sounded like *that.*"

"Sorry, but that's *exactly* how we sounded."

Matt grimaced at the thought, but rather than open a hermetically sealed can of petrified worms, he pushed through the stout iron gate and walked down the cobblestone alley.

A spiral staircase led up to Gus's second-story office, over the jewelry store. But that wasn't our destination. Instead, I followed Matt along the cobblestones, only to have my breath stolen again, this time by the splendor of a hidden treasure in the middle of Manhattan.

Nestled among the four-story buildings was a placid courtyard, completely buffered from any noise on New York's streets and sidewalks. A fountain's spray sparkled like diamonds in the noonday sun, and little brown mourning doves cooed among the ornamental shrubs and trees.

Lampposts topped with crystal bell fixtures marked each corner of this idyllic yard, and I could easily imagine their beauty at night, with the bell-shaped glass glowing golden.

On the far side of that magical space stood the Campana family home.

Even after a hundred and fifty years, the West Village was still dotted with Civil War–era buildings hidden from view — sheds or stables converted into garages or very small dwellings.

But the home tucked behind the Campana Family Jewelers was a restored example of a pre–Civil War "backhouse" — a hidden property built behind a main structure before building codes were put into place to prevent overcrowding.

Backhouses were commissioned by the wealthy to preserve their privacy and quietude in the busy urban landscape, and both wealth and taste were reflected in the white brick facade; the tall, arched windows; and the clean white balconies overlooking the courtyard.

Wide marble steps led to the white front door, the golden Campana bell once again embossed at the center. And on the door-step, a smiling Gustavo Campana waved to us.

FIFTEEN

Blessed with a full head of iron gray hair, a naturally lean physique, and a spine still straight as a flagpole, Gus greeted us with surprisingly powerful hugs for a man pushing eighty.

He still made jewelry by hand, melting, molding, and beating gold and silver with the ancient tools of his craft. The work gave him the wiry muscles of a blacksmith, along with scars from a hundred forge burns that freckled his forearms, and a face that appeared etched out of still-lustrous amber.

He led us inside and we settled in an airy parlor with a gleaming wood floor and tall windows facing the sunny courtyard. The Italianate furniture had cushions embroidered so finely that I hesitated to sit down.

Instead, I opened the pastry box to show off my cupcakes, made from scratch using the most buttery, melt-in-your-mouth Golden Cupcake recipe I'd ever baked.

(The first time I made them for Quinn, he asked why I didn't use a boxed mix. *"Wouldn't that be easier?"* My response was *"Not really."* Then I handed him the final product. One blissful bite and he never asked me about boxed mixes again.)

On top of these little golden cups of joy, I mounded my sweet, smooth Cannoli Cream Frosting. Some of the iced cakes I left plain, others I topped with grated dark chocolate or mini chips, and the remainder I finished with sprinkles of finely chopped pistachios.

When I showed them to Gus, he pretended to swoon.

"*Bella* Clare, you have brought me edible treasures!" He hugged me again and kissed my cheeks. *"Grazie!"*

"You are more than welcome . . ."

Then Matt presented him with three bags of our newest single-origin beans, and Gus looked genuinely overjoyed.

"Okay, you two," I said. "Sit down and catch up on family business, and I'll make us coffee . . ."

Gus's modern kitchen was spotless. Mason jars of cold brew were steeping in his fridge, each with a label marking their "ready" times, and bags of Village Blend roasts were lined up on a shelf.

I added Matt's premium offerings to the stash, found the burr grinder, and got to work.

Gus had several sizes of the famous Alfonso Bialetti stovetop espresso pot — an eight-sided marvel with the clean, faceted lines of a perfectly cut gemstone.

I put the largest one to use.

Ten minutes later, the glorious scent of strong coffee was drifting through the courtyard, and I was filling *tre demitasses* for our little party of three.

Settling in with the men, I caught my ex-husband's eye.

Okay, Matt, time to steer this conversation toward our reason for this visit . . .

"I'm sorry, Godfather . . ." he said, shifting uneasily. "I know you don't like to talk about the shipwreck, but —"

"But it would help our research" — I quickly jumped in — "if you could talk to us a bit about your memories. Maybe you can start with the reason you made the crossing. I know it was soon after World War Two, and Italy was still struggling to get back on its feet, is that right?"

Gus nodded, sitting back in his chair. "You are very right about the war, Clare. It destroyed so much. Angelica and I were sent to America to relocate the family business."

"Your jewelry business?" I assumed.

"The Campanas worked as goldsmiths and jewelers for generations in Florence, but the war was devastating, and moving to New York seemed like a good idea. So Angelica and I left Italy with a handsome young apprentice named Silvio . . . ah, I forgot his last name. I'm so old . . ." Gus smiled weakly.

"We three were supposed to get things settled before helping the rest of the family come over. But . . ." He paused, voice catching. "When the ship sank, poor Silvio drowned, and Angelica and I lost everything — everything but the clothes on our backs and our little Perla."

As a shadow crossed the old man's face, I spoke up again.

"I've seen photos of the *Andrea Doria,* but was the ship really as beautiful as they say?"

"Oh, yes . . . *sì, sì, sì!*" Gus smiled, this time more cheerfully. "We boarded in Genoa, and the city was still scarred by the bombs and fires of the war. But not the *Andrea Doria.* I still remember the first moment I saw her. She gleamed like a flawless diamond above the sad ruins of that port. So white and clean and pure, it made me proud again to be Italian."

"What was it like to walk the decks?"

"*Mamma mia!* Polished wood, marble, crystal in the bar, sterling silver in the dining rooms. And the public spaces were decorated with a fortune in art and sculpture."

Gus laughed. "There was fun, too. The *Andrea Doria,* she was the first ocean liner to have swimming on her outside decks — three different pools! For an Italian bumpkin like me, it was like life in an American magazine, or some glamorous pool party with the Beach Bums —"

"Beach *Boys,*" Matt corrected.

"Yeah, them. It was a beach party every day, a nightclub every night. Entertainment. Fine dining. *Eccellente!* Superb service, *notte e giorno* — night and day."

"Night and day," I echoed, suddenly getting a bright idea — one that just might win us this coffee competition.

"I remember a gala dinner party," Gus went on. "The ship glowed on the black ocean like a golden city floating in space. Elegant women danced with dashing men. At midnight everyone gathered on deck to watch the lights of Gibraltar fade from view. We were on our way to a new life, a new world . . ."

Matt refilled his godfather's cup. "I'm surprised you remember so much after all these years."

"You mistake silence for forgetfulness, Matteo. What happened on that ship is burned in my memory . . ."

With eyes misting, Gus gazed at a picture on the white marble mantel of his cold fireplace, where an image of a woman stood frozen for all time.

"No, I could never forget . . ."

When Gus rose and moved to the mantel, I joined him.

The picture he picked up was extravagantly framed in yellow gold. Inside that frame, a sad-faced woman wore an elegant evening gown. She was a dark-haired beauty, lovely and delicate, and so very young, yet with an expression of hardship that seemed to age her beyond her years.

"Is that your late wife?" I asked gently.

He nodded as I took a closer look — and blinked in surprise.

"That necklace she's wearing, is it a replica of the *Occhio del Gatto*?"

I'd first admired the legendary "Eye of the Cat" when I was a teenager, poring over art books in our small town's library. I saw it again in an Italian textbook when studying in Rome, and a few months ago on the Internet.

The huge, near-flawless ice blue diamond

had been cut and set in Italy with a design that mimicked a cat's eye. It was one of the world's most famous lost gems. And I expected Gus to tell me about the replication process.

But my surprise turned to shock when he spoke again.

"That is no replica, Clare. That *is* the lost diamond."

Sixteen

Taking the photo from his hands, I studied the jewel with renewed fascination. The blue diamond was surrounded in the unique setting by dozens of smaller, darker stones — "coffee diamonds," Gus called them.

"The piece is absolutely stunning," I said, "but I never knew the Campana family owned it."

"Very few knew," Gus revealed. "This picture was taken in Italy before we set out on that final, fateful voyage. It was taken as *prova* — proof."

"Proof of what?"

"That the *Occhio del Gatto* was personal property, not something to be declared at customs and sold in America."

"You mean you were smuggling the piece? You wanted to sell it and avoid the taxes?"

His smile returned, but this time his dark eyes carried a cunning gleam.

"As I told you, we left Florence with the

means to start a new life, and bring the family business to America. The family loaned the heirloom to us. They expected me to sell it and use the money to bring them over. When the jewel was lost, that means went away."

Matt snorted. "I guess it's water under the bridge. Or more like a giant diamond under two hundred feet of seawater."

I sighed. "It was such an exquisite gem. The shade of blue so sharply striking. It reminds me of Quinn's eyes."

"Oh, please." Matt groaned. "Where's a locked and loaded Panther Man when you need him?"

"Matt!" I cried, horrified. "That's a terrible thing to say!"

Gus stifled a laugh. "He says it because he still loves you. *La torcia.* His heart still carries the flame."

Matt waved his hands. "Don't go there, Gus. It's a lost cause."

"More like ancient history," I corrected. "And I wish Panther Man was, too."

"You are talking about that crazy man from the news? Or maybe not so crazy . . ."

"What do you mean?" I looked at Gus. "Do you know something? It could help me — and my boyfriend — a great deal."

He shrugged. "I know when someone acts

crazy, sometimes they're actually smart. Like Mussolini, maybe crazy is part of their act."

Gus saw my disappointment.

"You know, Clare, I've always liked you . . ." He reached for another of my cupcakes and sighed with happiness as he ate. "In my line of work I deal with many different people. They give me their dollars, their euros, their yens, their yuans, and I fashion jewelry for them . . . famous actors, businessmen, rappers . . . and people with less . . . *legitimate* occupations."

He paused to dab his mouth with a napkin. "I don't ask questions. If they pay me —" He shrugged. "I do the work. As for this Panther Man? Maybe I can ask around. You'd be surprised who this old man knows, and what he can find out. Like the *Occhio del Gatto,* eh?"

"Like the diamond?" I met Gus's gaze. "What do you mean?"

"The diamond was cut and set to honor the spirit of the bridge cat."

"Bridge cat?"

"You don't know about the guardian spirit of the Ponte Vecchio?"

"I know about the Ponte Vecchio . . ."

For centuries, the medieval covered bridge provided a home to the goldsmiths of Florence. I'd even visited the famous "Old Bridge" during my summer in Italy — and spent far too many lire on a twenty-two-karat-gold bracelet.

"According to legend," Gus went on, "a mystical cat prowls the bridge as a guard on dark and foggy nights."

"A guard against burglars?"

"Burglars, intruders . . ." He shrugged. "Any troublemaker to the merchants of the bridge."

"But what can a little cat do?"

"A little cat?" He laughed. "This is no ordinary animal. Inside, a protective spirit lives that transforms and attacks when threatened, killing if necessary."

He paused, dark eyes narrowing. "Heaven help the mortal who crosses it."

Seventeen

"Do you really think Gus can find something out?" I quietly asked Matt after our visit.

"About Panther Man? I doubt it. Gus is my godfather, not *the* Godfather. I think he was just humoring you. You heard him: he likes you, Clare — and your cupcakes."

As Matt and I left Gus's house and crossed the tranquil hidden courtyard, the shadows grew longer, and I slowed my steps to enjoy the coo of the mourning doves.

"Did you ask Gus about that tiff we overheard between Sophia and her husband?"

"Of course not. Sophia's marital problems are none of our business."

"I'm not looking for idle gossip. I'm worried about her. Did you at least ask how she's doing?"

"Sure, and her older sister, too."

"How is Perla? She must be in her sixties

by now? You know I always wondered about that huge age difference between the sisters."

Matt nodded. "My mother said Gus and Angelica tried to have children for many years, but Angelica had health problems. Apparently, the years in Italy were really hard on her — and she had some miscarriages. When they finally had Sophia, it was a happy surprise for them both. I remember Gus calling her his *piccolo miracolo.*"

"Little miracle?" I smiled. "That's sweet. But all the fuss must have been hard for Perla. What's she up to these days?"

Matt shrugged. "Gus says he doesn't see her much. She's too busy with her business. And before you ask, he thinks Sophia made a bad match in Hunter — that's her husband's name, Hunter Rolf. Apparently, their union was hasty. They hooked up last year on Aeroe."

"Aeroe? What is that, some kind of drug?"

"Aeroe is an *island* off the coast of Denmark. It's the quickie wedding capital of Europe. Like Las Vegas, only without slot machines or Elvis impersonators. And, actually, it's a very picturesque place."

"Hunter must have really swept Sophia off her feet."

"Hum," Matt said.

"*Hum?*" I echoed. "What's that supposed to mean?"

"Why is it women always want to pretty things up with phrases like *'he swept her off her feet'* when it was probably nothing more than animal attraction?"

"When did you get so cynical? If it was nothing more than animal attraction, then why would they get married?"

"Wild guess? Failed birth control."

I stopped dead and faced him. "What an *awful* thing to say. What is *with* you lately —" I was ready to say more, but clenched my fists instead.

Matt's mother had warned me there was something wrong with her son, and I agreed, but this was hardly the place to drill down on my ex-husband's latent bitterness.

"Forget it," I said instead and walked briskly ahead.

At the end of the alley, I popped the one-way lock on the iron gate, and tugged the heavy door.

"You, there! Hold that for me!"

The blunt command, in English but with an Italian accent, came from a fit-looking forty-something in a flowing black Valentino trench. The woman stood in the middle of Perry Street, speaking with her driver, a swarthy man in black with a U-shaped scar on his cheek, who cared not in the least that the vintage black Jaguar he drove was blocking traffic.

Impatient honks came from a taxi and delivery van stuck behind her car, which the woman completely ignored as she continued issuing instructions to her driver — or was it her bodyguard? He looked big enough.

Matt noticed this scene as he stepped through the gate behind me.

"Hold it open!" she commanded again, one leather-gloved hand hailing us as her sharp heels clicked across the West Village pavement.

Bright turquoise cat glasses exactly matched her thigh-high stiletto boots in a statement of high-fashion confidence that extended to her dramatic long hair, dyed with salon-ombre shading that moved from beetle brown to volcano ash. Her expertly made-up face displayed cover-girl cheekbones. But overly plumped lips and tightness around the eyes suggested some recent "work" — and not the kind you do with an apron or shovel.

Matt gently nudged me forward and pointedly released the gate, letting it loudly clang shut and lock tight.

"*Mannaggia!* Are you deaf?" The woman faced off with me and Matt. "I *told you* to

103

hold it! I *must* see Mr. Campana!"

Matt gestured to the store's front door. "Then I suggest you ask his staff for an appointment — *like everybody else.*"

Before the furious, sputtering fashionista could respond, Matt gripped my elbow and urged me toward Hudson.

"Did you know that woman?" I asked, glancing back over my shoulder.

"I know the type well enough from Breanne's circle. They're a soulless, self-centered, eternally entitled lot. This one probably has a complaint about an exquisite piece of jewelry that he's worked on tirelessly to her specification, yet it *'still isn't quite right.'* Let her go through Gus's staff. That's what he pays them for."

Matt stewed in silence for the rest of our walk. At the door to our coffeehouse, he checked his watch and sighed.

"It was nice to see Gus, but that visit was a waste of time. You didn't even ask him about cold brew."

"I didn't have to. Gus gave me the inspiration I needed. I know exactly what I'm going to create for the *Andrea Doria* competition."

"Great!" For the first time this afternoon, Matt looked happy. "Hit me with it. What's your idea?"

"Remember when Gus told us about the 'superb service' from the *Andrea Doria*? *"Notte e giorno,"* he said, night and day. It made me think *dark and light.* And then you mentioned that island off the coast of Denmark, and that sealed it. I'll do a Danish blend."

Matt clapped his hands. "Clare, that's perfect!"

A mix of dark and light roasted beans, Danish blend, when done right, gave consumers a superb coffee-drinking experience — beautiful smoothness with well-rounded body at any brewed strength. But balance was key, and the beans I selected had to bring enough richness, as "superb" as the luxury liner on which it would be served.

Matt knew it, too, and his joy quickly gave way to concern. "Do you know the coffees you're going to use?"

"I'm leaning toward your latest from Sumatra for the dark and that sweet honey-processed Costa Rican you found us for the light —"

"Brilliant! You'll get lots of wild complexity and sweet flavor from those honey-processed beans and the Sumatra will anchor it with richness, body, and depth."

"Sure, *theoretically,* if I don't blow the balance. So before I start testing roast times and ratios, I'll need one more thing."

"Name it."

"The phone number of the company that equipped the galleys on the ship. Can you get it for me?"

"You want to talk to the ship's contractors? Why?"

"Just get me that number, and I'll make your winning blend."

Eighteen

After Matt departed, I checked in with my staff, and all was well, apart from more rabid Panther Man fans lining up to take selfies.

At least they're lining up for lattes, too, I thought. *Matt's "silver lining."* But then business was business, as Gus said, even when your customers gave you the willies.

With Tucker overseeing the shop, I went to the basement to roast a few batches of green coffee. Then I finally knocked off for the day, climbing the back staircase to my apartment.

The furnished duplex above the coffeehouse was part of my compensation. I resided here rent free for as long as I managed the shop below.

Madame had lived here for years while running the place, and when her business finally took off, she splurged on her living quarters, decorating with a romantic's eye.

The main floor's cream marble fireplace, tall French doors, balcony with flower boxes, and fleur-de-lis ceiling molding had more in common with her Parisian roots than the building's Federal-style exterior. But I loved her choices nonetheless — the muted peach walls, ivory silk draperies, gleaming parquet floors with lush area rugs that perfectly complemented the carved rosewood and silk furnishings.

Off the parlor, the small dining room's décor was more in line with the Colonial history of the neighborhood. But upstairs, it was right back to the romantic with two lavishly furnished bedrooms and a luxurious marble bath, which is where I was heading.

With no time for bubbles, I stripped down and turned on the spa-quality showerhead, praying the pulsing stream of hot water would beat the stress out of my tense muscles and wash away the awful visions I couldn't shake since yesterday morning —

Sully bleeding on the cold concrete and Mike dodging deadly bullets aimed at his head . . .

Missing Quinn more than ever, I wrapped a bath sheet around me and checked my phone again. I'd invited him to dinner at seven and his terse *OK,* texted hours ago, was the last I'd heard from him.

With hope that he wouldn't cancel, I attempted to make myself presentable by crunch-drying my shoulder-length chestnut hair into (hopefully) attractive waves, and putting on light makeup — with the exception of my under-eye concealer, which (after my near-sleepless night) I applied with the gusto of a house painter spreading spackle over the Grand Canyon.

In the master bedroom, the coming evening had chilled the air, and I started a fire in the hearth before pulling on a clingy but comfortable jersey knit sheath with three-quarter sleeves and a sweetheart neckline. (I remembered Mike saying the color brought out the green of my eyes, although his eyes appeared more interested in the short length of the skirt. *Well, we both could use a distraction, so* . . . on went the dress.)

Downstairs in the kitchen, apron in place, I was ready to roll.

The first order of business, however, was feeding my overactive kitties: coffee bean–colored Java, and Frothy — a fluffy feline version of latte milk.

Long ago these furry ladies had decided that every time I entered the kitchen it was mealtime, and I had absolutely no say in the matter.

With the little beasties happily smacking their lips, I began putting together a human dinner of old-fashioned comfort food for *my* soul as well as Quinn's.

The first ingredient of tonight's feast was the foundation of most Italian American soul food — *tomato sauce.*

My nonna would have made it fresh with the ripe fruit from my father's garden; peeling the skins after flash-dips in boiling water; then de-seeding the insides; and finally cooking the mash down into a pot of sweet red bliss.

The smell alone of homemade sauce is like nothing else on earth. Tonight, however, I had no time for that particular joy.

While jarred sauce was convenient, it was nowhere near the quality I wanted for this dinner, so I began my 1, 2, 3 Magic Sauce, a handy little piece of alchemy that transformed canned tomatoes and three humble ingredients into a delicious pot of *nearly* nonna-worthy gold.

With the sauce simmering, I started the meatballs, mixing them by hand with just the right seasonings and binders. Thanks to my grandmother's "secret ingredient," they were fluffy perfection — as opposed to unappealingly dense.

Finally, I cooked the ziti, mixed it with

three different Italian cheeses, and layered it into the casserole with my quickie sauce. After sliding the dish into the oven, I uncorked a bottle of wine, poured a few fingers, and sipped it slowly as I sat down to close my eyes for a minute or two . . .

Thirty minutes later, the oven timer woke me from a nightmare of violent gunfire so vivid, I fell off my chair.

Two sleepy cats spied my backside's connection with the kitchen floor and rushed over for what they assumed was playtime — or, even better, an encore of mealtime.

That's when I realized someone was entering my apartment.

NINETEEN

Scrambling to my feet, I grabbed my phone.

Finger poised to speed-dial 911, I flew to the main room, where I sagged with relief at the sight of Mike Quinn coming through the front door, using (*oh, right*) that key I'd given him.

Still wearing his clothes from yesterday, including the NYPD jacket that nearly got him killed, Quinn nodded his greeting in silence.

His face was drawn, his color off, his lips thin and tight.

I never saw the man so tired.

But after thirty-six hours hunting the bastard who'd shot his colleague and friend, what else would he be?

By now, the umami aroma of my sauce, mingled with the creamy scent of melting cheese, had permeated the duplex. And, despite his fatigue, Quinn lifted his head with the keen interest of a starving bear sniffing honey.

"It's almost ready," I assured him with a smile.

There was no smile in return, just another nod. And I saw more than exhaustion and hunger embedded in Quinn's arctic gaze. Defeat was lodged there — and cold frustration.

I asked him about Sully, and the news was mainly positive. He was continuing to recover, although doctors were now closely monitoring an arrhythmia in his heart. But Fran and his family were keeping his spirits up.

I wanted more answers — about the pursuit of the shooter and Quinn's visit to One Police Plaza — but I could see he wasn't in any shape to be given a grilling, so instead I gave him a hug.

He wrapped his arms around me and dropped a kiss on my head. I touched his cheek and suggested he take a shower, although not for the reasons I'd advised my ex-husband to take one yesterday.

Holding my head under water had helped me feel like a new person. I hoped it would do the same for him. And, if I was lucky, the hot steam might just melt some of that blue ice.

■ ■ ■ ■

Twenty minutes later, Quinn was sitting at my kitchen table, his sandy hair still damp, his strong jaw freshly shaved. He'd grabbed a change of clothes from the bedroom, where I'd cleaned out drawers for his personals. Now his long legs were encased in NYPD sweatpants, his broad shoulders straining against the fabric of a light gray tee.

Unfortunately, the shower and change of clothes hadn't changed his mood. He remained stiff and uncharacteristically sullen.

The baked ziti was bubbling nicely as I removed it from the oven, and it still needed to set, so I served up an appetizer of what I hoped would be *literal* comfort food: freshly fried mozzarella sticks, each encased in panko seasoned with rosemary, thyme, garlic, oregano, and sea salt.

To wash down these hot, crunchy, gooey-hearted treats, I poured us the Lambrusco I'd uncorked. Fruity and sweet, it was a bright complement to the unctuous appetizer — and, hey, if it also loosened Mike's tight detective lips and let me in on some NYPD secrets . . . even better.

As he munched the mozzarella, he sent

me grateful nods. The wine appeared to relax him, and . . . sure enough, by the time I dished up my baked ziti and meatballs, he began to talk . . .

"The Crime Scene Unit searched the abandoned building where you saw the shooter, but found no evidence the suspect used anything but the fire escape . . ."

When he paused for more hungry forkfuls, I noticed Frothy and Java staring up enviously, their tails sweeping the kitchen floor with pre-pounce eagerness.

I quickly rose and pulled cat treats from the cupboard before Quinn became the victim of an eight-legged stampede.

"So this Panther Man got away clean?" I asked, bending down to placate my felines.

"Looks that way . . ."

When his voice trailed off, I turned around to see why. His attention had strayed from his plate to my short skirt. With unabashed interest, his focus continued moving up the curves of my clingy dress to the shiny waves in my hair and gloss on my lips.

"You look . . . very nice."

His blue eyes were much warmer now — and so was my face. I could feel the heat rising inside me, along with my (nearly lost) hopes for the night ahead.

"So," I pressed, sitting back down to dish

up my own dinner. "Did you pursue any leads?"

Quinn snorted. "Where do I begin? How about with Sergeant Sitko's advice for CSU to gather up every discarded garbage bag in our perimeter to check for DNA . . . They did. And believe me, DNA is one thing those bags have plenty of."

"Stop —" I raised my hand. "My garbage bag discussion with Sitko was a theory at best. What I want to know is exactly how the shooter tricked everyone with a badge into running into the wrong building."

"Buildings. Plural. You remember the pyrotechnics I mentioned yesterday?"

I nodded.

"These bangs also came from two additional rooftops. As soon as SWAT realized they hit the wrong building, they were diverted to another — and another, all leading us away from your lone gunman sighting."

"Sounds like a professional."

"A high school kid could have made the devices. The noise came from M-80s — fireworks you can buy on the street in Chinatown. But the way they were deployed?" Quinn nodded. "You're right, Clare. It was sophisticated. The explosives were wired to timers with disposable phones as triggers so the shooter could control the blasts. One call and boom, instant diversion."

"Couldn't you get anything else from the devices?"

"Forensics looked for fingerprints, clues to where the items were purchased, anything they thought could be a lead . . ." He shook his head. "We ran down everything — all dead ends."

"No leads at all?"

"We're still canvassing residents of the decoy buildings, and detectives reviewed plenty of digital recordings by the waterfront, but so far all they found were violations of the public urination statutes."

As Quinn drained his wineglass, my spirits drained with it, until I remembered my visit with Gus.

I told Quinn about Gustavo Campana's willingness to ask around about the shooter. "How his very 'diverse' clientele might have some useful information."

"He sells to the criminal element?"

"He sells to people with the money to buy. He doesn't question where the money comes from — in his view, that's for people like you."

Quinn snorted. "Guess I should get to know the man."

"I don't doubt he has a reach. You should have seen the woman who pulled up while we were walking away. Her driver was this big guy with a U-shaped scar on his cheek — like something out of *The Godfather Saga.* The Campana family's compound is really something, too. It's hidden off the street in one of those secret Village courtyards."

"Did you see Panther Man hiding there? Up a tree maybe?"

"No, but Gus's home wasn't in your dragnet, was it?"

"Too far north and east. Unless your superhero can teleport, there's no way he could have gotten by the police presence on Hudson."

"First of all, he's not *my* superhero. He's obviously a coldly calculating killer with professional skills — and some kind of dedicated plan or purpose."

"That's not what they think downtown. The brass believe we're dealing with a psychotic with a Panther Man fixation, like that nutjob — excuse me, 'troubled youth' — who dressed up as a comic book character before opening fire on a theater full of innocent people. They think *our* nutjob is only injuring cops because he's such a bad shot."

"That's not what I think."

"I don't, either. Neither do some of my men. They think it's revenge. Remember Eduardo De Santis, the one that got away?"

"How could I forget — I was tripping over stacks of his surveillance photos for weeks . . ."

A slight man with a hawk nose, aggressively tanned complexion, and close-cropped white beard, De Santis was a wealthy nightclub owner and fastidious dresser, his suit jacket's breast pocket never without a brightly colored handkerchief that always matched his silk shirt. After Quinn and his squad closed down Eduardo's club for distributing cocaine and heroin, he hired the best defense team money could buy — and managed to escape conviction.

"You think Eduardo is behind the shootings?"

"Some in my squad think so, but there's no proof, just a theory. He's not even in the country. According to Interpol, he moved to Cape Town and then to Dubai — probably too far away to worry about."

"Unless he hired someone to get even."

"It's possible, but it doesn't seem likely, and without evidence the brass rejected that theory outright. It's also conceivable this Panther Man stunt is connected to a known gang in the area who brands their drugs with superhero labels, Panther Man included. Remember that street dealer Sully and I flipped during our overnight interview? He's part of that crew, and that's the most reasonable revenge theory at the moment. But it doesn't really matter to me because the shooter's *motive* isn't my concern."

Quinn's tone was clear enough and so was the look in his eyes.

"You don't care *why* he's shooting cops, do you? You just want to find him and arrest him."

"Arresting is an option, sure. But if I see him take aim at another human being — in or out of uniform — I'll shoot the bastard dead."

TWENTY

I'd never seen such cold fury in Mike Quinn. It sent a shiver through me — and for more than one reason.

"Can I tell you something, Mike? You once said emotion has no place in police work. Wait. I misquoted you. Emotion has no place in *good* police work."

"You have a point to make, Cosi?"

"Yes. One I learned from you. When you're out for vengeance instead of justice, your judgment becomes clouded."

He grunted. "I'll keep that in mind."

"I wish you would. Because I'm worried about you."

"Don't be. I spent years on the street. I can take care of myself."

"It would kill me if anything happened to you."

"Nothing's going to happen."

"And you know that . . . *for sure?*"

Despite the seriousness of our argument,

the edges of Quinn's mouth lifted at my choice of words. He had shouted the same phrase at me yesterday when we were under fire.

"Tell you what," he said. "How about you trust me, like I trusted you. When you ran out, into the middle of the kill zone, to help Sully . . . you didn't think I was terrified for you?"

I shifted uneasily, knowing he was right.

I'd been afraid out there, but fear hadn't dictated my actions; something else had. Quinn was in the same position. How could I condemn that?

"Okay," I said at last. "You've made your point."

"Good. And if trusting me becomes too challenging, at least trust that I'm smarter than your Panther Man."

"He's not *my* Panther Man! Stop saying that."

"Sorry, but . . . that's how it's playing out. You're the only eyewitness."

"Are you kidding me? With all the smartphones in this town, didn't *someone* get a picture of this bizarre shooter? It's starting to make me believe he really does have superpowers!"

"He doesn't. At least not the power to be invisible. Two security cameras on private buildings caught Panther Man as he fled. But the pictures didn't tell us anything we didn't already know from your account."

"Then there *was* a Panther Man? I didn't imagine him?"

"You did not," Quinn said. "And the press would have been apprised of that fact this morning, at an *official* press conference. Until that sketch got out . . ."

He reached for the bottle and refilled his glass — to the brim.

I didn't blame him. The morning paper trumped the mayor with its front-page pencil sketch of the shooter and lurid headlines in comic bubbles, making the event into a joke and making the NYPD look ineffectual.

I hated to ask, but . . .

"What exactly happened when you were called downtown?"

"I caught hell, that's what happened."

"I'm so sorry, Mike. I should have stopped Sergeant Sitko from tossing that sketch into the waste can, but I never thought a reporter would get in there and search the trash."

"It wasn't your fault, Clare. Sitko should have known better."

"What's going to happen to him?"

"Nothing. The pair of us were dragged through the ringer this morning, but that's the end of it."

"Really?" I studied Quinn. "I don't believe you."

"I didn't say all was forgiven. It's over because I took the fall."

"But you weren't even in the room when Sitko tossed that sketch! Why should you take all the blame?"

"Because Sitko is six months from his pension, and the brass would have fired him over this." Quinn shrugged and dug back into his ziti. "Better me than him. They're not going to get rid of me."

"Because you've been decorated multiple times?"

"Because my case clearance rate is phenomenal. When I was off working in DC, my OD Squad's effectiveness nose-dived. They weren't aggressive enough at pursuing leads, circumventing jurisdictional roadblocks, building solid cases, or securing convictions. With me in charge again, *they are.*"

"So there are no consequences to your taking the blame today?"

He waved his fork. "A letter of reprimand tucked into my files. Not the first, by the way. I've forgotten it already."

"That's because you did the right thing."

"Not where it counted, I didn't." He took

another drink of Lambrusco . . . and continued drinking until he once again drained his glass.

"I let Sully down, Clare. I was just as fooled by that comic book shooter as the SWAT team."

"You were set up. All of you were."

"Maybe. But you weren't fooled, were you?"

"I didn't have a gun, Mike. I wasn't looking to return fire. You were the one trying to give me and Sully cover. You did what any good cop would have done: glued your gaze to the gunman's position — or what you thought it was."

"That's just it. What I thought wasn't good enough. Now the trail's gone cold, and we've got no leads. Not until the shooter strikes again."

And that's what my nightmares were made of . . .

Twenty-One

A few hours later, my sleepy eyelids opened, not to morning, but a semi-dark place . . .

Flames were still crackling in the master bedroom's hearth, casting their warm, red-orange glow on the art-covered walls. The feather pillows felt like clouds, softening the hard knocks of the last two days, and the mahogany four-poster was a solid ship for drifting away to dreamland.

But I wasn't dreaming now.

Rubbing my eyes, I rolled over to discover Mike's shoulder holster on the nightstand, its leather straps wrapped around his weapon. The empty bottle of Lambrusco sat next to it, along with a pair of drained glasses.

Mike and I must have brought the wine up here after dinner, I realized, although my memory was foggy. *We must have done something else, too . . .*

A simple conclusion, given my state of

dress — or more like undress. No emerald sheath, no lacy nightgown, not even a shred of underwear. The crisp sheets and soft quilt were the only things covering my naked curves —

Until a heavy arm draped itself around my midriff.

Mike's lips touched my neck, and I smiled into the shadows.

"You're so beautiful," he whispered. "Even with my eyes closed . . ."

Then his mouth and hands began to roam, exciting me all over again. I turned in his arms, and soon we were moving together beneath the bedcovers, making physical what we both felt in our hearts.

Breathing hard, our bodies finally collapsed against each other.

Exhausted but contented, that's how we fell back to sleep, my cheek on his strong chest, his chin resting on my dark hair . . .

A short time later, a strange noise woke me.

Sitting up in bed, I peered into blackness. The hearth had gone cold, its orange flames now white ash. And the shadows in the room were thick as sea fog.

The noise came again — a strange bumping — and then I saw it.

"Mike, wake up!"

I shook his shoulder, and he slowly stirred.

"What is it? What's wrong?"

"I saw something moving, just outside the bedroom window —"

"A tree branch?"

"Not a tree branch. A shadowy shape, in *human* form . . ."

Mike sat up, awake now, and stared at the dark glass.

"I don't see or hear anything, Clare. And there's no fire escape on this side of the building."

"I know that."

"So how could someone be outside your *fourth-floor* window?"

"I don't know."

"It's okay . . ." Mike yawned. "You had a nightmare, that's all. Go back to sleep."

"But I saw *something* —"

Hooking my waist, Mike pulled me back down, against his big, warm body. I struggled lightly until one of his long legs curled possessively around the pair of mine, and his lips began whispering things to ease my worries — sweet, thrilling, *very* distracting things. And then . . .

BANG!

BANG-BANG-BANG!

Omigod. "Mike, someone's shooting out there!"

By the time I sat up, Quinn had rolled out of bed and was going for his shoulder holster.

"Be careful —"

"Stay back!"

Crossing the bedroom, he pulled his weapon free of the leather and tossed the holster aside. With two hands on the gun, he approached the window from the side and quickly opened it.

Freezing night air swept in, and I shivered in bed, watching Quinn lean out the window to survey the street below.

"Be careful!" I warned. "There's someone out there. Not in the street. But much closer —"

BANG!

The shot rang out with horrific clarity, hitting Quinn directly in the head. He dropped his gun, and his body pitched forward.

I gasped in disbelief as the man I loved disappeared into the darkness.

Kicking off the bedcovers, I rushed to the open window and looked down. A body was lying in the street below, blood pooling on the concrete, but it wasn't Quinn.

The body belonged to Sully Sullivan.

What? I rubbed my eyes. *This makes no sense. What is going on?!*

Sirens began to wail, and a helicopter dropped like a spider, straight down from the clouds, its blades battering my eardrums. Flashing red lights drew my attention to the street, where two paramedics were now loading Mike Quinn's limp body into their vehicle.

"Wait!" I shouted out the window. "Wait for me!"

I threw on clothes and ran out of the bedroom, into the hall, but it wasn't a hall anymore. Suddenly, I was standing in a small paneled room with no doors and no windows.

Frantic, I turned around and around, looking for a way out. But there was none. Then I looked up and saw Panther Man above me!

I screamed so loud I hurt my own ears — until I realized the ceiling was a mirror. When I moved, Panther Man moved. I looked down at myself and saw no costume. Yet my reflection told me . . .

I was Panther Man!

Just then the room lurched and vibrated, moving like an elevator. With another lurch, everything stopped. One wall parted, swishing open on a brightly lit hospital ward. That's when I heard Mike's voice.

"Clare!"

"Mike!" I called. He sounded far away. "Where are you?!"

"I'm here!"

Down an impossibly long hall, I saw Mike's body, strapped to a gurney. Orderlies wearing white coats were wheeling him rapidly away.

"Stop!" I cried, chasing them. "Don't take him away!"

But the orderlies ignored me, pushing the gurney through a pair of white double doors. I tried to follow, but the white doors were locked tight.

"Let me in!" I shouted. "Let me through!"

I beat on the doors, but they wouldn't open. I was so frustrated, so angry, so scared. Tears were streaming down my face as I pounded and pounded.

"Excuse me? Can I help you?"

I turned to find a nurse standing there, reading a file folder.

"I'm looking for a shooting victim named Michael Quinn. I was told he was in this unit."

The woman in white closed the file she'd been reading and gave me a hard, bureaucratic stare.

"You're Mrs. Quinn?"

"No, I'm —"

"You're his friend?"

"Yes."

"Friendship has no legal status."

"You don't understand. I love him, and I *need* to know if he's okay."

"I can't give you any further information. You'll have to get it through the family."

"But I'm his family!"

I turned to try the doors again, but they were gone; in their place stood a stout iron gate. As I reached to open it, a masked figure slammed through, striking me down.

Flat on my back, I tried to see who'd hurt me, but the shadows closed in and the world went black . . .

I opened my eyes to darkness. The flames of the fireplace had turned to ash, and the bedroom window was shut tight.

Mike was snoring softly beside me, his heavy body curled possessively around mine. My limbs felt languorous from our lovemaking, but my mind was spinning from my nightmare, so vivid and so awful.

The particulars of the dream might fade, but I knew two things would stay with me: the image of Mike being shot; and a phrase, seemingly harmless, now stuck inside me like a dagger —

Friendship has no legal status.

TWENTY-TWO

The next day, I woke to a warm kiss on my lips and a masculine murmur in my ear —

"Good morning, sweetheart . . ."

Yawning, I squinted against the golden sunshine pouring through the tall windows. Mike's large frame was sitting on the edge of the bed, already dressed for work in chocolate brown dress slacks and a crisp white shirt.

My nose immediately detected two stimulating aromas: freshly brewed coffee and caramelized cinnamon. Sitting up, I spied two mugs of coffee on the nightstand, next to a plate of something that smelled amazing.

"You *baked*?" I asked, incredulous.

"I toasted."

As I adjusted the sheet to cover myself, he proudly presented the breakfast-in-bed plate. I marveled at the stack of freshly made cinnamon toast — so simple yet so wonderful. I sipped the coffee and crunched the toast.

"This is delicious."

"Yeah, but it *should* be smoked salmon on toast with champagne and flowers. You deserve it."

"This will do just fine . . ."

The coffee was hot and perfectly balanced, the toast sweet and spicy with the beautiful bite of Saigon cinnamon. Extra good because the man I loved had made it with his own handcuff-wielding hands.

"Okay, I'm off to work," Quinn said, getting up to pull on his shoulder holster. "I just wanted you to know how much I appreciated the TLC last night — the dinner, the wine, *that dress* . . ." He smiled. "Everything."

"You're welcome . . . but do me one favor."

"What's that?"

"Be careful out there."

He grabbed his suit jacket. "Try not to worry."

"Impossible."

"Why? It's a beautiful day. Focus on that. The sky is clear and the weather's warmed up —" He crossed the room to crack the window. "Breathe in some of that fresh —"

"Get away from the window!"

The shriek of my voice stopped Quinn dead. When he turned around, he found me in a state.

"Clare? What's wrong?"

I shook my head hard, trying to clear my mind of last night's awful images. But I couldn't. My fears and frustration finally got the better of me, not only because of the nightmare. My anxieties had been building since the first round of *Cops Shot* headlines.

Not knowing *where* he was, *how* he was — the weight of it was crushing.

"I'm sorry," I said, swiping my wet cheeks. "Bad dream, that's all."

"That's not all. Not if you're this upset. Talk to me . . ."

He sat back down on the bed, and I told him about my nightmare. He listened patiently until I was done.

"You know, I've had strange dreams like that," he said. "It's actually a good thing. It means your mind is trying to process the events of your life, make sense of it all."

"But it doesn't solve a thing."

"Solve?" Quinn sat back. After studying me a moment, he frowned. "Clare . . . you and I . . . we can't 'solve' the work I do. You know that."

"I know that."

For another long moment, he held my gaze. Then he looked away and nodded — almost to himself — as if he'd just made a decision. Finally, he turned back, took my hands in his, and said —

"Clare, do you think maybe you and I should . . . think about a change?"

"A change? What kind of change?"

"The way things are going right now, our situation may not be the best thing for you . . ." He squeezed my hand, and my breath caught.

Had Quinn understood my dream that well? Was he about to propose that we finally fix our "legal status"? *That's it,* I thought. *He's going to propose!*

"Go on," I said, leaning forward with hope.

"I think maybe we should take a break, you and I . . . for a little while."

"A break!" I jerked my hands away. "You want to break up?"

"I didn't say break up. I said *break.* A temporary cooldown between us. It might be the best thing —"

"For you?"

"No. For *you.* Some distance between us should help lessen your anxieties."

"*Distance* from you is the last thing I want — the very last. Please, don't *ever* suggest

136

we break up again. Look, the truth, *the real truth* about what upsets me is that we're not closer."

"Closer than last night?" Quinn's eyebrows arched. "I don't think that's possible. Unless we join molecules."

"No, but we can join something else."

He blinked. "You're talking *marriage?*"

I nodded.

"Clare, before we left Washington, I asked you to consider a next step for us. Do you remember what you said?"

"Yes, of course. I told you I wanted to wait, but only because we've had so many changes in our lives. I wanted to get back into a settled routine here in New York before we started planning our future."

"Well, *you* might feel settled now. But at the moment, I'm in the middle of a manhunt that's going to take most of my time and all of my energy. I can't think about the rest of my life right now, especially when —"

He cut himself off.

"When what?"

"Never mind." He got up and slipped on his jacket. "We should talk about this another time."

"I know what you were going to say. You don't want to think about the rest of your life right now because you're not sure you'll have a rest of your life — correct?"

"Let's not do this, Clare. I'm running late as it is —"

"Mike, wait! *Please.*"

He turned at the door.

"Do you remember when we tried to see Sully at the hospital? Do you recall what that nurse told me?"

"No. Too much was going on —"

"She said, *'Friendship has no legal status'* — and it tore me apart. All I could think was: What if you had been the one shot up and in critical condition? What would I be then?"

"I don't know . . ." Quinn rubbed his forehead. "Cops on the street, the smart ones, don't spend their time imagining being shot and lying in a hospital. We focus on positive outcomes, on coming home in one piece."

"That's all well and good, but I'm not a cop on the street. I just happen to love one. And what happened to Sully has woken me up to the fact that I've put you off too long. There are consequences to my decision to wait. And I don't want to wait anymore. I want us to be more than friends. I want us to have legal status."

For a moment, Quinn stared wide-eyed at

me, and then — he laughed. He actually laughed. I couldn't believe it!

"What is so funny?"

He folded his arms. "Sorry, but any man who used that phrase to propose — *'Darling, I'd like to give you legal status'* — would probably get a glass of champagne thrown in his face."

"Don't make light of this."

"I'm not. But try to understand — I cannot have this discussion now. And it's not something we should rush, anyway. Marrying a cop . . ." He shook his head. "It comes with a lot of baggage."

"Oh, for heaven's sake. At our age, who *doesn't* come with a lot of baggage?!"

Just then, Quinn's phone buzzed. He apologized, pulled it out, read the text, and cursed.

"What's wrong? It's not Sully —"

"No. A friend downtown sent me a warning."

"What kind of warning?"

He showed me the screen. "Read it for yourself . . ."

Just got out of commish meeting. Members of mayor's staff pushing idea that shooter dresses as superhero B-cause he has "legit" grudge, targeting "bad" cops.

They R pushing for any officers targeted by shooter to be investigated by IAB for police misconduct. Watch your back, buddy.

"Are you kidding me!" I cried, jumping out of bed. *Oh, crap, I'm naked,* I realized and snatched up a robe.

"These officers are *victims*! The mayor's office should be pinning medals on them, not having them investigated by your Internal Affairs Bureau for suspicion of misconduct! This is outrageous!"

I expected Quinn to start yelling, too. If I were him, I'd be punching a wall. Instead, he seemed more fascinated with my emotional reaction.

In silence, he studied me as I angrily shoved my arms through terry cloth sleeves and furiously tied the robe's belt. Whatever he was thinking, it seemed a cool, clear calculation. Only I had no idea what he was adding up.

"Don't tell Fran," was all he said in reply. "I don't want Sully to know. It might give him that heart attack they're trying so hard to prevent."

"I won't tell her, but please keep me updated."

He pocketed his phone. "The next few

weeks may get bumpy, Clare. Try to hang in there, okay?"

"I'm here for you. I always will be."

"I know," he said, touching my cheek. "And I know how lucky I am to have a woman like you in my corner."

Then he downed his coffee and headed out the door.

TWENTY-THREE

"Clare, look. Something's going down on Hudson . . ."

A week after my "legal status" discussion with Quinn, my assistant manager was directing my attention to a pair of police cars rolling up in front of the Village Blend. More sirens wailed in the distance.

As rippling scarlet beams cut the magic-hour glow of the Manhattan twilight, my curious, caffeinated customers looked up from their smartphones — well, some of them did.

When a third squad car arrived, I stepped out from behind the coffee bar. But before I could join Tucker at the door, the touch of a gently wrinkled hand gave me pause.

I faced Madame's violet gaze and genial smile. "It's rude to rush off in the middle of a conversation, dear."

"I'm sorry, but I'm worried there might have been another shooting . . ."

Leaving Madame, I stepped outside, checked with the officers out front, and quickly returned.

"They wouldn't tell me a thing," I informed Tucker. "Just asked me to stay off the street."

Far from reassuring, I thought, but then the entire city had been on edge for a week. Quinn and I hadn't seen much of each other these past seven days, and when we did, our encounters were heartbreakingly brief, nothing more than tense updates on our busy lives.

Every night, I lay alone in bed, aching for him — and wondering if he was consciously putting distance between us to "lessen" my worries. The longer it went on, the more I feared he had made his decision and was gradually breaking things off between us.

The more fool him.

Seeing less of him *didn't* lessen my worries. But it was accomplishing one thing — it was shredding my heart to pieces.

As I walked back to the coffee bar, Madame waved me over and patted the seat beside her.

"Sit down, Clare. Take a break. That sound and fury could be anything, or nothing at all. This *is* New York, you know."

"Ain't that the truth," Tuck said, and as

he distracted our customers with a few bars of "On Broadway" (in his *Off*-Broadway cabaret voice), Madame leaned close.

"Please don't worry, Clare. I hate to see you so troubled." She reset a strand of hair that escaped my ponytail and squeezed my hand. "Now let's get back to your presentation plan for next week's *Andrea Doria* competition."

I prepared a sample cup for Madame and held my breath as she inhaled the aroma, preparing to sip.

Earlier in the week, I'd created the Danish blend with a dark-roasted Sumatra and light-roasted Costa Rican, but this coffee needed something more. For days, I tested and retested ratios until one golden afternoon, I remembered something more from my talk with Gus.

The gold of the autumn sun reminded me of another afternoon, one I'd spent in Florence, shopping among the goldsmiths on the Ponte Vecchio, and I suddenly remembered the yellow caturra — a coffee plant that produces yellow instead of red cherries.

Matt had this unique varietal stored in his climate-controlled warehouse in Brooklyn. Grown in the volcanic loam of Puna, it was even honey-processed, like his outstanding Costa Rican.

Unlike the more common "washed" processing method, which used water to strip the coffee bean of the fruit surrounding it, honey-processing removed only the skin of the cherry. With the sticky-sweet pulp remaining, the beans were spread on racks and raked gently under the golden sun several times a day to quicken the drying process. The coffee then rested for months, developing exotic flavor and striking character in its sugary cocoon before the dried parchment layer was finally removed by machine and the beans sold for roasting.

Though the method was labor-intensive, it produced some of the best-tasting coffees in the world. The honey-processed Puna was one of them, with transcendent notes of floral and spice, apricot, caramel, and almond.

Unfortunately, Hawaiian coffees were highly priced — demand was high, supply limited. *But* if I used only 10 percent in my blend, I could bring our "Night and Day" *Andrea Doria* entry to a premium level for a price far less than our Billionaire Blend — which was Matt's directive.

Madame tasted the results of my honey-yellow experiment, closed her eyes, and swooned.

"Superb," she said simply.

She sipped again. "Beautifully balanced, Clare, with a plush mouthfeel. The flavors are dazzling, and they continue to unfold through the sip and swallow." With a nod, she continued sampling as the coffee cooled. "Ah . . . perfect caramelization. Like the perfect man: smooth yet exciting, sweet yet exotic, and" — she winked — "a little nutty."

"I didn't think I could produce a winner in the short time I had but —"

"You know what I say, dear. *No pressure, no diamonds.* And this is a jewel. *Un bijou!* A coffee diamond!"

I grinned with relief (and a little pride) explaining how I'd even done a little detective work, calling the ship's contractor to discover what machines they'd installed in the galleys for making coffee (a brand of super-automatic now popular with many of New York's top hotel kitchens).

"Now I can adjust the roast for that particular machine's optimum settings," I noted. "And the addition of a Hawaiian coffee will be attractive for the marketing and menu descriptions — luxury taste without an astronomical price."

"In plain terms, it'll make a nice profit — for them and us."

"No profit, no business. Isn't that what

you *also* say?"

"*Exactement!*"

As we chatted, I pretended to ignore the fact that more NYPD cars were arriving by the minute, or that our sidewalk was now a municipal sea of uniforms. Then several officers began cordoning off the area around the front door.

They're setting up a perimeter, and the Village Blend is ground zero. Why? Are they trying to keep people out, or rope us all in?

I was about to storm outside and demand answers when a parade of officers pushed through the door enough times to make our greeting bell peal like a country church on Christmas morning.

Detectives Lori Soles and Sue Ellen Bass, partners who'd been nicknamed the "Fish Squad," led the pack in starched slacks and navy blazers. I counted these women as friends, or at least friendly acquaintances — but you wouldn't know it from their grave demeanors.

Oh, God, I thought. *Something terrible must have happened to Mike, and they've come to tell me!*

Despite my worst fears and weak knees, I faced the police squarely. "Detective Soles. Detective Bass. How can I help you tonight?"

"We're here to place you under arrest, Clare Cosi."

I blinked, certain I'd heard wrong. "Arrest me?"

"Yes, you."

It was Sue Ellen Bass who spoke this time. The more volatile of the pair, she quickly reached for the handcuffs on her belt.

With their ridiculous charge came a realization. *There's no "bad news." Mike Quinn is fine, and the rest of this is just a stupid, silly misunderstanding!*

The rush of relief left me giddy. But my goofball happy grin infuriated Sue Ellen.

"Did you think you could get away with it?" she demanded, rattling the cuffs like a dungeon mistress.

"Get away with what?"

"Grand theft."

I gawked at the pair. "Are you kidding?"

Lori Soles shook her head. "This is serious, Clare. In New York State, stealing a police detective's heart is a Class A felony."

With the practiced perfection of a Rockettes chorus line, the wall of uniforms parted, and there was Mike Quinn, down on one knee, wearing a crooked smile and his best blue suit.

Time seemed to stop, the packed coffeehouse stilling with it, as his hand lifted a white ring box. My breath caught at the sight — of Mike, the box, and the tiny golden bell embossed on top.

"Clare," he began. "I love you, and I know you love me."

He opened the box to reveal a small but perfect diamond, its ice blue color shining as brilliantly as the good in Mike's eyes.

The uniquely Campana-cut stone had exceptional clarity — but it was no solitaire. Around the blue center, a circle of smaller coffee diamonds winked at me with shocking familiarity.

I knew at once that Gus's own hands had made this stunning piece, a perfect replica of the legendary lost Eye of the Cat, which I'd openly admired in his home just a week ago.

But how could Mike have known?

When I tried to ask him, he shushed me.

"First, I have something to ask you. And you better think hard about your answer. With these law officers as witnesses, it's going to be tough to change your story."

I nodded dumbly, waiting for the question to pop.

"Clare Cosi, will you marry me?"

TWENTY-FOUR

Mike's voice was firm and steady, his expression sweetly somber.

I had to admire the man's self-control. When I tried to speak, I couldn't find my tongue. I couldn't see straight, either. Yet even with my eyes blurred by tears, I sensed Mike's anxiety, along with his unspoken questions —

Did I do a good thing here or completely screw up? Are you thrilled or embarrassed? Are you going to make me the happiest man on earth or pierce my soul and say you've changed your mind?

Clearing my throat, I gave the man his answer.

"Of course I'll marry you —" My voice broke, and I swallowed hard. "I know it won't be easy. But I love you with all my heart. So . . ."

I met his eyes and smiled. "Let's give it a shot."

At the word *shot,* gasps hit my ears and every cop in the place froze.

Mortified, I froze with them — until Mike burst out laughing, along with the entire coffeehouse. Grinning with joy, and more than a little relief, he rose, took my left hand, and guided the tiny golden circle onto my finger.

I gazed at the dazzling blue center of what was now my engagement ring — the coffee diamonds flawlessly set around it — and realized this band not only fit perfectly, it felt perfect, too.

Then I wrapped my arms around my new fiancé and stiffened. The ring may have felt right, but Quinn's torso felt wrong, oddly rigid, his chest harder than Superman's. The fleeting perception was quickly banished when his lips met mine, and the cops, customers, Madame, and my staff began to applaud.

Amid all the congratulations, Mike and I were quickly separated.

While he endured a round of backslapping and good-humored "give it a shot" jabs from his buddies, I found myself cornered. Esther Best and Nancy Kelly were circling me like curious birds while Tucker loomed over my shoulder.

"So . . ." he said. "Let's meet your new

BFF, because everyone knows a diamond is a girl's best friend."

As we ogled the ring, Madame moved closer, and I lifted it for her inspection.

"See the coffee diamonds?" I pointed out excitedly. "They're just like the ones on that brooch Matt's father gave you."

"Not *like* the ones on my brooch, dear. Those *are* the very diamonds."

"What?"

"When Antonio died, I promised myself I'd never sell them. But I knew how much you admired them, so I happily *gifted* them to you and your future husband."

"But how?" I gaped at her. "How could you know that Mike would —"

"Your young officer paid me a visit," Madame confessed. "He wanted my advice on choosing your engagement ring. He said you were always behind him and his work, and he wanted a ring that would show you that he felt the same about you. He insisted on a token of his love that would convince you that he respected your life and wanted to join it, not take you away from it. I suggested we use the coffee diamonds, as a symbol of your ties to the Village Blend, and he happily agreed."

"What a beautiful gesture."

She opened her arms, and we hugged each

other tight.

"Thank you," I croaked, tears welling again.

"Thank that man of yours. He is something special. And, frankly, I'd consider losing *you* a much greater loss than those diamonds."

Twenty-Five

With eyes as wet as mine, Madame excused herself, announcing she wanted to get the ball rolling on this surprise party and see to serving all the guests who'd come — which looked to me like the whole Sixth Precinct and one entire floor of One Police Plaza.

That's when Nancy and Esther jumped in.

"Let's take a closer look at those rocks," Nancy said, seizing my hand.

My eyebrows rose when she produced a jeweler's loupe. With professional aplomb, Nancy flipped the compact magnifying glass open and placed it against her eye.

"This blue diamond is some piece of ice!" She whistled. "I'll bet that cost a pretty penny —"

"Nancy!" I whispered. "A public jewelry appraisal is hardly appropriate right now."

I tugged my hand, but she held firm.

"One minute, boss!" She activated the

loupe's tiny LED light and squinted into the glass. "Hey, some of those little brown diamonds have tiny stars inside. It's hard to see, but —"

"Okay, enough!" I pried my hand loose at last.

"Wow, Nancy. I didn't know you were training to be a pawnbroker," Esther cracked. "All things considered, it's a good career move. With a little more training, you'll be cheating junkies, drunks, and degenerate gamblers out of their heirloom watches and wedding bands in no time."

"Don't be silly." Nancy waved the device. "I'm using this to make coffee-themed charm bracelets to sell online — *and* whimsical wall decorations."

"Wall decorations?"

"Like that paper-clip sculpture I hung above our bathroom mirror. I call it *Galloping Unicorn.*"

Esther's eyes went wide. "*Galloping Unicorn?* And here I thought it was a three-legged mule in desperate need of rhinoplasty."

Nancy frowned. "That's harsh."

"It's the arts. Expect criticism."

Tuck groaned. "If you ladies want to talk art, join the Salmagundi Club! Right now we have cups to fill and goodies to serve, so

155

stop your tuts and move your butts!"

As Tuck herded Esther and Nancy toward the kitchen, Esther couldn't resist making one last comment —

"Are you sure pastries are a good idea? Don't you think these cops have enough padding already?"

The observation reminded me of my engagement hug with Mike. His torso did feel thicker and his pecs seemed harder than steel — or was it Kevlar?

I looked closer at this conspicuous police presence. *Oh, for heaven's sake.* I'd been too bowled over by Mike's proposal to realize. These officers were wearing bulletproof armor under their uniforms.

Were they really that paranoid about the shooter? Or was this little show more than an engagement prank?

I searched for Quinn, but he was still surrounded by backslapping policemen — though I noted that the boisterous congratulations were starting to recede. Now the cops were speaking in low tones, through poker faces.

Something's up. But what? I wondered, scanning the crowd for several minutes. *There must be someone here I can wheedle the truth out of . . .*

Sully Sullivan would have been perfect.

His strict Irish Catholic rearing left him with one brother a priest, another a missionary, and himself uncomfortable at being anything but completely truthful.

Quinn once told me that when he and Sully ran "good cop, bad cop" on some suspect, Sully had to play good because he couldn't lie — not convincingly, anyway.

Unfortunately, Sully was still recovering in the hospital, or he surely would have been here tonight.

Sergeant Emmanuel Franco, another member of Quinn's OD Squad, *might* be counted on for the straight story. After all, I was the young detective's ally in his battle to win my daughter's heart — and overcome my ex-husband's objections.

For that alone, Franco owed me.

I scanned the room for a pair of really broad shoulders (an embarrassment of riches with all these cops around) topped by a streetwise shaved head.

I spotted Manny Franco the same time he spotted me. Waving his smartphone, he beckoned me over.

TWENTY-SIX

"Hey, Coffee Lady, check this out." Franco displayed his phone. "I got your entire engagement on digital. I'm sending it to Joy tonight."

We watched the recording together.

"Do you think my daughter will be surprised?" I asked.

"More like surprised it took so long. She's been waiting for this. And I think we can guess why." He grinned. "Should I be getting the name of Lieutenant Quinn's jeweler?"

Oh, no, I thought. *Slow down!*

In less than an hour, I'd gone from single woman to pledged in marriage. My daughter was still happily adjusting to her new responsibilities managing our Washington, DC, coffeehouse. And I was far from ready to fight a war with Matt on accepting Franco as his new, shaved-headed, handcuff-wielding son-in-law.

So instead of encouraging Franco, I patted the young detective's giant shoulder and assured him — "There's *plenty* of time . . ."

Then I dropped my hand and felt his back.

"My, that's an awful lot of *armor* you're wearing."

"I . . . ah . . ." The boy choked on his own gravelly voice. "I just came off duty."

"And all these other policemen?" I eyed him sharply. "It's pretty obvious that everyone wearing a badge in this place is also wearing body armor, so you must have expected *something* to go down. Come on, Franco, spill it."

Blinking blankly, Franco groped for an answer — until he was saved by the belle.

"Hey, hey, it's the hero of the day!" Sue Ellen Bass slapped Franco's broad back. "Good to know there's a cop we can count on under that Vin Diesel–Telly Savalas thing you've got goin' on."

"Ah, it was nothing," Franco replied through gritted teeth, eyes pleading for her to *shut up* already.

"Did you say Franco is a hero?" I pressed, sensing a crack in the blue wall of silence. "He was far too modest to mention it to me."

"Last week, Kojak Junior here pulled a policewoman out of harm's way after she took a bullet."

My mind raced back to the discussion Quinn and I had about those initial newspaper headlines: *4 Cops Shot in 3 Days.*

"Are you talking about the shooting in Queens?" I asked. "The female traffic cop? The one the papers and NYPD 'believed' was due to random gang activity?"

"That's the one," Sue Ellen confirmed. "Franco was talking with this policewoman in the street. After she was hit, two more shots were fired, but despite the danger to that shiny head of his, Franco pulled the woman to safety and rendered aid and comfort until backup arrived."

Franco was frantically signaling Sue Ellen to stop talking when a uniformed officer called his name.

"Yo, Manny. They need us outside."

Before he left, Franco leaned close. "Sorry for keeping it from you, Coffee Lady. Lieutenant Quinn asked me not to tell you and Joy. He didn't want either of you worrying."

"I see."

As Franco left, I faced down Sue Ellen.

"And I suppose half the cast in *this* production is outside, in cars or on roofs. I hope they get a chance to sample the pastries and coffee, too."

Sue Ellen didn't even try to play dumb. "I wasn't aware you knew."

"I didn't. But all this Kevlar makes it pretty obvious."

"You've got a cop's eye, Clare, and you're a good sport," she said with a measure of respect. "I don't know how I'd feel if my big day was doubling for a perp trap."

I blew out air, but steam was slowly building. "Dangling a party of blue uniforms and hoping the shooter will take the bait? Seems like an awfully risky way to catch a potential cop killer."

Sue Ellen's lips tightened. "Guess you're not so happy, after all."

As I confirmed that observation, her smartphone buzzed.

She glanced at the screen. "Sorry, I have to get back to work. Like I said, this may look like a party, but it's also a police operation, and I'm on duty."

"Of course." I turned and headed for the coffee bar.

"Oh, Clare," Sue Ellen called. "Congratulations, you know, on the whole official engagement thing."

It was soon apparent that the same call Sue Ellen answered was simultaneously received by every law enforcement officer in the coffeehouse.

Almost immediately, the police began to leave, singly or in pairs. When Lori Soles and Sue Ellen Bass hurried out the front door and ran to a sector car, the exodus became a stampede.

As the coffeehouse emptied, a frowning Quinn touched my shoulder.

"I'm sorry, sweetheart, but I have to go. Something's come up. A police emergency. We'll have a long talk when I get back."

You bet we will, I thought.

But what I said was — "Be safe!" — and meant it.

TWENTY-SEVEN

Within two minutes you could hear a cricket chirp in my coffeehouse. A dozen local customers remained, but there was nary a blue uniform (with secret Kevlar Skivvies) in sight.

"Talk about rude," Esther declared.

"What's rude?" I asked.

"Gulp, dunk, thanks a bunch?"

"They had police business."

"Man, I am *never* dating a cop."

"Since you're already engaged to a Russian baker with dreams of being the next Eminem, I don't see that as a problem."

"Sorry for the knock, boss. Some days I can't stop the 'stupid' that flows out of my mouth amidst all the wisdom I impart."

"No offense, but your 'wisdom' could do with a little more filtering, as well."

"Excuse me," Nancy interrupted. "There's a Mr. Arnold waiting by the hearth. He's here to see Mr. Allegro. He says he can't locate him, and it's important."

I sighed, hoping it wasn't that *Andrea Doria* competition. *That is the last thing I want to deal with right now!*

"Goodness, what happened to the party?" Madame cried. "One minute I was reminiscing about an old television program with a pair of very charming vice detectives, and suddenly all the policemen were called away."

"You were discussing television?" Esther asked, astonished.

Madame patted her hand. "My dear, one cannot survive on the rarefied air of high art alone. Why, there was a time — well before you were born, of course — when I never missed an episode of *Mannix.*"

"What was *Mannix*? Sounds like one of those humdrum reality shows. You know, women of a certain age trying to nix men from their lives."

"Not quite," Madame replied. "More like women of a certain age nixing humdrum reality to spend time with a Los Angeles hottie."

"Forget *Mannix*!" I cried. "We've got another issue to deal with."

As Nancy and Esther returned to the coffee bar, I told Madame about Mr. Arnold.

"He *can't locate* my son?" Madame's

hands found her hips. "That's preposterous. Perhaps he went to the wrong address —"

"No. I did not."

In a tone of barely contained impatience, Sal Arnold, attorney-at-law, introduced himself, holding my gaze with disturbing intensity.

"I didn't wish to interrupt your celebration, Ms. Cosi, although it appears someone beat me to it."

Not the most politic opening line, but Sal Arnold seemed a direct man. The diminutive, forty-something lawyer sported a full, bronze beard, which seemed to stand on end as he spoke, and his jaw jutted as aggressively as his considerable midriff.

"This is about Matt?" I asked.

"It is. I visited Mr. Allegro's Sutton Place address this afternoon, to deliver a time-sensitive legal document. I was told by his wife's personal secretary that he no longer resides there, and that they had no forwarding address other than this place of business."

Madame and I exchanged shocked glances.

He no longer resides there! What happened? Did Breanne throw him out? Or was Matt the one who left?

Whichever it was, my ex-husband's second

marriage appeared to be in trouble.

"I told you something was wrong with Matteo," Madame whispered.

I turned to Mr. Arnold. "I'm Mr. Allegro's business partner. I don't know where he is this evening, but this is his place of business, and I can contact him."

"Good. Then I can legally turn this over to you."

He handed me a large white legal-sized envelope.

"See that Mr. Allegro gets this, and follows the instructions to the letter. If he has any questions, my card is inside."

"Is this about the competition?" I asked. "For the *Andrea Doria* coffee blend?"

Sal Arnold blinked. "Goodness no —" He tapped the envelope. "This letter relates to a legacy left in the trust of Matteo Allegro and his offspring, by his late father, Antonio Allegro. It's a dual trust situation that also involves the family of Gustavo Campana, so the matter is rather complicated."

"Gus?" Madame and I said in unison.

"Good evening, ladies. I'm off."

"Wait!" I cried as he headed for the door. "We have more questions!"

"The answers are in the letter, Ms. Cosi," he called over his shoulder. "See that Mr. Allegro opens it as soon as possible." Then

166

Sal Arnold paused at the door and said something even more mysterious —

"Tell him I look forward to our meeting, which will be quite soon."

TWENTY-EIGHT

"I don't understand any of this," Madame said with a baffled frown. "The only legacy Antonio left me was this building, and the mortgage that went with it."

We sat near the brick hearth. While Madame pondered these questions in the crackling flames, Esther served us a second round of espressos. The unopened envelope lay on the marble tabletop between us.

"I knew your husband didn't die wealthy," I said.

"To put it bluntly, we were flat broke. His family left him this building free and clear, but to grow our business, we took out a mortgage on it. You do know the origin of the word *mortgage*? In Latin it means —"

"Death pledge."

"Precisely. And after Antonio died, it nearly choked the life out of me. If not for Gus — and other good friends — helping me out financially, this coffeehouse would

168

be a mobile phone store."

I rubbed my brow, perplexed. "I don't understand. If Antonio had something of value, why not leave it to you immediately? Why delay it all these years? And why is Gus involved?"

"I have no idea. When Matt's father passed away, Gus was already a wealthy man. But you know . . ." Madame glanced my way. "I still remember when Gus didn't have a pair of shoes to call his own."

"Was that after the *Andrea Doria* disaster?"

She nodded. "Just days after the ship sank, Matt's father and I went to Pier 88, where the *Ile de France* was scheduled to arrive with a group of *Andrea Doria* survivors on board. We hoped his cousin was among them, but we didn't know . . .

Madame's gaze grew glassy as she looked back in time, describing the tense mood among the families as they watched the ship approach. Many survivors were standing at the rail as the ocean liner docked. They wore only pajamas or bathrobes — and there were several rescued women wearing nothing but bathing suits . . .

With one white-gloved hand, Blanche Dreyfus-Allegro held her hat against the wind whistling through the terminal while she used the other to turn her husband's young handsome head. Slim, stylish, and attractive, Blanche's striking violet eyes met his espresso-dark gaze.

"We're married now, Antonio. So no ogling. We're here to find your cousin, remember?"

Antonio laughed. "I'm not looking at the bathing beauties, my Bella Blanca. I'm trying to spot Silvio."

"You haven't seen him in years. How can you 'spot' him?"

"I got his picture. And he will know me by this." He tapped his lapel, where a red carnation was pinned.

She tweaked his cheek. "You get so many letters from Italy I don't know how you tell all your relatives apart."

"It's not easy." With a smile, he moved his warm lips to her ear. "They multiply like the rabbits."

Outside the terminal, past the ambulances waiting to receive the injured, thousands pushed against a police barricade. Many were women from New York's Italian communities — some clutching babies and children. Their husbands were aboard the doomed ship, and they had no word of their fates.

Anticipating this ugly circus, Antonio had

170

greased the palm of a longshoreman, who escorted them through a cargo entrance — with a wink for Blanche.

As the liner floated up to the pier, the hundred policemen could no longer hold the line. Soon a mob of three thousand filled the terminal. Desperate shouts and children's cries mingled with the hollow *boom* of the ship bumping the dock, and the chugging engines of trucks unloading clothing donated by area stores.

When the *Ile de France* finally offloaded its passengers, it was the *Andrea Doria*'s survivors who came out first. Joyous men and women immediately rushed forward to embrace loved ones. For the survivors, there were expressions of joy or relief — but just as many had dead eyes, the shock still etched on their faces.

The hugs lingered, and tears of gratitude were shed. Others clung only to one another, wailing inconsolably as a stranger delivered terrible news.

Blanche spied one of her favorite movie stars. Distraught and harried by the press, the actress hurried to another pier in search of her missing son. Meanwhile, the other survivors were led to tables piled with the donated clothing, where they took what they needed.

"There he is!"

Like Antonio, this young cousin had a beautiful head of thick black hair, now disheveled. He wore a once-fine, now ruined suit that somehow seemed too big for his lean, strong build. His silk tie was askew, and he wore no shoes.

A hollow-eyed woman in a ruined party dress and bedroom slippers clung to him. Beside her, a girl no more than four years old stoically looked on as she clung to her mother's hand.

Blanche halted, confused. *But Silvio Allegro is a bachelor. Antonio mentioned no wife, no child.*

Meanwhile, she watched her husband push through the crowd until the men embraced. Then Blanche saw Silvio whisper into her husband's ear, and Antonio react with surprise.

Suddenly, she was warned back by a nurse leading a parade of stretchers. When Blanche finally reached her husband, he and the other man had finished a serious discussion in Italian.

"Silvio died in the crash," Antonio proclaimed as he made the sign of the cross. "This man is Gustavo Campana, and this is his wife, Angelica. Silvio worked for their family business . . ."

Confused by the mix-up, Blanche forced a smile and nodded a sincere greeting. The woman timidly nodded back.

"We'll have to find a place for them to stay," Blanche declared, and Antonio nodded quickly, looking instantly relieved by his wife's quick and generous acceptance of the situation.

As the two couples left the terminal, a man cried out.

"Hey, wait a minute, pal!"

Gustavo appeared stricken with fear, until the man shoved a Florsheim shoe box into his arms.

"These should fit nicely," he told Gus with a grin, adding, "Welcome to America!"

As Madame finished her reminiscence, I leaned forward with more than a few questions.

"Are you *sure* Silvio Allegro died in that shipwreck? The way you tell the story, it sounds like he may have taken Gus Campana's identity."

"It may *sound* that way, but . . . I have no proof. And you have to remember that things were very different back then. We'd all endured a terrible war. We accepted without question that one did what one had to do . . . you understand?"

"I think so. Whatever you did, you did —"

"To survive, dear."

I had more questions, but Madame waved them away with a yawn. "Let's focus on the present, not the past. What time is it now?"

"Nearly eleven."

"And still no call back from my son?"

"I phoned him three times and sent several text messages. I could try again, but I doubt we'll hear from him until morning."

Madame sighed. "Why didn't he come to me if he was having marital problems? I'm his mother!"

"That's why he didn't come to you. Or mention it to me. I'm sure he's embarrassed. He probably feels like a failure, and that's the last thing he wants to be in your eyes — and mine. Or maybe it's a lot simpler than that."

"Simpler?"

"Maybe Matt and Breanne didn't break up for good. Maybe they had a fight and have separated temporarily with intentions to try again."

"But in the meantime, the poor boy has nowhere to live. He could have stayed with me. I have plenty of room."

Playboy Matt? Moving in with his mother? I nearly choked on my espresso.

"He's not in Manhattan very often," I

174

tactfully replied. "He's probably keeping odd hours. He wouldn't want to trouble you with all his comings and goings . . ." *(Not to mention his X-rated, X-tracurricular activities.)*

"You're right, Clare. But where could he be?"

"I have a clue."

TWENTY-NINE

Fifteen minutes later, I was behind the wheel of the Village Blend's delivery van, giving Madame a ride home. The night was crisp and clear, the arch in Washington Square Park glowing whitely against the Lower Manhattan skyline as we rolled up to her Fifth Avenue apartment building.

"Perhaps I should go with you," Madame said. "At times like this, men's fragile egos need mothering . . ."

I assured her the trip wasn't worth her time. "What if I'm wrong and Matt's not there? It's close to midnight now. You wouldn't be back here until two AM."

"Well, if you think it's best. But please, Clare, if you do find my son, remind him that my door is always open."

I squeezed her hand. "I will."

Matt's warehouse sat near the Red Hook piers, where the briny smell of the churning sea permeated the air. As I exited the van to open the security gate, a salty wind blew in from the dark, cold deep.

It chilled me to the bone — and so did my surroundings.

This industrial area of Brooklyn spooked me at night. The black silhouette of the warehouse looked more like an ominous prison than a state-of-the-art holding facility for green coffee beans.

Shaking off my shivers, I locked the gate behind me, parked the van outside, and entered the building through the office door.

As soon as I stepped inside, I detected signs of recent habitation.

An empty pizza box sat on the desk beside the remains of Italian seafood salad in a plastic tray. The French press pot was still warm, and there were wine bottles scattered about (way too many and all of them empty).

The big office couch was made up like a bed, and a brand-new flat-screen TV, sound muted, was playing an HD version of *Kramer vs. Kramer.* On a folding table I found a half bottle of tepid Chianti beside a wine-stained water glass.

This isn't good.

Leaving the office, I moved to the coffee storage chamber.

The door was hermetically sealed, the climate control system pinging happily. I peeked through the window at hundreds of agricultural sacks filled with green gold — freshly picked and processed beans from around the planet, waiting to be roasted.

Yet still no sign of Matt.

That's when I noticed the door to the warehouse garage stood open, the lights inside blazing. As I approached, I heard noises — a water hose gushing, followed by a loud and continuous burst of angry expletives.

"Matt! What's wrong?! Are you okay?!"

On the loading dock in back of the building, I found my ex-husband dripping wet, wearing nothing more than the briefest of briefs.

"Oh, God!" I turned away. "Where are your clothes? What are you doing?"

"Rinsing off from my shower," Matt replied, turning off the spigot. "A very, v-very cold shower."

"You're right. It's freezing in here."

"The central heating doesn't extend to the garage. Anyway, I was working late and I got sweaty. Sometimes the bathroom sink just won't do —"

"Stop telling tales. I've had my fill of them tonight."

"Huh?"

"You're not *working* late. I know about your breakup with Breanne, and I've seen your setup in the office. You've moved in. You're *living* here." I faced my ex and turned away again.

"Put some clothes on, will you? We need to talk."

Matt snorted. "What's with the prudery? There's nothing here you haven't seen before."

"And I shouldn't be seeing it now!"

THIRTY

"There," Matt declared back in his office. "All dressed."

He wasn't, but at least his extremely brief tighty-whities had been replaced by jogging shorts. Matt settled for a towel draped over his broad shoulders in lieu of a shirt, and I did my level best to ignore the water droplets speckling his tanned chest and hard biceps.

More than twenty years ago, when I first laid eyes on Matteo Allegro — shirtless, in cutoff combat fatigues, playing Frisbee with a black Lab on a Mediterranean beach — I'd found him undeniably attractive.

I was a nineteen-year-old art student at the time. He was a backpacking vagabond, a few years older, but light-years beyond me in experience, from speaking foreign tongues to sampling exotic cuisines — and exotic girls.

He'd been away from the States for over a

year, and he said I felt like home.

We became friends at first, not lovers; because, at twenty-two, Matt was not a cynical playboy (not yet, anyway). Joyous and genuine, he was still filled with youthful hope and carefree laughter, along with vivid personal stories from some of the earth's most glorious and dangerous places.

He and I might have been a one- or two-night affair, but a spinout on his motorcycle left him with a broken forearm and battered body.

Like a grounded bird, he seemed sad and lost when I found him reading at a small café. So I cheered him up by showing him — with an art student's eye — the treasures to be found in the Vatican Museums.

By the end of it, he said I'd completely charmed him, making him laugh and think and feel. His cast had made him vulnerable. It also slowed him down, preventing him from dashing off to another part of the world, or risking his neck on paragliding, cliff diving, mountaineering, or any of the other extreme sports he loved.

And so, as the adrenaline junkie healed, we began our relationship.

When the Italian sun went down on our first night together, I drank him in like a superb espresso, wanting more and more.

He wasn't grabby or pushy. Instead, he gave me time, waiting until I'd warmed to him before using his lips and fingers to relax, excite, and surprise me.

The result of our many-splendored summer was Joy — an unexpected treasure I've cherished with all my heart.

I still cared deeply about the well-being of my child's father. And like any straight woman with a heartbeat, I found Matt's globe-trotting daring and combustible energy hard to resist. But romance with the man was a dangerous rocket. No matter how high he took me, I knew where that magnetic pull would leave me — plummeting down into a world that would consume me completely before burning me alive.

"Is that why you came here in the middle of the night, Clare?"

Matt's tone had dropped an octave — his bedroom voice — and his eyes were melting into dark pools. "You came here just to talk? Or . . . for *something else*?"

As the edges of his mouth lifted in a let's-be-bad smile, he stepped closer.

I stepped back.

"I assure you. I am *not* here for 'something else.' If you had returned my calls, I wouldn't have come out here at all. And your secret would still be safe."

He blew out frustrated air. "Who else knows?"

"Your mother. By the way, she says you always have a home with her."

Matt winced. "And give up all this?"

"So why didn't you return my calls?"

"I'm ducking the phone." He ran the towel through his hair. "Breanne's secretary keeps harassing me about moving my stuff out of the condo. That or gleefully informing me which privilege was canceled that day: the health club membership, the lease on the BMW, the dry cleaners, the hairdresser —" His fingers snapped. "Gone with the wind."

"Tough break, Scarlett. Is the split that bad?"

"It's permanent. Breanne and I are over."

THIRTY-ONE

Matt threw the towel into a corner, tugged a *Rio Carnivale!* tee out of his backpack, and pulled it over his head.

"What happened?" I asked. "One too many afternoon delights in your many ports of call?"

"That's the sort of stuff that bothered *you.* Breanne was much more Continental about the whole thing. She agreed to an open marriage because she knew that with me, other women were just —"

"Conquests?"

"*Recreation.* On par with a good tennis match. Two consenting adults. Proper precautions. Where's the harm?"

I was tempted to give him an hour-long lecture on "the harm," including "proper precaution" failure; *Fatal Attraction* attachment; and homicidally jealous boyfriends. But his unchecked libido and haywire moral compass were no longer my problems.

Still, I was curious enough to ask —

"If you two were so 'Continental,' then why the breakup?"

"Familiarity breeds contempt."

"Excuse me?"

"When Bree and I were first married, my long-distance coffee-hunting thing was impressive to her and her crowd of sycophants. I was this great guy, helping the developing world bring their crops to market for a fair price, yada yada. Indiana Jones without the whip — or the colonialism. And I was gone weeks at a time, which ratcheted up the mystique."

He snorted. "Things changed when I stayed put in Manhattan, covering for you while you were in DC with the flatfoot. Six months of working at the Village Blend every day, and I'm suddenly an embarrassment to my trendsetting wife."

"That's overstating it, don't you think?"

"*She's* the one who said it! According to her, I'd become a glorified waiter, pouring cups of coffee for hipsters and tourists."

"But you've *gone back* to coffee hunting. Not that it isn't beyond superficial of her to break up your marriage over a simple job change —"

"It's not just that . . ."

He dropped onto the couch and reached

for that half-empty bottle of Chianti. With a gentle touch, I bent down to stop him.

"It's late, Matt, and the wine looks old."

Shaking me off, he took a heartbreaking swig.

"Bree's magazine is struggling. That's the reality. It's underwater and gasping for air. She saw her lifestyle going down with it — so she clawed for a golden life raft before the inevitable, something to get her to the shore in style. She found one in the Hamptons in the form of a seventy-year-old widowed owner of some media company, one she'll no doubt be in control of one day."

I sighed, feeling Matt's pain and humiliation — but secretly glad he was rid of that awful woman.

"You know what?" I said.

"What?"

"One day, Breanne will discover that in the sea of life, clinging to a warm body is a better way to stay afloat than jumping into a golden life raft. It's only a matter of time before that rich widower realizes how cold-hearted she is and throws her overboard. Then what will she do?"

Matt shrugged. "Find another golden raft."

He took a second swig from the sour

bottle. "Marriage is a mistake for people our age. Better to stay loose, free, unencumbered by —"

As I yanked the bottle from him, he finally saw it.

"My God, Clare! What is *that thing* on your finger?"

THIRTY-TWO

Eyes wide, my ex-husband stared. "Tell me that's not an *engagement* rock?"

"That's exactly what it is. Mike asked me to marry him. I said yes."

"Is that why we need to *talk*?! When did this happen?!"

"Earlier this evening. Your mother and the baristas threw a surprise party."

"And failed to invite me."

"I think your mother felt it would be awkward."

"Considering my current marital situation, or lack of one?"

"We didn't find out about your troubles until after the party, which — as it turned out — pulled double duty as a police operation."

"As a what?"

With a deep breath, I dropped on the couch and told Matt everything. It all poured out — the tense week of thinking

Quinn was breaking up with me, followed by the prank engagement arrest, Madame's gift of coffee diamonds, the party with guests in Kevlar underwear, and finally Sue Ellen's confirmation that the whole thing was a sting operation designed to draw the cop shooter into the open.

When I was finally talked out, I expected a wisecrack or three, and a ranted warning not to marry a guy who would do that to me. But on this night full of surprises, it was my ex-husband's turn to shock me.

"You shouldn't be upset by what happened, Clare. You should be flattered."

"Flattered?"

Matt nodded, looking almost defeated. "Tonight your Eagle Scout went all in. He's decided to make you part of his life. His *whole* life, including the most important thing to that glorified gumshoe — his law enforcement career."

He pointed to my engagement ring.

"That shiny piece of kitsch says it all. Those coffee diamonds he took the trouble to get from my mother show how much he respects what you care about, your involvement with my family's business. I hate to admit it, but even I'm touched."

Sliding close, he studied the ring. "Maybe he should have put a tiny NYPD shield on there, too, to remind you to accept his life's work, as well."

"I guess you're right . . . except for the fact that he wasn't forthcoming, and that really bugs me. He kept me in the dark about the reality behind tonight's engagement party, and I'm pretty sure he's keeping another secret, too."

"A piece on the side?" Matt cracked — until he saw my glare. "Relax. I'm kidding!" He nudged me with his elbow. "Okay, what secret?"

"Right before Sully was shot, Quinn twisted the facts about one of the shootings that made the newspapers. He told me a stray bullet hit a female traffic cop."

"Yeah, I remember that. The paper said something about it being a neighborhood with lots of gang activity."

"Well, tonight I found out that Sergeant Franco —"

"Stop. I do not *ever* want to hear that mook's name again. No joke. Not ever."

"Fine. I found out that *a young detective on Quinn's OD Squad* was right next to that traffic officer when she was hit. But Quinn failed to tell me the truth about that. Instead, he fed me a large helping of baloney, claiming that with all the cops in New York, the chances of someone I know getting hurt were miniscule."

Matt raised an eyebrow. "And?"

"A minute later, Sully was shot."

"So?"

"Add it up! What are the odds? *Two members* of Quinn's small OD Squad are fired on in *one* week? And I don't even have all the facts on the other shootings."

Matt weighed my words. "You might be right. You might not."

"But —"

"Listen, Clare, I'm no fan of men with badges —"

"That's putting it mildly."

"— but as cops go, Quinn's a good one. Maybe the only good one. If anyone can take care of himself, and bring this cop-hunting maniac to justice, your Mikey can. And, hey, if he happens to catch a bullet in the process, remember, I'm always here for you —"

I burst into tears.

"Oh, crap, what did I say? Stop, Clare, don't cry. It kills me when you cry. Come on, I was kidding!"

"N-no you . . . y-you weren't . . ."

As I swiped at my tears, I reached for that stupid bottle of soured Chianti. Now Matt was pulling it from me. He dropped it in the trash, went to his office fridge, and popped the cork on a demi-sec Moët & Chandon Nectar Impérial.

Grabbing two empty coffee mugs, he poured out the crisp, cold bubbly, pressed one into my hand, and sat back down.

"Since I missed the big event, I want to make a toast right now." He put an arm around my shoulders and squeezed, then clinked our mugs. "To your future with Detective Michael Ryan Flatfoot Quinn."

As Matt drained his cup, I took a few sips and felt better, until he added —

"And if your new fiancé ever fails to satisfy you — including and *especially* in the bedroom — I *am* always here for you."

"Okay, enough consoling."

"But not enough champagne!"

He refilled his cup, but when he moved to top off mine, I stopped him. "I'm driving, and we still have to talk."

"There's more?" He eyed me. "This isn't a shotgun wedding, is it? I mean, we won't be hearing the patter of tiny, flat feet? Please tell me Joy's not going to have a Quinn-jawed little sister or brother."

"Don't be ridiculous!" I fished the envelope out of my bag. "I came to talk to you about this."

I told Matt about the attorney, who insisted I deliver the letter ASAP.

"He's the one who clued us in about your breakup."

"I love this guy already."

"Quit complaining and open the letter. It's about a legacy your late father left to you and Joy. It's probably good news. It might be something valuable."

"Now *that* is ridiculous, Clare. My mother struggled for years after my father died. If he had anything valuable, he would have left it to her."

Matt set the bottle aside and tore into the letter. As he read, his bafflement increased.

"I'm supposed to go to 580 Fifth Avenue, Suite 400, at six PM tomorrow. This Sal Arnold guy is going to open a lockbox that has been sealed for decades. I'm named as a co-trustee with Sophia Campana —"

"Gus's younger daughter?"

Matt lowered the letter and took another swig of the champagne. A long one. "This makes no sense."

"Well, in about sixteen hours . . ." I tapped my watch. "Let's hope it will."

THIRTY-THREE

Sixteen hours later, I was back in Manhattan, riding uptown in a yellow cab, Matt's leg bouncing impatiently next to mine.

Thankfully, my ex was no longer half naked.

For this appointment, he'd donned a custom-tailored Italian suit. His longish hair was trimmed and brushed back, his jaw freshly shaved — so freshly that I could still smell the faint scent of jasmine from his imported *après-rasage.*

I'd cleaned up, too, but hadn't fussed as much as he had. A simple skirt, sweater, and low-heeled utility pumps were the extent of my primping. I hadn't bothered with jewelry, except my exquisite cat's-eye engagement ring, at which I couldn't stop staring.

"At least you quit looking at your phone," Matt cracked halfway to Midtown.

"It's in my skirt pocket, on vibrate. And

the second it *does* vibrate, I'll be riveted . . ."

I didn't bother adding that I was still upset about what happened with Quinn. After leaving Matt the night before, I got back to my duplex to find a red rose on my pillow next to a hastily written note.

Quinn said he was sorry he'd missed me, but he felt funny staying in my apartment without me there, and since he had to get up early and didn't know *where* I could *possibly* be at this time of night, he returned to his place.

I put the beautiful rose on the pillow beside me and fell asleep fantasizing what Mike had in mind with its soft petals, silently cursing my decision to drive to Brooklyn.

In the morning, when I failed to reach him by voice, I texted —

So sorry I missed you!

Thirty minutes later I received this reply . . .

Mike: Where were U?

Me: Urgent business. I went to see Matt in Brooklyn.

Mike: Till 2 AM?

Me: Will explain tonight. Dinner?

Mike: Can't promise.

Me: Call me, ok? I love you.

Mike: U2.

And that sad excuse for twenty-first-century communication — an echoed love declaration that looked more like the name of an '80s rock band — was the last I'd heard from him.

I (stupidly) showed the exchange to Matt, who said —

"Aw, how sweet. Not even married yet and he's already neglecting you . . ."

I bit my tongue on a caustic reply, only because I knew he was still smarting from Breanne's putting him out like trash. And, I hated to admit, he wasn't wrong.

Quinn's chilly silence grew louder as the day stretched on. I only hoped this Allegro-Campana "legacy letter" would be worth all the trouble.

Yes, I could have let Matt go to this unveiling alone. But whatever this inheritance turned out to be, it would involve my daughter, *and* it was seriously upsetting my former mother-in-law, which was why I wasn't about to learn the details second-hand.

"Pull up right here," Matt told the driver at 47th Street.

Two lampposts drew my attention as I exited the cab. They flanked 47th like Art Deco pillars to the entrance of a royal palace, each metal pole topped by a glowing lamp in a diamond shape.

That's when I realized where we were: Manhattan's Diamond District, one of the largest centers in the world for buying and selling gemstones and precious metals.

Well over two thousand independent jewelers, appraisers, and precious metal traders worked in this cluttered little plot of Manhattan, and (needless to say) security was tight.

I remembered joining Quinn and Franco one evening at a nearby sports bar. Officers who worked in the area shared hilarious tales of Darwin Award–worthy attempts by shoplifters who thought they could "run off" with thousands of dollars in jewelry.

Not on *this* block.

In addition to a constant NYPD presence, there were undercover guards in the stores, bodyguards for jewelers transporting gems, even armed patrols on the street by retired police officers. And then there were the cameras — high-tech, untouchable cameras everywhere, rumored to be partly funded by the Department of Homeland Security.

Tourists and casual buyers would notice none of this. But after hearing those cop stories, I glanced around self-consciously as we walked to our destination, wondering who on the street was packing . . . and who was watching.

THIRTY-FOUR

Matt's letter directed us to a suite in a skyscraper known as the World Diamond Tower.

The Art Deco building was also the New York headquarters of the Brink's company as well as Lyons Global Security and their massive underground security vault.

This concrete cavern of four steel-reinforced cinder block walls was built into the solid bedrock of Manhattan Island with chambers where millions of dollars in gold, platinum, silver, and palladium were stored along with nightly deposits of gemstones, a fortune in treasure worked with or displayed during the day by Diamond District merchants on the floors above.

The security company also guarded a room holding hundreds of privately owned safe-deposit boxes, and that's where we were headed — the "we" being me, Matt, Sal Arnold, and three men in Lyons uniforms. With their broad shoulders, thick muscles, and vests branded with the flashy lion's paw logo, you could put a cape on any one of them and he'd pass for Panther Man, which didn't calm my nerves any.

In their suite upstairs, Lyons had lovely viewing rooms where owners had their boxes brought to them, and they did their business in comfort and privacy, 24/7. But when we checked in, we were informed that "due to the extraordinary nature of this account" we would be brought to the mountain, so to speak.

The slow descent in a creaky steel mesh-walled elevator was unexpected, and rather unnerving. When we finally landed inside the vault, the concrete passageways and floor of leveled and polished bedrock felt like a claustrophobic catacomb for the dead.

It didn't take long for world-traveling Matt to feel trapped. "What are we waiting for? It's after six o'clock."

Sal Arnold's reply was equally impatient. "We can't do business until Sophia Campana or her legal representative arrives."

I touched Matt's arm. "Do you think your godfather will come?"

"I figure he'll show. Which begs another question —" Matt checked his watch. "Where is Mother? I texted her where to be and when."

"Oh, I forgot to mention. She called me this morning and said she had a change of heart. She said you should stop by tomorrow and discuss the matter. Frankly, Matt, I think she's upset that your late father never mentioned a word to her about this legacy. I also think she's afraid some dark family secret will be revealed."

"Like what? I have a long-lost brother, or sister? Then what's in the box? Their birth certificates, or their bones?"

"That's not even close to funny. You never know what sort of skeleton might pop out of this high-security closet."

Matt shrugged off my warning and fixed his gaze on the lawyer. "I have a question, Mr. Arnold. What is so *extraordinary* about this box that the security chief refused to move it upstairs?"

The portly man shrugged. "The two gentlemen who established this trust sixty years ago bought an unusual amount of insurance, not only from a Swiss company but from this security company, which required that the box should not be removed from the vault by anyone but the owners."

At the end of the passage outside, the noisy elevator thudded to a halt and the steel doors clattered opened. A minute later, a guard ushered in a natural beauty in a black A-line dress. Her amber-brown eyes were bright, her charming smile lined and glossed in a vibrant red that precisely matched her shoes, handbag, and glittering jewelry.

In a perfumed cloud of style and grace, Sophia Campana had arrived.

THIRTY-FIVE

"I wore my hair up, Matteo, so you wouldn't be tempted to tug on it."

As Sophia touched the glossy back of her dark golden French twist, I admired the ruby-and-diamond Campana originals dangling from her ears, matching pieces around her lovely, long neck and slender wrist.

"I couldn't help myself, Sophia," Matt said with a laugh. "You always wore those stupid pigtails. They made you a target."

With easy elegance, Sophia approached us, the strappy heels of her dramatic designer sandals clicking on the bedrock. She gave Matt a tight hug and Continental kisses on both cheeks. Then she warmly greeted me.

"Clare, it's been too long."

"I know, but it's good to see you again . . ."

The last time I'd seen Sophia was well over ten years ago.

She'd stunned me by schlepping all the

way out to New Jersey to deliver an early birthday present to my daughter. It was Joy's first birthday away from Manhattan, and she wasn't adjusting well to my divorce from Matt and our move to the suburbs. She didn't like the new school and was having trouble making friends.

I remember how touched I was by Sophia making the effort to find us. Her grinning arrival was a ray of warm light on a cold, rainy day.

As soon as Sophia handed Joy her gift, she tore open the wrapping to find a narrow white box with a tiny golden bell on the lid. Inside was a gorgeous chain of yellow gold with a topaz pendant the color of sunshine, masterfully cut into the shape of a many-faceted heart.

"The color of this stone makes it very special," Sophia explained as she gently lifted the treasure from its white velvet bed. "It's what we call *imperial topaz.* See the way my father cut it? You can tilt it this way in the light and it looks bright yellow, like a rising sun. Tilt it the other way and it looks more golden with a pinkish hue, like the setting sun in the late afternoon . . ."

As Sophia undid the chain and fastened it around Joy's neck, my daughter listened with big eyes and rapt attention.

"The ancient Egyptians believed their sun god, Ra, gave this jewel its magical color. Many still believe that wearing imperial topaz brings good luck, long life, beauty, and intelligence. It's my hope this gem will lend you its ancient earth energy and help brighten your days."

The moment Sophia finished telling Joy about the necklace, my daughter flew to the mirror to see how it looked.

"Joy!" I called, worried the girl had forgotten her manners. "What do you say to Aunt Sophia?"

"Oh, I'm sorry!" She turned and ran back. "Thank you! Thank you! Thank you so much! It's beautiful, I love it, I love it!"

Joy hugged Sophia with a brightness I hadn't seen in months.

In the days that followed, Joy's pride in her new pendant gave her the confidence to make two new friends. (No doubt relating the history and mythical power of the sun-colored gem she wore to school every day had helped melt some of the "new girl" ice, as well.)

The two classmates encouraged Joy to join their Girl Scout troop, and by the time her birthday arrived, we had a house bursting with the energy of laughing, happy kids.

Of course, I thanked Sophia, too — for

giving the gift of joy to my Joy — and I wouldn't let her leave that day without a delicious dinner.

It wasn't until Joy went to bed that Sophia admitted over coffee and a plate of my lemon-iced Anginetti and Chocolate-Almond Biscotti that one of the reasons for her visit was to tell me about Matt and how hard he was taking our split.

A little digging and I realized she had heard only half the story.

Matt's half.

As gently as I could, I told her the *other* half — about Matt's cheating and lying, and about his cocaine addiction. I confessed that I'd stayed with him until he got clean of the drugs, but I couldn't remain in the marriage, not for the long haul, not for my own sanity and self-worth.

I needed to stand on my own, apart from a young man who'd taken too much of my good faith, loyalty, and love — taken them for granted instead of cherishing them for the gifts they were.

I still loved Matt, but that wasn't the problem. What we lost — what *he* lost — was our ability to function as a married couple. I would never trust him with my heart again.

Sophia had listened with extreme kindness. But she was barely in her midtwenties back then, and (with memories of her girlish crush on Matt still fresh) she couldn't comprehend why I wouldn't give "a great guy like him" another chance.

Still . . . she was kind enough to listen to my side, and she did sincerely care about me and Joy — and that's what mattered most.

As we parted that evening, she hugged me tight, and wished me all the luck in the world.

We tried to keep in touch — a few cards and phone calls — but with her mother, Angelica, gone, Sophia had already begun taking on the responsibilities for the retail end of the family business.

In the years that followed, she encouraged her father to expand his market, and she spearheaded that vision by traveling to Chicago, Dallas, Los Angeles, San Francisco, and then London, Paris, Rome, and Tokyo.

The years had changed her, it seemed to me. She was so sophisticated now, so grown-up. And one thing I knew from overhearing that private argument with her husband last week in that strident, cynical voice that I barely recognized —

Sophia Campana finally understood heartbreak.

THIRTY-SIX

"We'll have to catch up," Sophia sincerely insisted as we finished our hug. "Promise?"

"Of course," I assured her.

"And you —" She poked Matt's hard chest. "How is it I never see you? You're married to Breanne Summour now, right? Why don't you go with her to Milan's Fashion Week this spring? We three can get together and go to some great parties."

Matt immediately looked uncomfortable. But before he could offer the awkward news of their split, Sal Arnold loudly cleared his throat.

"Might we postpone this little reunion? We have business to attend to."

The frosty lawyer faced the nearest uniformed guard. "So, where is this box, please?"

The Lyons man double-checked the key in Sal Arnold's hand against his itinerary sheet. He took five steps, pointed to a drawer no bigger than a toaster, and undid the top lock.

"Your key will open this one, sir."

After the security team stepped outside to give us privacy, Sal Arnold slipped his key into the second lock and slid it open. A smaller steel container was nestled inside, and the lawyer used yet another key to open it. Then he lifted out the contents.

We stared in disappointment at a sixty-year-old Florsheim shoe box tied with butcher's twine.

"May I?" Matt asked.

"Of course." The lawyer handed it over. "This belongs to you and Ms. Campana now, whatever it may be."

Matt shook the box. "It's not very heavy."

He carried it to a table in the center of the room. Sophia untied the knot and pulled off the lid. On a bed of ocean blue velvet sat a plain white envelope. Matt opened it and read the typed single-page letter inside, dated December 1956.

To our sons and daughters:
Six decades have passed, we are probably dead, and the world has most likely forgotten the treasure inside this box.
We now leave it in your trust, as a gift to a generation we will never know.

Divide the profits equally among your-selves and your children (our grand-children) with the love, devotion, and blessings of their grandfathers.

Antonio Allegro & Gustavo Campana

The letter was signed by both men. A few words of another language were scrawled at the bottom — *"ken eyne hore"* — along with a final name, "A. Goldman," followed by *"mazl un brokhe,"* but none of us wasted time questioning those notations. All eyes turned instead to the bundle of velvet inside the box.

"Open it, Matt!" Sophia urged.

It took a few painfully protracted seconds for Matt to unwind the velvet cloth. When he exposed its contents, Sal Arnold was the first to react.

"Holy cow!"

The rest of us gasped, or cried out — none louder than Sophia Campana.

"Madre di Dio! È L'Occhio del Gatto!"

Matt and I exchanged incredulous glances. Neither of us had ever seen a diamond so large or a setting so beautiful — except, of course, in Gustavo Campana's photo of his late wife.

This was it, we realized, and I silently

echoed Sophia's cry.

Mother of God! It's the Eye of the Cat!

THIRTY-SEVEN

Even in the harsh fluorescent lights of this high-tech dungeon, the glacial blue glow of the *Occhio del Gatto* was alluring, almost hypnotic.

"What a hunk of ice!" Sal Arnold gushed, his impatient aloofness suddenly gone. "A diamond that big can't be real, can it?"

"Let's find out." Sophia reached into her elegant Italian handbag and withdrew a jeweler's loupe considerably more impressive than my barista Nancy's economy model.

Feet together, one hand on bended knee, Sophia stooped on her stilettos to study the jewel. Her elegant style and graceful pose reminded me of a young Audrey Hepburn gazing through the window in *Breakfast at Tiffany's*.

"It's real," she declared a moment later. "All 59.6 carats' worth. The distinctive blue shade, the Campana cut — even the VVS cat-shaped flaw is right where it ought to be —"

"VVS?" I asked.

"Very, very small. And many of the coffee diamonds in the setting display the VS asterism flaws — another validation mark of the piece."

"Then this jewel is authentic . . . ?" A wide-eyed Sal Arnold had temporarily lost his tongue. "Why . . . it must be worth millions."

"Tens of millions, easy," Sophia replied absently as she studied the necklace itself. "The diamonds have intrinsic value, but these days it's the historical value that fetches the fortune."

"And what exactly is the history of this thing?" Matt asked, folding his arms. "I mean, I know it was famously lost on the *Andrea Doria,* but how did the Campanas end up with it?"

"They were given it as a gift, during the Renaissance — from the Medici family."

"Seriously?" I blurted.

"Seriously," Sophia affirmed.

"A Medici dug it up?" Matt asked in a doubtful tone.

"No. It originated in India from the famous Golconda diamond mines."

"That's where the Hope Diamond was

found, right?"

"Yes, Clare, those mines stretch back for centuries, to the first diamonds ever found by man — or woman. And *this* diamond was said to have originated as the orb of a pagan idol."

Matt scoffed, "Until Indiana Jones came along and stole it, right?"

"Don't be cynical, darling. The Eye of the Cat isn't the only jewel to formerly grace an idol. There's a black diamond called the Eye of Brahma, and the Orlov, on display at the Kremlin. It was the Eye of Vishnu, until a French soldier stole it in the 1700s."

"So who stole the Eye of the Cat?" Matt asked.

"Originally? No one. It was a gift from a Hindu goddess who served as the protector of children."

Matt snorted. "Sorry, Sophia, but Indiana Jones sounds more plausible —"

I elbowed Matt into silence. "Go on. I'd like to hear the story."

"According to the legend, centuries ago in Eastern India, a bandit chief kidnapped a widow's children. The chief told the woman he would only return them if she agreed to steal all the jewels from the crown of the Hindu goddess Shashthi, protector of children."

"Blackmail is nothing new," Matt cracked.

"The widow went to the temple. Instead of trying to steal the goddess's jewels, she prayed for help before her stone statue, rendered as a beautiful woman with a glittering crown, riding a giant feline with two ice blue diamonds for eyes. In answer to her prayers, the goddess appeared in a fountain of water and instructed the widow to appease the bandit by taking one of the cat's diamond eyes and leaving the rest of the jewels behind."

"I think I know how this story ends," Matt said, before I delivered another silence-inducing elbow to his midriff.

"Of course the bandit was angry that the woman brought only one jewel. But when he raised his sword to strike her and her children dead, the goddess's giant black cat appeared in a burst of fire. The cat slaughtered the bandit, and sent the mother and children on their way with his Eye as their eternal protector."

A black cat dealing vengeance? I thought. *Sounds like a Bollywood version of Panther Man — and not much different than the story of the guardian cat on the Ponte Vecchio bridge. Is this all a coincidence, or was Gus really onto something?*

"The Eye of the Cat was lost to history

until the sixteenth century," Sophia continued, "when it was used to pay part of a ransom by pirates defeated by Cosimo de' Medici, Grand Duke of Tuscany. Years later the duke presented the jewel to the Campana family, as thanks for their help in clearing the butchers off the Ponte Vecchio."

"How civic-minded," Matt said dryly. "Why did they want the butchers off the bridge?"

"The smell," I said, recalling the history. "The Medici palace was near the bridge, and the family didn't like the smell of the butchers' tables. They also wanted to give the bridge more prestige."

"That's right, Clare." Sophia nodded. "The butchers were moved out, forcibly in most cases, and the gold merchants moved in. In the years that followed, my family recut the diamond, and set it as a tribute to the Hindu legend, which is probably how the myth of the protective bridge cat came about in the first place. The jewel was passed down through the years, until the *Andrea Doria* sank and the jewel went down with it . . . except it didn't."

Sophia shook her head. "Do you know how many deep-sea treasure hunters perished searching the shipwreck for this very gem? All those lives lost, and the jewel hidden in this safe-deposit box all along . . ."

She returned her attention to the appraisal.

"I must say, this setting is in excellent condition, considering it spent sixty years in an old shoe box. The clasp is intact, the gold held its luster . . . but several decorative stones are missing. Two, four, six, ten . . . I count *sixteen* coffee diamonds gone from the setting. They must have been lost during the shipwreck."

I exchanged a guilty glance with Matt.

I was tempted to hide my left hand behind my back, but decided honesty was the best policy. With a deep breath, I was about to confess that eight of those diamonds were likely on my left hand. Nancy even mentioned seeing the tiny star flaws at their centers. But when I tried to raise my hand to show Sophia, Matt silently gripped it and forced it back down.

"If this is true," he loudly said, cutting off my attempted confession, "how in heaven's name did my father come to partially own it — or at least will it as a legacy?"

Sophia's expression grew increasingly baffled. "I don't know, Matteo. This is a total surprise to me, too — and a complete mystery."

Matt faced Sal Arnold. "I think you know

more about this than you led us to believe."

Sal Arnold's head slouched between his round shoulders as if he were dodging shrapnel.

"Yeah, okay," he said. "That name on the letter. A. Goldman. I know who it is. Abe Goldman was my grandfather on my mother's side. He was a diamond trader in this very building. His son founded the law firm that I inherited with my brother. When our father passed, we moved the business to Queens, and the trust moved with us."

"And?" Matt probed.

Arnold shrugged. "That's all I know."

"But there must be some kind of a paper trail," Matt insisted. "A registered appraisal. Something?"

When Sal Arnold shook his head, Sophia said she wasn't surprised.

"Look, Matt, you see here on the letter. The words *mazl un brokhe* are written at the bottom. That means *good luck and a blessing.*"

"I know what it means, Sophia."

"No you *don't,* not here in the Diamond District. That Yiddish phrase is never given or taken lightly. It's an oral handshake that can seal a deal worth millions, without lawyers and contracts. When you make *mazl,* you're staking the honor of your family on fulfilling your promise."

Matt threw up his hand. "Then how are we going to find out anything?"

Everyone in this cave was tiptoeing around the answer, which left me to state the obvious.

"Your father can certainly solve the mystery, Sophia. He signed the letter, along with Matt's father, who's long dead. That means only Gus can tell us why and how the Eye is here, and not at the bottom of the Atlantic Ocean with the *Andrea Doria.*"

Frowning, Sophia reached for her smartphone.

"Don't bother," Matt said. "No reception down here."

"But Clare is right! Dad knows the truth. I've got to speak with him."

"We all want to talk to Gus," Matt said, folding the letter and placing it in his pocket. "But we'll have to go upstairs to do it. Now let's lock this necklace back up and we can go — unless you plan on wearing it home?"

As the elevator lifted us out of Manhattan bedrock, my thoughts returned to the legacy letter in Matt's pocket.

"What does that other phrase mean?" I asked Matt and Sophia. "Mr. Goldman wrote it right after the *mazl.* Something like *ken eye —*"

"*Ken eyne hore,*" Sophia and Matt recited together.

"They're superstitious here in the Diamond District," Sophia explained. "They have been for years."

"I don't understand."

"*Ken eyne hore* is a talisman phrase," she said, "like knock on wood."

"Is that what it means?"

"No," Matt replied, exchanging a tense glance with Sophia. "It means *without the evil eye.*"

THIRTY-EIGHT

Unfortunately, our rapid ascent was not to street level. Matt and Sophia were obliged to return to the offices of Lyons Global Security where they signed a barrage of property transfer papers for Sal Arnold. Then more forms arrived from Lyons, and even more from the Swiss company insuring the gem. It was well after seven PM before we left the Diamond Tower.

We'd barely hit the chilly evening sidewalk before Matt and Sophia had their phones to their ears — Matt ringing up his mother; Sophia calling Gus.

I folded my arms and casually watched the parade of traffic and pedestrians heading down Fifth Avenue.

And then I saw something curious.

Across Fifth, a car was idling, and not just any car. This was a vintage black Jaguar, the same kind of car that had pulled up in front of the Campana store last week.

My gaze moved to the driver's seat, and sitting behind the wheel was the same big man in black with the same U-shaped scar on his cheek.

I remembered the woman who'd been with him — the fashionista with the cat-shaped turquoise glasses and dramatic two-toned hair. She'd imperiously commanded me to hold open that iron gate to the courtyard so she could get to Gus. Matt as good as told her to go fly a kite.

Was that woman in the Jag's backseat now? And was she also staring at these two new trustees of a long-lost gem and veritable fortune?

Unfortunately, I couldn't answer either question. Though the front seat windows were down, the back windows were up and heavily tinted.

Too curious not to get a closer look, I moved slowly away from Sophia and Matt, walking uptown along the sidewalk. Traffic on Fifth was light, and I managed to jaywalk (carefully!) through the passing vehicles to the other side of the street.

I approached the Jag from the rear — all the better to see through the back window.

Unfortunately, that window was tinted, too.

Now what?

I would need to stick my head through one of the front seat windows to see into the backseat, which seemed impossible — until I came up with a solution inspired by the U-shaped scar on the man's face.

Anxious but determined, I charged down the street, frantically waving my smartphone like a semaphore. I rushed right up to the Jaguar.

"Hello? Are you my Uber car? You *must* be my Uber car. I'm late and I've been waiting forev—"

I expected the driver to speak to me — which would have given me a chance to peek into the backseat and address the woman (if she was there).

Didn't I see you in front of the Campanas' shop in the Village? I was ready to ask, which would have opened the conversation to more urgent questions.

But instead of speaking with me, the driver threw the idling car into gear, and punched the gas. Tires squealed as the Jag leaped forward, into traffic. Yells and honks ensued. The driver ignored them and kept going.

I would have chalked that encounter up to paranoia or coincidence. (After all, Cat Glasses woman was a fashionista and we were in the Diamond District.) But before the black Jag's uber-scary driver screeched away, I'd caught a split-second sight of something too disturbing to dismiss. The driver wasn't just staring at Sophia and Matt. By the time I reached him, he had lifted a smartphone, as if he were taking photos *or* digital video.

"Clare! Over here!"

On the other side of Fifth, Matt was waving frantically with one hand while he held a cab door with the other. Sophia was already in the backseat.

"There's no time to window-shop!" he shouted. "You know we're in a hurry. Come on!"

THIRTY-NINE

"I can't reach my father, or the jewelry shop," Sophia told me as I slid into the cab's backseat.

Matt squeezed in beside me and shut the door. "I can't reach Mother, either, but that's nothing new. She's always busy with someone or something."

"Maybe a high-end client showed up unexpectedly," Sophia considered aloud. "I don't know, but it feels wrong . . ."

Her anxiety was palpable, and I didn't want to add to it, but I did need to find out if she knew anything about the driver in the vintage black Jag.

Sophia's brow wrinkled at my descriptions of the man — and the woman who'd asked to see Gus the week before.

"Neither sounds familiar, but then I don't deal with retail anymore or making appointments. Monica will know —"

"Monica?" I asked. "Is she the petite,

young blonde who greets customers?"

"The same."

"Matt and I met her the other day, but we didn't catch her name."

"She works full-time for my father. So she may know if he doesn't. When we get to the shop, we'll ask them."

The mood in the cab was beyond tense.

To calm my nerves, I began playing with Quinn's engagement ring — until I felt Matt's right hand cover my left.

With Sophia focused on her smartphone on one side of me, Matt took hold of my hand on the other and firmly pulled it into his lap.

I sent him a withering *You have got to be kidding*!

Rolling his eyes, his fingers did their silent work and he released my hand with Quinn's ring turned 180 degrees. Now the jewels, including those questionable coffee diamonds, were facing my palm and effectively hidden from Sophia's view.

"Why?" I mouthed.

"Tell you later," he mouthed back. "Trust me."

Two simple words in the English language, easy enough to understand — but when uttered by Matteo Allegro, I found impossible to believe.

■ ■ ■ ■

As soon as we pulled up in front of the Campana address, Sophia rang the bell for the jewelry store, and we waited to be buzzed in.

"Come on, Monica. Answer the door, you stupid girl."

High-heeled foot tapping impatiently, she tried a second time, but got no response.

"Fine, I'll let myself in."

She swiped her thumbprint over a tiny panel on the door frame, and a small hatch opened to reveal a security keypad. She punched in a series of numbers and letters, cursed, and did it again. After a third attempt, the panel light remained red.

"This isn't right. The security code won't work — I think it's been changed."

"Changed? When?"

"Today, Matt. The old code worked last evening. Nobody told me about a change!"

An anxious Sophia shoved a key into the door lock. Matt grabbed her hand. "This could be a robbery situation. You shouldn't go in there."

"Dad could be in danger. I have to go!"

"It's not smart, Sophia."

"Look, fifteen seconds after I open this

door, the alarm is going to go off — here, in the backhouse, and at our security's central station. The police will be here in minutes."

"Fine," Matt said. "But if you insist on going in, then I'm going with you."

Sophia nodded, turned the key, and the lock clicked.

Matt turned to me. "Wait here, Clare. When help arrives, explain the situation to the cops so some trigger-happy rookie doesn't shoot us by mistake."

With Matt in the lead, the pair pushed through the store entrance. I stepped out of the recessed doorway and along the sidewalk, counting down the seconds.

The alarm went off on cue, an earsplitting clamor that battered the quiet block and made my teeth rattle. The noise rattled someone else, too, as I discovered the hard way.

I was watching for the police like Matt's good little soldier, when, behind me, I heard metal crash against metal. Before I could turn, someone slammed into me. I stumbled and fell, landing on my Spanx-covered backside.

I tried to ID the fast-moving figure, but the most I could see from my unceremonious sidewalk view was a long black coat (a raincoat?) fluttering loosely with the black hood up. The figure moved fast as flickering light along Perry Street, disappearing into the shadows like an urban phantom.

As I stood and dusted myself off, I realized the Phantom had gone through the arch. I knew because the iron gate that had been closed when we arrived was now wide open.

I thought about giving chase — a futile gesture in low heels and a skirt, and an all-round stupid idea. Besides, I was more worried about Gus, now. *Had he been robbed? Attacked?*

I peeked around the arch and found the gate had been yanked open with such force that it wedged itself against the spiral staircase to Gus's upstairs office and workshop. I listened again for sirens — and heard nothing but the continuous jangle of the burglar alarm.

So much for the police showing up "in minutes."

Well, I couldn't wait. If Gus was hurt, then seconds counted.

I left the gate open to signal Matt and the police where I'd gone. Then I proceeded along the narrow cobblestone corridor, where shadows were so deep I couldn't see my feet. Soon I moved into the dim glow of the courtyard's bell-shaped lamps.

I hesitated before stepping into the clear.

What if the prowler had an accomplice, lurking behind the tinkling fountain, or among the manicured bushes?

Then I saw the front door to Gus's hidden backhouse was open, light from the foyer spilling onto the outside steps. I forgot everything else and hurried across the courtyard.

Moving through the door, I called out Gus's name. Except for the brightly illuminated foyer, the other rooms in the house appeared dark — until I spied the glow of a flickering fireplace in the sitting room, where Gus had shared his memories of the *Andrea Doria.*

"Gus?"

Standing at the doorway, I finally saw him, slumped in one of the beautifully embroidered Italianate chairs. His head was down, so I couldn't see his expression. A nearly finished glass of cold brew sat on the side table next to him. Another glass, still full, sat on the coffee table in front of the couch, as if Gus had served a guest.

Is he asleep?

I moved closer — and cried out when I saw flecks of black blood dotting his white polo shirt. I rushed forward and touched the man. His head lolled sideways, and I saw the mess around his mouth, on his chin.

231

I felt for a pulse and, miracle of miracles, found one!

Despite his lean frame, Gus was surprisingly heavy, but after some difficulty I managed to get him off the chair and onto the floor. I rolled him on his back and checked his mouth for blockage. I heard a gurgle with every labored breath.

I used chest compression to clear his breathing passage. Eight, nine, ten hard pumps, and suddenly Gus's body convulsed and he emptied the rest of his stomach onto the Persian carpet.

"Clare!"

Matt was at the door, along with two policemen. Sophia peeked over their broad shoulders and pushed her way into the room.

"Call 911!" she cried. "We need an ambulance!"

"It's on the way, ma'am," one officer said.

Then we worked in tandem, performing CPR on the still-unconscious Gus Campana, until the paramedics arrived.

FORTY

All hospitals feel the same. This building was a different facility, in a different part of town, and it was Gus, not Sully, wrestling with the Grim Reaper. But the anxiety was the same, along with the tears, the waiting, the dreading of the doctor's prognosis. Even the Spartan snack room was painfully familiar with its single-serve coffee machines that allegedly brewed "the perfect cup every time."

FYI: They don't — the preground beans are old by the time the hot water hits them, their complexity and vibrancy long gone. *But,* this coffeehouse manager and master roaster hadn't had caffeine in six grueling hours.

Time to compromise.

My taste buds were still protesting that first dead stale sip when Sophia appeared with Matt by her side.

"Dad's stabilized, but he's not out of

danger," she announced.

"What happened?"

"The doctors aren't sure. They found no signs of injury. He didn't have a heart attack, and there's no indication of a stroke, thank God. They hope to know more when the test results are in."

Tears welled up in Sophia's big, amber-brown eyes. Matt hugged her, and spoke into her ear. "Remember, Gus survived the *Andrea Doria.* He'll survive this."

"Why was Gus alone?" I asked. "You mentioned a girl when we tried to get into the shop —"

"Monica?" Sophia shook her head. "I don't know why Dad puts up with that stupid girl. Yes, Monica was *supposed* to be on duty, but she wasn't. And I haven't been able to reach her for an explanation."

"Have you told your husband?"

"Hunter texted me that he'll come soon. He's tied up with some important client meeting at the 21 Club, and can't possibly break off the engagement." Anger clouded Sophia's pretty face. "It's probably a woman . . ."

"I'm sorry —"

"It doesn't matter, Clare. I need your help with something else. You told the police you saw someone fleeing my father's property.

Do you think you could identify that person?"

"Only by the clothing. I never saw a face. And I only got a glimpse of the figure before it disappeared into the shadows. But I did see the person was wearing a long black coat, or raincoat, hood up."

"That's good enough."

Sophia used her smartphone and the waiting room's Wi-Fi to link to the jewelry shop's closed-circuit television cameras. We three sat around a table to review the surveillance video on the tiny screen.

"We'll watch the in-store video first to see if anyone broke in."

The fast-motion, herky-jerky recording began with Sophia kissing her father goodbye earlier in the afternoon. Matt and I recognized Monica, the nervous blonde we met on our last visit — the one in the minidress and high-heeled Louboutins with platforms so big they looked like her mother's shoes.

"What's this?" Sophia cried. "Dad's sending Monica and our armed guard home and closing the store. But the camera clock says it's only three thirty? This makes no sense."

"Maybe Gus planned to join you at the World Diamond Tower appointment," I offered.

"Dad would have left Monica in charge, the guard on duty, and his workshop staff busy upstairs. There was no reason to close altogether." Sophia bit her lip in thought. "Maybe he was preparing a private viewing for a VIP."

But after Sophia sped through a group exodus of the Campana staff via the front door, and the armed guard carefully locking up after them, there was no arrival of a Very Important client. We saw no figure in a black hooded coat arriving, either, or anyone else on the rest of the camera's recording — not until Matt and Sophia pushed through the front door hours later.

"Thank God no one got into the store," Sophia said, relieved.

"But who changed the security code, and why?"

Sophia shook her head.

"Okay. What about the *other* camera?" I asked. "The one I saw positioned over the arch at the entrance to your courtyard."

Sophia hacked into the second CCTV view. This time it took only a moment for the Phantom to make an appearance. Fortunately, our collision and my embarrassing pratfall happened off camera.

"I don't understand how this person got in! Only Dad, me, and my older sister,

Perla, have keys. Not even Monica has one."

"Go back to noon," I suggested, "and see who came through the archway's gate in the hours before the Phantom ran out."

Sophia nodded and ran the recording. The only person we saw was Gus, who left around one PM and came back at two. There was nothing after that, not until —

"What?!" Sophia cried, her manicured fingers tightening on the smartphone. "I don't believe this . . ."

"What is it?" Matt asked.

"Dad buzzed in a visitor at four twenty."

She displayed the phone. On screen, Matt and I saw a tall, broad-shouldered figure with an angular face and light blond hair.

"Who is that man?" I asked.

"It's my husband, Hunter Rolf."

FORTY-ONE

"It looks like your husband was the last person to see Gus before what happened, happened."

Sophia looked at me as if I'd spoken Martian. "It's not possible, Clare. Dad would *never* meet with Hunter. He disliked my husband from the start. And it's only gotten worse."

"Someone buzzed Hunter in," Matt replied. "If not Gus, then who?"

I interrupted with a better question. "Whether Hunter was with Gus or not, how long was he inside the compound?"

She continued to play the digital footage.

We all watched Hunter leave about an hour after he arrived and then . . . *nothing.* Just like the jewelry store's front door camera, there were no new arrivals or departures at the courtyard gate until we came on the scene.

"Looks like Hunter was inside the property for almost an hour," I said. "If he did meet with Gus, that's a long time for one man to tell another man he doesn't like him . . ."

I flashed back to the argument Matt and I overheard in the jewelry shop between Sophia and her husband. Hunter seemed pretty keen on talking with Gus. But Sophia had played gatekeeper and denied him entry — entry he obviously found today with Sophia preoccupied.

I also thought about that promise Gus made me to ask around about the Panther Man shooter and find out what he could. Matt thought it was idle talk, but now I wondered —

Could Gus's condition be a result of asking too many questions about the pattern of police shootings? Or . . . finding too many answers?

Whatever was going on, one man seemed to have some answers.

"Your husband was obviously determined to speak to Gus," I said firmly. "You need to find out why."

"I agree," said Matt, exchanging glances with me.

Reluctantly, Sophia nodded and put her smartphone to use. A minute later she was wiping away a tear. "Hunter won't pick up my call, or answer my text. He's probably

239

busy with some new —"

Sophia paused and perked up when she heard activity in the hall. But her shoulders slumped when she realized it wasn't her husband rushing to her, but some other man coming for another loved one.

After a moment of thought, she leaned across and touched my shoulder.

"Clare, I can't leave the hospital. Will you and Matt go find Hunter at that 21 Club meeting? Ask him why he visited my father, what they talked about, and . . . what my father's condition was when he left him."

"No problem," Matt said.

Yeah, no problem for the guy in the custom-cut Italian suit, but this was one of the most exclusive eateries on the West Side we were talking about, one with a strict dress code.

I faced Sophia. "I'm dressed fine for the sports bar on that block, but . . ."

Matt seemed baffled by my comment, but Sophia took one look at my simple black skirt, off-the-rack sweater, and low-heeled (slightly scuffed) New York walking shoes, and nodded.

"What size shoe are you, Clare — seven, right?"

I nodded.

She unfasted her stiletto sandals. "Let's swap. Handbags, too . . ."

Finally, she tugged off her ruby and diamond earrings, unfastened the matching necklace and bracelet, and gave the stunning treasure trove to me.

"Put these on. The shoes and bag are to make you feel better. But, honestly, most of the people in that place will only see the jewels."

You can't imagine the confidence boost a little fresh makeup and twenty thousand dollars' worth of jewelry gives a girl.

I even stood taller — *much* taller — although, I had to admit, the reason for that wasn't confidence as much as Sophia's Giuseppe Zanotti "Cruel" Wing shoes.

The strappy five-inch-heeled sandals (with the fifteen-hundred-dollar price tag!) included decorative metal "Firewing" appliques on the front and two thin ankle straps. With the matching designer bag, I felt like a celebrity exiting the cab, and even managed a short catwalk down the sidewalk — before Matt had to catch me.

FYI: I now know exactly what Giuseppe meant when he called these shoes "cruel."

I only hoped it wasn't an omen for the night ahead.

FORTY-TWO

Matt was still holding me upright as we paused outside the 21 Club entrance.

"So what's the plan?" he asked.

"Take this," I said, passing him my smartphone. "I asked Sophia to send me a photo of Hunter. See, I've called it up for you."

"I know what he looks like, Clare. I saw the CCTV images."

"The photo isn't for you. It's for the maître d'. Thanks to your famous editor wife, *you're* the one with the connections here. So claim Hunter is your friend and ask where the man is seated."

"Fine."

Our strategy settled, we moved toward the club's famous 52nd Street entrance, its wrought-iron facade more reminiscent of New Orleans's French Quarter than the West Side of Manhattan. On the balcony above, a chorus line of colorful little lawn jockeys extended their cast-iron arms in greeting — a surreal element of kitsch to an otherwise elegant portico.

"What is up with all the lawn jockeys?" I wondered aloud.

"Notice some of the *names* under those jockeys, Clare?"

I did: *Vanderbilt, Mellon, Ogden Mills Phipps* . . .

"It started back in the 1930s, with a gift from a horsey-loving customer. Then other patrons with stables wanted *their* racing colors represented. And, hey, if A. G. Vanderbilt had his jockey on display, well, Mr. Mellon had to have his up there, too, and on and on, ad nauseam . . ."

"Okay, Gatsby, speaking of filthy rich, are you picking up the tab for this foray into the upper classes or am I?"

"Neither of us. Breanne is."

Before I had a chance to object, my ex ushered me through the grand double doors, and into the golden glow of New York City's most legendary bar.

As we entered, I realized Sophia was right. Her stiletto stilts gave me height and confidence, and the maître d's admiring gaze brightened noticeably at the sight of my glittering gems — which magically rendered my cheap poly-blend sweater as good as invisible.

"Mr. Allegro!" cried the man with warm familiarity. "Welcome back to Manhattan. Would you like your usual table?"

"That depends . . ." Matt flashed the photo of Hunter on my phone and asked if we could be seated near him. "Is my friend upstairs tonight?"

The maître d' shook his head. "No. And I'm afraid Mr. Rolf is in a private meeting. I cannot seat you near him, sir. But your usual table is open, if you'd like it."

Matt nodded. "That's fine."

The host led us through the crowd and past the horseshoe-shaped bar. I scanned the well-dressed customers on the stools. No Hunter, which was no surprise, although I did recognize a number of famous faces and a surprisingly familiar one — that first-year NYU law student (*"I need coffee badly!"*) who'd become a new Village Blend regular.

Carla was her name, and her tall, slender form sat at the crowded bar alone, attractively dressed, auburn hair in a pretty twist, pale skin warmed with a dusting of rouge. With a drink in one hand, her smartphone in the other, I assumed she was waiting for a date — and in a place like this, that made me worry.

I hoped she wasn't getting herself involved

in a sugar daddy situation. I'd heard about young women solving their high-tuition problems by giving men, usually wealthy older men, "the girlfriend experience," and (frankly) it horrified me.

Whatever her business, I knew it was none of mine, so I refocused on staying upright as Matt urged me (and my cruel shoes) to keep up with the crisp steps of 21's maître d'.

The curved bar opened into a large room with a wooden floor and tables covered in old-fashioned red-checkered cloth. Most of the walls were paneled and held framed cartoons dedicated to "21" and drawn by the likes of Walt Disney and the *New Yorker*'s Peter Arno. But the most striking aspect of this otherwise typical tavern space was the colorful kitsch dangling from the ceiling — model airplanes and trucks, baseball bats and tennis rackets; the sheer number of items crammed up there was stunning.

As for the tables, most were occupied, and I spotted more famous faces as we strolled by — actors, politicians, TV news anchors — and once again, no Hunter.

At last, we were seated along the farthest wall, near the kitchen.

"Matt," I whispered, "we're supposed to be looking for Sophia's husband, not going into social exile."

"Trust me. This is the perfect spot to find him."

"We're in Siberia."

"No, Clare. These are the most exclusive tables. In fact, this one was Dorothy Parker's favorite. The one next to us was regularly occupied by Ernest Hemingway. And the one across from us, Frank Sinatra. I grant you, this isn't the most popular section with tourists — that would be over there —" He pointed across the room. "Table 30, 'Bogie's Corner,' where Humphrey Bogart and Lauren Bacall had their first date."

"That doesn't answer my question about Hunter."

"Keep your panties on. I have an idea where he is. Just be patient. In the meantime, try to enjoy the place." He gestured to the crazy clutter of memorabilia hanging above us. "There's a lot of history here."

"History? It looks more like somebody opened the trapdoor of an attic and tossed out all the kids' playthings."

"The staff calls them *toys* and, believe me, they're the kind Christie's would die to auction. The bat up there belonged to Willie Mays. Those ice skates are Dorothy Hamill's, that tennis racket is Chris Evert's — the smashed one is John McEnroe's. And those pool cues are from *The Hustler* with Paul Newman."

"I see a model of the PT-109. That's not — ?"

"Yeah, that was Jack Kennedy's. JFK gave it to the club. And that model of Air Force One came from Bill Clinton."

I studied the ceiling with new interest. "There are more airplanes up there than anything else."

"It's the same story as the jockeys out front. Years ago, British Airways hung a model of one of their planes over their table for a corporate dinner. Howard Hughes saw it and decided —"

"They'd better hang *his* plane, too. I get it. The millionaires' equivalent of roosters crowing." I had another thought and shuddered. "I would hate to have to dust all that stuff."

"Only you would think of that."

"Because I'm probably the only service industry manager seated as a guest in this room. With your new inheritance, on the other hand, it looks like you and Joy have just become members of the one-percent club."

"No, Clare. We haven't."

FORTY-THREE

Matt's remark was followed by a sullen silence that surprised me. But then so did his behavior in the bowels of the World Diamond Tower when he held my hand down; and again in the cab on the way to Gus's place when he forcefully turned my ring around.

"Well?" I said. "Are you going to explain why you think you and Joy haven't become millionaires? And while we're at it —" I lifted my engagement ring. "Why don't you want Sophia to know my ring might have some of the missing coffee diamonds from the Eye's setting?"

"Because I want you to *keep* those diamonds, Clare. You deserve them."

"Why on earth wouldn't I be able to keep them?"

"For the same reason I doubt very much that Sophia and I — and Joy — will be able to cleanly inherit that multimillion-dollar bauble. Gus and my father hid the Eye of the Cat for sixty years because they believed they couldn't sell it in their own time. I'm sure they thought that after more than half a century, no one would remember. But they were wrong. And there is going to be a legal tsunami roaring toward us that gives me a headache just to contemplate."

"You'll have to be more specific."

"Okay, issue one." Matt held up his index finger. "After the *Andrea Doria* went down, the Italia Line's insurance company paid passengers for their losses. From what I know, they didn't pay much, but if they cut a check to Gus, and he had the jewel all along, then *they* own the Eye, not us."

"You don't know all the facts yet. If Gus still had the jewel, he may have rejected the insurance payment."

"Maybe he did, which brings us to issue two." Matt's second finger joined his first. "Last week, Gus himself told us he was *loaned* the jewel to sell in America. He was supposed to use the money from the sale to bring over the rest of his family. All these years, he pretended the jewel was lost — and the family believed him. Now what will they think?"

"I don't know. But it's clear you and Sophia are going to need a lawyer."

"And maybe a bodyguard . . ." Matt curled one finger and raised a thumb, shaping his hand into a gun.

I blanched at that. "You think the Campanas will try to —"

"*Vendetta,* Clare. It's an Italian word. You should know it."

"In the twenty-first century, you're better off with an English word: *attorney.*"

"Sadly, I'm familiar with the word. The truth is, even before this mess, I needed one — a tax attorney."

"Tell me you're joking."

"I wish. Our friends at the IRS audited my returns over the last few years and denied a stack of deductions." Matt put his hand-gun to his head and pulled the trigger. "I'm a small fortune in arrears, not counting interest and penalties. I can make good over time, but it will be *much* easier if you help me get that *Andrea Doria* coffee contract."

"Maybe Sophia's right. Maybe that jewel is bad luck."

"Well, it sure was bad luck for Gus."

"I'm thinking the same thing. That he was stricken today of all days seems like more than coincidence — and now that you've brought up the idea of a vendetta, I'm wondering if that man who was watching you and Sophia outside the World Diamond Tower — the one I told you about with the U-shaped scar on his cheek — could he be working for the Campanas? And what about the stranger in black, that Phantom figure I saw running from Gus's property?"

"Too many questions," Matt said. "And the only man who can answer them is in the hospital, unconscious."

"Not the only one. Hunter Rolf might be able to clear up some of this mystery." I looked around the room. "But *where* is he?"

Before Matt could reply, a young woman approached our table, bent low, and purred into his ear.

"Why so glum? You look like you need a drink."

The ruby-tipped fingers that caressed Matt's broad shoulders belonged to a leggy blonde in a curve-hugging polka-dot dress. I'd noticed her on one of the barstools when we arrived. I wouldn't say she was gorgeous, but I would concede she was well-built — and enjoyed showing off the architecture.

"How about something sweet?" she cooed. "Like a Slow, Comfortable Screw Against the Wall?"

Did she actually proposition Matt, right in front of me?

"Sound's great, Trudy, but not tonight,"

Matt replied, squirming in his seat.

I glanced around quickly for rescue and signaled a nearby waiter. An older man with a black bow tie and hair nearly as white as his short jacket swept in smoothly with our menus. Matt appeared relieved.

"Let's start with cocktails," he told the waiter. "I'll have an Atlantic Sunset and my business partner will have a Southside." He caught my eye. "It's the club's signature drink. You should try it."

Trudy looked at me for the first time. "She's your business partner?"

"That's right," I replied, flashing my ring. "I'm engaged to a different hunk."

"Lucky you," she said, hungry eyes drifting back to Matt. "And *me . . .*"

Is Matt blushing?

Okay, I probably imagined it (who could tell in tavern light?), but his discomfort was obvious enough. Then his expression brightened, and he addressed the waiter —

"If possible, my business partner and I would love to have our dessert in Jimmy's special booth . . ."

That request seemed to annoy Trudy. Her disappointment was clear.

"Sorry, Mr. Allegro," the waiter replied. "There's a private party in there."

Matt quickly showed the waiter my phone

with Hunter's photo on it. "Is my friend Mr. Rolf part of it?"

The waiter silently nodded, and Matt thanked him with a handshake that just happened to include a folded green bill.

As the waiter departed with Matt's twenty, Trudy frowned. "Why are you so interested in that blond giant? Are you going for a threesome?" She glanced my way and winked. "Why not make it four?"

"Sorry, Trudy. This is just business. That's *all* I'm interested in tonight."

From the way the young barfly stormed back to her perch, I wouldn't have been surprised to find poison in Matt's drink.

"So," I said, "is that Slow, Comfortable You-Know-What Against the Wall a real cocktail, or was Trudy's drink suggestion as obscene as I thought?"

"It's real," Matt replied. "The *slow* comes from the sloe gin, it's *comfortable* because there's Southern Comfort in it, the *screw* is there because, like a screwdriver, it contains orange juice, and finally, it has Galliano, like a Harvey Wallbanger — hence, *against the wall.*"

His smiled turned devilish. "Cocktails aside, I recall you and I used to enjoy something like that in our shop's roasting room . . . Just remember, I'm always happy

253

to oblige."

"You'd have better luck with Trudy."

"I had better luck with our waiter."

"Really?" I lifted an eyebrow. "I hope your explanation is less obscene than that cocktail you just described."

"It's not obscene at all. He simply confirmed what I suspected."

"That Trudy is a lush, looking for a sugar daddy?"

"That I now know *for certain* where we can find Hunter Rolf."

"You found out where Hunter is? From that quick exchange?"

Matt's smile was suitably smug. "Guess you're not the only amateur sleuth in the family."

FORTY-FOUR

I regarded Matt's confident smirk with curious skepticism.

"So?" I prompted. "Enlighten me. If Hunter is in this club, where is he?"

"Look, I figured the woman he's with must really be something if he's dumping out on his wife while her father is in the hospital, which means he would have booked the most intimate private booth in this club."

"I doubt Hunter is with a woman. The man promised Sophia he would come to the hospital as soon as his 'important meeting' was over. Why would he make that promise if he was on a romantic tryst?"

"Maybe he lied about joining her. He sounds like a real cad."

"Uh-huh. Well, on that particular subject, I bow to your expertise. So where is this special booth?"

"In a secret room."

"Go on. Or is the secret room a secret?"

"Not anymore — although it was during the Prohibition years. This club was never shut down by the feds because they could never find any booze on the premises. When the doorman saw agents coming, he sounded an alarm, and the barmen activated a lever and pulley system that dumped all the upstairs booze into the sewers. Meanwhile, *downstairs* they kept the rest of their hooch safely hidden in a camouflaged wine cellar — and that's where the special booth is."

"You called it Jimmy's booth?"

"Jimmy Walker, the mayor of New York. He was a regular here, but he didn't think he should be seen drinking in public — given that it broke federal law — so the club gave him his own little booth in their secret cellar. Apparently, he also used it to dine with his lady friends, which is why I'm convinced Hunter is down there with another woman."

"That history is depressing, another example of a hypocritical politician skirting laws he expects the rest of us to follow — it makes me wonder how many public servants have done the same through the years."

"Don't expect to find out. Taking down the powerful is no easy feat, Clare. The feds once raided this place while the mayor was in his secret booth. Jimmy got so angry that he called the NYPD and had all the agents' cars towed — before going right back to his evening cocktails."

"Okay. I'm impressed you know the secret room's secret history, but does *getting us into that room* have to be a secret, too?"

"Why so eager?" Matt asked slyly. "Are you finally ready for that Slow, Comfortable Screw Against the Wall?"

"I'd kick you under the table, but I'm afraid these Cruel Wing shoes would sever an artery."

"That's your response to a friendly proposition?"

"Focus, Matt. How do we get to Hunter?"

"We don't. We wait until Hunter gets to us. That room can only be reached through a hidden passageway below the kitchen, and the entrance to the kitchen is . . . right over there." Matt pointed to the open doorway fifteen feet away. "Believe me, this is the best place to collar Sophia's husband. We just have to wait him out. So, like I said, we might as well sit back and enjoy the wait."

Thus began the most delicious stakeout I'd ever been on. Our drinks arrived, and I proposed a toast to Matt's promising detective skills then sampled my Southside. The cocktail was bright, like a mint julep, but with the fruity, juniper berry flavor of gin instead of woody bourbon.

"Wow. This is nice."

Matt nodded. "They really know how to mix a drink here. Now . . ." He rubbed his hands together, and his sly smile broke wide. "*What* shall we order for dinner?"

"Hold on. I don't feel right about putting this on your wife's tab."

"And how did you feel last Christmas?"

"Excuse me?"

"When I was in Nairobi for the December auctions, Breanne sent you and the flatfoot invitations, remember?"

I groaned. "*Trend* magazine's big holiday party. I was surprised she invited me."

"So was I, until I learned that your invitation was the only one sent without the glossy insert card bragging how Driftwood's star baristas would be serving drinks made with Driftwood Coffee — which also happened to be one of Bree's advertisers."

"And one of our competitors. God, it was awful . . ." I shuddered at the memory. "I spent an hour dodging attempts by Driftwood staffers to tweet me drinking from cups with their logo, until I begged Quinn to get us out of there."

Matt met my gaze. "You don't actually

think your 'special' invitation, sans any mention of Driftwood, was an accident, do you?"

"You're right. She owes me." I snatched up a menu and opened it. "I'm starving. Let's eat."

Though I didn't know much about 21's history, I knew about some of the most famous items on its menu.

This club had invented the concept of the "haute" burger, so common now in high-end restaurants, but I began instead with another of their signature dishes, a crab cake. The meat was the highest quality, as juicy as the sea and as fresh as an ocean breeze, and the peppery cucumber-ginger salad made a wonderful complement.

Matt almost went with the soup du jour, a traditional Senegalese curry and cream bisque. But ultimately he went full carnivore, starting with sweetbreads served with creamed corn and a sauce made of veal stock and truffles, followed by a dry-aged, grill-sizzled New York strip steak with a creamy peppercorn sauce, and a potato whipped to fluffy perfection with seasoned olive oil.

Since I needed comfort after my stressful day, I chose one of the club's most famous comfort foods for my entrée: Chicken Hash with Mornay sauce — a béchamel with plenty of Gruyère, which made the hash so creamy and rich that I pushed all thoughts of calorie counts out of my head (the bottle of Pinot Noir helped). A golden, cheese-crusted topping continued the Gruyère theme and was so delicious I decided this was something I'd try at home. Even the bed of spinach was special — Bloomsdale, grown since 1925, glossy, deep green leaves cooked to perfect tenderness.

I thought I was hungry, but Matt devoured his meal so fast I doubted he'd actually chewed.

We were debating dessert (over shots of liqueur) when I noticed a man emerging from the kitchen doorway who, for once, wasn't wearing a white jacket.

Young and olive skinned, this strongman wore a fine black blazer over an open-necked black shirt and slacks. His inky eyes scanned the Bar Room with such intensity that I pegged him as a bodyguard.

But whose body was he guarding?

I poked Matt when more well-dressed men began exiting the kitchen.

Wearing designer suits and sporting watches and bling I couldn't afford in a lifetime, three of the men were stout, middle-aged, and wearing traditional Arab head scarves.

The *keffiyeh*-wearing trio was followed by someone I *did* recognize.

In his fifties, this slight man sported salt-and-pepper hair, a hawk nose, and a snow-white beard that looked even brighter against his aggressively tanned complexion. He wore no tie with his pin-striped suit, but the lavender silk handkerchief in his pocket exactly matched the open-necked shirt, where gold chains flashed, even in this low light.

It's Eduardo De Santis, I realized, *the nightclub-owning drug dealer whom Quinn once tried to take down. What is this guy doing back in New York?*

Just then, a younger man came through the door, joining the rest of the group in backslaps and handshakes. Matt and I immediately tensed.

The last man was Sophia's errant husband, Hunter Rolf.

FORTY-FIVE

My first impression?

Hunter was tall and broad and scary big, like a Viking who'd docked his longship on a West Side pier and promptly visited a high-end barber for a shave and haircut before pillaging Barneys men's department.

Eduardo De Santis looked almost like a child beside him — if not for his close-cropped white beard and more wrinkles than one typically saw on a man in his fifties.

Despite their differences in complexion, age, and shoe sizes, however, the two men were alike in mood. As they shook hands, their eyes remained locked in silent communication, their expressions confident.

No, I thought. *More than confident . . . triumphant.* The question was *why.* What was their meeting about?

I leaned toward Matt. "Give me back my phone."

He handed it over. "Why do you need —"

"Time to play tourist," I whispered then loudly declared, "SMILE!"

Thank goodness Matt realized *what* I was trying to do, if not *why,* and positioned himself to give me the best shot of Hunter and the men around him. To the rest of the world, it looked like I was simply shooting photos of my date at the famous 21 Club. But I was actually snapping shots of Hunter and De Santis. Then I zoomed in and took four more snaps of the former club owner, including a close-up.

When Hunter moved to the center of the entourage to wish everyone a final farewell, I pretended to be enamored of the "toys" above us, pointing and snapping until I got more pictures that included the three smiling sheikhs.

I quickly sent the photos to Mike with the text message —

Look who's here!

When I glanced back to the group, they were still talking. None of the men had noticed my interest in them — none, that is, but the shifty-eyed bodyguard, whose dark focus was now frozen on me.

Crap, I thought, before shaking it off. The

photos were with Mike Quinn now, so let him stare!

Ignoring the young man's penetrating gaze, I pretended to chat with Matt about the memorabilia, pointing and laughing, while still keeping a peripheral eye on Sophia's husband.

When the group finally began to break up and move out, I signaled Matt, who rose to block our outsized prey.

Okay, so Hunter was only a head taller than my six-foot-two ex, and his shoulders weren't quite as broad as the Verrazano Bridge, but with the fashion of the day, his snugly tailored blue suit revealed an impressive shoulder span, a trim midriff, and arms that would do Mr. America proud.

Hunter was aptly named, too. He had a cat's vigilant gaze with dark blue pools that seemed serene but remained wary, reacting with alertness to any movement his way — including Matt's quick approach.

"You're Hunter Rolf?"

"That would depend on who *you* are," Hunter replied in that same vaguely European accent I'd overheard at Campana's jewelry store.

"I'm Matteo Allegro. A friend of Sophia's."

"Oh, yes . . . my wife has mentioned you.

You are the Bean Man."

I moved to join the two men, but Matt didn't bother with introductions. Instead, he stepped closer to Hunter, putting chest to manly chest.

"Well, this *Bean Man* would like to know why you're in a private meeting, when you *should* be at the hospital consoling your wife!"

Matt's raised voice turned heads. As a waiter moved to ask if anything was wrong, Hunter's arrogant confidence suddenly folded.

"We can't talk here," he hissed to Matt. "Come with me."

He turned and moved back through the kitchen doorway.

Matt threw me a look, and I followed him into the crowded stainless steel kitchen. We headed down a flight of crooked, rubber-coated utility stairs that landed us in a basement storage area.

With the clangs and shouts of the busy kitchen echoing above, Hunter paused in front of a bricked-up alcove, removed a metal meat skewer from a hook, and shoved it into a tiny crack between the bricks. With an audible *click,* the lock was undone, and Hunter pushed the two-ton "wall" inward.

For the second time that day, Matt and I

entered a secret underground chamber. Looking around, I had to admit this one was *much* cozier than the World Diamond Tower vault.

The muted glow of golden lamps and flickering candles illuminated a surprisingly inviting room lined with finished wooden wine bins. Their shelves gleamed in the romantic light, with the dark glass of vintage bottles filling every nook.

Hunter led us to a long dining table in the quiet, cozy space. Dessert and after-dinner drinks had recently been served on its polished expanse, the remains not yet cleared away.

Matt and I took seats while Hunter stood at the head of the table, arms crossed, glaring at my ex. Matt glowered back.

Great, I thought. *Another rooster fight.*

We weren't going to get anywhere like this. *Time for a woman's touch . . .*

FORTY-SIX

"Mr. Rolf," I gently began after politely introducing myself, "your wife is worried and upset. She sent us here to question you. After what happened to her father, she wants to know why you visited him this afternoon."

Hunter blinked in surprise. This was not the conversation he was expecting.

"How does she know I did?"

"Sophia and I both saw you come and go on the surveillance recording. You were with Gus Campana for over an hour, and you were the last person to see him before he was stricken."

Hunter lifted his chin. "Are you *accusing* me of something —" A faint chirp interrupted him, and Hunter checked his smartphone before putting it back in his dinner jacket. "I was discussing business with my father-in-law, that's all."

"The *jewelry* business?"

I doubted that. My mind raced back to the argument Matt and I overheard at the shop. Hunter had sounded desperate to speak with Gus, but not about precious gems —

"I have something far more valuable — information," he'd said. *"News that Gus will surely want to hear . . ."* It was about *"a man in Rome . . . who was aboard that sinking ship . . ."*

"I think you went to tell Gus about a man in Rome," I said, "a man who was aboard the *Andrea Doria* when it sunk. Who is this man? And why did you need to tell Gus about him so urgently?"

Hunter slapped his hands on the table and leaned into my face.

"Why does Sophia want to know this now? She turned deaf ears when I brought her this information. Now I fear it is too late."

"Too late for what?"

I saw Hunter's jaws working. "Not your concern. I'll discuss this only with my wife, not strangers."

Matt was already simmering about the demeaning "Bean Man" remark. Now he pushed his chair back and stood.

"We're *not* strangers. I knew Sophia long before you entered the picture. And Gus

Campana is my godfather. I've known him
—"

"You know nothing, Mr. Allegro. *Nothing.*"

Matt balled up his fists. "No? Then why
don't you enlighten me."

I jumped between them, backing Matt off
with a firm hand. Then I faced Hunter.

"I won't keep you from your wife much
longer. Just tell me one thing. What was
your business with Eduardo De Santis?"

"Eduardo? Why?"

"I'm a businesswoman, Mr. Rolf. De Santis is well-known in this city. I've always
wanted to make him a client — supply his
venues."

"There's nothing there for you."

"Why not? What are *you* doing for him?"

He threw up his hand. "It will be news in
a few days, anyway, so you might as well
know. I was commissioned to procure a
large number of gemstones for Mr. De Santis and his investors."

"For?"

"A luxury resort in Dubai called Ra's
Paradise. Their nightclub will have a gem-
encrusted sun illuminated by laser lights."

"How did you get involved with this
project? Was it through Mr. De Santis?"

That chirp again. Hunter pulled out his

phone, checked the screen, and frowned. "I really must be going —"

"Have you been friends with Eduardo for long?"

Hunter crossed his thick arms, then uncrossed them again — a nervous gesture that made me think I was going to hear less than the truth.

"I met him six months ago, on safari in Africa. Eddy is not a very good shot. I gave him a few pointers. That's the end of it."

I remembered Sophia remarks about her husband's shady business practices — *"What are you peddling now? Blood diamonds? Smuggled Russian amber? Pilfered European heirlooms? Contraband jade from Myanmar?"* — and doubted that was the end of it.

"So gem hunting is the only job you're doing for De Santis?"

"It's what I do, Ms. Cosi."

"But you're handy on safari, too. Have you hunted since that time in Africa?"

His placid blue eyes suddenly turned to ice. When his phone chirped again, Hunter Rolf didn't bother to check it.

"I have had enough of these ridiculous questions," he declared. "Now if you will excuse me, I am going to join my wife."

FORTY-SEVEN

As Hunter bolted for the secret door, Matt started to go after him.

"Hey, pal, we're not done here!"

"Let him go!" I tugged Matt's arm. "Sophia needs a shoulder to lean on — and Hunter's looks substantial enough. It's time he lent it to his wife."

"Fine."

Still agitated, Matt paced the long table of used plates, cups, and glasses from the final course of the group's lavish dinner. Among the bottles on the table, he caught sight of one in particular. A single glance at the label turned his grimace into a smirk.

After finding us two unused glasses, he gestured for me to join him at the old wooden booth, built into the wall of the wine bins at the far end of the room.

So this was it, I realized. This was Mayor Jimmy Walker's famous Prohibition-defying seat. *As fitting a place as any to discuss crime and corruption,* I thought, and slid onto a polished bench.

Matt sat down across from me, poured from the bottle of Glenfiddich, and clinked my glass.

Drinking the twenty-one-year-old single malt at 21 was heady, I have to admit. Aged in barrels once used to store premium Caribbean rum, the scotch was woody, warming, and supernaturally smooth with hints of vanilla, toffee, banana, and citrus — sweet aromas that appeared and disappeared on my palate like magic smoke.

"Well, at least Sophia will be glad," Matt said after a few quiet sips. "It actually was a business meeting and not another woman."

"Yes, but we still don't know anything about this 'man in Rome,' who Hunter implied knows something about the Campanas' family history with the 'sinking ship.' He must have been referring to the jewel Gus and your father hid for the last half century, don't you think?"

"You heard Rolf. He's going to come clean with Sophia. If we need to know about the guy in Rome, she'll tell us about it."

"What I want to know is whether we can trust Sophia's husband? I sincerely doubt it, considering the other company he keeps. That man I asked him about — Eduardo

De Santis — he used to have a nightclub in the Meatpacking District that —"

"Stop, Clare. I know *all about* 'Club Town Eddy.' "

"You do?"

Matt touched his nose and snorted.

I froze in unhappy understanding. With one gesture, Matt confirmed De Santis had been one of his cocaine suppliers in those bad old days, which gave me yet another reason to despise the man. Club Town Eddy had effectively contributed to ruining my young marriage.

"You're right, Clare. He's a creep, and a nasty one."

"Is he nasty enough to take revenge on the detectives who had him prosecuted?"

I told Matt about Quinn's involvement with De Santis a few years ago when his OD Squad had secured his arrest and indictment. I'd spent months stumbling over NYPD surveillance photos of the man, which was the only reason I was able to recognize him.

"Quinn and his team got the nightclub closed, and put a few low-rent dealers behind bars —"

"But Eddy De Santis walked. I remember." Matt leaned across the table. "I heard stories about Eddy's bad side. And there's one I know is true. He had a cocaine-fueled falling-out with his partner. It happened right in front of me and a few other party animals I used to know."

Matt swirled the liquid gold in his glass. "A week later, that partner was shot dead outside his Hamptons summer home by a man waiting for him. The cops said it was a botched robbery, but I doubt that's what went down. So if you're asking me if De Santis is capable of violence, I'd have to say *yes.*"

My stomach churned at this news. Still, I needed facts, as ugly as they might be.

"What do you think about Hunter? Is he capable of violence?"

"It might be the scotch, but I'm not following your logic."

"What if Eddy De Santis hired Hunter to play Panther Man?"

Matt just about fell out of Jimmy's booth laughing.

"Hear me out, because it's not so crazy. I saw Panther Man. He was a tall, muscular guy like Sophia's husband — a man who knows how to shoot so well that he gave pointers to De Santis in Africa." I met my partner's skeptical gaze. "They met on safari, Matt. Big-game hunting. And there is no bigger game than hunting humans."

As he considered my words, Matt poured another scotch. I covered my glass. The Glenfiddich was amber bliss, but on top of my Southside cocktail, half a bottle of Pinot Noir, and a dessert shooter, I'd consumed more alcohol tonight than my last New Year's Eve party.

After another savored swallow, Matt sank back in the booth.

"Well, either it's this second scotch, or your theory is starting to make sense. Enough sense to be possible, anyway."

"What changed your mind?"

"The deal Hunter made with Eddy is worth millions. He might be willing to go along with attempted murder for that kind of money."

Just then, a pair of busmen entered the wine cellar, gave us a polite nod, and began to clear the long table. Our privacy ended, Matt drained his glass, set it down, and helped me to my feet.

"It's time for you to go home to Sergeant Friday, and me to get some sleep in Brooklyn. Mother's been ignoring my calls all evening, and it's too late to upset her, so I'll deliver the news of the day tomorrow."

"I guess that's best. She's better off hearing about Gus after a good night's sleep, and you know how she felt about opening that box. She dreaded it."

"Well, with Gus in the hospital and that cursed diamond on our plate, now she has something real to dread."

FORTY-EIGHT

The autumn night was chilly, but not nearly cold enough to dispel the alcohol vapors from my brain. My knees felt wobbly — although strong drink was not to blame.

It was these darned cruel shoes.

Traffic was fairly light on 52nd Street, with not a cab in sight and a line of well-dressed patrons waiting for one in front of 21.

Matt took my arm. "Let's walk to Fifth and grab a cab there."

Unfortunately, the far end of the block might as well have been the summit of Everest. The cruel shoes had finally done me in.

As hobbled as a geisha, I halted in front of Halftime, the sports bar frequented by off-duty policemen, where I once joined Quinn.

"I can't go any farther, Matt. Hail a cab and swing around to pick me up."

"Clare, just take off those heels and keep

moving."

"Sorry, these feet may be made for walking, but they *do not* walk bare on New York City pavement. I'd have to get them sterilized before I opened the coffeehouse tomorrow."

"Hyperbole, anyone?"

"Just get the cab."

With the noise of revelers and throb of music from inside the busy bar, we had been speaking loudly. Now he leaned into my ear and lowered his voice.

"Are you going to be safe wearing all that bling?"

"This place is full of off-duty cops. Believe me, no one is going to mug me here."

As if to prove me right, two red-faced, middle-aged men in rumpled suits stepped outside and lit up cigars. A third joined them to argue local football. When he opened his coat to tug up his pants, Matt and I both noticed the gun in his belt and the badge hanging from his neck.

"See," I mouthed. "Armed guards."

With a nod, Matt sauntered off, and I texted Quinn to make sure he opened my first text and the attachment.

Will I see you tonight? I have more info.

Quinn's reply came immediately.

U R amazing. Luv the pictures. DEA
surprised. Almost done here. Cannot wait
to C U.

Despite the long and stressful day, I suddenly felt awake again. Quinn's text was a
lot warmer than the last one, like a sweet
gust of oxygen amid the choking cigar
smoke. I felt so happy some of my alcohol
fog began to dissipate.

Yes, all was right with the world —
Until a sudden string of explosions shattered the night.

FORTY-NINE

BANG! BANG! BANG! BANG!

For several seconds that's all I heard — one *boom* after another, blast echoes overlapping as the noise bounced between buildings.

Sheer instinct had me crouched behind a steel lamppost.

The detectives behind me had different instincts. They were hugging the sidewalk, too, but they'd also drawn their weapons and were searching for a shooter.

"There!"

The man who yelled fired off a shot, then another. His two colleagues followed suit. Suddenly, the deafening din was in front of *and* behind me.

Scrunched into a ball with my hands over my ears, I peeked around the steel pole and spied bright white flashes on top of a latticework of construction scaffolding across the street.

I saw something else, too. *Smoke.* And I remembered what Quinn said in passing about those SWAT team assaults on the wrong buildings the day Sully was shot. After the fact, everyone was embarrassed by the miscalculation. Modern firearms don't release smoke. Or as Quinn put it —

"We should have known: where there's smoke, there's fireworks."

A metallic *ping* shattered my thoughts. One of the cops had clipped the *No Standing* sign high above me. Then the pole itself vibrated like a metronome, raining silver paint chips on my head.

I heard a grunt, turned, and saw a detective had been hit — no doubt by fragments ricocheting off the pole. He was on his back, clutching his shoulder.

More men rushed headlong out of the sports bar, some waving guns. They saw a man down, two cops shooting, and reacted instantly.

"Stop! Stop! Don't shoot!" I cried. But in the heat of the moment, mine was the only cool head. "It's fireworks. Just fireworks!"

Nobody listened, and the battlefield clamor went on until another ricochet cracked the sports bar's plate glass window. Inside, customers still on their feet hit the floor.

The explosions across the street finally stopped around the same time as a wiry plainclothes detective flew out of the bar like an angry bird, frantically flapping his arms and squawking —

"Cease fire! Cease fire!"

The racket died, and in the sudden stillness I heard the urgent wail of approaching sirens — and then a long string of colorful curses. The diminutive man was now walking in a circle, ranting at the others. One man timidly interrupted him.

"Ah . . . Lieutenant McNulty . . ." He sheepishly pointed to the ranking officer's gaping pants.

With a grunt, the lieutenant zipped his fly and continued berating his men.

"I can't take a leak without you Keystone Kops screwing up? Who the hell ordered you to fire? Did you even *see* who you were shooting at —"

"Excuse me, sir. I saw the whole thing," I firmly declared. "The explosions came from fireworks. I'm sure of it. On top of the scaffolding on that building across the street."

One man helped me to my feet. The rest stared in shock and awe.

Apparently, one does not interrupt the great and powerful Lieutenant McNulty — unless one has news about his fly being down.

The lieutenant walked right up to me and glared. "You are mistaken. You hear me, little lady?"

Little lady? What was he talking about? In these red stilettos, I was eye to eye with him. And my eyes glared right back!

"I know what I saw, Lieutenant."

"You don't know a thing. My men don't pop off at phantoms."

"Well, there's no shooting now, is there? And I saw smoke. So naturally, I thought: where there's smoke, there's fireworks —"

"Are you drunk?" He leaned in and sniffed my breath.

"I am *not* drunk. And I know what I saw."

"I got a man *down,* here," he pointed. "And over there a bullet punched a hole through that window. Fireworks didn't do that!"

"Clare! Clare!"

Matt pushed through a gathering crowd to reach me.

"Are you okay? I heard the fireworks and came running."

"Did you hear this guy?" McNulty threw up his hands. "Fireworks again!"

I had hoped the pyrotechnics were over, but, as it turned out, the evening's explosions were just getting started.

First, my smartphone buzzed — a text

from Quinn.

SRY Will B late. Crime Scn on 52 ST

At that same moment the police cars arrived.

One by one the sirens faded. Then an unmarked car rolled to the curb right in front of me and Matt. Two men stepped out. One was the young Sergeant Franco.

The other was his boss — and my brand-new fiancé.

FIFTY

"Clare?" Quinn's jaw dropped when he spotted me, but he was quick to regain his composure. "You want to tell me how you ended up in the middle of another crime scene?"

"In two words — cruel shoes."

Quinn's eyebrows rose as he took in my obscenely expensive stilettos. Then his gaze traveled up my legs, to my embarrassment of jewelry, and back down again to those fetish shoes.

"Hmm . . ." was his only response, until he haltingly added, "You look . . . *very nice.*"

For some reason this remark cracked up Franco — but his chuckling stopped when he noticed my ex-husband hovering over my shoulder.

Matt glared at the young officer with the shaved head who'd been dating our daughter over his strong objections. The animosity was completely one-sided. Franco continually tried to pass the peace pipe. Matt preferred war.

"Well, if it isn't Dwayne Johnson's mini-me. What are *you* doing here? Hoping to score another false arrest?"

Franco greeted the verbal slap with a good-natured grin. "Hey, Mr. Allegro, long time, no see."

"Not long enough."

Now Lieutenant McNulty joined the party — and his bad mood just got worse.

"Crazy Quinn. What got you out from behind a desk? I don't see any dead junkies here." He jerked his thumb in my direction. "Or was it these two troublemakers?"

"Troublemakers?!" Matt and I cried in unison.

Quinn's attention reluctantly left my legs to refocus on his prickly peer in the NYPD. "What happened here, McNulty?"

"I'll tell you what happened. We had an active shooter in an elevated position across the street. Sound familiar?"

He pointed to the scaffolding, where several determined cops had already climbed, without benefit of ladders, and were now hunting clues.

"— And we got a man down with a shoulder shot. We're waiting for the bus on that. Meanwhile, these two inebriated civilians are trying to claim it was a Macy's Fourth of July spectacular!"

Quinn gave me a sidelong glance, which probably meant I should keep quiet. I didn't.

"It was fireworks, Mike. I'm sure of it. And I am *not* inebriated!" (I would have offered to walk a straight line, too, if I'd been steadier on those ridiculous heels.)

Ignoring me completely, McNulty turned to Mike. "Listen, Quinn. I'm not so sure I want you around."

Quinn's eyes narrowed. "And why would that be?"

"I've heard the rumors. After that last shooting, they say IAB might be looking at your squad. I don't want my team tainted by your presence."

"Is that so?" Quinn stepped forward. McNulty moved to meet him.

Oh, brother. Not another rooster fight!

Thankfully, an excited shout from across the street broke the standoff.

"Hey, Lieutenant! There's a whole rack of blown M-80s up here. It looks like the fireworks were set off by throwaway phones."

Quinn cracked a justified smile. McNulty cursed. Then he turned to me — the "little lady" who was right all along! I folded my arms, waiting for an apology followed by a polite request for my detailed impressions of the incident.

Unfortunately, my expectations were slightly off.

"Get her out of here!" McNulty roared.

"What?" I squeaked, momentarily stunned.

That's when Quinn took my arm. "Clare, it's better if you leave."

"I am not going anywhere!"

"Go with Franco," Quinn pressed, making eye contact with his sergeant. "Get her home safe," he ordered. "With all that bling, I want her escorted all the way through the front door. Got it?"

"You got it, Loo."

"But I'm an eyewitness!" I protested. "Don't you want my statement?!"

It took two strong men to drag me and my cruel shoes to the unmarked police car; Matt on one arm, Franco on the other. *Hey, at least they were working together.* But the team spirit ended after I was "helped" into the front seat.

"How about a ride, Mr. Allegro?" Franco asked from behind the wheel. "Where are you going?"

"To my warehouse in Red Hook, Brooklyn. It's nine miles away, but if you're driving the car, I'd rather walk."

"Suit yourself," Franco said — and left Matt in the New York dust.

FIFTY-ONE

After flashing his gold shield to get us through the crime-scene perimeter, Franco turned onto Fifth and switched on his siren.

For twenty-plus blocks of Manhattan traffic, I vented enough steam to make fifty espressos, ranting my head off over the unmarked car's wail.

Eyes on the road, Franco said nothing during my diatribe, save for the occasional "uh-huh" and perfunctory nod of his shaved head.

Around 25th Street, he hung a right, and finally cut the siren.

In the ensuing silence, my volcano melted down to an exasperated stare. The young sergeant sheepishly glanced my way.

"Sorry, Coffee Lady. Try not to take it personally."

"But I saw the whole thing. I'm a *witness*!"

"Not to Lieutenant McNulty and his men.

To them, you're an *uncooperative* witness."

"What are you talking about? I was willing to *cooperate* fully with any investigation."

Turning south on Seventh, Franco suppressed a smile.

"What's so funny?"

He shrugged his big shoulders. "When you're on the Job, *cooperative* has a more . . . *nuanced* meaning."

"Oh, really?"

Franco nodded.

"Fine. Educate me."

"Okay . . . if you had told McNulty, 'Gee, Lieutenant, I was sure I heard gunshots, but then I realized it was fireworks,' then he'd consider you a *cooperative* witness."

"But that's not what happened. I was sure it was fireworks, right from the start."

"That's why he sent you home. We have a name for that, too: *witness correction.*"

"Excuse me?"

"As tactics go, it's unofficial, but effective."

"I need more."

"Right. Say there's a hit-and-run. You have four witnesses. Three will testify they saw a black car do the deed, and one says it was blue. It's not smart to confuse the issue in your report by including the one dude who insisted it was a blue car, especially when you find a black car with a drunk driver and the victim's blood on the grille. *That's* witness correction."

"But what if you didn't find the black car right away with all that forensic evidence? Maybe the three witnesses who saw the black car had a bad angle. But the guy who saw the blue car was right."

Franco took a breath and blew it out. "His testimony would be something we'd consider . . ."

And ignore. The sergeant's tone made *that* perfectly clear.

"I just can't believe Mike went along with sending me home."

"Aw, don't go blaming Lieutenant Quinn. It's not his crime scene. And he's got to pick his battles — especially with McNulty."

I collapsed back against the seat. "I suppose if anyone actually wrote up my view of the incident, it would make McNulty's men sound blind and trigger-happy."

"Not to mention tanked up."

"Well, I admit — I had a few drinks tonight, too. But I kept a cool enough head to figure out the truth of what was happening. Why couldn't they?"

"Because two members of McNulty's special task force were shot."

"No, Franco. Just one — and it was a ricochet. I saw it."

"Not tonight. Ten days ago, give or take. They were the third and fourth victims of our cop-hunting shooter."

FIFTY-TWO

I'd been slouched in my seat, gazing up at the city's buildings. Now I sat up straight as a skyscraper and stared at Franco.

"Two men from McNulty's squad were shot by the same shooter who hit Sully? Can you be sure it was the same person?"

"The ballistics are a match. One of McNulty's men walked out of the hospital the same day; the other had a short vacation. But both were targeted by an active shooter in an elevated position, just like Sully — and me, too, the day they winged that poor traffic cop instead. And I can tell you, the feeling of being hunted can make *anyone* jumpy."

"I don't doubt that. I'm just surprised the other two victims were also part of a special unit. Is McNulty's team focused on narcotics, like your OD Squad?"

Franco shook his head. "Something else entirely."

"*What* else entirely?"

"It's an elite grand-theft unit. The official name is a tad unwieldly."

"Try me."

"Specialized Felony Theft Investigations and Embezzlement and Extortion Task Force."

"SFTIEETF?"

Franco laughed. "Nobody abbreviates it like that, Coffee Lady."

"Okay, so what's the acronym?"

"No acronym, either, just a nickname. You know, like everyone calls us OD Squad because we start our investigations with citywide incidents of illegal and prescription drug overdoses."

"Yes, Franco, I'm all too familiar with your squad's work."

"Oh, yeah, of course. I guess Lieutenant Quinn and you . . ." He winked. "You know, pillow talk."

"I'll forget you said that. Tell me more about McNulty's unit. What exactly do they do?"

"They investigate one-time or habitual thefts, including embezzlement or extortion, involving an office, store, construction site — whatever and wherever doesn't matter. They catch the case when the thefts are suspected to involve someone who works for the company. That's why their nickname is the Inside Job Squad."

"Inside Job Squad. I see . . . catchy."

"You think so?"

"What I think is that I don't remember the press reporting a single thing about Mc-Nulty's squad. Not the work they do or the strange coincidence of two men from the same unit being targeted. In fact, they gave very few details about the incidents."

"What did I tell you? Witness correction at work."

"Yes, but why?"

The big shoulders shrugged again. "Mc-Nulty primarily catches perps the same way we do — with surveillance and undercover work. When you're using those kinds of tactics, the less the press and general public know, the more effective you can be."

I couldn't argue with that. And I wasn't all that surprised members of the NYPD brass were less than forthright with civilians. Quinn selectively withheld information from me on a routine basis.

"Subterfuge must be the first subject they teach you at the Police Academy."

"Not the *first*," Franco said with an amused glance.

I sighed and returned my gaze to the passing buildings. The farther south we traveled, the more they shrunk in size — from skyscraping offices to fifteen-story apartment houses. Now Franco made a right onto West 11th and the buildings reduced even more, to human scale.

That's how the NYPD brass should be looking at this crime, I thought, *in human terms . . .*

Two members of Quinn's squad and two members of McNulty's squad were targeted. Tonight it appeared someone was targeting McNulty and his people again. Maybe not with a gun, but those M-80s panicked his men enough to shoot wildly and cause a friendly-fire ricochet.

"Franco, do you know if Eduardo De Santis was ever investigated by McNulty and his crew?"

"No. Never. And I know that scumbag's file from front to back."

"Then why would he bother going after McNulty's men?"

"Why not? If De Santis is out to make the NYPD look bad, I'd say he accomplished that tonight."

"I don't know . . . It seems more calculated than that."

"Calculated how?"

"I'm not sure, but there seems to be a strategic plan here."

"Yeah, to create chaos for revenge."

"I'll agree the plan is to create chaos, but if he's after revenge, why not kill the cops? Why just wound them?"

"He doesn't want to martyr us or make us into hometown heroes. He just wants to scare us. That's my theory. Force us into making mistakes, looking bad to the public . . ."

"That makes sense, and I understand De Santis's resentment toward you and Mike and the other members of your squad. You all tried to put him in prison. But why would he go after members of McNulty's squad ten days ago? And target them again tonight? I think there might be a connection we're all missing . . ."

"Maybe, Coffee Lady, maybe not. I just hope Lieutenants Quinn and McNulty find a way to bury the hatchet and move on to what's important."

As the car swung onto Hudson Street, I made a point as close to home as we were: "You know, I could say the same about you and Joy's father."

Franco seemed astonished. "Hey, I'm willing to powwow, anytime, anywhere. But I get the impression the only place Mr. Allegro wants to bury a hatchet is . . ." He tapped his shaved head.

"I wouldn't go that far. And I'm certain Matt's hailed a taxi by now, but you should have tried harder to get him into your car. Maybe if you two sat down and —"

"Face facts, Coffee Lady: he doesn't like me."

"You arrested him. *Twice.* Have you ever apologized?"

"Come on. You and I both know those false arrests are not why Mr. Allegro can't stand the sight of me."

I didn't have to go full-on Freud to know Franco was right. This wasn't the rooster syndrome as much as Matt's maturity issues. In his mind, he was still thirty and Joy barely ten, so . . . *How dare this cocky cop try to steal the heart of Daddy's Little Girl!*

Franco rolled into a parking spot within sight of the Village Blend and cut the engine.

"Okay, you heard Lieutenant Quinn. I'm under orders to escort you — and your bling — all the way inside, and that's what I'm going to do."

"Well, since you're coming in anyway, I could fix you something to eat. Are you hungry?"

Franco's eyes lit up. "If you're cooking, I'm *always* hungry."

"That's very sweet. And smart. Flattery will get you dessert, too."

"Hey, you wouldn't happen to have any of those Fried Mozzarella Sticks, would you?"

"How do you know about those?"

"Are you kidding? Lieutenant Quinn wouldn't shut up about them! At every crappy lunch for the past week, his eyes would glaze over and he'd talk about these *unbelievable* mozzarella sticks you made him, all hot and crunchy and gooey and —"

"I get the idea . . ."

I hated to disappoint Franco, but I was low on bread crumbs and completely out of mozzarella. Thinking fast, and with the memory of my own dinner's cheesy béchamel still blissfully lingering on my tongue, I offered him a nice, big bowl of fettuccine Alfredo instead.

"Wow, that's four-star restaurant stuff. Isn't Alfredo hard to make?"

"Not at all. It's so easy I could make it in these cruel shoes."

"You don't have to do that for me, but . . ." Franco cracked a smile. "I *know* your new fiancé would appreciate it."

"Really? I didn't think he liked the shoes."

"What? Didn't you see his reaction?"

"Reaction? All he did was stare with a blank face and say I looked 'nice.' I thought he was being polite."

Franco laughed out loud. "First of all, he

didn't say 'nice,' he said '*very* nice' — and he couldn't take his eyes off your legs. HR translation, he thought you looked hotter than hell."

"Really?"

"Scout's honor."

"Sorry, what's an *HR translation?*"

He shrugged. "Human resources. The new department brass made all the supervising officers go to Politically Correct boot camp. These days you couldn't get the words *you look sexy* out of Lieutenant Quinn's mouth if you beat him with a nightstick."

FIFTY-THREE

"My God, Clare, you look sexy."

"I do?"

Three hours after Franco left my duplex, I was standing on my bedroom rug, watching Quinn snap on a nearby lamp and prop himself up for a better view. His smile spread slowly in the soft light, but his ice blue eyes were already wide, which surprised me.

A few minutes ago, he was snoring away in my four-poster. Now he'd caught me in the light, blinking as blankly as the proverbial deer on a country road — not quite as buck naked, but close.

"Do me a favor, sweetheart, don't move."

"Why?"

"I'm taking mental pictures . . ."

I could feel the blush creeping up my cheeks, but Mike's eyes took me in with such love, I let the moment linger.

During my brief trip to the bathroom, I'd

thrown on my short terry robe, which was now gaping open rather lewdly. Sophia's stunning ruby earrings were still dangling from my lobes. And strapped to my feet, like Hans Christian Andersen's red shoes, were Sophia's stilts — the reason for the latter was a story in itself . . .

A few hours earlier, I'd kept my promise to Franco and made enough creamy fettuccine Alfredo for two generous helpings plus leftovers. I fulfilled my dessert promise, too, by serving him a stack of our Village Blend "Globs" — fudgy circles of chocolate decadence with hints of espresso in the deep, rich background (a storied recipe once served in Soho decades ago, now insanely popular on our menu downstairs).

Taking his coffee to go, along with a few Globs for the road, Franco wished me a good night. Then I cleaned up the kitchen and settled in on the living room sofa to wait for Quinn.

I'd kept the extra Alfredo warm for his midnight snack. More than a thoughtful gesture, I hoped to grill him (between enriched forkfuls of pasta) about his feud with McNulty.

But by the time Mike got back to my duplex, he wasn't hungry for food. Or much interested in talking.

I didn't blame him. It was our first night together since he'd proposed. He'd even stopped somewhere between Midtown and the Village to pick up a bouquet of flowers.

They never made it to a vase.

The reason? Though I'd taken off Sophia's stilts to make Franco's Alfredo, the moment I heard Mike's key in the lock, I decided (for the heck of it) to strap back into those stylish torture devices and strike a pose.

My toes protested, but I persuaded them it *might* be worth it.

Sitting on the sofa, I crossed my legs. When Mike's broad shoulders filled the doorway, I attempted an alluring smile.

"Franco claimed you liked the shoes. But I have my doubts. What do you think?"

Mike didn't say a word. He simply gave me the flowers, dropped a kiss on my lips, and lifted me in an old fireman's carry. My feet were more than willing to accept the lift upstairs.

As it turned out, they wouldn't have to bear my weight again until I woke up, hours later, in the master bedroom, thoroughly naked, except for the ruby earrings and "very nice" shoes, which I realized, upon rubbing my eyes clear of sleep, were *still* strapped to my feet . . .

And that's how I came to be standing on

those stilts in my bedroom's low lamplight, watching the smile widen on the face of my new fiancé.

"Looks like Franco was *half* right," I told Quinn.

"Excuse me?"

"I can see you do like the shoes. But he was wrong about the beating."

"What beating?"

"Franco said because the brass sent you through some kind of sensitivity training, the words *you look sexy* wouldn't come out of your mouth if I beat you with a night-stick."

Quinn arched an eyebrow. "Sounds like fun. You wanna try it?"

"What? Beating you with a nightstick? No need, Detective, you *just said* the words!"

"Oh, sure, in the privacy of the bedroom. But outside that door, believe me, it's back to 'you look *very nice*' . . . and, for the record, I haven't carried a nightstick in years. So if you want to use one on me, you'll have to find your own."

"Well, I am resourceful."

"That you are."

"And observant."

"Agreed."

"Which is why I'm fairly sure I'll find a stiff object under those covers."

"Clare Cosi! I'm shocked, *shocked* at your bawdy insinuation!"

"I'm sorry, Officer, did I offend your delicate sensibilities?"

"I think I need a safe space."

"Hey, you're the one who brought it up."

"Another actionable innuendo."

"I said *brought* it up, Quinn, not get it up."

"So you did . . ." He turned down the bedcovers. "Care to investigate?"

"Absolutely," I said and slowly walked toward him.

I'm sure Mike thought I was trying for a sexy sashay, but (frankly) between the blisters on my feet and these cruel shoes, slow was the only speed possible.

FIFTY-FOUR

The next day's dawn was frosty, and I dressed swiftly after my shower in comfortable jeans, a warm sweater, and (thank goodness) a happily worn pair of *flats.*

With Mike still in slumberland, I quietly opened the bedroom drapes. Soft light trailed in from the sleepy West Village streets. As I cracked the window, a salt breeze from the chilly Hudson refreshed the air and rustled the branches of a nearby elm, its yellow-gold leaves a primary contrast with the red brick of the low town houses and lightening blue of the coastal sky.

I breathed them in, these little beauties of the new day when all was quiet and peaceful and good.

Like most things in life, the moment wouldn't last, but the calm center was worth finding, something to hang on to before life's grind began with all its stresses and stumbles, mistakes and regrets.

Below me, a loud motor rumbled, and our baker's van arrived, bringing me back to the duties of the day.

Texting my opening team of baristas, I asked if everything was on track downstairs. They assured me all was well. That's when I noticed a familiar unmarked police car pulling up across the street.

In the front seat were Detectives Lori Soles and her partner, Sue Ellen Bass. The Fish Squad came by every morning for their caffeine fix, but today was an unusually early start for this pair. We wouldn't be open for another fifteen minutes.

And since Mike and I were already engaged, I knew they weren't here for another false arrest.

Texting down to Tucker, I asked him to have complimentary drinks taken out to their car: a cappuccino for Lori, and for Sue Ellen a triple espresso.

Tuck texted back, *no prob,* and asked if he could use our second floor for a morning read-through of his new superhero script.

As I typed *OK,* I noticed an unread message from Sophia. She'd sent it late last night . . .

Dad no better. Praying for improvement in

AM . . . Thank you for sending Hunter to me. We are talking. Really talking. Finally!

They're talking. Really talking? I thought. *About what? Their rocky relationship? Gus's condition and how he got that way? The mysterious man in Rome? Hunter's deal with that creep De Santis? Or all of the above?*

I knew a list of questions like that couldn't be sent in a text message or over voice mail. So I tossed Sophia's designer shoes and handbag into my canvas tote, carefully wrapped up her jewelry in a silk scarf, and went down to the kitchen.

My list of concerns continued mounting (and agitating me) as I fed my demanding felines. While Java and Frothy chowed down on cat chow, I preheated my oven, pulled out six loaf pans, and assembled ingredients.

By now, Hunter would have heard about Sophia's share of that priceless inheritance. My worries increased at the thought — and I took it out on the eggs in my mixing bowl.

Certainly, I could see why Sophia had been drawn to her husband. Hunter was a sophisticated world traveler; a big, blond Viking who spoke her language when it came to her passion for those shiny, precious stones of the ancient earth.

But what were Hunter's true intentions?

Did he really love her? Or was he using her?

With renewed vigor, I whisked maple syrup and brown sugar into the beaten eggs. Next came vanilla, cinnamon, nutmeg, baking powder, baking soda, and salt. Finally, I whisked in the pumpkin puree, stirred in the flour, divided the lumpy batter among my pans, banged my frustrations out on the counter (which also nicely removed air bubbles), and slid the quick bread into the oven.

After cleaning the mixing bowl and whisk, I got to work on the bacon. Not just *any* bacon — not for my new fiancé. Quinn would be getting my special Coffee Bacon with Maple-Espresso Glaze and my mustard and brown sugar variation, which drenched the tongue in a smoky-sweet tang of bliss.

The process for glazing complex flavors into plain old thick-cut bacon was incredibly easy. To start, however, I had to brew a pot of coffee. It would be the first of many this morning as I continued preparations for the upcoming *Andrea Doria* blend competition.

Ninety minutes later, with my pumpkin bread baked, my glazed bacon sizzling, and my thoughts about Sophia and Hunter still in knots, I heard Mike's deep voice ask —

"What smells so good?"

"Your breakfast," I replied, my short tone revealing my anxieties. "Sit down. We need to talk . . ."

FIFTY-FIVE

With a relaxed stride, Quinn's long legs moved into my kitchen.

Showered, shaved, and *nearly* dressed for the day, he hung his leather holster and suit coat on the back of a chair and, following the order of my pointing finger, rolled up his white shirtsleeves and settled his forearms on the table.

As I poured him a fresh-brewed cup, he surprised me by hooking one of his strong arms around my waist. "Can't a guy get a good-morning kiss before coffee?"

"You sure about that? There's no caffeine on these lips."

"Let's find out . . ." He tugged me closer, and I set down the pot. "Yeah," he agreed after testing his theory. "No caffeine, yet incredibly stimulating . . ."

"That's nice," I said as our morning kiss ended — or so I thought.

When I began to move away, Quinn not

only tugged me back, he pulled me off my feet and onto his lap.

"Mike! What are you doing?"

"I just remembered. We're officially engaged, so . . ."

"So what?"

"So you deserve more than a 'nice' kiss . . ."

With a smile in his eyes, Quinn took over my mouth, his lips and tongue leaving me breathless. When his callused hands slipped under my sweater, I gave in to the moment, my fingers tangling in his short sandy hair.

Aromas of hot coffee, sizzling bacon, and fresh pumpkin bread filled the kitchen, but he was still hungry for me — a realization that convinced me, for the next few minutes anyway, that I was the happiest woman alive.

"I guess I better get my own pair of those shoes," I rasped against his lips, a few minutes later.

He laughed. "It's not the shoes. It's the woman they're strapped to."

"Well, I'm sorry to tell you: *this* woman has a busy day ahead of her, and so do you."

I gently pushed his chest, and he reluctantly let me go.

On shaky legs, I moved to the counter, fighting hard to rid my molecules of the need to either pull Mike back upstairs or (with last night's suggestive cocktail coming to mind) unbuckle the man's pants and initiate a slow, comfortable coupling against the kitchen wall.

I could see him wrestling with the same temptations, so I supplied another: a plate of glistening, sweetly glazed bacon. While I didn't relish putting myself in competition with fatty strips of meat, the tactic was (to quote Franco) *effective.*

Quinn's focus quickly shifted from me to the caramelized pork belly. Then his own belly took over, trumping his libido, and the kitchen fell silent, save for the sounds of meat being munched to that ancient but universal music — guttural sounds of manly pleasure.

The primitive noises roused Frothy and Java from their postbreakfast napping. Like a pair of hungry raptors, the two circled Quinn's legs, little pink tongues licking their cat lips, long, straight tails petitioning like furry raised flags.

"Mike, I'm afraid you're going to need a lint roller for your pants."

"What?" he asked, emerging from his bacon trance.

I pointed to the fur-covered fabric below his knees.

Far from annoyed, he reached down and

stroked the lucky felines. "Should I share some of my bacon?"

"No, I'll take care of them . . ."

After bribing my nervy pair of pusses into the living room with a rattling faux mouse and an indulgent trail of catnip, I returned to the kitchen table, sliced up a loaf of my maple and brown sugar pumpkin bread, and slathered a few pieces with Quinn's favorite high-fat Irish butter.

My new fiancé closed his eyes as he sampled the fresh-baked slice. "Better than catnip," he garbled around his stuffed mouth.

"I iced three more loaves for your squad," I said. "And a fourth loaf for Sully — I know you visit him every day in the hospital. I'm sure Fran and the kids will enjoy the bread, too."

"I know they will, sweetheart. That's incredibly thoughtful."

"I made one final loaf. But I'm taking it to another hospital."

"What?" Quinn stopped chewing. "What hospital? What's going on?"

"That's what we need to talk about . . ."

FIFTY-SIX

I started from the beginning, telling Quinn about yesterday's trip to the Diamond District and the strange legacy left there in trust to Matt and Sophia — and my own daughter.

I told him how I found Matt's godfather, Gus, alone and stricken. How he was still in the hospital, unconscious and unable to answer any questions about how he got that way.

I also reminded Quinn what Gus had told me last week. "He promised to ask around about the Panther Man shooter."

Quinn studied me. "You think his condition had something to do with that?"

"I told you Gus made jewelry for people on both sides of the law, rap artists, and nightclub owners, including — I'm guessing — people like Eduardo De Santis . . ."

Finally, I told Quinn about Sophia's husband, Hunter Rolf, and how he'd gone to see Gus just hours before we found the poor man close to death.

"You wouldn't happen to have a picture of this guy?"

"I already sent it to you . . ." I showed him my phone with the photos I took at the 21 Club. "That's him, the big blond. And, let me tell you, when Matt and I confronted him, he was a nasty piece of work."

"Okay, Cosi," Quinn said, eyes smiling with a cross between astonishment and admiration. "I guess you better brief me on your suspect . . ."

I did, and Quinn listened the way I imagined he did with detectives under his command — with a complete poker face. Even more annoying, in the middle of my little "briefing," he pulled out his smartphone and told me to keep talking as he began to type a text message. Burying my frustration, I finished my spiel.

"So? What do you think?"

"Well . . ." Quinn began, face still frozen. "You know Eduardo De Santis is now under surveillance. Thanks to you."

"That was luck."

"No. Luck would have been you showing me a photo of your ex-husband with De Santis in the background, completely by chance. What you did was ID De Santis

317

from an old case and meticulously photograph him and those around him. That's not luck, Cosi. That's good detective work."

"Thank you. But in the light of a new day, I'm not sure it matters. Last night, I grilled Franco during my little mandatory ride home —"

"Listen, I'm sorry about that. I didn't want to send you away. But McNulty and I —"

"It's okay. Franco explained the reasons for it — or tried to, anyway. And I took the opportunity to find out more about that loudmouthed lieutenant and his unit. Franco says there is no history between McNulty or his Inside Job Squad and Eduardo De Santis."

"That's right."

"So doesn't that blow your current theory? I mean, if De Santis is out for revenge on you and your squad for trying to put him in prison, then why risk exposure going after McNulty's men?"

"I don't have to prove why De Santis did the latter. What I *can* prove is that he's in town, he has a grudge, he has the money to hire a sniper, he was in proximity of last night's fireworks display that ended in a wounding ricochet, *and* . . . after you sent me those photos, I had my squad do some more digging."

"Is that so?" I leaned forward with interest at the sudden sharp glint in Quinn's eyes. "What did they find?"

"Only that the owner of that empty building half a block away — the one you'd been complaining about; the one the sniper used to target my man Sully —"

"The one where I saw Panther Man descending on his trick rope?"

"The very same. That building is owned by a shell corporation."

"A shell for whom? Wait. Not —"

"The building belongs to Eduardo De Santis."

The news hit me like a physical thing. I sat back in my chair. "That bastard. It really is him."

"Looks like it. But we need more than a theory and circumstantial evidence. We need the kind of proof that will hold up in court."

"So what do you think of my concerns about Hunter Rolf?"

"He's a known associate of De Santis. The surveillance now includes him."

"Oh, okay. You already suspected him?"

"No, you did, Cosi, and you made a more than reasonable case. You found motive, proof of skill from that safari statement, excessive defensiveness when questioned, and proximity to last night's fiasco."

"But if I just made the case now, how could the man be under surveillance already?"

Quinn lifted his smartphone. "Because while you were talking, I ordered it."

Thirty minutes later, Quinn was heading for the front door. As he slipped his suit jacket over his shoulder holster, I hurried to catch him —

"Wait! You forgot something!"

"No, I didn't. I have your wrapped pumpkin breads right here in the shopping bag you gave me. And, no, I won't forget to take one to Sully at the hospital — that's my first stop."

"It's not that."

"Oh? You want another good-bye kiss?" He bent down. "Pucker up —"

"It's not that, either, although I'm happy to go again."

"Okay, I give. What did I forget?"

I pointed to the pressed pants of his charcoal gray suit. "Look down."

"Really?" He arched an eyebrow. "You're *that* ready to go again?"

"No, Mike, *farther* down, where Java and Frothy loved up your shins during breakfast, remember?"

"Oh, hell. The fur. Do I need to change my pants?"

"No, Lieutenant. I've got you covered. Because this" — I lifted my locked-and-loaded lint roller — "will get you un-covered."

He took the roller, handed me the shopping bag, and got to work.

"You know, Cosi, when I'm done *down here,* I expect another kiss *up there.*"

"Keep your pants on, Quinn, I'm not going anywhere."

Unfortunately, neither were Java and Frothy, who decided the lint roller "game" should include them.

I did my best to hold them off as Mike finished his de-furring.

Fearing a repeat offense, however, he planted the quickest ever kiss on my lips before bolting for the door — and left me holding the bag!

"Mrreeoooow," my girls complained, watching their favorite playmate depart *without my pumpkin bread!*

"Mike, wait!" I shouted through the door. "You forgot the —"

Suddenly, the door cracked open and a long arm poked through.

With relief, I handed over the goods, and

my fiancé finally left the building.

With a sigh, I gazed down at my girls. "You know, you two were no help at all."

Their reply consisted of a lazy stretch, an aloof yawn, and a double-teaming herding of their gullible owner to the kitchen cupboard — the one with the catnip.

FIFTY-SEVEN

"Shoo! Scat! Move along!"

Shortly after I helped Quinn de-fur his shins, I was dealing with another cat problem, this one on the sidewalk.

"Go on! Get!" I shouted, waving my broom at the offending feline — a big one, on two legs.

"Please!" he cried. "I'm expected —"

"Not here, Panther Man. Go climb a tree!"

Over the past week, we had no less than three different Panther Man impersonators stake out in front of the Village Blend at various times. They posed for pictures, aggressively shilled for "tips," and generally intimidated our customers.

I'd had enough!

So had this Panther Man, apparently. He suddenly ripped off his cowl to reveal a darkly handsome face wearing an expression of wounded dignity.

"I'll have you know I played the Marquis de Lafayette in the *Hamilton* road show," he declared with a toss of his dreadlocks. "I don't deserve such cavalier treatment."

I was ready to poke him with the broom one more time when Tucker burst through the front door and snatched it out of my hand.

"Stop, Clare! That's not a Panther Man imposter! That's *my* Panther Man."

Oops.

I'd completely forgotten that Tucker had scheduled a read-through of his superhero extravaganza. *But honestly, none of the other actors showed up in costume, only this guy!*

Tucker tried to smooth things over, but after my broom assault, this Panther Man was as skittish as a feral feline, and temperamental as an aging starlet.

"It's clear I'm not welcome in this production!"

"Come on, Wendell. Don't be silly. The play needs you."

"I'm not sure I'm right for the part."

"Of course you are. The role was made for you." Tuck began quoting his own script in an old-time radio show voice —

"Dick Nelson, crusading DA from New Kirk City, was so tough on crime that he had to go. Kidnapped, shot, and dumped in the deep forest, Nelson was saved from death by a pride of mountain lions who bestowed on him the speed, strength, and agility of a predatory feline. Now, in the guise of Panther Man, he defends the innocent and wreaks vengeance on the corrupt."

Tuck wrapped his arm around the big cat's shoulder. "This is your hour, Wendell. This is *your* part. Get in there and give it a hundred percent."

In the end, Tucker Burton's persuasive charm — and the promise of a private dressing room — convinced Panther Man to join his fellow thespians on the Village Blend's second floor.

When the temperamental talent was gone, I cornered my assistant manager. "So why the costume, Tuck? You're holding a casual script read-through, not a formal dress rehearsal."

"Wendell's a great performer. No matter the role, he gives one hundred and fifty percent. But he's also a Method actor, which comes with a whole lot of baggage. To understand motivation Wendell needs to live and breathe his character, 24/7."

"Dressed in *that* costume, I'm surprised he isn't living and breathing in a jail cell."

"I know Wendell is a little . . . *eccentric,*

but he's the only actor willing to play Panther Man after all that's gone down."

"You mean the shootings?"

Tuck shook his shaggy head. "I mean the police harassment."

"What?"

"I thought I was going to end up in jail myself. My crime was calling every rental place in town for a Panther Man costume. What I got was a very unfriendly visit from two surly NYPD detectives who wanted to know why I wanted the suit —"

"You explained everything, right?"

"Of course, only to find out I'd been *profiled.* Costume shops were ordered to provide authorities with a list of Panther Man requests. My name was on a list, Clare. A suspected terrorist list!"

"I'm sorry you had to go through that, Tucker."

"So am I. After the detectives interrogated me, they questioned Wendell. I hear they even grilled that Panther Man hustler in Times Square. I was ready to cut the character out of my play completely. But in the end the comic publisher provided a costume. They really want Panther Man to appear at a kid's charity event to counter all the bad publicity."

After Tuck greeted the last arriving cast

member, a strapping Amazon playing Wonder Woman, he announced: "Well, that's my cue. I'd better get upstairs before the talent start counting their lines and complaining they didn't get enough dialogue."

"I'd say break a leg, but those spiral steps are already an insurance nightmare, so good luck!"

When Tuck was gone, I put the broom to a more traditional use and swept the sidewalk. I looked up minutes later to find Nancy, my youngest barista, running toward me at top speed, her wheat-colored braids flying behind her.

She should *run. The girl is over an hour late!*

But if I was expecting an apology — and I wasn't — I would have been disappointed.

"Is he here? Is he here?" Nancy asked as she screeched to a halt. I caught the covered sheet-cake pan before it slipped from her grip.

"Whoa, slow down. By *he* you mean — ?"

"Superman . . . I mean David. Is he here yet?"

"The actors have arrived, according to Tuck. Superman is being played by David? David who?"

"It's David. Just David. Isn't that so perf? He models for Abercrombie and Fitch and

Hanes underwear. His last ad was so steamy and revealing that the MTA had all the posters removed from the subway!"

An image of Michelangelo's *David* in tighty-whities came to mind.

"David wouldn't happen to be Italian?"

"Oh, no," Nancy replied. "His accent is so cute. He was born in Australia — or was it New Zealand? And then his family moved to Wales . . ."

"I thought Superman was from the planet Krypton."

"Ha-ha." Nancy rolled her big doll eyes. "David just relocated to New York, so I baked him a welcome-to-America treat. It's my version of Blueberry Boy Bait."

"Well, the prey is waiting —" I pointed upstairs. "So I guess you better deliver the bait."

FIFTY-EIGHT

An hour later, Tuck gave the actors a fifteen-minute break. While Esther served coffee and pastries to the super heroic cast, Nancy presented her crush with a generous slice of blueberry heaven, cradled in a lacy doily.

"Enjoy, David . . . I baked this just for you."

The undeniably handsome underwear model flashed the blushing barista a toothy smile. "Thank you so much, luv. This looks super. Simply super."

Nancy waited expectantly until he took his first bite. As he chewed, David threw her a wink with one of his Paul Newman blue eyes.

"Oh, it's super good. Really, really super," he cooed around a mouthful of sweet, tender cake.

Nancy's smile was bright enough to light the second floor. "I'm so happy you like it. Let me get you another slice!"

Esther was beside me at the serving cart. "Seems like everything is *super* with Superman."

"He *is* super, isn't he?" Nancy gushed, arriving at our side. As she spoke, David raised his half-eaten cake with a smile.

Nancy giggled with glee and whispered, "Blueberry Boy Bait . . . it never fails."

"Ouch." Esther slapped her own forehead. "My feminist soul just cringed."

"Oh, what is it now?" Nancy demanded.

"Your choice of vocabulary is so . . . prehistoric. I mean, this is the twenty-first century. Who talks about 'boy bait'?"

David's perfect mouth took another bite of cake, and he winked again at Nancy. She tiny-waved back.

"What's wrong with boy bait?"

"Nothing, if you wear white gloves, a pillbox hat, and voted for Eisenhower!"

"Eisenhower? Is he one of your stupid Beat poets?"

"Oy gevalt," Esther wailed into her own hands. "Those who don't know history are doomed to wear aprons!"

"Look around, Esther. We're *all* wearing aprons."

Tucker and I laughed at that one while Esther steamed.

"You're like a broken clock, Nancy," she

said, tapping her *Powerpuff Girls* watch. "You're right twice a day!"

Unbowed, Nancy went toe-to-toe with her roommate. "How about you make like the Powerpuffs and go take a flying leap —"

I was about to intercede, but Tucker moved faster, jumping between the battling baristas. "Ladies! And, believe me, I use the term loosely. Let's not make a scene!"

"Come on, Tuck! Don't you find the words *boy bait* sexist and offensive?"

Hands on hips, Tucker challenged: "You're the poet, Esther. Come up with a new name."

"Okay. How about *mate bait*? It's perfect. Gender neutral and free of power trips and social convention, because there's no wife and no husband. Just a mate."

"Fine, call it whatever you want," Nancy said. "It made David happy and that's what counts. Isn't he a dream?"

Esther took a closer look at Superman. "I don't know. I couldn't go for a guy with Botox lips."

"David doesn't have Botox lips!"

"Sure he does, look at him. He's gone full Mick Jagger. He's got the pale complexion of Elvis, too."

"Pale? David's got a gorgeous, golden tan!"

Esther blinked. "Your gorgeously pale David is clutching his throat —"

"He's . . . he's probably practicing his death scene or something," Nancy said, her voice uncertain.

"He plays Superman. Superman isn't supposed to *die* —"

"He's not supposed to fall off his chair, either!" I cried, rushing to the stricken actor's side. "Call 911! David's going into anaphylactic shock."

FIFTY-NINE

"I think he'll be okay," I said to a tearful Nancy after the ambulance had gone. "Why, I'm pretty sure David's at the hospital already."

"I almost killed him. I almost killed Superman!"

"Come on, Nancy," Esther said, putting an arm around her. "How could you know David was allergic to blueberries? Anyway, you heard the paramedics. They got the air tube in him just in time —"

"Waaaaaaaahhhhhhh!"

"I'll take over," I insisted, stepping around Esther.

For the next ten minutes I consoled my youngest barista, giving her hugs and drying her tears. Nancy had finally settled down, when Tucker climbed the spiral stairs and sank into a chair across from us.

"My Superman is down for the count. Jeez, who knew a little old innocent blueberry had the potential to be Kryptonite?"

"I . . . I didn't mean it," said Nancy, her sobs dissolving into hiccups.

"I know," said Tuck, leaning forward to pat her hand. "He would have been all right if he hadn't sprained his wrist when he fell to the floor. But now . . ." With a dramatic sigh he sat back, then slapped his knees. "Well, the show must go on — with or without David!"

"You always tell me the world is full of actors," I said.

"Actors, yes. But actors who are also acrobats — they're not so easy to find on short notice." Tuck snatched a piece of the offending boy bait from the serving cart.

"What does he have to do?"

"Perform aerial stunts onstage. Superman has got to fly, Clare. Fly! And David was experienced. He'd learned the ropes of rope performing when he played the winged Car Insurance Angel in that 'Heavenly Rates' commercial. Plus he has the physique of Superman. Even if I can find a last-minute understudy with rope skills, he'll probably have to wear an inflatable muscle suit to look the least bit super heroic."

Tuck took a bite and chewed absently. Suddenly, his eyes lit up. "Hey, this is really good."

Nancy wiped her wet cheeks. "It's the award-winning Betty Crocker recipe with my own little tweaks —"

"Tweak away, kiddo. It's delicious."

I was happy to see Tuck smiling for the first time since the Fall of Superman. But poor Nancy was still miserable.

"Hey, Nancy, I have an idea. Why don't you and I go to the hospital and visit David?"

"I can't!" Nancy cried. "I feel so guilty. He probably never wants to see me ever again!"

"I'm sure he doesn't feel that way. Look, if you like, I could go and check on him for you."

"You'd do that?"

"Of course . . ."

I was heading that way anyway because David had been taken to the same hospital as Gus Campana, and I knew that's where I'd find Sophia.

With a deep breath, I got moving. I had a king's ransom in jewelry to return, pumpkin bread to deliver, and a list of questions I was anxious to have answered.

SIXTY

Beauty has tamed the savage beast . . .

My first thought when I arrived at Gus's bedside after checking on David — who was doing fine and (thank Cupid) didn't blame Nancy in the least.

With good news on my first visit, I was feeling positive about the second. That's when I found Gus's lovely daughter on a hospital couch, cradled in the arms of her Viking-sized husband.

The room was peaceful with ambient forest noises floating through the air from a small machine on the windowsill, and there was another sound, too.

Hunter Rolf was stroking his wife's dark golden hair while quietly singing in another language, his voice a whispered purr accompanied by the soft *ping*ing of the medical monitors.

"Byssan lull, koka kittelen full," he sang.

Just then, he spied me in the doorway —

and without breaking rhythm he put his index finger to his lips. As he finished his song, he slipped out from under his sleeping wife, put his jacket under her head for a pillow, and draped his coat over her for a blanket.

In shirtsleeves, he led me into the hallway.

"I'm sorry, but I do not wish to wake her. She slept very little in the past twenty-four hours."

"Of course."

"You are Ms. Cosi, from last night?"

Hunter was clearly embarrassed that he had to ask, but I didn't blame him. With my hair in a ponytail, and my jeans and flats, I looked a lot different today.

"Call me Clare."

He nodded, and when he spoke again, I could better hear the lilting Swedish rhythms in his speech.

"Please accept my apology for my behavior last evening. I was not sure that I could trust you. And when you asked about the man in Rome, I became protective. Perhaps overly so. But my dear wife explained what a trusted friend you are, and she is grateful you found me at the club. So am I. We talked all night and worked out many misunderstandings . . ."

It seemed Hunter had transformed overnight, from angry lion to purring kitten. Of course, Sophia had warned me that her husband was a charmer — so I viewed this gentler version of the gem dealer with a skeptical eye.

"I'm glad we had a chance to meet again," I told him with reserve, and pointed to my tote bag. "I brought something to eat."

"How kind of you, Clare. Sophia will be happy. Lately, it seems the first two words out of her mouth every morning are 'I'm hungry.' "

"I brought coffee, too. If you've tried to choke down the brew here, you know why."

"I am sure Sophia will enjoy it, but I cannot drink coffee. I have an allergy to caffeine."

"Really?"

He nodded. "I get the hives."

Resisting the urge to ask how he felt about blueberries, I glanced at Gus. "How is Mr. Campana?"

"Not good, I am sorry to say . . ." Hunter gravely shook his head. "The toxicology tests revealed that Gus was poisoned —"

"Poisoned?"

"Acute exposure to beryllium salts. His condition is very serious. But there is hope. Now that the doctors know the problem, they have begun a proper treatment."

"*How* was he poisoned?"

"Beryllium is used in metal processing, so it was probably an accident at the forge. Early this morning, two female police detectives visited us here at the hospital. They wanted access to the Campana property, so Sophia called her security man to let them in. I'm confident the police will find out how this accident happened."

"Did Gus show any symptoms of poisoning when you talked to him yesterday?"

"None at all. He seemed fine. Happy. I brought him good news."

"I see. And the news . . . I assume it was connected to that business meeting you had last night?"

"Yes, that was a celebration. As I explained to Sophia last night, the deal is sealed and will bring millions of dollars to the Campana family business over the next few years. I will no longer be the freeloader in this family."

"Freeloader? That's a harsh word. Is that how Sophia felt?"

"No, not my wife. But her father did. He did not believe I truly loved his daughter. He thought my marriage to her was a scheme to profit from their successful family business."

"Why would he believe that?"

Hunter lowered his eyes. "He had good reason. My old business, and the way I conducted it, bothered Sophia terribly."

"Did you do anything illegal, Hunter?"

"Not illegal, but, I admit . . . some would not view it as ethical. You see, in addition to hunting gems, I procure heirloom jewelry. I act as a middleman between buyers and sellers. Because my clients are almost exclusively women, I try to be amiable, persuasive — even charming — in order to detach a valuable piece from a widow, a divorcée, or a neglected wife."

"You seduce the jewelry out of them for a fraction of its value — is that what you're trying to tell me?"

"These are very wealthy women, Clare, and they part with their items by choice."

"But you persuade them — charm the stones from them, by your own admission. *Romancing the Stone* is a term I've heard —"

"Yes, yes, I saw that movie years ago." He smiled weakly. "But that is now behind me."

"Behind you? You gave it up?"

He folded his arms. "Sophia would see a client's text messages or overhear a phone conversation, and she'd fly into a jealous rage. She would not accept that my heart was hers alone and my brief associations with these women was simply business, so . . ." He shrugged. "I decided to make it my business no longer."

"You gave up romancing the stones? Completely?"

"Completely, yes. With what the three sheikhs have paid me, and the new connections I have made through Eduardo, I will be able to invest in the Campana business and work with Sophia. We will no longer be apart. No more traveling for our separate businesses. Together, Sophia and I are going to help Gus with the family business, and with my investment, we can begin planning for a profitable expansion."

The noises in the hospital corridor increased, and Sophia made a sound in her sleep. Hunter paused to check on his wife and partially closed the door.

His concern for Sophia seemed so tender and genuine, his demeanor so gentle, that it was hard to reconcile my suspicions that Hunter was the coldhearted shooter who'd targeted so many good cops.

But Hunter was undeniably an associate of Eduardo De Santis, a known — if unconvicted — drug dealer. And Hunter went on safari with De Santis, which meant this kindhearted hustler was capable of killing a helpless animal. It also meant he had the skills to act as a hired sniper.

"One more question, if you don't mind."

"I don't mind."

"I asked about the man in Rome last night. I'll ask again now. Who is this man, and why did you want to speak with Gus about — ?"

"Hunter? Is that you out there?" called Sophia through the door. "I'm hungry. I hope you got us something to eat!"

Sixty-One

As Hunter and I returned to the hospital room, Sophia was slipping into the flats I'd swapped with her last evening.

"Your friend Clare is here," he announced. "She's brought you something special."

Sophia jumped up and hugged me tightly.

"I'm also returning your jewelry," I said as I returned the hug. "It's here with your beautiful handbag and your designer heels —"

"Please, keep the bag and shoes," Sophia said, "if you'll let me keep your flats. They're the most comfortable shoes I've ever worn!"

I smiled. "Absolutely, keep my shoes as a *gift*. But you must take back yours. It's not even close to a fair trade —"

"I received them gratis, Clare. I have two more pairs at home, ditto for the designer bag. I get so many freebies and deals with my work in the fashion trade. Please keep them. I insist!"

"Well, if you insist." I leaned close. "I know my new fiancé will be happy."

"Do tell?"

At my slight blush, she smiled. "You know, the rubies I lent you to wear may have helped in that department." As she spoke, she unwrapped her jewelry from my silk scarf and lifted one of the earrings up to the light. "Look at the brilliance of that red, a magnificent stone with intense energy. Historically, many cultures believed it gave the wearer confidence and power. It's also the stone of passion — a gemological aphrodisiac."

"Really?"

"The ruby's glowing red hue is said to ignite an inextinguishable flame between couples, inspiring great and long-lasting love . . ."

With care, she transferred her necklace and bracelet into a safe pocket of her handbag on the couch. When she returned, she still held the earrings. To my shock, she presented them to me.

"Keep these, Clare. They look amazing on you." She held them up to my ears. "They even bring out the red in your chestnut hair."

"That's incredibly generous, but I can't possibly —"

"Please accept them — as an engagement present." She wrapped the earrings back up in my scarf and pressed them into my hands. "Now let's sit . . ."

Over slices of my iced pumpkin bread and paper cups of coffee from my thermos, we discussed Gus's condition. Hunter declined sampling my Winter's Dawn blend, sipping fruit juice instead, though he clearly enjoyed the bread, eating three pieces in a row.

"Too bad you missed Perla," Sophia said, nibbling on her first slice. "She brought that ambient music box in hopes that Dad can hear it. It's very pleasant, but I'm afraid the forest sounds put me right to sleep."

"That or the song I heard Hunter singing to you."

Sophia nodded, her face glowing with love for her husband. "It's a Swedish lullaby. Hunter learned it from his mother. When we were first married, he sang that song to me nearly every night. But I haven't heard it in a long time."

"It's called 'Galley of Riches,' " Hunter said. "A sweet little song about things grouped in threes. Three wanderers from afar, three ships that sail to port, a treasure box with three gifts —"

"And how three people make a family," Sophia added. "A mother, a father, and a child . . ."

The way Sophia looked at Hunter made me think that remark was more than rhetorical. *Is Sophia pregnant?* The glow in her face and revved-up appetite sounded awfully familiar.

I recalled how my own little family of three began. The tender way Matteo treated me when I was pregnant with Joy, including his many trips to all-night bodegas and neighborhood delis to satisfy my cravings.

The three of us certainly weathered the ups and downs together, like a rocky ride on a volatile sea; but even after Matt and I split, the ship didn't sink. We kept our bond to support our daughter.

My gaze found Gus, still unconscious, on the hospital bed, hooked up to machines and monitors.

I tried to imagine what his little family of three had gone through aboard the *Andrea Doria* on the harrowing night it went down. It must have been terrible and terrifying. But somehow he'd gotten them through it — his wife, Angelica, and their young daughter, Perla.

Perla.

My thoughts stalled on Gus's eldest child as a crucial question occurred to me that hadn't before —

The day Gus was poisoned, Sophia had joined Matt and me for the opening of the safe-deposit box. Why wasn't Perla with us?

Sixty-Two

"Sophia, can I ask you a question about your sister?"

"Sure."

"How did Perla react to news about the Eye of the Cat?"

"Funny you should ask, because I wondered about that myself. She seemed curiously *unsurprised* when I told her about it. But then, Perla is Perla. She never reacts the way you think she will . . ."

Perla Campana was not only Gus's daughter; she was his first child. In every Italian American household I knew, the eldest held a special place in the family. The oldest child was usually entrusted with more responsibility — including legal ones like assignment as executor of a parent's will.

"But why wasn't Perla at the vault?"

Sophia shrugged. "Because Sal Arnold didn't have orders to serve her a letter of notice. She wasn't named as one of the trustees."

"Only Matt and you? Do you know why?"

"You'd have to ask my father for sure, but I suspect Perla's total lack of interest in the family business might have been a factor. My sister made it clear when she went off to college that she wanted nothing more to do with my parents' jewelry business. She announced she wanted her life to be her own."

"But don't you think Perla will want a say — and a big share — in the fortune that the Eye of the Cat will bring?"

Hunter had been listening quietly, but he laughed out loud at that question.

"What's so funny?" I asked.

With a shake of his head, he echoed Matt's sentiments.

"You think that jewel will bring a big fortune, but what it really brings is big trouble. That man in Rome, the one you asked about. He is only the beginning of the storm that is coming."

Hunter explained that while he was doing business in Rome, he was approached by an elderly but dapper man in a white suit, who refused to give his name but claimed to have been aboard the *Andrea Doria* with Gus.

"He showed me money transfers that proved Gus paid him a small fortune over

349

the decades since the shipwreck — close to a million dollars. This man freely admitted it was blackmail money. He said he witnessed something on the sinking ship, something that involved Gus and the Campana family. He refused to tell me what, only that because Gus had recently cut him off, there would be a reckoning."

"Reckoning how exactly? What do you think he was blackmailing Gus about?" I asked, thinking I might know the answer — and it had to do with a young apprentice named Silvio.

Sophia jumped in. "Isn't the answer obvious? This man in Rome must have known Dad snuck the Eye off the ship and hid it all these years. Dad cut off this man's blackmailing payments because he knew it was time for the safe-deposit box to be opened — and the secret would be out anyway."

My theory was no better, so I didn't dispute hers, not out loud.

But it seemed to me the blackmailer's threat implied something darker than a hidden jewel. In Hunter's words, *"he witnessed something on the sinking ship, something that involved Gus and the Campana family."*

While Gus was on that ship, he was in rightful possession of the jewel. His unethical act of concealing the truth occurred *after* the ship had sunk. Yet the blackmailer claimed to have "witnessed" something *on the sinking ship.*

To my ears, it was worse than one man assuming another's identity. It sounded as if the blackmailer had watched a crime take place, something awful enough for Gus to pay off this witness for sixty years.

I turned back to Hunter. "What did Gus say when you told him about this black-mailer in the white suit?"

"He seemed unfazed," Hunter replied with a shrug. "Gus knew all about the man and his threats, and he assured me that he would deal with the problem himself."

"If Gus was stricken after you left, isn't it possible that this character had something to do with Gus's poisoning?"

"What are you saying, Clare? That what happened to my father wasn't an accident? You think someone tried to murder him?"

"I have no proof, but the timing makes me suspicious. Doesn't it make you suspicious? I'm sure it will make the police *extremely* suspicious —"

Just then, a knock on the open door made our heads turn.

Detectives Lori Soles and Sue Ellen Bass strode into the room, followed by two uniformed police officers.

The last time I'd spoken to the Fish Squad was at my engagement party. They put on a good false-arrest act that time. This time, I was certain their grim demeanors were no act.

"Ah, Detectives, back so soon?" Hunter said, rising.

Without breaking her stride, Sue Ellen Bass pulled out her handcuffs as she stepped behind Sophia's husband.

"Hunter Rolf," Lori Soles announced, "you are under arrest for the attempted murder of Gustavo Campana. You have the right to remain silent —"

A stunned Hunter put up no resistance as Sue Ellen cuffed him. Then the shocked silence was obliterated by a shriek of anguish so loud and sharp that members of the hospital staff came running.

"No!" Sophia cried. "You can't take him away! You can't!"

Using her manicured nails like claws, Sophia launched herself at Detective Bass. The uniformed officers jumped in and pulled a sobbing Sophia back as Sue Ellen dodged back and forth to avoid getting slashed, while valiantly keeping her hold on the prisoner.

I quickly stepped up and took Sophia off

the officer's hands and into my arms.

"Hunter!" she cried.

"I did nothing," he assured her.

An annoyed Sue Ellen hustled him out of the room, followed by the uniforms. Lori Soles touched my shoulder, and tilted her head at the tearful woman in my arms.

"Get her out of here, but don't let her go home. Their place is being searched. That could go on for hours."

"What are you basing this arrest on?" I asked.

"This morning Mr. Rolf freely admitted that he visited with his father-in-law on the date and time shortly before the poisoning. We also lifted his fingerprints from the glass of cold brew coffee that Gustavo Campana drank from, which contained the poison." Lori met my gaze. "Another full glass sat by the sofa, it remained untouched. The untouched glass also carried Mr. Rolf's fingerprints."

Sophia was so distraught I doubted she noticed our exchange. After Lori left, I helped Sophia to her feet.

"Come on," I said. "There's nothing more you can do here. You're coming home with me."

SIXTY-THREE

An autumn cloudburst caught us as we flagged a cab outside the hospital.

Though we were soaked when we arrived at the Village Blend, Sophia refused to go upstairs to my duplex because she "didn't want to impose."

So I took her to the most comfortable spot in my coffeehouse, the second-floor lounge, a place to dry off, and speak in private.

I stoked the fireplace, and soon the crackling flames dispelled the dampness and the gloom. All we needed was something warm and soothing.

"How about a *caffè corretto* or maybe an Irish coffee?" The moment I made the suggestion, I wanted to take it back.

"Irish coffee, please!" Sophia replied. "I don't think Sambuca is going to be sufficient to drown my sorrows."

"But . . . maybe you shouldn't. I mean, if you're . . ."

"If I'm what?"

"Sophia, are you expecting?"

"No. But that's prescient of you. Among the many things Hunter and I discussed last night was our agreement that we would start a family — as soon as my father recovers, if he recovers . . . and if I can keep the man I love out of prison."

"Try to stay positive."

Despite her down tone, I knew Sophia had a resilient spirit — because I'd seen it. The moment we climbed into the cab outside the hospital, she pulled out her phone and called her company's legal team, firmly demanding they spring Hunter from custody. If she was going to get through this in one piece, she needed to keep summoning that strength.

As we settled into our armchairs by the fire, Tuck delivered a tray with a plate of treats, along with a pot of hot coffee, four shots of Jameson, fresh whipped cream, and a bowl of brown sugar.

As Sophia nibbled one of our sweetly iced Pretty in Pink cookies, she watched me place a bit of brown sugar into each of our glass mugs, stir in the shots of whiskey, pour on the hot coffee, and finish the drinks with generous dollops of whipped cream.

Sophia hit the spiked coffee hard.

"Oh, that's good," she said, already appearing more relaxed. "Clare, I can't thank you enough for all you've done."

"You might not remember, Sophia, but it was a rainy day like this when you came out to New Jersey to visit me and my daughter. It was right after my divorce from Matt, and Joy was really struggling with all the changes in her life. The confidence you gave my daughter was a priceless gift. I can't thank you enough for that, so no more talk of 'imposing,' okay?"

"Okay . . ." She gave me a weak smile before her expression clouded again. "You know, it's ridiculous the police think Hunter is a murderer. If you saw the way he mourned after we lost our child — he was completely inconsolable."

"You lost a child? I'm so sorry. I didn't know . . ."

"A few months after Hunter and I met, I got pregnant. I told him he was the father, and assumed our affair would be over. Considering his reputation in Europe, it was a reasonable assumption. To my surprise, Hunter wanted us to be married immediately. It was a quickie wedding on Aeroe Island, but it was so beautiful, right on the bluer-than-lapis Baltic Sea, and afterward, we traveled across Europe, and we were so happy together, and then . . . I miscarried."

Sophia swiped at a tear. "After that, I got it in my head that Hunter only wanted the child, not me. I treated him badly. Pushed him away. I became very jealous and said awful things. Until last night, when you convinced him to come back to me."

"It wasn't me, Sophia."

"It *was* you, Clare. I called and called last night. I texted him, too, maybe a hundred times. But Hunter didn't come until you and Matt talked to him . . ."

I tensed, recalling the distracted way Hunter had looked at his phone last night while speaking with me and Matt. After the fireworks caused all that chaos in front of the cop bar, I had suspected Hunter's rush to leave had something to do with setting them off. Now, it was clear, his rush to leave had everything to do with his wife. And yet . . .

He was an associate of De Santis, owed the man for a multimillion-dollar deal, fit the physicality of Panther Man, and was a marksman by his own admission.

"Sophia, I have to tell you something — and it's going to be upsetting, so brace yourself. I believe Hunter may have been picked up by the police for more than one reason, more than suspicion of poisoning your father."

"What are you talking about?"

"Last night, Hunter's meeting at the 21 Club showed him to be an associate of Eduardo De Santis, a man who was tried a few years ago in this country for distributing drugs in his nightclub. He wasn't convicted, but members of the NYPD believe De Santis may be behind the recent spate of cop shootings as revenge. And because Hunter is now a known associate, there is concern that he's also involved —"

"Involved in shooting cops?! That's insane!" Sophia adamantly shook her head. "Hunter is the gentlest man I've ever known. He abhors violence!"

"If that's true, then why does he shoot innocent animals? He told me last evening that he met De Santis on an African safari —"

"Yes, a *photo* safari! You should see his pictures — they're spectacular. If he stopped hunting jewels tomorrow, he could probably get a job with *National Geographic.*"

"Does he own a gun? Has he ever?"

"No! He hates guns. He won't even carry when he's in dangerous parts of Africa."

"And what about his business in Africa? Last week, I overheard you arguing with him in your family's store. It sounded to

358

me like he deals in blood diamonds."

"God, no, Clare, he doesn't! I was enraged at him last week after I saw a series of text messages from a Danish woman who will not stop chasing him — and she's far from the first. You see, Hunter started out in this business by buying heirloom jewelry from wealthy women and reselling the pieces at a higher price —"

"Yes, he told me about that."

"Well, let *me* tell you, it became a very bad habit, like excessive gambling or drinking. He'd see a woman in a restaurant or hotel and charm the jewels right off her neck. It became a game to him, and I hated that he kept playing it after we were married. What you overheard was one of our many arguments about my wanting him to stop. My 'blood diamond' remark was a trade insult. It's as if you told Matteo that his latest crop of beans were garbage. It was a charge that I knew would hurt Hunter because when he buys heirloom gems, he *may* be buying blood diamonds or their equivalent, and these days he is a stickler about legally sourcing his stones."

With each new revelation, my body tensed a little more.

This was clearly a very different picture of

Hunter than the one I saw last night — and, worse, the one I painted for Mike Quinn.

SIXTY-FOUR

"What can I do to help my husband, Clare? Tell me!"

The words I used to comfort Sophia were a salve for my own racked conscience.

"First, try not to worry. All of these facts about Hunter will come out as detectives interview him. And the search of your home will yield nothing incriminating — no guns, no fireworks, no evidence of any involvement with the shootings here in the city. They'll check his phone and any digital messaging account and see that he's innocent, not only of plotting to hurt police but of plotting to hurt Gus. I'm sure they're looking at you, as well, to see if you colluded with him to kill your father so you could inherit the business — you see where I'm going?"

"Yes, and none of it's true."

"I know that now. Clearly, Hunter is a victim of circumstance. But the police won't know that for hours, and because of his association with Eduardo De Santis, they'll be questioning him for the next twenty-four, pressing him for any information he can give them on Club Town Eddy and his business in the city."

"I should tell my lawyers all of this."

"Yes, you should . . ."

As Sophia made the call to her attorneys, I sat back and now considered (ironically enough) how to prove Hunter's *innocence*. By the time she was done, I had an answer.

"Sophia, Detective Soles told me the police found Hunter's fingerprints on Gus's glass of poisoned coffee while his own drink was untouched —"

"It was untouched because Hunter can't drink coffee. It makes him ill."

"I know that. But the police didn't, which is another reason they picked him up today."

"What about that person who knocked you down, the one in the black raincoat?"

"My Phantom?"

Sophia nodded. "Why aren't the police tracking him down as a suspect?"

"It's possible they already did — and dismissed him. By now, a routine investigation would have included interviews with your father's employees and close associates. But the forensics yielded Hunter's fingerprints. He had opportunity, proximity, and motive since Gus's death would mean you'd inherit the business and as your husband he would profit. So my next question is important. Did your father know that your husband is allergic to caffeine?"

"No. There's no reason he would. I'm sure Hunter accepted the glass of cold brew out of politeness. He was already on pins and needles facing Dad. I know how tough my father can be."

"So there's a valid reason Hunter's glass went untouched. And a good lawyer would say that just because Hunter's fingerprints are *on* Gus's glass doesn't prove that he put the poison *in* it. Your husband could have held or moved Gus's glass for any number of reasons. And maybe the poison wasn't put in the glass at all. Maybe the poison originated from somewhere else."

"His forge?"

"No. His cold brew jars. I saw them lined up in the refrigerator when I visited last week."

Sophia finished her second Irish coffee. "I don't follow."

"Cold brew can take anywhere from twelve to twenty hours to make, depending on the type of coffee and the batch size. You add ground coffee to cold water and place

363

it in the refrigerator to steep. After the flavor is extracted, the grounds must be filtered out. Your father made his cold brew in quart-sized Mason jars. He staggered the steeping and clearly labeled each jar. Some jars were just started, a few were in the middle of the steeping process, and others were already filtered and ready for drinking."

"And you think someone poisoned one of the jars?"

"Yes. You can store cold brew coffee for up to a week, but Gus went through his much quicker than that. That's why I think the person who poisoned Gus's coffee could have been someone who visited him a day or two before we found him poisoned. It's ingenious because whoever did this would be long gone by the time Gus drank it."

"So what can we do?"

"Well, a logical investigation has to start somewhere. So let's check your surveillance cameras again. Hopefully, they go back a few days —"

"They go back seven days."

"Good. If we see any possible suspects who visited Gus in the hours — and days — leading up to his drinking the poison, then we show them to your lawyers."

Sophia thumbed her phone and cursed.

"The battery died."

"The Village Blend has Wi-Fi. Can you hook up your surveillance system to any device?"

"Sure. The passcodes are in my head."

Tuck returned, glanced at the empty cups and shot glasses. "Would you like more Irish coffee?"

"Just bring the bottle," Sophia replied. Suddenly embarrassed, she covered her mouth. "I'm sorry. I know you don't have a liquor license."

"Oh, don't you worry about that," Tuck said with a wink. "We never make a liquor *sale* here — just complimentary service for family and friends."

While my assistant manager fetched Sophia's bottle, I went to my office and grabbed my laptop.

She was logging on when Tuck got back.

"Here you go. For the ladies who *liquid* lunch."

Not only had Tuck delivered the Jameson, he'd dug tumblers out of our catering closet, and brought water and a bowl of ice, too. Sophia passed on the amenities and downed a quick shot.

"You know, honey," Tuck said, "my mother was quite the drinker. And *her* mother, Granny Chestnut, used to warn her: '*People who drink to drown their sorrow should be told that sorrow knows how to swim.' "*

I arched an eyebrow at my assistant manager. "That wasn't your grandmother, Tuck, that was Ann Landers."

"And Granny read that column every single day!"

"It's all right," said Sophia, French-tipped fingers hovering over the computer keys. "I may have had a few, but I'm not about to drown — or let my family sink. Now, let's get started."

SIXTY-FIVE

"Hold that picture!"

Sophia froze the security camera image of my Phantom in the hooded raincoat — the one who'd slammed through Gus's iron gate and knocked me on my assets.

We were no longer squinting at a tiny phone. We were watching the surveillance footage on my laptop's fifteen-inch screen, where I quickly discovered the devil is in the details, and there were several significant little devils I'd missed the first time.

This Phantom figure wasn't very tall when measured against the size of the gate, the figure's shoulders were narrow, and the raincoat was not completely black. The sleeves had cuffs with a gray and black flower pattern. All of which suggested a woman, not a man.

Stopping frame by frame, we zoomed in close on the Phantom's hand gripping the gate. It appeared my menacing Phantom was wearing pink nail polish.

"Thanks," I told Sophia. "Now let's go back in time."

She jumped the recording back to six AM the day before we found Gus poisoned. In fast motion we watched deliverymen come and go along with the mail carrier. Neighbors moved up and down the sidewalk.

Then, in the early evening, Gus had a visitor.

"It's Perla," Sophia said, slowing the recording to normal speed. "You can't miss that hair."

Or lack thereof. Perla's pixie cut was extreme but attractive with her high cheekbones. Strands of gray-white hair heavily salted the raven black color.

For a woman in her sixties, she was in superb shape with a strong, athletic build. She wore chunky-heeled boots and loose, outdoorsy clothing — khaki pants with an open Windbreaker over a Henley. From the quality of the cut and the material, they looked more like J.Crew or Patagonia than Old Navy.

Perla used her own key to let herself through the gate. She wasn't in the habit of wearing makeup, let alone nail polish, and I could see, measuring her height against the gate, that she was much taller than the

Phantom figure in the raincoat.

Perla's visit with her father lasted nearly two hours.

"Longer than her hospital stop today," Sophia said. "Perla had to rush off to explore a just-discovered fallout shelter inside the Brooklyn Bridge . . ."

I nodded. Perla was a doctor of urban archaeology, so I wasn't surprised. Her work took her to some of the oddest places in the five boroughs.

The recording of the next day's activities revealed more deliveries, mail, and the neighbors again. At around two o'clock Gus had another visitor. This one was about the same height as our Phantom.

Sophia didn't have a clue who the tony, middle-aged woman with the cat glasses was. I didn't know her name, but I'd seen her before — in front of Gus's gate a week ago, demanding entry.

As we watched the footage, Gus buzzed the woman in, but she didn't stay long. After fifteen minutes she stormed out the gate and angrily hailed a taxi.

"From her body language, it doesn't look like her conversation with your father went well."

"I don't recognize her," Sophia replied. "What I can tell you is that those glasses are Bulgari, and that particular jeweled frame is only sold in Italy, so she's either Italian or visited Italy recently."

"You're getting good at this detective thing."

Sophia downed another shot and patted my shoulder. "I have a good teacher."

On the morning of the day Gus drank the poison, we discovered the last visitor Gus had before Hunter showed up in the late afternoon.

"Matt's mother!" Sophia and I cried out together.

Sixty-Six

The recording that followed told a disturbing tale in silent-movie fashion, but maddeningly lacking those all-important dialogue cards that give viewers the rest of the story.

Madame arrived at nine in the morning — about the same time she'd called me to say she had a change of heart about attending the box opening. During the call, she also mentioned being upset about her late husband keeping this mysterious legacy a secret from her.

Clearly, she'd gone to Gus for answers.

When she arrived, Gus greeted her sweetly at the gate with a kiss on each cheek, and they went inside the property, where the visit lasted for over two hours.

Did Gus tell Madame the truth about the Eye of the Cat? And why he involved Matt's father in a scheme to hide it? Or was the conversation even more revealing? Did he confess why he was being blackmailed? And what really happened all those years ago on the sinking Andrea Doria?

Whatever they discussed, the real mystery began when Madame and Gus parted ways.

Gus took the trouble to escort Madame across the hidden courtyard and through the exterior gate. On the sidewalk, they hugged, and Gus waved as Madame strolled down the block.

Before she got very far, a familiar black Jaguar rolled quickly up to the sidewalk in front of Gus. He must have recognized the car, because instead of walking back inside the courtyard, he waited until it stopped.

The camera angle was bad, and there was glare, so I couldn't tell if the driver was the man with the U-shaped scar. Still, I expected the woman with cat glasses to climb out of the backseat.

This time I was wrong.

When the door behind the driver opened, an old man in a spotless white suit climbed out with the help of his walking stick. That man used that stick to close the car door. Then, smirking, he faced Gus.

Sophia froze the picture so we could study more detail.

"The suit is very good quality, but it's an old-fashioned cut," Sophia said. "It was likely purchased in the last century. And that hair is too thick, too dark, and too long to be real. It certainly doesn't match his age. The skeevy mustache is dyed too dark, too. This man is trying to disguise his appearance. He must be —"

"— *the blackmailer from Rome!*" we cried in unison.

Sophia restarted the footage.

The visitor took two steps toward the gate, and Gus exploded in absolute rage. The wild gestures were threatening enough to stop the man in his tracks.

Meanwhile, just inside camera range, Madame turned to watch the entire exchange with wide eyes.

The argument was cut short when Gus made a final universally obscene gesture and retreated back through his iron gate, slamming it shut behind him, which left the man in the white suit locked out.

It should have ended there, but it didn't. In fact, the worst was yet to come.

Madame had a curiosity like mine, and when it was piqued, she couldn't let it go. Now I watched in helpless dread as she approached this blackmailer in the white suit.

The man's demeanor instantly changed when he faced Madame. The smirk vanished, replaced by a snake charmer's smile.

He bowed graciously, and even kissed her hand.

After Madame and he spoke for a few minutes, the man pointed to the black Jag, offering Madame a ride.

To my horror, she accepted, allowing him to help her into the backseat. He climbed in on the other side, and the Jag sped away.

I gritted my teeth as Matt's one-word warning popped into my head.

Vendetta.

The tension was so thick in the coffee lounge that the rattle of my smartphone startled both Sophia and me.

"Yes!" I answered.

"Clare, it's Matt." His voice was tense, and I knew why. "It's Mother. I can't find her. When her housekeeper arrived this morning, the apartment was empty. I've tried texting and voice mail, but she hasn't responded. I don't know what's happened to her."

God help me, I did know — and the truth scared me to death.

SIXTY-SEVEN

"Matt! What took you so long?"

"So long? I got here from my Red Hook warehouse in one hour, in heavy traffic, in the *pouring rain!*"

Matt didn't have to tell me it was pouring outside. As he stepped into my apartment, he shook off his yellow slicker and water sprayed everywhere.

"It's been over an hour, and you should have been here sooner." I jumped clear of the Matt monsoon. "Did you stop along the way?"

"Only once." He held up a speeding ticket.

"Great," I called from the kitchen. "I hope Emmanuel Franco didn't write that."

"No, it was some other *poliziotto fascista.*"

"So you weren't actually speeding?"

"Yes, of course, I was speeding! I was trying to get here! And I'd appreciate your leaving the Mook's name out of our conversations from this day forward . . ." Shaking his shaggy dark hair, Matt continued shedding water like a wet dog. "So when can I see this security camera recording?"

I handed him a fistful of paper towels. "As soon as we mop up Lake Allegro."

While we dried the flood, I told Matt about Gus being poisoned, Hunter's arrest for the crime, and Sophia's more than understandable freak-out.

By now, the poor woman was passed out in my bedroom.

In the hour and twenty minutes it took Matt to drive here, I'd even convinced her to have actual food — a smart idea on top of all that whiskey and a single Pretty in Pink cookie. And since I wanted to provide something delicious and nutritious for her, I whipped up a big batch of my Pumpkin Alfredo, which also made good use of the leftover pumpkin puree from my morning baking. The beautiful pastel orange fettuccine had all the buttery fall flavor of pumpkin ravioli and the rich and decadent creaminess of regular Alfredo, but with more fiber and vitamins from the winter squash.

After swooning over the bowl and inhaling the mound of pasta, Sophia showered in my upstairs bath and borrowed a change of clothes: a pair of my jeans with a belt notched tightly enough to hold the roomier size on her slender frame. And because chic styling was second nature to her, she automatically knotted my oversize T-shirt, adjusting it cleverly enough for a casual-girl-at-home magazine spread.

By the time I finished cleaning the dishes, she was sleeping soundly on my bed, Java and Frothy curled up, almost protectively, on either side of her.

Fortunately, she left my laptop linked to the jewelry store's security system, and the software was user-friendly. I jumped around a bit to confirm my suspicions, then I sent several screen grabs to my printer.

I'd just finished up when I heard my waterlogged ex at the front door . . .

After mopping up the rainwater, we moved to the kitchen, where I ran the footage of Madame and the mystery man in the white suit.

"That's got to be the guy from Rome," Matt said, pacing the length of the counter. "The blackmailer Hunter talked to you about, don't you think?"

"Yes, and so does Sophia. But we don't have his name, or the name of the others I saw in that same car — the thuggish guy with the U-shaped cheek scar or that fashionista with the cat glasses, a woman who is suspiciously close to the same height as the

Phantom."

"The Phantom? Another comic book character?"

"The Phantom is how I think of that figure in the black raincoat, the one who ran me down on the day Gus was poisoned."

"Do you think this woman poisoned him?"

"It's possible, but we need more answers. And real evidence."

Matt bent over the screen, squinted, and shook his head. "I can't make out the license plate on the car. The angle is wrong."

"The question is: Do you believe your mother is in danger?"

"I don't know, Clare, we could be over-reacting . . ."

I had to admit, I was leaning in that direction. While waiting for Matt, I had calmed down from my initial emotional response and tried to think things through logically.

"It's possible the man in the white suit only wanted information from your mother and simply took her for a drive and maybe to dinner. Whatever Gus and this blackmailer told her may have been deeply upsetting to her, especially if it involved your late father. Maybe she decided to get out of town for a while to think things through. She could have hopped a plane to visit a friend — she has them all over the world.

And if she did, she'll be in touch soon, right?"

"I guess so. My mother does act on impulse."

"Not unlike her son."

"And she's often taken trips at a moment's notice — or no notice."

"Ditto."

"She could have taken off for Europe or Brazil or Bali —"

"So we could either wait another twenty-four hours to hear from her, or we could call the police now. What do you want to do?"

As Matt started pacing again, he noticed the extra Pumpkin Alfredo on the stove. Grabbing a fork, he began eating straight out of the pot.

"Mmm . . . this is good," he absently garbled, shoveling in the food.

Hungry much?

"Matt?" I prompted. "You can eat your feelings but there's no time to chew on this decision. Should we wait? Or err on the safe side and call the police now?"

I could see he hated the idea of calling the police, because (frankly) he hated the "fascist" *polizia.* Not so much Mike Quinn, not after all that Quinn had done for him in the past. But Franco and those false arrests

Matt had been subjected to were another matter, along with every cop who ever wrote him a speeding ticket, every corrupt official he'd had to pay off in the developing world, and . . . authority figures in general.

Which is why I knew how worried Matteo Allegro truly was when he finally said —

"Let's call the police."

Just then, my smartphone alerted me to a new message.

"Esther is texting me from downstairs," I said, scanning the words.

"What is it?"

I met Matt's gaze. "Looks like the police came to us."

SIXTY-EIGHT

I grabbed my printouts, scribbled Sophia a quick note in case she woke up. Then Matt and I hit the stairs.

We found Detective Lori Soles at a table by a rain-spattered French door, dressed in her usual crisp slacks and pressed blazer, which barely hid the bulky weapon at her hip. Her short blond curls looked damp from the downpour, her expression beyond agitated.

Between angry swipes of her smartphone screen, she gulped her Iced Vanilla Latte — which did little to cool her off.

We hardly slipped into chairs at her table before Lori let loose —

"Who the hell is this Hunter Rolf we arrested today?! Did he steal the Hope Diamond? Commit high treason? Plot to kill a world leader? What?"

Matt blinked, surprised. "And here I thought cops in this city actually *knew* who they were arresting and why —"

I laid a hand on Matt's arm to silence him.

"I know his name, Allegro," Lori shot back. "Now I'd like to know why our collar was taken away from us."

"What do you mean?"

"I mean we're out, Clare. No interview room questions. Not even a *Thanks for your work, Detectives.* Sue Ellen's so pissed she went on a Tinder date. I feel sorry for the person she swiped right on this time!"

Lori's loud voice was turning heads. "McNulty just marched in, took over, and had us relieved for the day. You know, some of us actually like to be kissed before we get —"

"Shhh. Calm down," I said. "Are you talking about *Lieutenant* McNulty, the man who heads the Inside Job Squad?"

Now it was Lori's turn to be surprised. "You know him?"

"We've met. I was a victim of the man's brand of 'witness correction.' "

"Do tell."

I did. About the fireworks. And the panicked shooting outside the bar where McNulty and his men were drinking. I also confessed that I was the one who fingered Hunter when I spoke to Quinn about him.

"So, you think *Hunter Rolf* is the cop

shooter?"

"Not now . . ." I explained how Hunter was the victim of circumstance, for the shootings and the poisoning of Gustavo Campana.

"Well, I can tell you that Lieutenant Mc-Nulty won't be taking your word for it. All interviews and investigations of both crimes are under his command. And he did not want Sue Ellen and me on his team. We're out."

"What about Mike?"

"Last I heard, your fiancé and his squad have been temporarily diverted from their own casework and put under McNulty's authority for the duration of the cop shootings investigation. As of this afternoon, Quinn and his people are scattered across the five boroughs, tracking down Panther Man 'leads.'"

"Why are you putting finger quotes around the word *leads*?"

"Because they're obviously bogus. Mc-Nulty's not about to give anyone the chance to solve a case he's running, especially his chief rival in the department. That's why he sent me and Sue Ellen off to see the wizard. He knows we're tight with Quinn, and he obviously believes Hunter Rolf is a prime suspect. He wants the glory of a confession all for himself and his detectives."

"Well, he's not going to get a confession! Hunter is not guilty!"

Now Matt put a hand on *my* arm. "Take it easy, calm down."

But I couldn't. I was livid!

"Why in heaven's name is Lieutenant McNulty in charge of the investigation? Mike's team was targeted *before* the Inside Job Squad. He's been working the case longer than McNulty!"

"That's true, Clare, but McNulty is in favor right now at One Police Plaza, not your fiancé."

"Why?" I squeezed my eyes shut, already knowing the answer. "It's because Mike embarrassed the mayor and police commissioner, isn't it? They blame him for the newspapers publishing that Panther Man sketch."

"I'm sure that's part of it. But don't forget, Quinn went off to DC to work for Justice. He may be back in New York now, but those bureaucrats downtown are all too human — they have resentful streaks and short memories, and some of these new appointments in the commissioner's office seem to have amnesia."

"Are you saying Mike's career with the NYPD is in jeopardy?"

"No, of course not. Mike Quinn is a thoroughbred. He's a decorated narcotics officers, highly valued. The brass is not about to risk losing him in their stable. But they *are* pissed. So they're spanking him by temporarily putting him under McNulty, who has much more political power at One PP —"

"Okay! Enough with the career counseling!" Matt threw up his hands. "This pee-pee talk is pissing *me* off. It's time we talked about my mother!"

"Shhhh," Lori and I hissed in unison.

Then we all calmed down and got down to business.

Sixty-Nine

Ten minutes later, Matt finished explaining his worries to Lori Soles. "So what do you think?" He rubbed the dark stubble on his chin. "I know I'm supposed to wait forty-eight hours to file a missing person's report but —"

"Actually, you don't have to," Lori replied, reaching for one of the fudgy Chocolate Globs that Nancy brought from our pastry case. "If you have serious concerns for the safety of someone whose whereabouts are unknown, you should *immediately* report them missing."

Then she sighed and looked again at the screen grabs I handed her. "Unfortunately, from what you've told me, and what I see here, this hasn't reached the level of a missing person's investigation."

"But you *just* said —"

I settled Matt down again.

"Look, I can see you're worried, but from

a law enforcement perspective, there's little here to indicate a threat to your mother. She's greeted pleasantly and responds in kind. She's invited into a nice car and goes willingly. If she were a child, an Amber Alert would be issued instantly, but she's as far from a minor as a hawk from the moon. If she were senile, that would be another matter — but she's not, right, Allegro?"

"She's as sharp as a blade grinder."

"You haven't received any threats to her well-being or any messages from her that indicate she's in danger. Did you check to see if your mom's passport was missing?"

Matt shook his head. "Missing isn't a factor. She carries it with her all the time. My mother likes to be ready to fly off to visit friends on a lark."

"There you go — another reason an investigating officer would be skeptical and suggest that more time needs to pass. Otherwise, what we're looking at could be a very innocent incident."

"But what if this incident isn't innocent?" I said. "What if it's connected to Gustavo Campana's attempted murder?"

"How so?"

I explained what we knew about the man in the white suit. "What if this blackmailer tried to kill Gus?"

"Clare, from my perspective, your theory is valid enough to investigate further. But from the NYPD's perspective, the prime suspect for Campana's murder was already arrested. The forensic evidence incriminating Hunter is all wrapped up with a nice fingerprint bow. And witnesses who know them both have gone on the record swearing that Gustavo and Hunter were not on good terms. The motive is easy enough to establish since Hunter's wife would inherit the business. That's why the DA's office believes it can prosecute."

"But Hunter is innocent."

"I know you, Clare, and if you believe that, I'm inclined to think it's true. But Mc-Nulty is in charge now, and he's not going to pursue any theory that doesn't involve Hunter poisoning Gus. That charge is the only way he'll be able to pressure Hunter into giving up information on Eduardo De Santis — his ultimate goal . . . and prize."

Matt sighed. "So we're on our own?"

"No. You have me. And I believe you."

"Then help us," Matt urged, leaning across the table. "Get that black Jaguar tracked."

Lori sighed patiently. "If you had a license plate, I could easily run it for you. But the screen grabs don't show us a license —"

"What about traffic cameras?" I asked.

"A nonemergency request for a detective to track that Jag through the archived data feeds would take at least a day or two to process."

"What if someone checks just one camera?" I suggested. "By watching an intersection near the Campanas' place, at the date and time indicated here" — I pointed to the CCTV screen grab — "the observer is sure to see the Jag pass by within minutes and might be able to zoom in on a license plate. All someone has to do is take a quick look."

"Once again, it would take a day or two for a request like that to go through channels."

Matt's jaw clenched and the veins on his neck twitched.

"But you're in luck. I have a friend in the Traffic Division. I'll reach out to her," Lori said as she reached for another Chocolate Glob. "She might agree to do me this favor out of school, without the red tape."

"That would be great," I said. "And tell her she's got free coffee for a week and all the Village Blend Chocolate Globs she can eat."

Lori took the screen grabs and rose. She put her hand on Matt's slumped shoulders. "Don't stop looking for your mother. Call her friends, check the hospitals . . ."

Wincing at the word *hospital,* Matt raised a hand to silence her. "Okay. Enough."

"Sorry," Lori said, taking one last Glob for the road. "These are amazing, Clare. Good bribery material." She gave me an encouraging wink. "I'll be in touch."

"What now?" Matt asked. "Before I called you, I texted her friends. Do we check hospitals?"

"Not yet. There's one person on that security camera footage who may be able to answer a lot of the questions we've been asking over the last two days."

"Who —" Matt cut his own question off when he realized the answer. "Perla Campana."

I nodded. "Gus's eldest daughter was on the sinking *Andrea Doria* at the time this blackmailer claims he saw something — something so terrible that Gus paid him off to keep silent for sixty years."

"But Perla was only four years old at the time. Do you think she actually remembers anything?"

"Let's find out."

SEVENTY

"That's it!"

I pointed to the stately sign above the fashionable TriBeCa address. White letters floated against a sea green background: *Urban Salvage and Artifact Recycling Co.*

Matt pulled our Village Blend van over to the curb, tires bumping loudly on the old Belgian blocks that still paved the historically preserved side street.

A century ago, this southern Manhattan neighborhood was a bustling center of textile and cotton trade. By the 1970s, it looked more like a ghost town, a decrepit blight of run-down properties on the city's crime-ridden landscape. That's when artists and urban pioneers like Perla moved in, converting the dingy, abandoned factories and warehouses into livable lofts and art studios — even naming the area TriBeCa, a catchy abbreviation of the neighborhood's location: Triangle Below Canal.

No longer a struggling artist, Perla was now a respected academic with an adjunct position at Cooper Union. She was also a highly successful businesswoman who was often hired to consult on historic preservation projects throughout the Tri-State Area.

Her retail-store-cum-art-gallery occupied the first three floors of this former warehouse, which boasted soaring ceilings, cast-iron pillars, and plate glass windows passing plenty of light, even on this overcast day.

We entered the vast space like divers moving through a great sunken shipwreck, gawking at pieces of salvage Perla had plucked from urban landscapes here and abroad.

To our left was a slab of the Berlin Wall, one side oppressively gray, the other freely painted with colorful graffiti. A video screen beside it played 1989 footage of Berliners sledgehammering away at the Cold War artifact.

To our right were antique lampposts from London. Ahead, gargoyles from Paris. A scarred wooden slab was labeled as the original front door to Edgar Allan Poe's Brooklyn residence, and part of a demolished building from Alphabet City displayed a mural of superhero characters by a world-famous graffiti artist.

"Panther Man again," whispered Matt,

pointing to the Art Deco–style rendering of more than a dozen men in tights. "Looks like you can't get away from him."

"Don't remind me . . ."

There were pieces of sidewalk, subway signs, antique traffic lights, and more front doors, lighting fixtures, and window frames labeled as once attached to residences of famous New Yorkers from Teddy Roosevelt and Walt Whitman to Madonna and Lady Gaga.

"A store dedicated to historical trash," Matt whispered.

"And you know what they say? One man's trash is another man's treasure."

"Especially when you have an excessive amount of treasure . . ." Matt tilted his head toward a trendy-looking couple, arguing over whether to put an SPQR sewer grate in their penthouse apartment or Hamptons' beach house.

Behind them on the wall, I noticed a timeline of framed black-and-white photos showing the evolution of Perla's store, from an abandoned linen warehouse to the upscale showplace it was today.

A parallel set of photos illustrated Perla's personal journey, from a young sharpshooting competitor in the 1972 Olympics, to a pro-anarchy antiestablishment activist in the early 1980s, to her academic career in the 1990s.

Finally, we came to the end of the floor and a giant squared and polished chunk of Manhattan schist. A nearby video showed Perla in a white hard hat, leading a tour somewhere beneath the city . . .

"This bedrock was formed over 300 million years ago under the Manhattan skyline," she told the camera. "Not unlike the formation of diamonds, the hardest naturally occurring substance on our planet, heat from the core of the earth and pressure from the mountains above turned fifteen miles of fragile shale into this super strong stone. Without this foundation to anchor the city's skyscrapers, builders couldn't reach for the stars. Ironically, stars are what appear to twinkle around you here, so deep underground, as crystal deposits in the schist — of mica, milky quartz, and blue kyanite — sparkle and wink in the urban builder's industrial light . . ."

"May I help you?" An intense young woman in a short skirt and ankle boots adjusted her horn-rimmed glasses for a top-down evaluation of us.

"Hello," I said politely. "We're looking for Ms. Campana —" I pointed to the screen, where Perla continued lecturing the camera on the qualities of Manhattan bedrock. "Is she here?"

"I'm sorry, *Professor* Campana is *very* busy today. But I'm happy to help you!" She gestured to the big chunk of New York like a game show model presenting prize number one. "Are you interested in our *Schist Squared* piece for your residence or an office space?"

"We're not customers," I clarified. "We're friends of Perla's family, and we really do need to speak to her. It's urgent."

The young woman pursed her lips with a kind of skeptical superiority. "I don't think I understand. If it's *urgent,* and you're really 'friends,' why don't you *text* her?"

"We prefer to speak in person."

"Well, she's not even on the premises . . ." The young woman glanced at her smartphone. "At this hour, she's consulting on the Track 61 Project at the Waldorf Astoria — or more precisely *under* it." She flashed us a smug smile, as if she'd made an inside joke that only she could understand. "Would you care to make an appointment?"

"No. That won't be necessary," I said. "I'm familiar with the hidden VIP track connecting Grand Central with the Waldorf, the one historians believe FDR used to hide his handicap. Did you know Andy Warhol threw an underground party down there in 1965?"

"He did?" The girl blinked at me in shock, as if a trained monkey had just recited a Shakespearean sonnet.

"Yes, dear," I said, channeling Madame, who'd attended that very party. "And even Andy would agree. Trendy glasses and a few short years of college are a poor replacement for a lifetime of experience and decent manners. Good day."

Before Matt could close his dropped jaw, I tugged him away from the sputtering girl and out the chic junk store's door.

"You sounded like my mother back there," Matt said as we climbed back into the van.

"I consider that a compliment. Your mother knew more about Manhattan's geology than Perla Campana. And her advice to me is still truer than ever."

"Really? What did she tell you?"

"That surviving New York boiled down to one maxim: If you want to build anything on this island, you better find some bedrock underneath."

SEVENTY-ONE

As we headed uptown, Matt turned to me. "Tell me again where we're going?"

"Under the Waldorf Astoria."

"And how do you propose we get there? Dig?"

"Don't be silly." I held up my phone. "A friend of Joy's in high school is now an assistant front desk manager at the hotel. I'm texting her for a favor."

"You really think she'll help us?"

"Of course! I employed her part-time back in New Jersey and gave her a great reference to get her started in hospitality. She's also a former Girl Scout. We Scouts stick together . . ."

Twenty minutes later, Matt and I were waiting by a mysteriously unmarked brass door near the Waldorf's garage on 49th Street.

Joy's friend met us with a security guard who used a pass card to open the door, and we were in!

Escorted by the guard, Matt and I descended several sets of stairs, coming to a dimly lit subbasement. After thanking the guard for his help, he headed back up while we moved into a vast and shadowy underground space.

Rusted train tracks crossed the dingy, dusty area, which was cluttered with construction materials and scaffolding. In the center of the space stood the famous armored train car believed to be Franklin D. Roosevelt's, now a grimy shadow of its former glory years as a presidential Pullman.

"I still don't get it." Matt gazed down at me with a perplexed expression. "What's the point of having a secret railroad track?"

"You have to remember, back in FDR's day, trains — not planes — were the way most people crossed the country; and when the president's train pulled in to Grand Central, about a thousand feet away, this track allowed him to arrive in New York in complete privacy. His bulletproof limo would roll right off the train car and onto that reinforced elevator, which lifted him to street level."

"Then it was a security issue, during World War Two?"

"Yes, but also a public relations tactic. It saved the crippled president from being gawked at or photographed while he was struggling to get into or out of a vehicle. He was determined to keep his image looking strong for the good of the country and the world . . ."

"So why is this place still so secret?"

"It's been this way for decades, sealed off from any access by the public — although it appears Perla has been hired to change that . . ."

I pointed to a high scaffold, across the long space. Perla was moving around up there, photographing the area and taking oral notes with her smartphone. In overalls, a hard hat, and her tough-as-nails stance, she looked ready for any construction crew in the city.

"Perla!" Matt called, cupping his hands around his mouth.

"Who's down there?"

"It's Matt — Matt Allegro. We need to talk."

"One minute!"

I watched as Perla secured her gear on a work belt and within the deep pockets of her overalls. Then she used a rope to rappel smoothly down the wall. When she reached the ground, she worked some kind of magic.

With one swift movement, the entire rope fell to the ground.

As she neatly wound it up, I leaned toward Matt and whispered —

"Did you see that? She has a trick rope, like Panther Man."

"It's not a trick rope, Clare. It's a rappelling technique called South African abseil. I use the same method when I'm traveling down from high altitudes in shade-grown territory."

"How do you —"

"I wrap a doubled-up rope around a tree and around my body. When the rope runs out, I release and repeat, until I reach the bottom of the incline. If you're on mountainous terrain and have only one rope, that's the way to manage it."

"Manage what?" Perla asked, moving over to us.

"Manage the coffee-hunting business. How are you, Perla?"

"Nice to see you, Matt. My God, it's been years, hasn't it?"

The pair firmly shook hands and Perla nodded down at me. "It's Clare, isn't it? Are you two back together? I thought you —"

"We're still divorced," I said. "But we're working together now at the Village Blend.

You should stop in for coffee sometime."

"I should, but I'm addicted to Driftwood."

"The coffee or the flotsam?" Matt said with a tight smile. "It's hard to tell the difference."

"I use a lot of cream and sugar," she said with a shrug. "And it's a lucrative business connection. They hire me to hang pieces in their chain stores. Mostly of . . . you know . . ."

"Driftwood?" I finished for her.

"That's right."

We talked a few minutes more in pleasantries, and her reason for being down here. According to Perla, a group of developers were hot to turn this secret train platform into a nightclub.

Matt glanced around. "In this wreck of a place? It'll cost a fortune."

"It will." Perla nodded. "And the men who hired me claim they're lining one up."

"What exactly are you doing for them?" I asked.

"They want a feasibility report, and my seal of approval that they can preserve the historical integrity."

"Can they?"

"Yes, if they follow my directives. Ultimately, it will be up to the city and state to approve the construction. Metro North is the owner of this platform, but the city would be involved in the permits, so it's a sticky wicket — with *plenty* of wheels to grease."

I nodded politely and gently changed the subject. "Perla, the reason we came to see you has to do with another sticky wicket, one involving your father."

"You mean Gus?"

The way she said it sounded strange, as if she wasn't comfortable with my referring to him as her father. *Could it be because Madame's suspicions were correct, and the man we know as Gus is really Silvio?*

"You may not have heard," I continued, "but the police arrested your sister's husband today. They believe he poisoned Gus's cold brew coffee, but we don't believe it — we think someone else tried to hurt your dad."

"Really? Who?"

"That's what we're trying to find out. And in the process, we discovered Matt's mother climbed into a vintage black Jaguar at the invitation of a man in a white suit. A man we think has been blackmailing Gus for going on sixty years."

"Blackmailing him? Do you know why?"

"No," Matt said, jumping in. "Apparently, he was on the *Andrea Doria* and witnessed something involving your father on the night it sank. We hoped you might remember what he saw . . . or at least help us identify this mystery man by name."

She folded her arms. "I'm sorry. I can't tell you anything more."

"We saw you on the security camera footage," I pressed. "You met with your father for two hours the day before he was poisoned. Why?"

"Gus was the one who called me. He wanted to talk — and tell me the bad news."

"Bad news?"

"He was recently diagnosed with cancer. The doctors gave him a year, maybe two. That's why we had a lot to discuss . . . personal things."

Matt appeared upset by the news, and I squeezed his shoulder.

"I'm sorry to hear that diagnosis," I said to Perla — and Matt. Then I stepped closer to Perla and instantly regretted it. At her height, I had to crane my neck to meet her gaze. "Could anything Gus told you shed light on what's happening now? Did he mention something about a man from Rome or the two people this man appears to be in league with . . ."

"I'm sorry, Clare. Like I said, I can't tell you anything more."

I gritted my teeth at her repeated choice of words. It seemed to me she did know more and wasn't willing to tell us. For what reason? I had no clue — unless she herself was involved in this crime.

Matt also picked up on Perla's stonewalling. "My mother is missing," he said, impatience growing. "Do you understand that we're worried for her safety? Are you telling us there is *nothing* you know? Not one thing that will help us find this alleged blackmailer who drove off with her?"

"If you think your mother is in danger, Matteo, you should contact the police. Look, I'm sorry, but I'm running late. I have an event tonight, and I've got to get ready."

Before Matt could press her again, Perla's smartphone rang.

"That's my Uber car arriving. Come on, let's go up together . . ."

As we stepped out into the chilly, damp air of 49th Street, I half hoped to see a black Jaguar waiting for Perla, driven by my old buddy, the U-scar man.

But Perla's Uber car turned out to be a Toyota Prius, driven by a slender young man with a neo-pioneer beard and J.Crew hoodie.

"Now what?" Matt asked as we slammed

our van doors.

Before I could reply, my smartphone buzzed. I read the text.

"Sophia's awake and her phone is recharged. She wants us to give her a ride back to the hospital so she can be with her father."

SEVENTY-TWO

Traffic was heavy and we couldn't find parking so I sent Matt and Sophia into the hospital while I slipped behind the van's steering wheel and circled the block for fifteen minutes.

The rain ended for a time. But big drops began falling as Matt made a dash for the driver's side.

"Slide over!"

"How is Gus doing?" I asked, moving to the passenger's seat.

Matt slammed the door and pulled on the shoulder harness. "Still no improvement. Sophia's going to stick close to him tonight."

"Did you check with Admitting?"

He nodded. "No sign of Mother. Now what do we —"

"Matt! Look!"

I pointed to a woman wearing a familiar black raincoat, hood up. She was just leaving the hospital — the same hospital where

Gus Campana was fighting for his life.

"That looks like my Phantom!"

"How can you be sure? It could be any woman in the same coat."

"Move the van up. Try to get in front of her so I can see her face. If it's that fashionista with the cat glasses, she could lead us to your mother!"

But the traffic was too heavy and slow moving — and our Phantom was outpacing us down the block.

"That's it! I'm getting out to chase her on foot —"

"Wait!" Matt yanked me back and pointed. "She's getting into that taxi up ahead."

"Then you know what to do. Follow that cab!"

As the rain poured, we headed to Second Avenue, then straight downtown.

"Don't get too close!" I warned. "We don't want to spook her."

We passed 14th Street and then 10th and 8th and 6th . . .

"Where is she going?"

"If we're in luck, she's leading us straight to your mother."

By the time we reached 1st Street, the rain tapered off and the clouds began to recede.

With no need to protect her hair from the rain, my Phantom finally flipped down her hood as she exited the cab at the corner.

I fully expected to ID that haughty middle-aged woman with the cat glasses. But I realized with a jolt that the woman we were following was much younger, much skinnier, and much blonder. She was also someone Matt and I had seen before.

"Who is that?" Matt asked. "Why does she look so familiar?"

"Because she works for Gus. Do you remember that young blonde who greeted us in the jewelry store? The girl in the baby blue minidress and giant Louboutins?"

"Good God. It's Monica!"

"She must have been the one who knocked me down outside of Gus's courtyard."

"What the hell was she doing inside that compound when everyone was gone?"

"Poisoning Gus is my guess."

Matt's jaw clenched. "Clare, what are we going to do?"

"For starters, make the turn onto 1st Street and keep following her. We need to see where she's walking . . ."

He did as I advised. Then, halfway down the block, she completely disappeared.

Matt cursed in three languages. "Where did she go?!"

"She couldn't have ducked into a building. There are no doorways up there. Drive forward, closer to where she vanished . . ."

As Matt drove the van to the middle of the block, I realized where our prey had gone: down a secret New York street called Extra Place.

"Oh, man!" Matt slapped the steering wheel. "I should have remembered. This is the cruddy alley where my friends and I used to sneak into CBGB's back door."

"Yes, Matt, *'used to'* is the operative phrase in this neighborhood."

The famous music club was long gone, its legendary 315 Bowery address now a John Varvatos store for men's designer clothing, an apt reflection of the area's radical gentrification.

The rugged bohemian roots were nearly wiped out, along with the grime, debris, and freewheeling graffiti. The Lower East Side tenement houses on either side of this hidden lane had vanished, too. Slick glass and steel luxury buildings stood in their place, with first-floor retail space rented to three upscale restaurants and a minimalistic home goods store.

Unfortunately for us, this hidden New York half street was a pedestrian-only affair.

"I'm jumping out to follow on foot," I

said. "You park and catch up, okay?"

"Be careful, Clare, and *wait* for me before you do anything stupid."

"Don't worry, Matt. If anything stupid needs to happen, I promise, we'll do it together."

SEVENTY-THREE

When Matt caught up with me, I was loitering outside a casual seafood restaurant at the very end of Extra Place. The eatery served four kinds of lobster rolls, peel-and-eat shrimp, and New England clam chowder.

"Hungry?" I asked.

"I am if Monica is inside."

"She is." I pointed through the plate glass at one of the butcher-block tables. "The moment she sat down, she began typing into her smartphone. I say we grab seats across the room, order a couple of lobster rolls, keep our heads down, and watch to see if she meets up with one of our three suspects. With luck, it will be our blackmailer or one of his associates . . ."

But it wasn't.

To my shock — and especially Matt's — the man who strode into this glorified version of a lobster shack was the last person we expected.

"I can't believe it," Matt said.

Neither could I.

Clad in blue jeans, boat shoes, polo shirt, and Windbreaker, the man of wealth who took a seat across from Monica appeared to be the successful entrepreneur who'd passionately put together a consortium of investors for his dream-come-true project — the re-creation of a lost Italian luxury liner.

"Is that Victor Fontana?" I whispered.

My ex-husband's shocked expression was confirmation enough. This was the very man who'd invited Matt to submit a last-minute entry in the *Andrea Doria* coffee competition.

"Stay put and keep your head down," I commanded. "Fontana's met you, but he doesn't know me . . ."

Before Matt could object, I grabbed our table's tray and sauntered over to the condiments bar to gather ketchup, mustard, cocktail sauce, and napkins from the tall dispenser, anything that would lengthen my eavesdropping time.

Unfortunately, the restaurant was crowded and too loud to overhear one word of Monica and Fontana's conversation. But I was able to *see* one very important exchange.

Monica reached into her black raincoat pocket and pulled out a small brown bag. Out of the bag came a white velvet box. She handed the box to Fontana, who opened it with intense interest.

Then his fingers dipped inside, and when they came out, I heard Matt's loud gasp at my ear. Whipping around, I found him lurking behind the napkin dispenser.

"Matt, what are you doing?!"

"Shhh. Stay quiet."

I tried, but it wasn't easy.

Victor Fontana seemed pleased as punch by the treasure Monica had brought him. With glee, he pushed up his Harry Potter glasses — small, round frames that seemed calculated to emphasize the boyish good looks gradually fading from his forty-something face.

Then he tapped his smartphone. As he lifted it up for Monica to read the screen, I got the impression he was showing her a wire transfer.

She clapped her hands and thanked him.

Then he thanked her.

With exuberant awe, he lifted the jewel higher, examining its beauty in the day's fading light. Seeing it this clearly, Matt and I knew.

The little blond store clerk just sold Victor

Fontana the Campana family's priceless Eye
of the Cat.

SEVENTY-FOUR

Matt and I stayed quiet until Fontana left the restaurant. He appeared to be in a hurry, and we knew how to find him — along with the stolen jewel he'd apparently just purchased.

But Monica was another matter.

Suspecting her of attempted murder, as well as grand theft, we confronted her on 1st Street.

"We're going to have a long talk in the back of our coffee van," I told her, taking hold of one arm while Matt took the other. "And you're going to answer *every one* of our questions. Or we're driving you straight to the Sixth Precinct and you can answer official questions after a night in jail."

The young woman was clearly in a panic, sputtering over and over that we "got it all wrong."

"Okay," I said, as Matt slammed the van

doors shut. "Then tell us how to get it right."

"What I sold to Victor isn't real! It's a facsimile! Two months ago, Victor met with Gus and asked him to make a replica of the Eye of the Cat, using synthetic diamonds. Victor offered plenty of money, but Gus turned him down."

"So how did you get involved?"

"I followed Victor out to his car and told him I could do it. So he hired me. It's that simple."

Matt folded his arms. "You expect us to believe you were capable of imitating the famous Campana cut, and creating an identical copy of a world-famous piece like the Eye?"

"Yes! I have the skills Gus taught me. He's been mentoring me for five years. He knew, from the start, that Sophia didn't like me — and after he's gone, she'll inherit the whole business, and will probably fire me. Gus wanted to make sure I was good enough to start my own business on the West Coast — that's my dream."

"Why did he care so much about you?" I hated to ask the next question, given their age differences, but . . . "Monica, are you having an affair with Gus Campana?"

"Of course not! It was my mother who

had the affair, twenty-two years ago."

"You mean to say —"

"Gus is my father. And before you ask, Sophia and Perla don't know. Gus and I both wanted it that way. I'm just happy he was willing to bring me into the business when I was barely seventeen. He's treated me dearly and taught me a lot."

"Then why did you run away the day he was poisoned?"

"Gus let everyone go early, and I pretended to get my things together and leave with them. But I lagged behind the others and snuck up the back stairs into the workshop, so I could finish my Eye facsimile . . ."

How could I have missed that? I thought.

Then I remembered how rushed Sophia and I were when we reviewed the security camera footage. After seeing Gus dismiss his staff, we watched the employees exit the store in a bunch. But we never counted heads — never actually saw Monica leave.

"When the alarm went off that day, I thought I'd triggered it. We have night motion detectors, and I convinced myself I'd tripped one. I ran because Gus didn't know I was working on the copy, and I didn't want him to be angry with me."

"And you expect us to believe you didn't

poison Gus?" Matt said. "He had an affair with your mother, never married her, and won't even come clean about your identity!"

"I would *never* harm Gus! Never! And I'm not upset in the least with how he became my father. Years ago, my mother was divorced and miserable. Gus had lost his wife and was lonely. My mom went to Gus for an appraisal of jewels her ex-husband had given her. They became lovers. I was the result."

"But he never married her?" I pressed.

"Gus proposed, but my mother didn't want to marry again, or stay in New York. She took me to California, where she'd been born and raised. When I found out Gus was my father, I contacted him. I had zero interest in college, or my mother's real estate business, so he and Mom agreed I'd come to New York and apprentice in his shop. I'm grateful to him . . . and I love him."

"Then who do you think poisoned him?"

"Hunter Rolf, obviously! And that's what I told the police when they came to interview the staff early this morning. I told them I was in the workshop when Hunter came and went. I witnessed his visit. The only thing I can't figure is *how* he did it."

"What do you mean?"

"Gus was poisoned with beryllium salts."

"How do you know that?" Matt asked.

"The police detectives told me. They wanted to know if it was on the premises, and I told them that it was. And there is no way you could drink that by accident. It would burn and taste awful. I'm sickened by the idea that Hunter forced Gus to drink it — or even knocked him out somehow and inserted a tube down his throat."

I shook my head at her theory. "I don't believe Hunter poisoned Gus."

"But Hunter was there that day. And I know Gus never got along with him, especially lately with Sophia convinced he was cheating on her."

"He wasn't. And Hunter's visit was to repair the damage of misunderstandings they've had."

"Then who else could have done it?"

When I considered everything I'd learned today, including Monica's statement, I came to a firm conclusion. A sad one. But now wasn't the time to reveal it.

"Let's get back to the Eye of the Cat," I said. "By now, you must know it was never lost, that Gus had been hiding it all these years. Did you know he was being blackmailed?"

Monica nodded. "Gus confided in me that he was paying off a terrible man to keep him out of our lives. That's all I know."

I described the blackmailer in the white suit. "Did you ever see this man? And do you know his name?"

"I don't know his name, but I've seen him visit Gus a few times in the last week. They always argued in Italian."

"Did you understand any of it?"

"Every word. They fought about money. The man kept demanding that Gus 'sell it' and split the profits. I asked what 'it' was, and that's when he told me the Eye of the Cat was never lost. He said Sophia — and you, Matt — were named as its trustees. Gus also said that he didn't want you or Sophia or any of us to be harassed by this jerk. He said, *I'm going to take care of this man for good and forever.* "

"What did he mean by that?"

"He was enraged when he said it. I think Gus was willing to kill if he had to."

"I have no doubt he was . . . *and attempted it,*" I added under my breath. "Monica, do you have *any* idea where we can find this blackmailer?"

"Only tonight. He told Gus he was going to the 'Survivors' party on the new *Andrea Doria.* He wanted Gus to attend with him since he was also one of the shipwreck's survivors. He said they should work out their differences and make a deal. Gus told him to go have sex with himself . . . in Italian."

"So the new *Andrea Doria* is here in New York?" As I asked the question, Matt jumped in —

"She came in last night. I saw her from my warehouse this morning. She's docked at Pier 12, the Brooklyn Cruise Terminal."

Monica nodded. "Victor was thrilled I finished my work on the Eye in time for his party. He's putting it on display — marked clearly as a facsimile — with a series of video clips showing deep-sea divers who've searched the shipwreck looking for it over the years."

Before Matt and I parted ways with Monica, she had a final warning. "I told Victor already. But you should know, too, so you see it coming."

"See what coming?"

"That awful blackmailer swore that if Gus refused to make a deal, he was going to 'tell the truth' at tonight's party. He said the story would make a big bestseller or even a movie — and he'd get his money that way."

Matt narrowed his eyes. "What exactly does he plan to do?"

"He's going to make a scene and announce some kind of shocking truth about 'the real' Gus Campana and what happened to him on the night the first *Andrea Doria* sank."

After Monica left, I turned to Matt. "Tonight's party is our best lead at finding your mother. Can we get in?"

"It's a strict guest list. It's really a PR event to show off the ship to the press and media. Survivors of the first *Andrea Doria* are supposed to share their memories of the night it sank. Fontana's also inviting the mayor, the governors of New York and New Jersey, and a boatload of VIPs."

"If it's that exclusive, how can we possibly crash it?"

"Easy. I have an official invitation. With Mother missing, I was going to skip attending. But if that blackmailer's going to be there, and we can nail him, I'm all for it."

"Good."

"Clare, what was that bit about Gus you said to Monica?"

"What bit?"

"You said you had *no doubt* Gus was willing to kill — *and attempted it.* I heard that last part, under your breath. So who did he try to kill? The person who poisoned him?"

"Yes, and they're the same person."

"Who?"

"Matt, given all that we've learned about

the blackmailer's threats, the nature of the poison, and the fact that Gus knew he was dying of cancer, I believe Gus Campana poisoned himself."

For a silent minute, my ex-husband looked stricken.

I put a hand on his shoulder. "I'm so sorry. But we did get to him in time. And he still may recover. You need to focus on that — and finding your mother." I checked my watch. "We have to get to that party, and the clock is ticking. Does your invitation allow you to bring a plus-one?"

"Only by name. You'll have to pretend to be her."

"Her?" It took me a second to figure it out. "Oh, no."

"Oh, yes."

"There's *got* to be another way. Can't you explain that your marital partner couldn't make it, and you brought your business partner instead?"

"Sorry, it's a nontransferable invitation. It's also a press event, and they invited Breanne because she's the head of *Trend* magazine."

"But —"

"Look, Clare, I need your help tonight. And I don't want to risk them not admitting you. So get ready to impersonate your favorite editor in chief . . . Please?"

I considered my short-notice bag of tricks and took a deep breath. "Fine. If an insufferable fashionista is what they want, that's what they're going to get."

SEVENTY-FIVE

I tracked my assistant manager to a rehearsal space at HB Studio on Bank Street. Apparently, I wasn't the only one looking for a floppy-haired director of a superhero stage show. My favorite shaved-headed police sergeant greeted me in front of the red steel doors.

"Hey, Coffee Lady, fancy meeting you here."

"What are you doing at an actors' studio?"

Franco shrugged his big shoulders. "Time sink. McNulty has me re-interviewing everyone who tried to rent a Panther Man costume . . ."

Another good cop sidelined, I thought. *Lori Soles was right about McNulty scattering Mike's squad to the winds . . .*

"It could be worse," Franco added. "Poor Lieutenant Quinn is in the boondocks."

"Where?"

"Staten Island. McNulty has him 'overseeing interviews' of staff and customers at a comic book store. Some wiseass posted the Panther Man credo onto the NYPD Facebook page."

"Panther Man has a credo?"

"Sure. 'Do not ask on whom Panther Man pounces. He pounces on you!' "

"That sounds an awful lot like Hemingway."

"Yeah, the whole 'bell tolls' thing." Franco shrugged. "But my job isn't to investigate crappy comic book plagiarism. I'm here on a bogus follow-up to a crappy lead. And for the record, I never liked Panther Man. My guy's Captain America."

"Do you have a minute?"

"For you? Sure."

While we loitered in front of HB, I quietly told Franco everything I knew about Gus, his blackmailer, and Madame's vanishing act. He asked what he could do to help, and I told him a little (unofficial) NYPD backup could be useful.

"Do you know any officer who might be working security at the Brooklyn Cruise Terminal in Red Hook tonight? We could use some help . . . from the inside."

"There's a guy at the station house who coordinates that kind of thing," he said, pulling out his phone. "I'll reach out to him

426

and see what I can do."

I thanked Franco, and sent him off to his final "interview" of the day, an Irish pub offering a Panther Man special: two shots for the price of one — for anyone wearing blue.

A few minutes later, I found Tucker in the empty HB theater, dangling Superman on the end of a nearly invisible set of ropes.

"Stop wiggling and strike a pose!" Tuck directed.

My assistant manager clearly had found the perfect Superman. Though the actor's back was turned to me, his muscular physique was impressive.

Nancy is going to be happy, I thought, as I watched Superman relax his body, high off the ground, and find a stilling balance.

At Tuck's cry for "action," Superman thrust out his arms and straightened his legs. With the help of a stagehand, the Man of Steel was able to fly like a superhero over the practice stage.

"Brilliant!" Tucker clapped excitedly. "It's going to work!"

"I told you it would!" Superman replied from above. "I only weigh one fifty on a fat day. You don't need thicker ropes. These work better —"

"Oh, my goodness!" I blurted. "Is that

Punch up there?"

Superman squinted in my direction.

"Hey, CC, is that you? I don't have my contacts in!"

It *was* Punch, Tucker's boyfriend and one of the most accomplished cabaret drag singers and female impersonators in the Big Apple. And he made a pretty good Superman, too.

"You've been bulking up, I see."

Punch laughed and pulled a cord. Before my eyes, the Man of Steel's muscles sunk to nothing but limp vinyl.

"It's an inflatable suit," Punch explained. "You put it on, use an air can to blow it up like a balloon, and you're instantly Mr. Universe. A handy little suit for Grindr profiles, too!"

Tuck snapped his fingers. "Bite your tongue. Remember, you're taken!"

After scolding his partner for even *thinking* about using a dating app, Tuck turned to me.

"So what's up, Clare? You look tense. Is something wrong?"

"I need your help. Can you turn me into Breanne Summour for the evening? It's an emergency."

Tuck's eyes gleamed as he rubbed his hands together. "You came to the right theatrical genius! I have a locker downstairs, and it's full of goodies."

"You want my advice?" Punch called down from above. "Give her my Marc Jacobs. She's got the assets for it — no padding necessary."

"Perfect!" Tuck cried.

"And those tinted Bulgari glasses I wear when I'm doing Jackie O."

"Will do!" Tuck put his hands on my shoulders, and urged me toward the door. "I also have a blond wig that looks way better than that over-processed mane of Bree's. Now let's get to work —"

"Hey!" Punch shouted, still dangling from the ceiling. "What's the deal here? I lose my muscles and you forget all about me?"

"Don't be silly, honey," Tuck replied, hurrying back to help him down. "Air muscles or not, you'll always be *my* Superman."

SEVENTY-SIX

"I still remember the first moment I saw her. She gleamed like a flawless diamond . . . So white and clean and pure . . ."

I recalled Gus Campana's words when our limo passed the final barricade of Brooklyn's low-rise town houses, to reveal the new *Andrea Doria* in all of her nautical splendor.

Docked on the Red Hook waterfront, just a stone's throw from Matt's coffee warehouse, the ship radiated a silvery glow. It helped that the earlier storms had blown through, leaving in their wake a clear, crisp autumn night.

"She does gleam like a diamond, doesn't she?"

Matt, in Versace evening wear, wasn't looking at the ship as he said it. He was looking down at me.

"Oh, come on. Don't make me blush."

With an encouraging wink at my makeover miracle, he tugged on his own handsomely tailored cuffs.

"Look at this sight," I said, redirecting his attention to our destination. "There are so many spotlights on this ship she's probably visible from Earth's orbit."

The re-creation of the classic Italian cruise liner was two-thirds the size of the original, but when standing this close, she seemed immense. Her shiny black hull and gleaming white superstructure towered over the terminal's service buildings, and powerful spots on her upper decks shot columns of light high into the heavens.

"I have to give it to Victor Fontana," Matt said. "The man knows how to build a boat."

"And show it off . . ."

The show continued at the terminal entrance, where a prosecco fountain burbled, and bubbling flutes of the sparkling Italian joy were offered to the guests as a stunning soprano from the Metropolitan Opera sang "Musetta's Waltz" from Puccini's *La Bohème* (with full orchestral backup).

With a slow parade of guests, Matt and I moved through the glass-walled terminal, to the base of a wide, roofed gangplank illuminated by flickering party lights.

Matt presented his invitation to a young man in an electric blue skinny suit.

"Welcome, Mr. Allegro and . . ." He

glanced twice at the invitation. "Ms. Bre-anne Summour?"

The man in blue gave me a strange look, and I prayed my blond wig hadn't slipped. But his sharp eyes drifted instead to the ruby earrings Sophia gave me, and with a gracious smile he was about to wave us through, when Matt raised a finger.

"My wife is the editor of *Trend* magazine, of course, and she would like to do a human interest story on one of the original *Andrea Doria* survivors. I encountered the man, but I didn't catch his name. An Italian, elderly, most likely in a white evening suit? I believe he's come here from Rome."

The valet shook his head. "Sorry, sir. If he's a 'survivor,' he's one of the VIP guests. They came through another entrance."

"Thanks, anyway."

Matt took my arm and pulled me to the gangplank.

"At least we know not to wait for the mystery man. But I wish I knew where that other entrance was."

As we ascended the gangplank's gentle incline, I began to regret my reacquaintance with these cruel shoes.

Remember, Clare, I lectured myself. *You're doing this for Matt's mother . . .*

Then Matt lectured me: "When we get to

the party I want you to speak as little as possible, and only when spoken to. If Bre-anne's acquaintances approach you, greet them with aloof silence and an air kiss. They will compliment your dress or something. When they do, don't reply. Just strike a pose."

I didn't think that was the best advice, but Matt knew his wife better than I did, so I agreed. It helped that a smartphone text conveyed good news.

"We have police backup," I whispered, slipping the phone back into my purse. "There's a friend with a badge aboard this ship right now. If I call, the detective will come running."

"I hope it's Lori Soles, and not her crazy partner, Sue Ellen. But I'll take whoever's willing to help us locate my mother."

I planned to hold Matt to those words . . .

We boarded the ship through a glittering lobby, where a brace of hostesses waited to escort us to the festivities topside. Matt and I joined a clutch of well-heeled guests as we followed a perky young woman giving a bubbly info-talk about the ship's amenities.

Truly, you only had to open your eyes to see the elegance.

With all the Italian marble, shining brass fixtures, and polished wooden decks, doors, and trimmings, I found it hard to remember we were aboard an oceangoing vessel, and not in some landlocked luxury hotel.

Everywhere I looked, the walls were decorated with original art, and every nook in the public space displayed an eye-catching sculpture.

I heard laughter and clinking glasses, accompanied by a lounge pianist's tinkling keys, and I knew we were approaching the *Lido Prima Classe* — or the First Class Lido Deck. (Visiting the *Andrea Doria* was like taking an immersion course in Italian. Aboard this vessel, English was a second language.)

Beyond the bar and buffet, I saw a sizable ballroom; beyond that, the wide-open ship's deck. The view was spectacular, with a harvest moon rising and stars twinkling.

The skyline of Manhattan blazed with light, and headlights flickered between the support columns on the Brooklyn Bridge. Farther out, the Statue of Liberty held her golden torch high and the Verrazano-Narrows Bridge became a ribbon of light before the dark, cold waters of the Atlantic swallowed the horizon.

We'd just entered the ballroom when the moment I'd been dreading finally came.

"Breanne! There you are!"

An aggressive middle-aged woman with albino hair, a tanning salon complexion of parchment brown, and eyes so violet they had to be tinted contacts threw her jewelry-laden arms around me.

"Darling, you look smashing. I haven't seen you since Saint-Tropez!"

And I've never seen you — ever! What do I do now?

I responded to her messy hug with a quick air kiss, praying this woman couldn't see around the big round lenses of my tinted Bulgari glasses.

I sniffed tonic and juniper berries on her breath.

No wonder she's so effusive. The woman is as drunk as a skunk!

Finally, she stepped back, to offer me a lopsided smile.

"That's a lovely new scent for you —"

My guess? You're sniffing Finesse Revitalizing Shampoo.

"And that neckline — *very* saucy!"

I struck a pose.

"I have to say — Oh! Look! There's Ariana. I must say hello. Well, it was great to hear your voice. Don't be a stranger."

And just like that, the woman made a beeline for the famous former Interweb queen, now chatting with a white-haired cable news star and NY1 anchorman at the Art Deco cocktail bar.

"You handled that well," Matt said, squeezing my hand . . .

I hardly had time to bask in the afterglow of my ex-husband's compliment (sarcasm), before we came face-to-face with our supremely charming and conspicuously wealthy host.

After greeting Matt with a quick handshake and a "good to see you again," a smiling Victor Fontana took my hand in his.

"Ms. Summour, it's delightful to meet such an accomplished woman."

"The pleasure is mine, Mr. Fontana," I replied, gamely mimicking Breanne's affected manner of speech. "Your ship is quite the work of art!"

"Coming from this century's voice of style and taste, that means a great deal to me."

Fontana's smooth reply, and his intense gaze, which, in the briefest flicker, took in my décolleté — then the rest of my figure — more fitted his reputation as a ladies' man of Europe than the boyishly enthusiastic entrepreneur I'd seen in the exuberant video Matt had shown me.

The man's Harry Potter glasses were missing tonight, and his shaggy "surfer dude" hair was now combed back, into a slick Wall

Street bouffant.

Though he was a slim, average-sized man in a sea green suit and coral tie, Fontana's commanding presence exceeded his physical stature. The man's intelligence and confidence were broadly on display, but up close and personal, the glint in his aquamarine eyes was definitely more predatory than playful.

Our moment ended with the arrival of the mayor and First Lady of New York City. Matt hooked my arm and we moved along.

We passed the busy bar, crossed through the ballroom, and walked onto the expansively open Lido Deck, all the while searching for the man from Rome. It was a chilly fifty degrees outside, but strategically placed space heaters kept the guests comfortable. At the stern end of the deck, the illuminated pool was filled with clear blue water. There, Matt and I strategized, and decided to split up for a more effective search. Matt would case the bar, while I opted to "investigate" the buffet, but we agreed to stay in touch through our smartphones.

Despite my plan — and shameful salivation over the siren scent of chicken cacciatore (in both red *and* white varieties!) — I never made it to the glitterati's food trough. Mere moments after Matt and I parted, I came to a dead stop at the sight of a shockingly unlikely pair.

Standing at a high table near the bar, Eduardo De Santis was drinking and laughing with a shockingly familiar face — Gus's eldest daughter, Perla Campana.

SEVENTY-SEVEN

When I saw Perla so friendly with De Santis, I was shaken. The sight disturbed me so much that I had to sit down and process the implications.

Fortunately, a high bar table had just been vacated, and I grabbed a cushioned stool. A steward came by with prosecco, and I snatched one up, draining the flute in a single long gulp as I added things up . . .

Perla is a former Olympic sharpshooter. She knows the South African rappelling rope trick. She's athletic. And with an inflatable suit like the one Punch wore to look like a superhero, any illusion is possible . . .

Could Perla be the sniper shooting at cops? Could she be Panther Man?

On the face of it, the idea seemed crazy. But maybe that was the genius of it. Now that I saw her relationship with De Santis, it all made sense.

But what about murderous intent?

Perla was a tough and brittle person, but it was hard for me to see her as a cold-blooded cop shooter.

And what would her motive be? Her old radical, antiestablishment politics? Or money?

Perla appeared successful, but in towns like New York, ambitious people never had enough of it. For the same motive I'd ascribed to Hunter, she could be doing De Santis's bidding.

Then I remembered: *Track 61!*

Perla talked about the men who were lining up a fortune to convert the secret train station. Just like that abandoned building near the Village Blend, De Santis could be behind the Track 61 project, using a shell corporation and other investors to avoid scrutiny.

There was an easy familiarity between Perla and De Santis. Could there be more to their relationship . . .

Is it possible they're also lovers?

That theory went out the porthole with the arrival of another familiar face.

I almost didn't recognize Carla, the law student and recent regular at the Village Blend. She certainly didn't look like any hardworking grad student I'd ever known.

For tonight's party, she wore a daring minidress in lacy black, with mesh panels in places that revealed more than they hid. Her auburn hair was piled onto her head, save for a few stray ringlets that bobbed around her ears. Her eyebrows were manicured; her eyelashes, false.

I recalled seeing Carla last night at the 21 Club where we cornered Hunter Rolf. At the time I was worried she might be shopping for a sugar daddy. Now my fears for the naïve young student were realized tenfold because her sugar daddy turned out to be Eduardo De Santis.

They probably hooked up at 21 last night!

My stomach churned as I studied them from behind my tinted Bulgari lenses.

De Santis greeted Carla with a sloppy kiss and a clumsy grope.

"Hey, now! Watch the hands!" she protested, pushing back against his roaming fingers.

With a pout, De Santis returned to his conversation with Perla, a discussion that went on for ten more minutes. Carla grew so bored she began to play some app game on her smartphone, laughing in triumph when she scored.

I used my own smartphone to communicate with Matt.

Looks like 1 of our VB customers is hooking up w/ your old friend De Santis. If we can get her away from him, she might have good intel on his connection to the cop shooter.

I did not add that I thought that shooter might be Perla.

I didn't know how Matt would react to that theory, so I decided to keep it to myself — for now.

As Matt texted back a quick *OK,* my attention was diverted by several ship's stewards, who rolled out a podium, and the largest LED screen I'd ever seen. They were followed by another familiar face — attached to an olive-skinned man in a dark suit and open-necked shirt.

I stared hard at this well-built young guy. The last time I'd seen him, he was acting as bodyguard for Eduardo De Santis and the sheikhs at the 21 Club.

Last night at 21, he'd given me a cold, dead stare, one so intense that I was sure he'd recognize me if we met again. For the first time that night, I was glad I was in disguise.

Minutes later, after a short exchange with the intense bodyguard, Victor Fontana mounted the platform and faced his quieting guests. The guard positioned himself to the right of the podium, his hawkish gaze continuously scanning the partygoers.

So did this man work for Eduardo De Santis? Or the sheikhs? At the moment, he didn't appear to be working for any of them. Tonight he was very obviously guarding the body of Victor Fontana.

"This evening, I will introduce you to some of the surviving members of the first *Andrea Doria,* but right now, I want to tell you a story about a remarkable picture taken by an unknown photographer."

The lights dimmed, and the photo filled the massive screen.

Against a gray sky, the red keel, black hull, and white superstructure of the original SS *Andrea Doria* cut through the choppy blue waves as it steamed forward, moving to pass the towering Rock of Gibraltar before heading into the open ocean.

"Ten years ago, I bid on — and won — the auction for the negative of this photograph from 1953 because it intrigued me," Fontana said. "I hung a print of it in my office, and another in my home, all the while wondering why this picture continually captivated me.

"Then I discovered that the ancient Greeks and Romans saw the Rock of Gibraltar as one of the Pillars of Hercules, pillars that marked the boundary of their known world. What lay beyond was a complete mystery. Thus, to sail beyond Gibraltar, into the open ocean, was the greatest of all risks. As so many of you know from experience, in this voyage of life, daring to take the greatest risks requires the greatest stamina, courage, and nerve."

Fontana turned to gaze at the screen.

"In this photograph, this frozen moment in time, I realized I saw a different *Andrea Doria* than everyone else. I saw her as more than a great ship. With her beauty, her art, her culture, her design, and her culinary offerings — the *Andrea Doria* became a symbol of the best in our culture. And in this picture, she, like all of mankind, is sailing toward an unknown future, but doing so with the most precious cargo — the traditions, discoveries, and creative spark that give human beings worth."

Fontana faced the crowd again.

"I felt the world was a poorer place without the *Andrea Doria,* so I built her again. Tomorrow morning, we're taking this brand-new and improved *Andrea Doria* out to sea on her first shakedown cruise. And in a few months, we'll begin booking passengers."

He finally displayed that disarming,

crooked smile of his.

"Of course, many people believe what I was really attracted to was the tragic history of the original ship, rather than its legacy. I assure you, nothing could be further from the truth. Now, as for my own future —"

Suddenly, the screen displayed the infamous black-and-white photograph of the zeppelin *Hindenburg* crashing in flames over Lakehurst, New Jersey.

"Oops!" Fontana cried in mock horror. "How did *that* get in there?"

The partygoers laughed.

"Not simply a joke," he went on. "I'm thrilled to announce that my next project will be a re-creation of the *Hindenburg*!"

Holy cow, I thought as enthusiastic applause erupted. *Most men are satisfied building tabletop models. How rich is this guy?!*

Just then, Matt appeared at my side, face pale.

"While we're on the subject of volatile and explosive gasbags," he whispered in my ear. "I've got some bad news, Clare. I just found out . . ."

"What?"

"Breanne, the *real* Breanne, my soon-to-be-ex Breanne is at this party, too."

SEVENTY-EIGHT

"Breanne, *here*?! But you said she was out of town!"

Matt turned sheepish. "I thought she was. But now that we're no longer together, I'm less informed about my wife's itinerary than I used to be."

"How did she get in? I'm already here."

"She came with her new meal ticket, the media mogul widower. He's richer than Fontana, so he got her in with the other VIPs."

This gigantic ocean liner suddenly seemed very, very small. I pulled Matt onto the empty stool beside mine.

"There are only a few hundred people at this party," I hissed. "And the rest of the ship is sealed off to the public. This Lido Deck isn't big enough for *two* Breanne Summours!"

"Are you kidding? Manhattan Island isn't big enough for two of you — I mean *her.*"

"So what do we do?"

"Why don't you go back to the pool, behind that big screen they rolled out. The lights were dimmed when Fontana spoke, and as you can see, they never turned them on again."

"That's your big plan? Hide me?"

"You can't very well walk around. You'll be spotted. If that tipsy, overtanned socialite who hugged you runs into the *real* Breanne . . . well, let's just say my wife won't let news of an 'imposter' stand without getting to the bottom of it."

"How long am I supposed to cower in the dark, and how will that help Madame? We *are* looking for the man from Rome —"

"Listen, if I know Bree, she will only stay long enough to be seen by the 'right' people. And her new boyfriend needs all the rest he can get. The guy is so old I think he knew Julius Caesar *personally.*"

"Fine, I'll go. Call me when I'm freed from exile."

I was angry and frustrated as I crossed to the end of the Lido Deck.

How are we going to find Madame if we can't even find this blackmailer?

Another flute of the excellent prosecco helped ease some of my frustrations. I found a table far enough away from the pool to

447

stay out of its light. Holding my phone, I uselessly watched steam rise from the pool's glowing blue waters.

A few minutes went by before another figure emerged from the darkness. It was Perla. She was moving toward me.

My heart jumped, until I remembered I was Breanne, and there was little chance she'd recognize me. As she passed, I ducked my face, held the phone to my ear, and made noises as if I were immersed in conversation.

Perla, meanwhile, leaned on the rail not fifteen feet away, a half-empty cocktail glass in her hand. She quietly contemplated the cityscape — until, out of nowhere, that brittle fashionista with the cat glasses appeared.

In a rush of Italian, she confronted the professor. "I knew I would find you here, and not at the bedside of that man they call your father."

Perla whirled. "Careful, Donatella," she warned in English.

"You're the one who should be careful, my cousin. Like me, you are a Campana — the *only* one in that family who stole our name. Why can't you be loyal, and help me and my brother secure our Eye of the Cat?"

Now Perla switched her responses to Italian, too, and her tone turned sharp. "I told you. I have nothing to do with it. I'm not a trustee. If you want the diamond, hire a lawyer and take Sophia and Matteo to court."

The woman I *now* knew was a Campana named Donatella pulled a cigarette from her purse and lit it with a sterling silver lighter. "There are other ways. Easier on everyone. You could help."

"But I won't."

"You won't because you don't know the truth —"

"You're wrong. I know everything," Perla hissed. "I know my biological father was a brute who abused my mother. I know that his family in Italy — your people — did *nothing* to stop him. And I know that he tried to kill us both on that ship, until my mother stood up for herself and saved us —"

"And how do you know all this?"

"On her deathbed, my mother told me everything — about the abuse, and the hatred she felt for the monster she'd married. She confessed that she'd fallen in love with a young apprentice jeweler, and how the shipwreck changed everything."

Donatella cursed. "That apprentice stole your father's legacy, his identity. How could you not hate him for that?"

"I could *never* hate Silvio Allegro. He was nothing but kind and loving to me and my mother. He helped us create a new life in America — which is more than my biological father offered us."

"Listen to me, Perla. Events are moving fast. You are either with the Campanas, or against us. And if you are against us, you will get hurt, just like your sister . . ."

Donatella sucked in a lung full of smoke and blew it in Perla's face.

Perla's response was immediate. With a vicious slap, she dashed the cigarette out of the woman's mouth and knocked her cat glasses askew.

"You listen to *me,* you bitch, because I will only say this once. Stay away from Sophia, and stay away from the man who now calls himself Gus —"

"I did *nothing* to that man!"

"And you're lucky you didn't," Perla fired back. "If I thought you were responsible for poisoning him, I'd throw you over this rail. Then I'd hunt down that brother of yours and skin him like an animal."

"Bruno and I are the last real Campanas — along with you. We're the grandchildren of the *real* Gustavo's brother, your true cousins, and we have a *right* to the Eye of the Cat —"

"I don't care what you claim your rights are," Perla stated with finality. "I want nothing more to do with the Italian branch of the Campana family. Do you hear? Nothing."

"Why? Because of your murdering mother? Gino Benedetto told me and Bruno what happened on that ship. He was there. He saw it all. He said your mother acted like a crazy animal when she attacked your real father and held his head under the rising water —"

Perla raised her open hand, and Donatella stepped back.

"Say another word and I will kill you where you stand. It's done, Donatella. Over. *Finito!*"

Perla whirled and strode toward the light and music. Behind me, I heard the Campana woman call out a final threat. "My family is not done with yours, Perla. Not yet!"

Then Donatella Campana lit another cigarette and walked away. As she retreated, I could hear her chuckling over the chords of the distant piano.

Shaken by what I'd just witnessed, my mind raced.

Donatella mentioned a man named *Gino*

Benedetto. That had to be the blackmailer from Rome who claimed he knew about the crime that took place on the sinking *Andrea Doria.*

Now I knew the crime, too — murder.

I was willing to bet this woman, Donatella Campana, and her brother Bruno were also behind Madame's disappearance, even as Matt's warning echoed in my head.

Vendetta.

I texted Matt that I found us a solid lead and told him to meet me on the Lido Deck. Then I rose to follow Donatella, who was heading for the bar. But as I moved along the cool blue glow of the pool to catch up, someone moved to confront me — and refused to let me by.

Looking up, I found myself face-to-face with a spitting-mad blonde, Matt's estranged fashionista, Breanne Summour.

SEVENTY-NINE

The expression on Bree's face was priceless.

For her it was like being confronted by her own mirror image — albeit a slightly shorter one, even with my cruel stilts. For me, peering at the original model gave me an even greater appreciation for the theatrical tricks Tuck and Punch so earnestly applied on my behalf.

Hands on hips, Breanne (the real one) looked me up and down, her stare colder than the pool's frosty light.

"I don't believe this," she hissed. "When Cora Taylor-Chase asked what happened to the Marc Jacobs dress that so awesomely displayed my new boob job, I wondered if the poor drunken woman was delusional. *Then* I saw Matteo slinking around, and I knew *something* was up. Who are you?!" she demanded.

By now, I had pressed the panic button

on my smartphone — the one that connected me directly to my police backup at this floating shindig.

"Why are you *here beside the pool on the Lido Deck,* Breanne?" I said, loudly stressing the words I wanted my cop to hear. "Did you come to start *trouble?*"

"My God," Breanne cried when she heard my voice. "Is that Clare Cosi under that fright wig?" She threw up her hands. "Of course it is. You and Matt are like Laurel and Hardy. He's the big dumb cluck who does what he's told while he follows your fat ass all over town!"

I gritted my teeth. *Easy, Clare. You don't want to get yourself thrown off this ship. Just remember what Nonna used to tell you. Count to ten before you react . . .*

Bree folded her twig arms. "You know, I never understood Matt's fascination with such a *common* woman."

One, two . . .

"But then, Matt Allegro turned out to be as big a loser as you are. You're both nothing more than glorified waiters, living on tips — the dribs and drabs of your betters . . ."

Three — Oh, forget it!

"Listen, you witch, if you say another insulting word you won't need Botox injec-

454

tions to get a fat lip."

"I'm calling security," she said, lifting her phone.

"You stupidly gave up a good man, for what? Down deep, Matt is a better person than most I've known, and he's way too good for an aging East Side gold digger like you. Sure, he's not perfect, and he's made a lot of mistakes. But one of his worst was saying 'I do' to a shallow, superficial, aging vampire, clinging desperately to her sinking career and floundering social status —"

Breanne cut loose with a banshee scream and lunged at me.

"Take that wig off!" she howled, groping for my headpiece. "Let's see your mousy, mud brown hair so I can pull it out by the roots!"

Breanne was strong — hours of Pilates, probably — but she wasn't a street fighter so she didn't know the score. If she was going to grab my wig, then I was going to grab her hair.

Breanne howled, but her screams made me tug harder.

She tried to slap me, but only managed to send Punch's Jackie O glasses into the posh pool.

That's when the heels of my cruel shoes got tangled in the leg of a stool. I went down on one knee, but I never let go of her yellow straw. As I pulled Breanne forward, she tripped over my leg and did a somersault right into the water.

Wow. What a spectacular splash, I thought, as cold spray rained down on me. Then I stared at the wad of Breanne's salon hair extensions still clutched in my hand.

In the pool, Breanne broke to the surface, sputtering. Then she began to yell —

"Security! Security! Help! Help!"

I heard footsteps and turned to see Matt was already here. Right behind him, our police backup arrived with a pair of ship's stewards in tow.

"What's going on here?" Sergeant Franco calmly asked, his voice a low rumble. Then he spotted Breanne. "Isn't it a little chilly to go for a swim?"

Franco was in uniform tonight, his wide shoulders stretching the blue material. The two stewards seemed relieved that someone with authority was taking charge.

The big cop helped Breanne out of the water and sat her on the edge of the pool. Then Franco stripped a table, and draped the white cloth around her.

Matt joined me. Breanne pushed her wet hair back and spied her husband. "Are you both happy you've humiliated me?"

"You humiliated yourself when you let a good man go," I shot back, letting the sea breeze take her extensions.

A small crowd gathered. Breanne, shaking with rage, didn't notice she had an audience.

"Matt, a good man?" She laughed. "He has nothing. He works with his hands . . . in the dirt, for goodness sake, and takes losses to help farmers halfway around the world with less than nothing — the stupidest businessman in New York." She shook her wet head. "No, I have a real man now. Someone who can take care of me in the manner I deserve. A man with an empire I can help him run after I become his wife!"

"Okay, calm down," Franco commanded. "Now what's with all this fighting and ranting? What's the problem here?"

"That woman." Breanne pointed at me. "She's the problem. You need to arrest her for theft of my identity."

Franco flashed me a glance. *Or was it a wink?*

Then he scratched his shaved head in mock puzzlement. "But I know that woman. She's Breanne Summour, editor of *Trend* magazine."

"No, I'm Breanne Summour. The real one!"

"Do you have ID on you?"

"I only have my smartphone — and it's at the bottom of the pool. But you can ask my date —"

"Tall guy? Older man? White hair? Brought his own bodyguard?"

"That's him, Officer."

"He left the ship fifteen minutes ago with an Instagram model."

Breanne looked stricken. "That can't be true!"

"No worries, though. Breanne Summour's husband is standing right there." Franco met Matt's gaze. "So, Mr. Allegro. What's the verdict?"

Matt didn't hesitate.

"That one — the one who's all wet —"

"See!" Breanne cried.

"She's the *phony.*"

"You heard the man," Franco said to the stewards. "Let's get this gate-crashing mermaid out of here."

Cursing like a sailor, Breanne tongue-lashed Franco and the stewards as they led her away.

"That was nice of you," Matt quickly told me. "How you defended me, I mean."

"How long were you watching? And why didn't you intervene?"

"And miss a good catfight?"

As I shot him a dirty look, Matt draped a protective arm over my bruised shoulder. *Ouch!*

"We still make a good team, you and I," he said, making up for my postfight pain. "Now let's get back to that party and find the SOB who took my mother."

EIGHTY

I hit the ladies' room to freshen up — I'd been in a feline fight, after all. My makeup was smeared, my wig was falling off, and one of my false eyelashes threatened to drop into my plunging neckline.

While I was busy restoring my disguise, Matt went off to track down Donatella Campana. Unfortunately, when I came out, I found him waiting for me *alone.*

"She's gone, Clare. I cornered that steward at the entrance and he told me she left in a taxi."

"What!"

"Calm down. I found us an even better lead. The man from Rome is here, and I know his name."

Before I could tell him, *So do I!* Matt stepped aside and pointed to a standing sign with the names and photographs of the *Andrea Doria* survivors in attendance tonight, in alphabetical order. Perla Campana was one of them, of course, and right above her picture, I recognized the man from Rome.

"Gino Benedetto," I read under his photo. *Just as I thought.* "It says he was a first-class steward on the ship." *(Okay, that I didn't know!)*

"Now all we have to do is find him," Matt said.

I almost did a double take when I glanced over his shoulder. "Don't look now, but he's right behind you."

Of course Matt looked, but it didn't matter. Benedetto, wearing a white evening suit as predicted, was in animated conversation with Victor Fontana. They continued to talk, and gesture, as the pair crossed the crowded ballroom.

The pair shook hands. Then Fontana moved toward the podium, while Benedetto backed away. As the ship owner mounted the platform, the lights dimmed.

"Call the Mook, quick!" Matt urged. "This is the moment we've been waiting for."

I grabbed my phone, only to find a text message from said Mook waiting for me.

Gotta go. PD emergency. Quinn ordering all in. Good luck!

I told Matt we'd lost our backup, and he let out a string of curses, not unlike Breanne's, but in five different languages. A woman at the bar heard Matt and laughed. I pegged her as a UN translator.

"Calm down, Matt, you're making a scene."

"Calm down? That jackass left us high and dry, just when we need him most."

"It's a police department emergency."

"What? The Doughnut Plant is about to close?"

"We have to be our own police now. Do you understand?"

"How? We don't have badges. And we're not armed."

Fontana launched into a speech accompanying scenes of the ship's construction. All eyes were on the show.

"Watch Benedetto," I told Matt. "Don't let him out of your sight. I'll be right back."

"Clare! Where are you going now?"

"To the buffet."

I hadn't eaten for hours, but hunger wasn't the reason I raced to the food tables — though, I must confess that when I got there, my stomach nearly overrode my brain.

The dishes were mostly Italian, several I recalled from an original *Andrea Doria* menu I'd found. Other foods were distinctly modern.

There was that heavenly chicken cacciatore I'd smelled earlier, and Marsala (chicken and veal), several different pastas, including a red sauce simmered with pork, and a white carbonara with pancetta.

At the cutting board there was Italian-style pork roast, an impressive selection of meats on a spit, and portobello mushrooms grilled like steak and served on warm semolina rolls. There were Chicken Lollipops with a slew of savory dips, and much more. I don't even want to remember the desserts. I regard them as a lost opportunity, never to knock again.

Sadly, I was there for one thing. I found it, picked the biggest and heaviest, and raced back to Matt.

"Here," I said, slipping him the ripe banana. "Now you're armed."

"Great, I'm all set if I have to fend off a gorilla."

A few minutes into a time-lapse film showing the new *Andrea Doria*'s construction, Benedetto headed off to the men's room. When he came out again, Matt and I were waiting for him.

I blocked the elderly man, while Matt stepped behind him and shoved the banana into his spine.

"Don't make a sound, Mr. Benedetto, or this gun might go off."

Under his too-large, too-long, too-dark hairpiece — and a pasty layer of foundation — the old man appeared to pale.

"Is this a robbery? What do you want?" he asked, in solid English, with a slight but detectable Italian accent.

"I want you to tell me what you did with Blanche Dreyfus Allegro Dubois —"

"I never heard of —"

Matt dug the banana deeper into the man's back. "Don't lie. We have surveillance footage of you luring her into a black Jaguar."

Matt leaned over his stooped shoulder to whisper into Benedetto's ear. "I don't know about Italian law, but in America kidnapping is a capital crime. Do you know what that means, Mr. Benedetto? The gas chamber, the electric chair, or maybe a lethal injection. And you know how they botch those."

"All right, all right! I know where she is, and who she is with."

"Your accomplices?"

He nodded. "There are two of them. Brother and sister, both named Campana —"

"Donatella and Bruno," I said.

"That's right." Now Benedetto's head was bobbing like a life raft on the Hudson. "I can take you there now, if you want."

Matt's mirthless grin scared even me. "Let's go."

EIGHTY-ONE

"Hey," Gino Benedetto cried. "What kind of *polizia* are you, that you have to take a taxicab?"

"The kind who doesn't want to alert your accomplices we're coming," Matt countered, in a fair imitation of Franco's "cop voice."

"Makes me wonder," said Benedetto.

"Don't wonder. *Worry.* We have backup just minutes away." Matt shifted the banana hidden inside his jacket. "And remember, I'm armed."

At Matt's urging, Benedetto gave the exact address to the cab driver.

"Where are you taking us?" I asked the old man.

"Not far. They are here in Brooklyn. A home in Carroll Gardens."

"A private home?"

"It's a rental. Airbnb. The Campanas don't have a lot of money to stay in a fancy hotel."

I thought about Donatella's expensive clothes, sterling silver lighter, and designer eyewear. "That doesn't jibe with the facts. I've seen Donatella, and she dresses like a queen."

"It's all on the credit cards," he said. "The Campanas of Florence have fallen far. Their once-honored jewelry business now consists of selling trinkets made in China to gullible tourists. But they put on a good show. Keeping up with the Smiths, as you Americans say."

"It's the *Joneses,*" I corrected. "If the Campanas of Florence are so poor, why did you go to them after Gus cut off your blackmail payments?"

"It's true, *signora,* I did hope Donatella or Bruno would pay me money for the news that the Eye was not at the bottom of the ocean. That didn't work out so well for me, so we made another arrangement."

"You would help them get the Eye for a piece of the action . . ."

He nodded.

"Your English is pretty good for a man who lives in Rome."

He shrugged his narrow shoulders. "I worked for the Italia Line a long time ago. English was required."

"And since then?"

"After the *Andrea Doria,* that man you know as Gus sent me the quiet money —"

"*Hush* money."

"Whatever!" he said. "It was a lot of money. So I stopped working. For a while I entertained ladies: eager tourists, lonely housewives, bored little rich girls. My English got pretty good. I became so popular the women were soon entertaining *me.*"

"What exactly do you mean by *entertaining*?"

"A gift here, a gratuity there, gold cuff links, diamond stickpins. A Rolex. Maybe a month's rent. Just little tokens of their esteem —"

"Good God, Clare. This man is a *gigolo*!"

"Eh, *scusami*! It's a living. And I do it well. Customer satisfaction has always been my goal."

"So why did you grab Mrs. Dubois?" Matt demanded.

"We had a plan," Benedetto confessed. "The Campanas and I. We know the woman means something to Gus, so we were going to trade her for the Eye of the Cat. Gus going to the hospital ruined that plan."

"How were you going to fix it?"

"Bruno says the lady's son inherited the Eye along with Sophia Campana. We are going to send him a ransom note —"

"With the poor woman's finger, or her ear, included in the envelope?" Matt growled. "You're no better than those ruthless kidnappers in South America —"

"*Che schifo!* We are not barbarians, sir! I would never touch a hair on that sweet woman's head. Why, if she were younger, I would make the love to Mrs. Dubois. *Si, fare l'amore!* Sadly, Blanche is too old for a virile man like myself."

Matt stared at Benedetto. "You're at least eighty. What are you, delusional?"

He shrugged. "I prefer younger women." His leering interest shifted to me — or more accurately, my cleavage. "Like this *belladonna* beside me."

If I'd *had* dinner, I would have lost it then. Suddenly, I wanted out of this cab as fast as possible. Fortunately, we'd arrived at our destination.

When the cab sped away, it left us on a quiet one-way street with three- and four-story brick and sandstone row houses on either side. A few blocks away, a revitalized Court Street teemed with bistros, bars, bakeries, banks, and boutiques, but on Union Street you could hear a diamond stickpin drop.

Benedetto led us up a flight of concrete

469

steps. He reached for a doorbell, but Matt stopped him.

"We cannot get in unless they buzz the door," said Benedetto.

Matt shook his head. "We need the element of surprise." He studied the sturdy door, and the leaded glass panels on either side.

Benedetto smirked. "I told you —"

Before he could finish his sentence, Matt reached into both of the old man's white pants pockets and turned them inside out. Coins scattered on the ground.

Matt ripped one pocket free, then the second.

"Eh! These are tailored pants!"

"Don't worry. I'm sure you'll find someone who will *entertain* you with a new pair."

Matt slipped both pockets over his right hand. With the makeshift boxing glove in place, he punched the glass panel. The first blow cracked the glass, the second shattered it. Then he reached through the gap and turned the doorknob from the inside.

A wallpapered foyer led to a short hall with three doors. Benedetto stopped in front of Number Two.

"Are there any guns in there?" Matt asked.

"What do you care? You have a gun, too."

Matt grabbed his scrawny neck. "That's

not an answer."

"I never saw a gun," Benedetto wheezed. "But Bruno might carry one."

"Knock," Matt commanded. "Then call Bruno to the door."

He did. It took a moment for a muffled response. "Who is it?"

"It's me, Bruno. I have news."

A shadow crossed the peephole. Matt and I stayed out of sight.

"Gino! What's going on?"

As he spoke, Bruno unlocked the door.

As soon as it opened a crack, Matt surged forward and kicked it the rest of the way in.

EIGHTY-TWO

The door bounced off Bruno Campana's head, sending the man with the U-shaped scar crashing to the white carpeted floor.

Matt rushed in, to deliver a second blow. But he paused when he found Bruno sprawled on the carpet in natty pajamas, nursing a bruised noggin.

There was nary a weapon in sight.

"Mother! Mother!" Matt called. "Are you here?"

Still standing in the open door, Benedetto's jaw dropped. "Did you say *mother*?! *Mamma mia!*"

There was a small kitchenette off the main room. I was about to push past Matt and rush in, when I saw a shadow backlit by fluorescent light.

"Matt! A gun!"

Donatella Campana, in a flowing nightgown, raced out of the kitchen. Arm outstretched, she clutched a dainty silver pistol in a manicured hand. Matt froze as the scowling woman leveled it at his forehead.

Then a second figure burst out of the kitchen — Madame!

With a satisfying crash, Matt's mother smashed a bowl of red sauce pasta over her kidnapper's head. The pistol, and a squiggly torrent of pasta and sauce, hit the virgin white carpet at about the same time Donatella did.

Ouch. Somebody's not getting their deposit back!

"So much for your appalling cookery, you dreadful woman," Madame declared, wiping her hands.

Matt snatched up the gun and pointed it at the man with the U-shaped scar. "Hands on your head, Bruno, where I can see them."

Frowning, he complied. Matt tore a drapery cord off the curtained window and tossed it to the gigolo.

"Tie him up."

Madame rushed forward for a tearful group hug.

"I knew you two would come for me," she proclaimed. "I only wonder why it took so long."

Donatella stirred and Matt dragged her beside her hog-tied brother. Meanwhile, Bruno groaned and began to pound his head against the wall.

"Bruno! Stop! Stop!" Donatella hugged her brother protectively, while shooting me an accusing stare.

"When the jewelry business started to fail, Bruno got a job in a shipyard. A steel pipe struck him in the side of his face. Since the accident, he gets migraine headaches." She turned her dark gaze on Matt. "And now that awful man has hurt Bruno again!"

"He helped kidnap my mother, lady. He's lucky I only hit him with a door."

"Blanche!" Gino Benedetto cried. "In all of our charming conversations, you never once mentioned your son was so strong and so manly. And now, with the Eye of the Cat under his stewardship, so wealthy, too."

Benedetto faced Matt. "No need to thank me for all I have done to rescue your beloved mother, *signor,*" he announced with stunningly silky nerve. "But you might *entertain* the notion of a small reward. A token of your appreciation."

Before Matt went ballistic, I spoke up.

"Now that we're all together, I'd like our kidnappers to go on the record with a very important question." I stared at Benedetto. "Especially you."

He gave me an innocent shrug. "Whatever, my *belladonna.*"

"A young woman who works for Gus told us that Mr. Benedetto knows a secret, something so terrible that he blackmailed Gus for sixty years, demanding payments to stay silent. She says something happened aboard the SS *Andrea Doria* that you witnessed, Mr. Benedetto. A secret so sensational that you were going to reveal it at tonight's party in hopes of peddling the story as a bestselling book or Hollywood movie."

Benedetto was squirming and adjusting his collar.

By now, I knew the answer. I'd overheard Donatella reveal it at tonight's party, but I wanted this man to say it — with Matt and Madame as witnesses.

"Come on," I coaxed. "I know this secret is more than the Eye of the Cat being stashed away, and I want you to state it for the record, get it out in the open for good."

Benedetto stubbornly shook his head.

Matt displayed that scary grin again as he waved his smartphone.

"Tell us, Benedetto. What is this secret? Mother wasn't hurt, no harm done. If you come clean, I *might* let you walk away. If you don't, you can all spend the rest of your days in a US federal prison."

Benedetto looked at Bruno, who seemed

oblivious to what was going on around him. The gigolo shifted his gaze to Donatella, hugging her brother.

"Tell them," she commanded. "Gus is in a coma; there is nothing more to do. If the story will make them go, then tell it. You can *still* sell it. The truth is the truth and you witnessed it."

"Okay," Benedetto said with a nod. "Here is the real truth —"

Before Benedetto could say another word, we all heard an odd, unidentifiable sound. Not an explosion, more like a muffled *thud*. It came from the hallway outside the apartment.

Suddenly, Gino Benedetto jerked as if struck.

I watched in horror as a scarlet blossom of spouting blood stained the front of his white tux. Without uttering a sound, the man from Rome sank to the floor, dead.

"Get down, everyone!" I cried as I took my own advice.

Matt scrambled behind a chair, dragging his startled mother with him.

Bruno, still tied, reacted in helpless horror to his co-conspirator's fate. In shock, Donatella's eyes went wide, but she failed to move. Her arms merely tightened around her brother.

An eerie silence ensued for five long seconds, until the only sound I heard was my own breathing. I'd found dubious protection behind a heavy glass coffee table. But in truth, I was waiting for the bullet that would kill me.

Good-bye, Mike, I thought. *Wherever you are, I love you . . .*

But instead of a bullet, there was a loud *pop,* then a long, sustained *hiss.* A smoking canister bounced through the open door, followed by a muffled voice saying something really odd.

"Lekker dux."

I expected to be suffocated by a choking, poisonous gas.

Instead, I smelled posies — and then everything went black.

EIGHTY-THREE

I woke up with a mouth full of bad taste, and an aching head. It only got worse when I opened my eyes — then blinked against the glare of a single naked lightbulb in the center of a mildewed, spiderwebbed ceiling.

"Clare! You're awake." Madame hurried to my side.

I sat up — and immediately felt woozy.

Lekker dux.

Those cryptic words from a muffled voice were the last thing I remembered before the knockout gas. I repeated them aloud.

"Sweet dreams," Madame said.

"What?"

"That's what it means — in Afrikaans." She shrugged. "I have a friend who grew up near Cape Town."

"We're not in South Africa, are we?"

"No, dear. I'm fairly sure we're still in New York," Madame replied. "We've been dumped in a one-room basement apartment. We're locked in, but not alone. That's the only door out, and there's a man with a gun guarding us on the other side."

I rose — not from a piece of furniture but something soft.

I'd been stretched out on stacks of old newspapers — New York papers, I noted — piled on a rickety bed frame used as a makeshift couch. Broken, mismatched chairs had been arranged in a circle. Empty beer cans, wine bottles, and crumpled cigarette packs were scattered around as if the place had been used by street kids as a party room.

The room had two windows spray-painted over in black. A fist-sized piece of glass had been knocked out of one of them, revealing iron bars.

Wobbling on my cruel shoes, I moved to examine them. The floor was warped and sagging in spots, and my too-tall heels didn't make walking any easier, so I took them off.

All I could see outside was a dark courtyard with dead leaves, dying weeds, and more beer cans.

There's no getting out that way. And, according to Madame, a man with a gun is behind door Number One. Actually, it's the only door. If we scream, he'll hear us — and

probably do something awful to shut us up.
So now what?

Madame shook her silver-white head. "Kidnapped twice in one week. I feel like the Lindbergh baby . . ."

"Can you please tell me why you got into Benedetto's car in the first place?" I asked. "Didn't you know he was a very bad man?"

"Of course I knew! I also knew why that horrid little man was blackmailing Gus, and I wanted to put a stop to it."

"I don't understand . . ."

"I went to see Gus instead of joining you at the vault because I wanted him to confess the truth, and he did."

"Gus confessed to you?"

"He admitted that he'd stolen a dead man's identity, and his wife. The person we know as Gus Campana is an imposter. His *real* name is —"

"Silvio Allegro," I finished for her.

Madame nodded. "It's true. The young man who stepped onto that New York dock with Angelica and Perla was my late husband's cousin — in Gustavo Campana's clothing."

"Yes, but why the six-decade deception?"

"He did it for love."

Madame explained that as a young apprentice, Silvio fell in love with his employer's sad, mistreated young wife. At first his relationship with Angelica was platonic. But soon the young woman's own passion began to burn for the kind, gentle apprentice.

Meanwhile, the fires of rage and injustice roared inside of Silvio.

"When the real Gustavo Campana tried to lock his wife and young daughter inside of their stateroom to drown in the sinking ship, he was killed for it —"

"But not by Silvio. It was his own wife who murdered him."

"Yes!" Madame gawked at me in surprise. "How did you guess?"

"Not a guess, a discovery . . ." As I told Madame about my little undercover project on the new *Andrea Doria* (and my Lido Deck eavesdropping), a tantalizing scent tickled my nose.

"I smell coffee," Madame whispered.

I jumped to my bare feet. *That's not just any coffee,* I realized. *That's my Village Blend Fireside roast!*

I hurried to the window again and took a deep breath through the little opening. "I know where we are. We're inside that vacant building near the Village Blend!"

"The one you complained about to the community board?"

"The same . . ."

It was *also* the building that Panther Man used to shoot Sully. And, according to Quinn, Eduardo De Santis was the silent owner.

"But taking us here makes no sense . . ."

If Eduardo De Santis is engaged in criminal activity, why would he have us knocked out in Brooklyn and dragged all the way here to the West Village to be kept prisoner in the basement of his own building? I shook my head. *It's simple. He wouldn't!*

And that's when I knew. *This is a frame job!*

I didn't want to alarm Madame, but I was certain we were being kept alive only temporarily. Very soon we'd be shot dead. And having our dead bodies found here would continue the incrimination game that a genius was playing on Eduardo De Santis.

"What are you trying to figure out, dear?"

"Hold on . . ."

I tiptoed to the front door and looked through the peephole.

In the dim light of the shadowy hall, I saw our guard. He was talking distractedly, a Bluetooth in his ear, gaze locked on his smartphone, his face clearly illuminated by the screen.

I know this man!

He was the same olive-skinned bodyguard

with the dead cold eyes I'd seen at the 21 Club with Eduardo De Santis. But did he actually work for De Santis? When I spied him on the new *Andrea Doria,* he was shadowing every step of *Victor Fontana!*

"I wonder where they took my son?" Madame said. "I pray Matteo isn't hurt."

"I'm sure he's fine," I said. "The people who shot Gino Benedetto and kidnapped us need Matt alive."

"Why?

"The same reason the Campanas wanted him. So Matt can get them inside the Lyons vault, unlock that safe-deposit box, and hand over the Eye of the Cat. He'll do it for them because we're hostages, and they will kill us if he doesn't . . ."

I was certain they were going to kill us anyway, and leave our bodies here for the police to find, but there was no need to worry Madame about the inevitable, so I held my tongue.

"Who are *they*?" Madame asked.

"Victor Fontana, his bodyguard, and a small crack team of jewel thieves. They're setting up Eduardo De Santis as a patsy. He's going to be blamed for everything — and I'm betting he won't have a chance to defend himself. Fontana is too smart for that. He'll make sure the police find De

Santis's body in some kind of deadly traffic accident or sudden fire, along with evidence that he committed a host of crimes. Then Fontana and his tight crew of criminals will sail away clean."

I dropped to my knees and started digging through the garbage.

"What are you doing, Clare?"

"Looking for something that will get us out of here — aha!"

I held up a smudged and dirty disposable Bic lighter someone had discarded. At that moment, it was more precious to me than a sixty-carat diamond.

"It's truer than ever," I said.

"What?"

"One man's trash is another man's treasure!"

EIGHTY-FOUR

I had to flick the Bic a couple of times, but once the flint was free of dirt, I got a flame.

"What do we do now?" Madame asked.

"First we very quietly move that bed frame . . ."

Madame and I positioned the metal frame so it would barricade the front door. If our guard tried to get in, the angled frame would dig into the floor and make it difficult to enter — without time and effort. And that critical bit of time was what I needed to buy if my escape strategy was going to work.

"Now what?" Madame whispered.

"Now we're going to set a fire outside that window. The smoke will go into the courtyard, and someone in an adjacent building is sure to dial 911 . . ."

I remembered Esther's *"Open fire!"* complaint last week about Nancy's failed cookout, and I prayed for the same alarmed reaction among the neighbors.

"With luck, by the time our guard realizes firefighters are on their way, he'll choose to make a clean getaway rather than risk sticking around and getting caught."

Madame nodded with enthusiasm. "The plan is afoot!"

We quickly and quietly tore up the newspapers and dropped balled pieces through the hole in the broken window. Soon we had a nice pile of kindling on the ground next to the brick building.

I struck up the Bic again and lit a paper and dropped it on top of the pile. Soon there was a bonfire. As the flames rose, Madame and I used more papers to wave the smoke away from us.

The fire spread, as I kept feeding it. We were starting to cough when we heard the sirens. A moment later, I tensed at the sound of our armed guard trying to get in.

"The firefighters and police are here!" I shouted through the door. "And we have weapons to fight you!"

While I was yelling through the door, trying to scare away our would-be killer, Madame was breaking the windows and shouting, "Help! Help us!" at the top of her lungs.

My plan worked. Within minutes, two

firefighters heard our cries and came to break down the door.

By then, the bodyguard with the dead cold eyes took my advice and ran. I didn't care. I could ID him, and I knew where to find him.

I had a much bigger concern at the moment — finding Matteo Allegro!

EIGHTY-FIVE

With my arm around Madame, we pushed through the Village Blend's front door, just as Esther Best was preparing to lock up for the night.

"Wow, boss lady! You look terrible!"

"I smell worse."

"Yeah," Esther said, holding her nose. "Like a fire sale."

I sat Madame down into the nearest empty chair. "What time is it?"

"Twelve fifty. Last call was five minutes ago. We only have one customer left."

"Clare!" Lori Soles was already hurrying toward me. "I've been trying to call you for over an hour. I thought I would stop by to see what happened to Matt's mother —"

"I was kidnapped, twice, that's what happened." A breathless Madame patted my hand. "But Clare rescued me both times."

Lori blinked. "So you know the black Jaguar was rented to —"

"Bruno and Donatella Campana."

"And that they are staying at —"

"An Airbnb apartment in Brooklyn. I know."

"Then, should we pick them up?"

"You might want to dispatch the Crime Scene Unit. An Italian man named Gino Benedetto was murdered there. The Campanas didn't kill him, although evidence will look like they did. I'm a witness and can testify to their innocence — at least to murder."

"Talk about behind the curve," Lori cried. "Why did I bother to get out of bed?"

"To make the bust of your career."

"Huh?"

"We have to go to the Diamond District, right now. I'll explain on the way."

"But I just heard from my commander. Everybody's being called in. All hell's broken loose in Washington Heights, and down in Battery Park, too. *Nothing* is going on in Midtown."

"Yes, and that's exactly the plan."

"What plan?"

"I'll tell you on the way . . ."

The Diamond District was three miles from the Village Blend — a thirty-minute drive under "normal conditions."

Detective Soles was determined to make it in under twenty.

At nearly one AM, traffic was light. Lori used that fact as an excuse to weave around the buses, cabs, cars, and pedestrians we *did* see. She blasted through a few red lights, too, but at least she didn't blast the siren.

"Tell me again what you think is going on," Lori said. "And why you don't want me to use the siren?"

"Victor Fontana is behind a jewel heist that's taking place right now. His hired people have taken my ex-husband hostage. They're going to make Matt take at least one of their crew down to the Lyons Security underground vault, to steal the Eye of the Cat — and probably much, much more. There's a fortune down there for the taking. And they likely have an accomplice inside."

Lori seemed unconvinced. "And you think this has something to do with the NYPD alert tonight?"

"Everyone has been led to believe that Eduardo De Santis is behind the Panther Man shootings — Quinn, McNulty, and their squads."

"You know, right now, there are 'shots fired' incidents coming from uptown and downtown?"

"Exactly," I said. "Uptown and downtown, but not *Midtown.* Not anywhere near the Diamond District. Lyons Security runs an all-access vault, 24/7. This late at night, with the police intensely focused on alerts far from the area, it will be much easier to disable security systems, gas guards, and get away with hundreds of millions if not billions in precious gems and metals."

"Why don't I just call this in?" Lori asked. "And warn Lyons Security that something is up."

"Because these thieves are holding Matt hostage, probably at gunpoint. If they're trapped by security, they will use him as a shield if they have to shoot it out, and Matt may die."

"So we're just going to sneak up on them?"

"Kind of . . ." I said reluctantly.

Lori stated the obvious. "That's not a plan, Clare."

"No, it isn't. But according to your own ETA, I still have five minutes to come up with one . . ."

Four minutes later, I still had nothing.

"Okay, we're here."

Lori pulled up to the Fifth Avenue main entrance to the Diamond Tower. The lobby

491

lights were dim, and there was no sign of activity, normal or otherwise.

"Nothing to see here," Lori said.

"Circle the block. Let's look for a garage entrance . . ."

We parked within sight of a large metal door. Sure enough, after ten minutes of waiting, it rose to reveal an illuminated loading dock. I saw the Lyons Security cat's paw logo on the wall. A panel van and a black SUV were the only occupants. As they rolled onto the street, the SUV in the lead, I spied the logo on the side of the van — *Village Blend Coffee.*

"Oh, for the love of — that's them!" I cried. "Follow that van!"

Lori hit the gas.

"Why are we following your Village Blend coffee van?"

"Because it's not our van! Someone wants you to think it is."

"Why?"

"To go where the delivery of a van full of coffee would not look out of place."

"Where?"

"An ocean liner!"

It all made sense, now . . .

Victor Fontana invited the Village Blend to participate in the very public *Andrea Doria* coffee competition. It was a last-minute invitation, and now I knew why, because the Village Blend was the only coffee roaster that had a warehouse in Red Hook. And, thanks to Monica, Fontana knew all about the real Eye of the Cat and Matt's connection to it!

"They're going to Pier 12, the Brooklyn Cruise Terminal," I told Lori.

From behind the wheel, she looked skeptically at me. "How can you be so sure?"

"It's perfect camouflage. A coffee delivery to an ocean liner sailing in the early morning. Only below the coffee sacks, this van is filled with billions in treasure from the Lyons vault. Once they had Matt get them inside, the sky was the limit. I'm sure they grabbed as much as they could."

"I think Matt might be safe so far," Lori speculated. "If they're smart, Matt's driving. That way, if they're stopped, your average officer will check his license and think, *Well, it's the co-owner of the Village Blend, so it must be legit.* And let them walk."

"Just like the cops let a woman walk through their perimeter the day Sully was shot."

"What?"

"It wasn't their fault. Thanks to my eyewitness account, patrolmen were on the lookout for a strapping male in a Panther Man

493

costume, not a pretty, wide-eyed grad student from South Africa in a short skirt — even if she was carrying a backpack with a deflated Panther Man costume and a dismantled sniper rifle."

"Clare, the crime in progress now is my concern. And right now we need reinforcements."

"Reinforcements we can trust," I noted. "Which means no McNulty or any of his people. For this collar, we need Mike Quinn, Sergeant Franco, and the entire OD Squad."

EIGHTY-SIX

Lieutenant McNulty had dispatched Quinn's squad to Lower Manhattan, to investigate the "fireworks" that panicked citizens around Battery Park. That's what they turned out to be, too — more remote-controlled pyrotechnics meant to confuse and distract law enforcement.

But I was onto the deception, and I laid it all out to Quinn while Lori kept a discreet distance behind the suspect vehicles.

"Eduardo De Santis is being framed," I explained. "That's why your OD Squad was targeted. And the whole Panther Man thing was about rattling the cops, diverting the police from doing their jobs. Right now, Midtown is quiet because the jewel thieves wanted the police somewhere else while they robbed the vault in the World Diamond Tower . . ."

We spoke over the phone instead of using the police radio. We both knew these thieves could be monitoring the police band.

"Why has no one from Lyons Global Security raised an alarm?" Quinn asked. "By now someone must have discovered the robbery."

"They used some kind of knockout gas on Madame and me. Maybe they used it on the security guards, too. I'm sure the thieves have someone on the inside who prevented alarm triggers from going off."

"I follow you," Quinn said. "And now we know why McNulty's Inside Job Squad was targeted, too. His men were so distracted by the shootings they dropped the ball on what could be the biggest inside job of all time . . ."

All caught up, Quinn now described his plan of action.

"My guys are a lot closer to the Brooklyn Terminal than that Village Blend van. We'll arrive ahead of time and set up a trap at the terminal entrance. It will look like a routine security check, until it isn't."

"Be careful," I pleaded. "Matt's a hostage. If things go wrong, they might kill him."

Quinn's reply was garbled, as I temporarily lost the phone signal.

While I imagined Mike and his crew racing to the terminal to spring their trap, the Village Blend van and the SUV rolled downtown at a leisurely pace — a little too leisurely, like they had nothing to hide, and nowhere in particular to go.

After thirty minutes, we'd tailed them all the way to City Hall. That's when McNulty's gruff voice barked over the radio.

"Ten-seven, Detective Soles. Ten-seven. Ten-seven, immediately . . ."

Lori groaned. "I never reported to my precinct commander. Now McNulty wants to know my situation. If I don't reply, I'm officially AWOL."

"Detective Soles, ten-seven, at once . . ."

Ignoring the radio voice, she gave me a sidelong glance. "I hope you're right about this, Cosi."

Me too . . .

Minutes later, as we rolled across the Brooklyn Bridge, something magical occurred. It was almost as if the spirit of the bridge cat — that legendary supernatural guardian of the Ponte Vecchio — suddenly filled our hearts, until our doubts were dispelled, and we were electrified with a new sense of resolve.

Or . . . maybe it was the cop calling for help over the police radio.

"All units, Midtown, respond immediately. I have a ten-twenty B on the corner of Sixth and 48th Street. Need assistance at Lyons

497

Global Security. There's been a robbery —"

"You *are* right, Cosi!" Lori clutched the steering wheel, her expression determined. "Let's nail these thieving, cop-shooting SOBs!"

On the Brooklyn side of the bridge, the Village Blend van headed to the Cruise Terminal, just minutes away. But the SUV unexpectedly split off, heading deeper into the industrial section of Red Hook — an area I knew well.

"Quick! Do we follow the SUV or the van?" Lori demanded.

"Quinn's intercepting the van. So let's follow that SUV. I'm pretty sure I know where they're going, and if I'm right, Matt isn't in the van. He's inside that car right now."

EIGHTY-SEVEN

Red Hook was quiet as Lori dimmed the headlights and rolled to a stop in front of a shuttered auto-glass shop. Halfway down the block, the SUV we'd followed halted in front of the gate to Matt's coffee warehouse.

In the glow of a streetlight, I watched Matt exit the vehicle and punch in the code to open the gate.

"He should run for it," Lori whispered. "Lots of places to hide around here."

"He won't. Matt doesn't know his mother and I are safe. He'll do whatever they demand of him in order to protect us."

We both started when the police radio crackled to life.

"Detective Soles, ten-seven, at once . . ."

Lori muted McNulty's voice. "Call Quinn. Tell him we need backup."

I'd tried to call him before, to warn that the vehicles had split up, but Quinn didn't answer. He didn't pick up this time, either.

We both knew our timing wasn't the best. The Village Blend van should be arriving at the terminal right about now, and anything could be happening, including a firefight.

In desperation I sent a text message:

Thieves SUV at java warehouse red hook. Send help, ASAP

By now, Matt had deactivated the warehouse alarm, and opened the building's big garage door. The SUV rolled into the bay, and the steel door descended behind it.

"What do we do while we're waiting for reinforcements?" Lori asked.

"Go in."

Her eyes bugged. "That's crazy, Cosi. We wait for backup."

"There's no time. I watched Matt. He didn't reset the gate alarm —"

"So?"

"So they won't need him to unlock it, which means they're not taking him when they leave." I paused to let that sink in. "They're going to kill him, Lori. Just like that bodyguard was supposed to kill Madame and me."

"But that SUV had tinted windows. We couldn't see inside. We don't know how many perps are in there!"

I shrugged. "How many could there be?"

"That model seats eight."

I swallowed hard.

"Call Quinn again," Lori insisted.

I popped the door. "*You* call him. I'm going in."

"Fine!" Lori threw up her hands. "We'll both go. But I take the lead. I'm the detective, remember?"

We exited the car and stuck to the shadows as we approached the warehouse. Clouds blocked the moon as we slipped through the gate and across the parking lot. We didn't stop until we hugged the warehouse wall.

In my wobbly heels and party dress, I felt like a heroine in a French Resistance movie. Then Lori drew her weapon and things turned serious.

"Here." She passed me something hard and cold. "It's Mace, and not the wussy kind. With *that* you could stun a horse."

Lori showed me how to use it, and I slipped the cylinder into my bra.

"Okay, Cosi. You know the layout. What's the plan?"

"We'll go in through the front door and slip into Matt's office. They won't even know we're inside."

"Unless they're *in* Matt's office," came

Lori's less-than-heartening reply.

Fortunately, once we got inside, we could see the office was dark and empty, except for dirty laundry and too many additions to Matt's empty wine bottle collection.

"I hear voices," Lori whispered.

"Me too. They're still in the garage."

We peeked around the door, into the empty hall.

"Give me the layout, Cosi."

"The door on the left, the one with the window, leads to the hermetically-sealed, climate-controlled space where coffee beans are stored. The door on the right is a bathroom. At the end of the hall there's a door to the garage and interior loading dock."

We paused as more voices echoed from the garage.

"Stay here," Lori commanded. "I'm going to find out how many we're dealing with, and figure out a way to get the drop on them."

Leading with her weapon, Detective Soles left the office and cautiously approached the climate-controlled room. She was about to peek through the window when the door flew open, striking her with a loud *crash*. Lori bounced off the opposite wall and tumbled to the floor.

A Lyons Global Security guard burst out of the room, fist raised for a fight. But Lori was already down for the count.

With an angry grunt, he very gently closed the climate-controlled room's door. When he faced the unconscious detective again, his expression was anything but gentle.

With a bull neck and broad shoulders, this rogue security guard could have easily played Panther Man. I watched while he used gloved hands to scoop up Lori's gun and yank the clip free. He cursed when he spied the NYPD shield, but continued to search until he found a spare ammunition clip in her belt.

He dropped the empty gun beside the detective's still form. Still clutching the ammo clips, he turned — and headed right for me.

EIGHTY-EIGHT

I raced across the darkened office and dived under the desk. But the Lyons man ignored the room and went directly to the front entrance. I heard the door open, then a long silence while he made sure the place wasn't surrounded by police.

He grunted from exertion. Then I heard a faint, faraway clattering.

The man had tossed Lori's ammunition into the parking lot.

What the? Why did he do that?!

The door closed and he stomped down the hall, passing the office again.

This was my chance and I took it. I grabbed the nearest heavy object — which turned out to be a beautiful magnum of Moët & Chandon Nectar Impérial.

Clutching the full champagne bottle with both hands, I peeked around the door. The guard was bent double and grunting again, as he went through Lori's pockets, scattering the contents on the floor and stealing what he wanted.

This new violation turned some switch inside my brain, and righteous anger filled my being — or maybe it really was the spirit of the bridge cat!

Whatever it was, I didn't hesitate.

I kicked off those cruel shoes, and in five quiet-as-a-cat steps I padded up to the Lyons guy. He was still bent over his victim when I brought the bottle down on the back of his head with all my rage-fueled might!

He'd grunted a lot in the brief time I'd known him. But the Lyons guy didn't grunt this time — he silently toppled to the linoleum like a felled ox.

Amazingly, the bottle didn't even crack. I set it down, fearing the shaking would cause the cork to pop. Then I dropped to my knees to check on Lori.

She was breathing — labored because her fast-purpling nose was probably broken. Beyond that I didn't know how she fared, only that I couldn't wake her.

I reached for the gun. Then I remembered the clip was gone.

What was the point of tossing the ammo into the parking lot?

My silent question was answered by a voice coming from the garage — a disturbingly familiar voice. Trying to place it, I listened harder . . .

"A diamond is the hardest natural substance on Earth, Mr. Allegro, but place one in an oxygen-rich environment and heat it to fourteen hundred degrees, and that gem will vanish without a trace. Not even ash will remain. . . ."

As the voice droned on, I peeked into the climate-controlled room and saw the usual bounty of coffee packed in agricultural sacks. Then I noticed something sinister. Several industrial-sized oxygen canisters were scattered about, their valves open and hissing.

I checked the climate-monitoring controls. The nitrogen in which the raw cherries were stored had been replaced by pure oxygen — enough to blow up this entire building with a single spark.

No wonder the Lyons man was scared, I realized. *A gunshot could ignite the gas, and Matt's warehouse will blow like the* Hindenburg —

Wait. Did I just say Hindenburg?

That's when I fully realized that the voice I overhead speaking in Matt's garage had mentioned that doomed airship just a few hours ago.

My "theory" wasn't a theory anymore.

Victor Fontana really is behind it all!

"Think of it, Mr. Allegro," Fontana went on. "A diamond as large and precious and ancient as your Eye of the Cat, gone in a flash. But you needn't worry. I won't let that happen. The Eye of the Cat belongs to me now, though I must make the world think it's lost forever."

Inside the folds of my battered Marc Jacobs dress, a vibration announced a text from Quinn.

Gang + loot grabbed. No Matt! On way
ETA 15 mins.

I texted back.

I M in warehouse. HURRY! Lori down.
Needs RX. NO GUNS!!! Place like a bomb,
will blow!

I quickly tucked the phone away and left the empty gun. Grabbing my trusty champagne bottle, I carried it like a bludgeon as I padded silently to the garage doorway.

EIGHTY-NINE

"Take the Eye and shove it down your smokestack, Fontana," I heard Matt say. "And I hope the jewel's bad luck sinks your new *Andrea Doria,* too!"

I peeked around the half-open door.

Talk about a captive audience!

Matt was in the middle of the loading dock, perched on a stack of steel storage boxes, the Lyons paw logo clearly visible on each one. His hands were tied behind his back, but his feet were free.

Stacked around him were more containers. One had spilled, and a torrent of diamonds glittered on the rough concrete.

Leaning against Matt just to remain upright, Eduardo De Santis, still in his tux, seemed to be fading in and out of consciousness, and I wondered if he'd been given the old *"sweet dreams"* treatment.

That was more than a possibility, because Carla, the South African "law school student" and *"lekker dux"* girl, was standing beside Fontana, expertly spinning an open switchblade between manicured fingers.

Both had their backs to me, but suddenly I was spotted — by Matt. I saw relief in his eyes. Hoping for a rescue, he attempted to distract his captors.

"I know how you tricked De Santis," Matt goaded. "But how did you pick me for your patsy?"

Fontana folded his arms. "I heard your story from your soon-to-be ex-wife. Yes, I knew the woman at the party wasn't Breanne, but I played along until I had the opportunity to kidnap her along with your mother — all the better to insure your cooperation."

Matt cursed him, but Fontana just laughed. "I know it's not fair, but you've had a lot of bumps lately, haven't you? Tax liens, Third World charity cases bleeding you dry. Now a nasty divorce. You're close to losing it all — and desperate men are easy to manipulate."

Fontana paused to pull his Harry Potter glasses from his lapel and clean them with a silk handkerchief.

"Club Town Eddy was easy to frame," Fontana continued. "A near-conviction, shady shell corporations, ties to places and things that could be used to incriminate him. Like you, De Santis needed money. So I enlisted him in my jewel heist before I turned on him. You were a little tougher — that honest streak of yours — and I thought about putting my Carla on your case."

"That would have been fun," Carla said with a lascivious smile. "More fun than old man De Santis."

"My apologies, Carla, but I needed someone to keep close tabs on him."

"And you obviously needed my warehouse and my business," Matt spat.

"Which is why I baited you with a chance at winning a lucrative contract." Fontana smirked. "Mission accomplished. And when the dust settles, the police will be convinced De Santis was the mastermind behind the robbery and the cop shootings. And they'll easily believe you helped."

"Yeah, genius, except I haven't *spoken a word* to De Santis in years!"

Fontana's smirk turned into a grimace. "With the mountain of evidence I'm providing, the police won't care. They'll assume you brought the vault contents back here when they find these metal cases. They'll find the weapon used in the cop shootings. And they may even find a few of the low-quality diamonds we're intentionally leaving

510

behind —"

He kicked the gems at Matt's feet, scattering them.

"The police will conclude that you and De Santis planned to ship the jewels overseas in sacks of coffee. Unfortunately, a tragic accident ended your lives — an oxygen fire so intense it burned this warehouse to the ground and turned the stolen diamonds into smoke. The real diamonds, the valuable ones, won't be gone, of course . . . they will be *mine.*"

I checked my watch. Only two or three minutes had passed. Reinforcements were still a long way off!

"Do I kill them now?" Carla asked, licking her red lips.

"Her blood is up, Allegro." As Fontana spoke, his gaze admiringly raked Carla and her revealing party dress.

They exchanged a smoldering look that spoke volumes. The pair were lovers, that was clear, and I got the distinct impression Fontana's little lecture to Matt was some kind of sick baiting game, like a predator playing with prey before the kill.

"You see, Carla comes from a long line of Afrikaner guides and trackers," he bragged to Matt. "A big-game hunter since she was ten, my Jungle Queen was raised on blood sport. In fact, she rather enjoys it. Carla was one of the most sought after safari guides on the continent, and her career might have continued apace, but poor dear Carla helped a rich American tourist kill the wrong lion, a protected lion. So she fled into my waiting arms to avoid an African prison."

Fontana caressed the young woman's shoulder.

"She made the perfect Panther Man. A sharpshooter who could wound but not kill, then escape while the police searched for a burly man in a ridiculous costume, and ignored the pretty girl with a disassembled rifle in her backpack, one who'd shrewdly established herself in the neighborhood coffee shop as a bright new law student . . ."

As Fontana spoke, Carla moved behind the bound men. Her party hairdo was coming undone, and her eyes were wild as she twirled the long, thin blade in her hand.

"I had those stupid cops chasing their own tails," she boasted. "And tonight Victor's plan of distraction worked like a dream."

"A dream, yes, my love . . . and now it's time to put our prey to sleep." Fontana faced Matt again. "Since we cannot use a gun in here, I must rely on Carla. You see, she knows how to kill a wounded animal without damaging its trophy head. A simple jab behind the ear, into the brain, and life ends. Give Mr. Allegro a demonstration."

I bit my lip to keep from crying out when Carla plunged the blade into Eduardo De Santis's skull. As he slid to the floor, blood pooled around the scattered diamonds.

I saw the paralyzed horror in Matt's eyes. Still hiding behind the partially open door, I felt the same cold shock freeze my limbs.

"It's been delightful to speak with you, Allegro. I seldom have the opportunity to boast of my accomplishments. But now, I fear, our time is up." He checked his watch and nodded to Carla. "Yes, we're on schedule. It's time . . ."

Omigod, omigod, they're going to kill Matt, too! I have to do something!

I knew I couldn't rush them. They were too far away. Fontana or Carla would notice me long before I reached them. She'd kill Matt in one move and have more than enough time to stop me.

As the assassin cleaned her blade on De Santis's jacket, I longed for a loaded gun, fireworks, a bottle rocket — *anything* to surprise and confuse Fontana and Carla, distract them long enough for Matt to escape. But all of those things could send this warehouse up in flames. And all I had in my hands was warm champagne.

Wait a minute. Maybe champagne is all I need . . .

From my catering days I knew two things: with all that carbonation under enormous pressure, you never shook a champagne bottle, and you never opened one that was warm.

To save my ex-husband, I was about to do both.

After a good shaking, I broke a nail while I shredded the paper around the bottle's tip. As I watched Carla step behind Matt, I worked the cork.

The *pop* was as spectacular as I hoped it would be — it echoed like a gunshot inside the cavernous garage, making it impossible to pinpoint the source. The cork punctured a neat hole through a high window on the opposite wall, and the noise of breaking glass enhanced the chaos. I added a McNulty-inspired yell to the mix.

"Freeze, scumbags! NYPD! You're all under arrest!"

In a panic, Carla dropped her murder weapon and kicked it away as she faced the broken window.

Fontana turned to look, too — long enough for Matt to leap off the containers and head butt the billionaire. Both men went down in a heap.

Carla must have thought a SWAT team or tear gas was about to burst through the windows because she ran right for the door I was hiding behind.

The sparkling wine was still gushing from the bottle, so I gave her a face full of it, followed by a chemical Mace chaser.

"That's for Sully, you twisted bitch!"

Despite the wine and toxins, Carla had plenty of fight left. But she couldn't see, so after she slapped me the first time, I sidestepped her second charge and tripped her.

Carla sprawled flat on her face in the hall, where a grinning Sergeant Franco powercuffed her.

Oh, thank goodness, they're finally here!

"Stay down," Franco warned his groaning prisoner. "Or I'll sic the Coffee Lady back on ya."

More officers had arrived through the office door. Two were helping a dazed Lori to an ambulance, so I ran back to the loading dock to check on Matt.

I found him on his feet, hands still tied, kicking the squealing jewel thief — right up to the moment the garage door rolled open, and Quinn and the rest of his squad stormed in.

It was Quinn who pulled Matt off his tormentor.

"Whoa, buddy! Take it easy! We need Fontana alive."

I tried to calm Matt by assuring him that his mother was safe, but when Quinn cut the ropes on his wrists, he rushed Fontana again. This time he yanked the Eye of the Cat out of the man's lapel pocket. Then he slugged the jewel thief, shattering those insufferable boyish glasses.

"That's for kidnapping my mother — and my partner!"

When Quinn and I caught up with him, Matt was swaying from residual shock. Looking a little dazed, he seemed distracted by something on the floor.

I followed his focus and realized he was staring at his depleted magnum of champagne.

"Matt? Are you okay?"

"I will be, Clare," he said, draping an arm around my shoulders to steady himself. "As long as you didn't ruin the rest of my Nectar Impérial."

"Don't worry, Allegro," Quinn said, throwing me a wink. "After the night you've had, I'll buy you a drink."

EPILOGUE

No pressure, no diamonds.
                    — THOMAS CARLYLE

Weeks later, I threw a coming-home party for Gus Campana at the Village Blend. His daughters — all three of them — attended, along with Hunter Rolf, lawyer Sal Arnold, and the entire staff at the jewelry shop. We celebrated his return with cannoli cupcakes, cold brew coffee, some lively duets performed by Tucker and Punch, and . . . plenty of champagne!

Gus's escort for the evening was Madame, who'd gotten much closer to him since the ordeal — and his confession that he was born an Allegro, like her late husband.

Weak from his suicide attempt and the cancer that was slowly killing him, Gus held court beside the warming hearth, and for those few hours, the travails of the past, the difficulties of the present, and the uncertainty of the future were thrust aside for a celebration of life and hope.

The mystery of his poisoning boiled down to a simple solution. Gus had lived for the love of his family, and for that family he was willing to kill. But not another.

To protect his loved ones from a predator, Gus had chosen to kill himself.

It was a miracle that he failed, but now, with his tormentor gone, Gus discovered that he could live out his remaining year or more in peace — time that would allow him to see wounds healed, harms forgiven, and a family not only reconciled, but expanded. I had no doubt he'd live to see Sophia's child — his and Angelica's first grandchild — for the baby was already on the way.

And what about that other treasure?

In the months that followed, the Eye of the Cat, that priceless jewel that had divided a family for sixty years, served to unite them in the end. After the failed Diamond District heist, the world learned of the Eye's existence. And as Matt and Hunter predicted, many greedy hands reached out to grab it.

The Italian Campanas were the first but not the only sharks to participate in the feeding frenzy. More "interested parties" joined the fray, and by the time it was over — amazingly quickly, by legal standards —

the US State Department and the Italian government had become entangled, along with the Smithsonian Institution, the Uffizi Gallery in Florence, and those friendly folks at the Internal Revenue Service.

The Byzantine settlement satisfied no one, which was probably best. No party could claim sole ownership, so it was decided that the jewel would be broken up.

No, the Eye was not divided — the gem was far too precious for that.

The historic blue diamond, with its distinctive Campana cut, was purchased by the Smithsonian for a small fortune. It would soon be on display in the same hall where the Hope Diamond resided.

The famous *setting* that held the Eye was donated to the Uffizi Gallery Museum in Florence with synthetic diamonds replacing the missing stones. Sophia presented it in a formal ceremony, in which (to her delight) she was made an official citizen of Florence.

In the interest of unity, Sophia also presented a check to the near-destitute Donatella and Bruno Campana. They had avoided prosecution for kidnapping and extortion because Madame refused to press charges. Madame's gesture — along with Sophia's check — worked wonders to bridge the long family divide.

Donatella and her brother Bruno accepted their share with expressions of remorse for following the vicious scheme brought to them by the greedy and delusional black-mailer, Gino Benedetto.

With the threat of blackmail gone, and the Campanas in Italy appeased, Silvio was free to remain Gus Campana for the rest of his life, and take his secret to the grave — with the exception of a few confidants.

Perla, of course, had known the truth for years since her mother had confessed on her deathbed, not only to her elder daughter, but (as we all learned from Gus) to her priest. Angelica Campana had murdered her husband in self-defense aboard the sinking *Andrea Doria,* to save the lives of herself and her young daughter.

It was Angelica who convinced Silvio to exchange papers, and clothing, with the drowned corpse. From a secret distance, she had grown to love Silvio as he had loved her. Now they could be together, beyond Gibraltar, in a brand-new and unknown world — and just like that, he became her husband in America.

Gino Benedetto had been the only thorn in their new garden, and he became a lifelong one. He demanded payment for his silence, so Silvio came up with a plan to get the man his hush money. He would tell the world the legendary Eye was lost.

He sought the help and advice of his first cousin, Antonio Allegro, owner of the beloved Village Blend coffee business. Antonio introduced Silvio to a trusted friend, Sal Arnold's grandfather Abe Goldman, who confidentially appraised the Eye for insurers and sold eight of the coffee diamonds to give Silvio and Angelica the funds to start their own jewelry business — and make their first of many payments to Benedetto.

The other eight (of the "missing" sixteen) coffee diamonds were given to Antonio as a grateful gift for his help, which Silvio fashioned into a brooch for Antonio's beautiful young wife, Blanche, who (years later) gifted them to one Michael Ryan Francis Quinn for my engagement ring.

Now I knew the whole story. And what a story it was . . .

Gus's daughter Sophia took the truth in stride about her parents, along with the news she had another unexpected relative (in addition to the Allegro family). *This* relative was much closer to home — her half sister, Monica.

Not wanting to leave Monica out of the legacy, Sophia set aside a small trust for her, too. More importantly, after taking over the day-to-day operations of her father's business, Sophia learned of Monica's secret dream and commanded the talented girl relocate to the West Coast to launch a Los Angeles–based Campana Jewelry Design Studio.

The lion's share of the money, however, went where Antonio and Gustavo wanted it to go. A pair of trusts were established — one for my daughter, Joy; the other for the child Sophia and Hunter would soon have — which meant the Eye of the Cat did more than unite a family; it also reunited one very special couple.

Matt came up short in these negotiations, but he did get his IRS debt forgiven with enough left over to invest back in our business. And, from what I could see, he was plenty satisfied with the outcome, grateful to come out ahead — and alive. With his divorce from Breanne Summour finalized around the same time as the Eye of the Cat settlement, Matt was once again free to roam the savage, Tinder-swipe jungle that was the twenty-first-century dating scene.

All these things were still in flux when Gus left the hospital, and I contemplated the brutal past, and uncertain future beside our wall of French windows, as the welcome-home party wound down . . .

A sweet kiss on the top of my head clued me in to the arrival of my new fiancé.

"I was hoping you'd get here while there were still a few cannoli cupcakes left."

After inhaling two of the delicious treats, Mike leaned back in his chair with a fresh, hot Americano.

"It's been a crazy couple of weeks, and the most insane part is wrapping my head around the fact that Eduardo De Santis was set up as a patsy. That guy slipped out of so many legal nooses, I lost count."

I shrugged. "I guess even the shrewdest man on the planet can be blinded if you dangle enough carats in front of him."

"Too true. Apparently, Victor Fontana planned to frame Club Town Eddy from the moment he lured the man into his consortium. Just as he planned to frame your ex-husband."

"It was a clever scheme, hatched by an ingenious man."

"Not so ingenious." Mike smiled. "He didn't count on the panther-like Clare Cosi pouncing on his perfect plan."

"Happily without a mask or cape."

"Or even a gun," Mike noted. "But then, as elegant weapons go, you can't beat a magnum of champagne."

"Hey, it all worked out."

Even the coffee part . . .

After Fontana was arrested, the new head of the *Andrea Doria* consortium decided to ditch the coffee competition and go with a famous Italian coffee brand for their galleys. I was disappointed — but then I'd said from the start the job was bad luck.

So, I thought, *why not make lemonade out of the whole sour mess?*

I took a chance and pitched my Night and Day blend to a hotel chain that used the same super-automatic espresso-cappuccino machine as the *Andrea Doria.*

They were so happy with the results that word got out, and my new blend became the talk of the hospitality trade. I could hardly keep up with sampling meetings, let alone delivering the goods to my new clients.

Consequently, Matt promised to invest in an expansion of his Red Hook warehouse to include a roasting facility, and I looked forward to the new challenge.

"You know, sweetheart," Quinn continued, "if it weren't for you, that ex-husband of yours would be dead and his warehouse burned to the ground."

"You're giving me way too much credit.

Lori Soles risked her life to help us."

"I haven't forgotten Lori. And neither did the NYPD."

"I'm sorry I missed her decoration ceremony. But I'd promised to cater Tucker's superhero extravaganza . . ."

I was happy to do it, too. The show was a hit — along with our food, especially the "Comic Book" Carbonara that Nancy suggested. Based on a recipe in a famous graphic novel, the mouthwatering marriage of bacon, cream, garlic, and pasta even persuaded a certain "super" model to forgive Nancy for her blueberry Kryptonite. He was so tickled by her attention, he gifted her a framed and signed tear sheet of his latest underwear ad.

As for the besmirched character of Panther Man, the comic company was so grateful the shootings couldn't be pinned on a rabid fan, they funded a special Panther Man hospital wing to care for children with cancer.

They could afford it, too.

The moment the very wealthy Victor Fontana was revealed as the mastermind behind the Panther Man shootings, the comic company and its deep-pocket Hollywood partners filed suit for infringement of copyright "for nefarious purposes that had the potential to damage the property."

"It's one thing to shoot a few policemen," Tucker Burton quipped. "Quite another to mess with a media giant's franchise!"

Indeed, the *New York Post* only half joked that Victor Fontana would probably pay more dearly for stealing Panther Man's likeness than all his other crimes.

And there were other crimes.

Interpol began working with member countries to review suspicious heists worldwide with the same MO. Several cases that had been closed with the prime suspect dead and much of the fortune lost would now be reopened and examined with an eye toward Victor Fontana's proximity to the case.

Carla, the actual police shooter and faux Panther Man, was offered no plea deal despite her willingness to cooperate. She was placed on Rikers Island without bail, to face consecutive life sentences for the attempted murder of several police officers and the premeditated murder of Eduardo De Santis.

If by some miracle, Carla managed to beat all of those raps, Interpol was waiting to help hang a few more charges on her, just like Fontana — with assistance from Lori Soles and her partner, who accepted a temporary assignment to follow up on international leads that landed in our Tri-State Area.

"So how did Lori's decoration ceremony go, by the way?"

"Great," Mike replied. "The police commissioner and mayor congratulated her personally."

"She had to be happy about that."

"So was Lori's husband. But I think her partner, Sue Ellen, was beaming brighter than anyone."

"I guess the only person not celebrating is Lieutenant McNulty."

Mike grunted. "He's got a promotion, too. A *lateral* promotion. He's been bumped from the Inside Job Squad to the brand-new Out of School Squad."

"What do they investigate? Truancy?"

"Goods and supplies that mysteriously vanish from the public school system. The Board of Ed reached out to the NYPD, and they got McNulty. I won't miss seeing him, but I will miss Sully."

"Oh, I think he's more than ready to enjoy retirement with Fran."

"Yeah, but now I need to promote a second-in-command for my own squad."

"Got anyone in mind?"

"A certain shaved-headed sergeant — if

he ever comes back from his vacation in Washington."

"I'd say he earned time off. He's also got good reason to linger in DC — and it's not to visit the monuments. I got a text from Joy. She's never been happier."

"Watch out. Franco gets a raise with this jump. He might just go shopping for an engagement ring."

I looked again at my own ring. I was grateful that Matt and Sophia insisted I keep the coffee diamonds. Gus agreed that Quinn and I more than deserved them for our help saving his life, his daughter's happiness, and the Eye of the Cat itself.

Like Madame and her brooch, I knew I would enjoy the shining jewels in this circle for the rest of my life. But I also knew the true treasure in my life wasn't something I could wear. It lived in the people around me, who'd become my family, the work that gave me pride, and the daughter who gave me joy.

As Mike took my hand and whispered sweet promises for the night ahead, I thought of the Swedish lullaby Hunter often sang to Sophia. I had looked up a loose translation, and hummed it now with happiness . . .

This galley of riches has three things to
    treasure.
The first one is faith. The second one is
    hope.
The third one is love.

RECIPES & TIPS FROM
THE VILLAGE BLEND

Visit Cleo Coyle's virtual Village Blend at
coffeehousemystery.com
for even more recipes including:

★ "Comic Book" Carbonara
★ Maple-Glazed Oatmeal Muffins
★ Snickerdoodle Muffins
★ Anginetti (*Iced Italian Lemon Cookies*)
★ Chocolate-Almond Biscotti
★ Pumpkin Pie Muffins (*Dairy Free*)

HOW TO MAKE
COLD BREW COFFEE

To see step-by-step photos of this method, visit Cleo Coyle's online coffeehouse at coffeehousemystery.com.

Cold brew coffee is a smooth and refreshing beverage. When made correctly, the flavor is outstanding — never weak or watery as many iced coffees can be. Cold brew is also insanely easy to make. On page 535 is the "Mason-jar method" that you read about in this book. There are many other ways to produce cold brew — with a French press, for example, or with appliances specifically created for cold brew. But all methods are essentially the same: coarsely ground coffee is stirred into cold water and allowed to steep for 12 to 20 hours.

The ratio of coffee to water and the length of steeping time depend on many factors, including the type of coffee you choose (light or dark roast) and your own taste. After steep-

ing, the coffee must be filtered and can then be stored in the refrigerator for about a week.

One last thing to keep in mind: the coffee made with the cold brew method is really a coffee concentrate, and should be diluted in some manner before enjoying. Some people use cold water. Others pour it over ice (and allow the ice to melt slowly). You might also add milk, half-and-half, or light cream. Sugar and flavored syrups are your call, as well. However you make and serve your cold brew coffee, may you drink with joy!

RECIPES

MASON-JAR COLD BREW COFFEE

The Mason-jar method of making cold brew coffee is highly popular. The jar's efficient lid seals the coffee in an airtight lock, keeping it fresh as you steep it — and after you filter it. This method is easy, convenient, practical, and (best of all) inexpensive. So let's make some cold brew!

Makes about 3 2/3 cup of concentrated cold brew
(Or about 48 ounces of drinkable beverage, once diluted)

3/4 cup (50 grams) coarsely ground coffee
2 wide-mouth Mason jars, quart size
4 cups cold water
Coffee filter cone (aka pour-over cone), size #2
Paper coffee filters, cone shaped, size #2 (or #4)

Step 1 — Choose and grind your coffee: The best coffee to use for cold brew is one with a strong, bold flavor, which is why Clare suggests a medium-dark or dark roast. Be sure to use freshly roasted coffee and grind your coffee fresh, on the *coarse* setting, as you would if making hot coffee in a French press.

Step 2 — Steep your coffee: Place your ground coffee in the wide-mouth Mason jar. Add your water. Note that because of the amount of coffee grounds, you will not be able to fit all four cups of cold water into the quart-sized jar, and that's okay. Stir the grounds between pours and you will be able to fit more water in. Pour all the way to the top of the jar and stir well. Seal the jar, gently shake it, and stand it in the fridge with a label that indicates when 12 hours will have elapsed.

Step 3 — Steeping time: Although cold brew can take up to 20 hours, start with 12 hours and see how you like the results. If the coffee tastes weak to you, increase the next batch to 14 hours, then to 16, 18, and finally to 20 hours. The longer you steep the coffee, the stronger it becomes — but you risk allowing it to become bitter, as well.

As mentioned in the opening of this recipe, it's a question of what kind of coffee you're using and your own subjective taste. So experiment with what you like best.

Step 4 — Filter the coffee: After the cold brew has steeped, filter it. While you can use cheesecloth and a kitchen strainer, Clare suggests that you invest in the purchase of an inexpensive coffee filter cone (aka pour-over cone) size #2. This is the perfect size for placing right over the mouth of your Mason jar. (FYI: This size cone also can be used over a coffee mug to make a single, pour-over cup of hot coffee.) Note that you will also need disposable paper filters (cone-shaped size #2 or #4), to place inside your plastic cone. Slowly pour the steeped cold brew through the filter, into your second, clean Mason jar. This process will take a few minutes, as the coffee drips down into the jar, leaving the grounds and silt in the filter.

Step 5 — Coffee concentrate service: As mentioned above, this is a concentrated coffee. To drink it, you will need to dilute it. You can add cold water and/or pour it over ice and/or add half-and-half (or milk or cream). Sugars and syrups are up to you.

Experiment with what makes your taste buds happy.

CLARE COSI'S CANNOLI CREAM CUPCAKES

To make these simple yet amazing cupcakes — which had Matt Allegro making "annoying orgasmic sounds" — you must start by baking Clare's Golden Cupcakes recipe (below). When the cupcakes have cooled completely, apply a generous dollop of Clare's Cannoli Cream Frosting (recipe on page 541).

While these frosted cupcakes are delicious served simply, with no garnish, you can also do what Clare does and finish some of the cupcakes in the manner of Italian cannoli. Garnish some with grated chocolate or mini chocolate chips and others with chopped pistachio nuts. A whole or half candied cherry is another idea for a festive, cannoli-esque topping. May you eat with joy!

CLARE'S GOLDEN CUPCAKES

The first time Mike Quinn saw Clare making these cupcakes, he asked why she didn't use a boxed mix. Aren't those cake mixes supposed to be "easier"? Clare never thought so. After all, you're already dirtying bowls and utensils and mixing ingredients. Why not make the cupcakes from scratch? After one bite of these tender little cakes, Mike never asked about a boxed mix again.

Clare's culinary note: This recipe is designed to be a quick and easy way of making scratch cupcakes. That's why she uses self-rising flour, which not only includes most of your leavening and salt, but also gives you a lower protein flour. In other words, for best results, use the ingredients listed and do not substitute all-purpose flour. Finally, be sure to use fresh self-rising flour that has not gone beyond the expiration date; otherwise, the leavening agent may not be potent enough to give you good results.

Makes 12 cupcakes

1 cup self-rising flour (use fresh, check expiration date)
1/2 cup granulated sugar
1/4 teaspoon baking soda
8 tablespoons (1 stick) unsalted butter, softened to room temperature
2 extra-large eggs at room temperature (*see Clare's tip)
1/2 cup whole milk
2 teaspoons pure vanilla extract

Step 1 — Make batter: First preheat your oven to 350°F. Start the batter by sifting the first 3 dry ingredients together into a large mixing bowl. (Yes, you must sift for a light, tender cupcake.) Add the softened butter (must be softened to room temperature) and the room-temperature eggs. Using an electric mixer, blend the ingredients together briefly. Now add the whole milk and pure vanilla extract and beat for a good 2 minutes.

Step 2 — Bake: Line 12 cups of your cupcake pan with paper liners and lightly coat the papers with nonstick spray. Divide the batter evenly among the cups. (Each cup should be about 1/2 full of batter and no more.) Bake at 350°F for 18 to 22 minutes. Do not overbake or cupcakes will dry out. Cupcakes are done when the top springs back after a light touching. You can also insert a toothpick into the middle of a test cupcake. If it comes out with no wet batter clinging to it, the cakes are done. (Moist crumbs are okay, but if you see wet batter, return the cupcakes to the oven for a few minutes more before testing again.) Once baked, allow the cupcakes to cool for 5 minutes before gently removing them from the pan to finish cooling on a rack.

*Clare's quick egg tip:** To get cold eggs down to room temperature quickly, place them in a bowl of warm tap water. Warming the eggs is important for proper blending of the egg proteins into the batter.

CLARE'S CANNOLI CREAM FROSTING

This frosting mimics the sweet, creamy, satisfying filling of a freshly made Italian cannoli. Now, the first thing you might notice about this recipe is its lack of ricotta. That's intentional. While ricotta is traditionally used in Italy, Italian American bakeries usually turn to mascarpone cheese to make their filling, and for good reason. The ricotta you find in Italy is drier and sweeter than the ricotta in the United States. To get the right consistency, Clare would have to wrap her American ricotta in cheesecloth, suspend it over a bowl, and allow it to drain overnight in the fridge — mamma mia, how much trouble is that? Which is why she finds the mascarpone solution to be far easier!

Makes 3 cups, enough to generously frost 24 cupcakes or 13-by-9-inch sheet cake or 8- or 9-inch two-layer cake

8 ounces mascarpone cheese, softened
6 tablespoons fresh, unsalted butter, soft-

ened (*see Clare's note)

3 1/2 cups confectioners' sugar

1 teaspoon pure vanilla extract

1/8 teaspoon table salt

(optional) 1/4 teaspoon good-quality cinnamon

(optional) 1/2 teaspoon zest of lemon or orange or mixed

1–2 tablespoons whole milk, half-and-half, or light cream

*Clare's butter note: Unsalted butter will be the freshest at your local store. While it's certainly not required for this recipe, for a real treat, look for imported butter with a higher fat content, such as Irish or European butters or "European-style" butters made locally. You can research the subject yourself by typing "high-fat butter brands" into an Internet search engine.

Be sure to allow your mascarpone cheese and butter to soften to room temperature before starting. Using an electric mixer, beat both ingredients in a large bowl until light and fluffy. Add 1 cup of the confectioners' sugar, vanilla, salt, (optional) cinnamon, and (optional) citrus zest, and beat well. Scrape down the bowl and beat in the remaining confectioners' sugar, a little at a time, and you will achieve a smooth frosting. If frosting seems too thick, add 1 to 2 tablespoons of whole milk, half-and-half, or cream. If too loose, add a bit more confectioners' sugar.

THE VILLAGE BLEND'S FARMHOUSE APPLE CAKE MUFFINS

A light, tender muffin with a hint of sweet apple and the rich "farmhouse" flavor of buttermilk makes these muffins a morning glory for Clare Cosi's coffeehouse customers, especially when enjoyed with a hot cup of her freshly roasted coffee.

Clare's culinary tip: Buy a quart of buttermilk, reserve 1/2 cup for this muffin cake recipe, and use the rest to make the delicious Buttermilk Fried Chicken featured at the relaxed jazz supper club, atop the new Village Blend, DC. Find that fried chicken recipe and many more in Coffeehouse Mystery #15: *Dead to the Last Drop,* in which Clare attempts to caffeinate the nation's capital and solve a capital crime.

Makes 12 muffins

1 1/2 cups all-purpose flour
2 teaspoons baking powder

1/4 teaspoon baking soda

1/2 teaspoon table salt

1 teaspoon cinnamon

1/4 teaspoon nutmeg

1 large Golden Delicious apple (*see apple note)

1 cup granulated white sugar

1/2 cup butter (1 stick), softened to room temperature

2 large eggs at room temperature

1 teaspoon pure vanilla extract

1/2 cup buttermilk (or light buttermilk)

(optional) Cinnamon-Vanilla Glaze (recipe follows)

Step 1 — Mix dry ingredients: Sift together flour, baking powder, baking soda, salt, cinnamon, nutmeg. Set aside.

Step 2 — Shred apple: Peel the apple. Using a boxed grater (or food processor), shred the apple. (Do not chop or finely dice. *Shred it* as you would cheese.) Set aside.

Step 3 — Beat wet ingredients: Using an electric mixer, beat the sugar and butter until light and fluffy. (Make sure butter is softened to room temperature.) Add your 2 eggs one at a time (use room-temperature eggs for best results), whipping well between each addition. The whipping will help make your muffins delightfully tender. Finally, mix in vanilla and buttermilk.

Step 4 — Marry dry and wet ingredients: With mixer on a low speed, add the premeasured dry ingredients to your wet ingredients, mixing just enough to create a smooth batter. (Do not overmix or you will develop the gluten in the flour and toughen your muffins.) With a spoon or spatula now gently fold in the shredded apple.

Step 5 — Bake: Either line muffin pans with paper liners and lightly coat the papers with nonstick spray, or use the spray on the muffin tins (or grease with butter or oil). Divide batter among the cups; filling to the top. Bake at 375°F for 18 minutes. Test doneness. If a toothpick comes out clean, with no wet batter clinging to it, the muffin is baked. Otherwise, bake 5 minutes more and test again. Cool the muffins 5 minutes in the pan and carefully remove to finish cooling on a rack. (If left in the pan, muffin bottoms may steam and become tough.) See Clare's "toothpick method" below.

Toothpick method for de-panning hot muffins: Gently insert a toothpick on each side of the muffin, below the visible muffin tops. Use the toothpicks as handles and carefully lift the muffin from the pan. This is a fast, efficient way to get the muffins out of their hot pan without squashing or flattening them.

*Apple note: The type of apple that you use will affect your muffins. That's why Clare is recommending Golden Delicious — not to be confused with Red Delicious. Golden Delicious apples have wonderful flavor and texture for baking, and will give you good results. Using a single shredded apple, as the recipe directs, is what keeps these muffins tender and light.

CINNAMON-VANILLA GLAZE
Makes enough glaze for 12 muffins

2 tablespoons unsalted butter
1/8 teaspoon table salt
1/2 teaspoon ground cinnamon
2 tablespoons whole milk
1 teaspoon pure vanilla extract
1 1/2 cups sifted confectioners' sugar

Melt butter in a saucepan on low heat. Remove pan from heat and whisk in salt, cinnamon, whole milk, and vanilla (in that order). Return pan to low heat. Whisk in the confectioners' sugar, a little at a time, until you have a smooth glaze. If glaze is too thick, add a bit more milk; if too thin, whisk in a bit more confectioners' sugar. Dip tops of muffins into glaze or use a fork to drizzle the glaze in a zigzag fashion across the tops. If glaze hardens, place over heat and whisk again until smooth.

THE VILLAGE BLEND'S PECAN PIE MUFFINS

An amazingly delicious cross between a mini pecan pie and a fresh-baked muffin. The dark brown sugar brings especially earthy goodness to this popular Village Blend morning breakfast or afternoon coffee-break treat. You can even serve these muffins as dessert by placing them on pretty, doily-covered plates with dollops of whipped cream on top.

Makes 6 muffins

1 extra-large egg
1 teaspoon pure vanilla extract
1/4 teaspoon table salt
2/3 cup dark brown sugar, packed
8 tablespoons unsalted butter (1 stick), melted and cooled
1/3 cup all-purpose flour

1 cup finely chopped pecans

Step 1 — One-bowl mixing method: Using a whisk, beat the egg until foamy. Whisk in the vanilla, salt, and sugar. Whisk in the melted and *cooled* butter. (Take care to cool the butter or you may cook your egg!) Switching to a rubber spatula, add the flour and gently stir until all of the raw flour is blended into the batter — but take care not to overmix at this stage or you'll develop the gluten in the flour and create toughness in your muffins. Fold in 3/4 cup of the finely chopped pecans, reserving 1/4 for topping.

Step 2 — Bake: Generously coat 6 nonstick muffin cups with nonstick spray (or grease with butter or oil and dust with flour). Do not use paper liners. Sprinkle top of unbaked muffins with reserved 1/4 cup of finely chopped pecans. Divide batter evenly among the cups. Bake in preheated 350°F oven for 20 to 25 minutes. Do not overbake. Muffins are done when a toothpick inserted in the center comes out clean. Cool muffins 5 minutes in the pan before gently running a butter knife around the edges of each cup to loosen. Then gently remove muffins from pan and finish cooling on a rack before starting that pot of coffee!

CLARE'S BAILEYS IRISH CREAM CHOCOLATE CHIP COOKIES

The great American chocolate chip cookie gets a superb spike of flavor from a wee bit of Baileys Irish Cream — a blend of real Irish whiskey and rich cream (from real Irish cows). No wonder they're a favorite of Clare's new fiancé, NYPD detective Mike Quinn. When she made a batch for a small dinner party, "Sully" Sullivan (Quinn's second-in-command) not only raved about the cookies, he ate half the plate — Quinn consumed the other half — and Sully's wife asked for the recipe. Clare was happy to share it with Fran Sullivan. Now she shares it with you.

Makes about 3 dozen cookies

11 tablespoons unsalted butter, softened
1 cup light brown sugar, firmly packed
1/2 cup granulated white sugar
1/4 cup Baileys Irish Cream (*see "tipsy tip" below)
1 large egg, lightly beaten with fork
1/2 teaspoon salt (use table salt or finely ground sea salt)
1/4 teaspoon baking soda
1 3/4 cups all-purpose flour
1 1/4 cups (by volume) semisweet chocolate chips

*Tipsy tip from Clare: 1/4 cup of Irish Cream equals 4 tablespoons. If you don't wish to buy a large bottle of Irish Cream, look for 2 minibar bottles of Baileys Irish Cream (50 ml size). This will give you enough for the recipe (about 6 tablespoons, a little over 3 tablespoons in each bottle).

Step 1 — Make the dough: Preheat oven well to 375°F. Cream the butter and sugars. Blend in the Irish Cream, egg, salt, and finally the baking soda. Beat in the flour just until it's completely incorporated. Do not overmix or you will develop the gluten in the flour and your cookies will be tough instead of tender. Finally, fold in the chocolate chips. You can either make the cookies now or place some or all of the dough in a tightly sealed plastic container (or wrap tightly in plastic) and store in the refrigerator for up to 3 days. *See Clare's tip below about baking chilled dough.

Step 2 — Bake the cookies: Your oven should be well preheated to 375°F. (Oven timers often lie so let it preheat for at least 30 minutes.) Line a baking sheet with parchment paper or a silicone sheet (do not grease your pan or your cookies will turn out greasy). Using clean fingers and the teaspoon from your measuring set, create generous rounded balls about 1 inch in diameter. Bake 8 to 10 minutes; do not overbake. Bottoms should be a lovely golden brown and not dark brown or black. Allow the (slightly underbaked) cookies to finish baking on the cookie sheet (at least 5 more minutes — time it, no kidding — on the hot pan).

Step 3 — Over-the-top finish (optional): For a "wow" finish that really boosts the Baileys flavors, make Clare's Baileys Irish Cream Glaze (recipe follows). Once the cookies cool, dip the crescent-shaped edge of each cookie into the warm glaze and immediately dip the wet edge into a bowl of finely chopped nuts (hazelnuts, almonds, or walnuts). OR skip the nuts completely and simply allow the glazed edges to dry by placing the cookies on a wax paper–covered plate or tray.

*Clare's chilled dough baking tip: Cold cookie dough is going to be hard — and difficult to work with. If you're in a hurry to make cookies from this cold dough (instead of allowing it to warm to room temperature), then form it into little round balls and flatten the cookie on your baking sheet with the palm of your hand or a spatula. This will give the cookie a head start to spreading inside the oven into a rounder, flatter cookie.

CLARE'S BAILEYS IRISH CREAM GLAZE

For an even more powerful taste of Baileys, create this easy glaze to dip the edges of Clare's Baileys Irish Cream Chocolate Chip Cookies in. This glaze also brings great flavor when drizzled over a plain pound cake, Bundt cake, or spice cake. You can dip the tops of cupcakes or muffins in the glaze to finish them. Or use a fork to create a zigzag drizzle pattern on shortbread or sugar cookies.

2 tablespoons butter
4 tablespoons Baileys Irish Cream
1/2 teaspoon pure vanilla extract
2 cups powdered sugar

In a medium saucepan, over low heat, melt the butter. Take pan off heat and stir in Baileys Irish Cream and vanilla. Whisk in powdered sugar, a little at a time, until all of it completely melts into the liquid. Whisk to remove any lumps and blend into a smooth, thick glaze. If the glaze is too thick, whisk in a bit more Baileys Irish Cream.

Use the glaze while still warm. As the glaze cools, it will harden. If the glaze begins to harden in the pan, simply return the pan to the stovetop and warm the glaze while whisking. Add a bit more Baileys Irish Cream, if needed, to thin the glaze back to the proper consistency for drizzling.

THE VILLAGE BLEND'S CHOCOLATE-ESPRESSO "GLOBS"

A chocolate cookie to end the need for all other chocolate cookies, this chunky, seductively dark and fudgy treat with a hint of espresso was inspired by the "Soho Glob," a cookie beloved for years at the now-defunct restaurant Soho Charcuterie.

The two women who opened the eatery (Frannie Scherer from Brooklyn and Maddie Poley from Jersey City) had little professional experience but great talent and passion. Soon after opening, they nearly went out of business, until their waiter enticed the New York Times's restaurant critic to give them a try. After a week of serving the critic meals, Frannie and Maddie received a two-star rave. Dinner covers instantly went from 10 to 110 a night, and a star-studded clientele became regulars throughout the 1980s.

Although the restaurant eventually did close, this cookie lives on. When one of Clare's longtime customers mourned the loss of her daily Chocolate Glob fix, Clare decided to re-create it with the help of her baker, who made only a few minor changes from the original. One last note: if you're ever in Boston, Massachusetts, be sure to stop by Rosie's Bakery, where you can sample it there, as well!

Makes 24 cookies 2-inches in diameter

8 ounces bittersweet chocolate
6 tablespoons (3/4 stick) unsalted butter, softened
2 extra-large eggs, room temperature
2 teaspoons pure vanilla extract
1 teaspoon instant espresso powder
3/4 cup sugar
1/4 teaspoon table salt
1 teaspoon baking powder
1/3 cup all-purpose flour
3/4 cup semisweet or dark chocolate chips
1/2 heaping cup chopped pecans
1/2 heaping cup chopped walnuts

Step 1 — Melt your chocolate: First preheat your oven to 325°F. Next melt your bittersweet chocolate and butter together in one bowl. You can do this in a microwave, stirring between short bursts to prevent burning. Or you can use a double boiler, or simply place a heatproof bowl over simmering water, making sure not to allow the chocolate to come in contact with the water or it will seize up. Whatever method you choose, be sure to stir together the melted chocolate and butter until smooth and set aside to cool.

Step 2 — Make the dough: Using an electric mixer, briefly beat your (room-temperature) eggs with the vanilla extract and espresso powder. Add the sugar and salt, and blend for a full minute, until thick. Add your melted and cooled chocolate-butter mixture and blend for another minute. Next add your baking powder and briefly mix until well blended. Now turn the mixer to low, and add the flour, blending until all of the raw flour is incorporated but taking care not to overmix. Finally, gently fold in the chocolate chips and nuts.

Step 3 — Bake: Line baking sheets with parchment paper or silicone sheets. Drop your dough from tablespoons, flatten slightly, and leave room for spreading. Bake in your preheated 325°F oven for about 12 minutes. Cookies are done when you see a shiny crust forming and cracking, like the top of a brownie. Baked cookies should be

2-inches in diameter. Cookies are fragile when hot, so be sure to cool on the baking sheet for 5 minutes before using a spatula to transfer them carefully to a cooling rack. Then start that pot of coffee or pour that glass of milk because you are about to go to Chocolate Glob heaven!

THE VILLAGE BLEND'S "PRETTY IN PINK" COOKIES

A popular cookie at Clare's coffeehouse, especially around Valentine's Day, this pretty, pink cookie is also delicious — a tender, sophisticated cream cheese dough with a sweet, light note of raspberry (or, if you prefer, cherry or strawberry). The cookie is easy to make, yet the pretty color and "Pink Chocolate" Icing make it an impressive-looking cookie for holiday party trays and dessert plates. As noted, you don't have to use raspberry preserves in this cookie. Cherry or strawberry preserves will work, as well. One last tip from Clare: because the eyes eat first, present your cookies in pastry-chef style with loose, whole raspberries or sliced strawberries or fresh cherries as a decorative accent on plates or trays.

Makes about 30 cookies (depending on size)

3/4 cup granulated, white sugar

1/2 cup butter, softened

1/4 cup packed (2 ounces) block (not whipped) cream cheese, softened

3 tablespoons raspberry preserves (or cherry or strawberry)

1/4 teaspoon table salt

1/2 teaspoon vanilla extract

1 egg yolk

1 cup all-purpose flour

Extra granulated, white sugar for finishing

Step 1 — Make the pink batter: Using an electric mixer, cream sugar, butter, and cream cheese. Add raspberry (or cherry or strawberry) preserves, salt, vanilla, and egg yolk. Beat until smooth. Mix in flour until well blended. Do not overmix.

Step 2 — Chill: The dough is too wet and sticky to work with at this stage. You must wrap it in plastic and chill it about 1 hour in the freezer or 2 in the fridge. After chilling, it will be firm enough to handle.

Step 3 — Roll, flatten, and bake: Preheat your oven to 375°F. Roll dough into balls, drop in granulated sugar, and coat.* Place on a lined baking sheet. Butter the bottom of a glass, dip the bottom in sugar, and flatten your first ball of dough. Dip the glass in sugar again, and repeat until all the dough balls are flattened. Bake for 8 to 10 minutes. Cool cookies completely before finishing with "Pink Chocolate" Icing (recipe follows).

*Note on the rolling and flattening: The larger you make the ball of dough and the harder you press on the glass, the larger and thinner your cookies will be. Experiment with the size and thickness of your cookies until you get the kind you like best.

"PINK CHOCOLATE" ICING

2 tablespoons whole milk, half-and-half, or light cream (do not use low-fat milk)

1 cup (good-quality) white chocolate chips

2 tablespoons raspberry (or cherry or strawberry) preserves

Heat the milk (or half-and-half or light cream) in a microwave-safe bowl for about 30 seconds — the milk should be very hot to the touch. (*See note below if you do not have a microwave.) Add the white chocolate chips and stir for about a minute. If the chips are not fully melted after a minute, place the bowl back in the microwave for 10 seconds and stir again. Finally, add the raspberry preserves and stir until you have your beautiful "pink chocolate" icing.

Work with this icing while it's still warm. Clare spoons it onto the Pretty in Pink cookies and uses the back of the spoon to lightly spread and smooth it into an even layer. Once spread, the icing will set in about 30 minutes (faster if you chill the cookies in the fridge).

*Stovetop directions: If you do not have a microwave, create a double boiler by placing a glass or other heatproof bowl over a saucepan of simmering water. Warm the milk, then add the chips and stir continually until melted. Take the bowl off the heat and stir in the raspberry preserves.

Warning: Be sure to mix the preserves as instructed in the recipe — i.e., after the chocolate is melted into the milk. If you try to "save time" by adding the preserves to the milk before heating, you will end up with an ugly gray mess.

CLARE'S PERFECT PUMPKIN BREAD WITH BROWN SUGAR AND MAPLE SYRUP

Clare Cosi knows the trick to baking up an excellent quick bread is not unlike the secret to a good relationship: keep the structure strong enough to prevent it all from falling apart — without sacrificing tenderness. She and Mike Quinn work on that delicate balance every day. In both cases (the bread and their relationship), the added spice makes it nice. While cinnamon and nutmeg are traditional in pumpkin bread, Clare's recipe also layers in earthy-sweet maple syrup and brown sugar. Both combine with the vanilla to create a delightful note of caramel. This beautiful bread is great for gifting as well as eating. Mike found that out the morning Clare handed him wrapped loaves for his squad and his hospitalized second-in-command. Now Clare gives you *the gift of her Perfect Pumpkin Bread.*

Makes one 9-by-5-inch loaf

2 extra-large eggs
1/2 cup vegetable oil
1/3 cup pure maple syrup
1 cup light or dark brown sugar, firmly packed and free of lumps!
1 teaspoon pure vanilla extract

1 teaspoon ground cinnamon
1/2 teaspoon ground nutmeg
1 1/2 teaspoons baking powder
1 teaspoon baking soda
1/2 teaspoon table salt
1 1/2 cups pumpkin puree* (most of a 15-ounce can)
2 cups all-purpose flour
(optional) 1/2 cup finely chopped pecans or walnuts
(optional) Clare's Cream Cheese Glaze (recipe follows this one)

*Pumpkin puree can be homemade or canned. If using canned, be sure to use 100 percent pureed pumpkin and not "pumpkin pie filling."

Step 1 — Make batter: First preheat your oven to 350°F. Coat bottom and sides of a 9-by-5-inch loaf pan with nonstick spray or grease the pan with oil or butter. With a fork or whisk, beat eggs in a mixing bowl. Whisk in oil, maple syrup, and brown sugar. Whisk in vanilla, cinnamon, nutmeg, baking powder, baking soda, and salt. Finally, whisk in the pumpkin puree and blend well. Switching to a rubber spatula (or spoon), stir in flour until a lumpy batter forms. Be sure all the raw flour is well incorporated into the batter, but do not overmix. If adding nuts, fold in now. Pour batter into prepared loaf pan. Even off the top and bang the pan a few times on the counter (to remove air bubbles). Allow the pan to sit undisturbed for 10 minutes before baking.

Step 2 — Bake: After about 50 minutes baking in your well-preheated 350°F oven, test for doneness by inserting a toothpick deep into the center of the bread. If the toothpick comes out with wet batter clinging to it, place aluminum foil over the top of the pan to prevent overbrowning and continue baking 5 minutes at a time, testing until toothpick comes out clean or with only a few moist crumbs clinging to it.

Step 3 — Glaze, cool, and slice: Bread should cool for at least 10 minutes before removing from the pan. If your pan is nonstick, it should come out easily. Otherwise, run a knife around the pan edges.

Optional: *While still warm* frost with Clare's Cream Cheese Glaze — the recipe follows with instructions for glazing. Before slicing, cool bread another 15 minutes or you may risk crumbling the slices. Slice gently, using a serrated knife. Delicious plain or with a spread of butter or whipped cream cheese.

CLARE'S CREAM CHEESE GLAZE

4 tablespoons butter, softened
2 ounces cream cheese, softened
1/2 teaspoon pure vanilla extract
2 tablespoons milk (whole, skim, or almond)
Generous pinch of table salt
3/4 cups sifted confectioners' sugar

Using an electric mixer, beat the softened butter and softened cream cheese until light and fluffy. (Tip: Be sure to allow these ingredients to soften to room temperature or you may have trouble getting the right texture.) Beat in the pure vanilla extract, milk, and salt. Finally, mix in your confectioners' sugar, a little at a time, until the glaze is smooth. Use a pastry (silicone) brush to generously brush this glaze over the top (and a bit over the sides) of Clare's Perfect Pumpkin Bread *while still warm*. The glaze will melt into the bread and set as it cools. This glaze is also delicious on spice cookies and muffins.

CLARE'S PERFECT COFFEE BACON WITH MAPLE-ESPRESSO GLAZE

Once you start eating this beautiful smoky-sweet bacon, you will not want to stop. Clare served it to her new fiancé in an effort to divert his amorous attentions. (There were, after all, mysteries to solve.) As the bacon caramelized in the oven, the incredible scent attracted the attention of Clare's feline friends, Frothy and Java, and the fur flew — until the catnip appeared. As for human catnip, you've found it. Serve this glazed bacon with coffee and slices of melon for a heavenly breakfast.

Makes 2 servings

6 thick-cut bacon slices (must be thick-cut)
2 tablespoons dark brown sugar (must be dark)
1/4 teaspoon espresso powder
1 tablespoon hot coffee
1 1/2 teaspoons pure maple syrup

Step 1 — Prepare the baking pan: Preheat oven to 375°F. Line a rimmed baking sheet with parchment paper. Place bacon slices flat on the paper. Allow the slices to warm a bit before going into the oven, so lay out the bacon *before* making the glaze. (Note: The parchment paper is there to absorb grease and prevent the bacon from sticking to the pan. The process is messy, so be sure to use the paper.)

Step 2 — Prepare the glaze: Place dark brown sugar and espresso powder into a small bowl. Add hot coffee and whisk with a fork until sugar and espresso are completely dissolved. Whisk in maple syrup. Brush each bacon slice evenly with your coffee-maple glaze, using about half the amount.

Step 3 — Bake the bacon: Bake for 10 minutes at 375°F. Flip the bacon, brush the other side with the rest of the glaze. Increase the oven temperature to 425°F and bake for another 10 to 13 minutes. Watch closely to prevent burning. The key to perfection is a *slight char on the edges,* which guarantees that the sugars have properly caramelized.

Step 4 — Drain and serve: Allow the bacon to cool enough for the sizzling to stop. Then move the hot bacon to a plate or baking sheet covered with wax paper or parchment paper to continue draining the grease. Do not use paper towels; the glazed bacon will stick! Serve hot or cold and you will definitely eat with joy!

CLARE'S SWEET AND SAVORY MUSTARD-MAPLE BACON

Like Clare's Perfect Coffee Bacon, this quick and easy glaze infuses your ho-hum breakfast with new and exciting flavors. Sweet, savory, and delicious, this Mustard-Maple Bacon is also fantastic in a BLT.

Makes 2 servings

6 thick-cut bacon slices (must be thick-cut)
2 tablespoons dark brown sugar (must be dark)
1 tablespoon Dijon mustard
1 teaspoon hot coffee or hot water
1 1/2 teaspoons pure maple syrup

Step 1 — Prepare the baking pan: Preheat oven to 375°F. Line a rimmed baking sheet with parchment paper. Place bacon slices flat on the paper. Allow the slices to warm a bit before going into the oven, so lay out the bacon *before* making the glaze. (Note: The parchment paper is there to absorb grease and prevent the bacon from sticking to the pan. The process is messy, so be sure to use the paper.)

Step 2 — Prepare the glaze: Place dark brown sugar and Dijon mustard into a small bowl. Add hot coffee (or hot water) and whisk with a fork until the sugar is completely dissolved. Whisk in maple syrup. Brush each bacon slice evenly with your mustard-maple glaze, using about half the amount.

Step 3 — Bake the bacon: Bake for 10 minutes at 375°F. Flip the bacon, brush the other side with the rest of the glaze. Increase the oven temperature to 425°F and bake for another 10 to 13 minutes. Watch closely to prevent burning. The key to perfection is a *slight char on the edges,* which guarantees that the sugars have properly caramelized.

Step 4 — Drain and serve: Allow the bacon to cool enough for the sizzling to stop. Then move the hot bacon to a plate or baking sheet covered with wax paper or parchment paper to continue draining the grease. Do not use paper towels; the glazed bacon will stick! Serve hot or cold.

CLARE'S MEMORABLE FRIED MOZZARELLA STICKS

Sometimes a food just sticks — to your memory. After Clare whipped up a batch of these hot, crunchy, melty delights for Mike Quinn, he couldn't stop raving about them, prompting his subordinate in the OD Squad, Sergeant Emmanuel Franco, to put in a request to Clare for a batch of his own. Unfortunately, Clare was fresh out of mozzarella, so the "poor guy" had to settle for a generous bowl of freshly made Fettuccine Alfredo (see Clare's recipe on page 576).

Makes about 16 sticks

1/2 cup flour
2 large eggs, beaten with 1 tablespoon milk
3/4 cup panko bread crumbs (for crunch)
3/4 cup Italian-seasoned bread crumbs (to boost coating and flavor)
3/4 cups grated Parmesan or Pecorino Romano
1/4 teaspoon coarsely ground sea salt
1 pound block whole milk mozzarella cheese (such as Polly-O)*
2 cups vegetable oil

*For convenience, you can use mozzarella "string cheese" (cutting each stick in half before coating), but Clare warns that these preformed sticks are made with part-skim mozzarella, and will not give you the level of creaminess, melty gooeyness, and flavor you'll get by taking a few minutes to cut sticks from a whole milk mozzarella block.

Step 1 — Prepare dipping ingredients: (Clare suggests using 3 shallow bowls or cake pans or pie plates for this dipping process.) Into first bowl, measure out flour. Into second bowl, beat 2 eggs with 1 tablespoon milk. Into third bowl, blend panko bread crumbs, Italian-seasoned bread crumbs, Parmesan (or Pecorino Romano), and sea salt. Cut the mozzarella block into sticks of about 3 inches long and 1/2 inch wide.

Step 2 — Bread and freeze: Coat each cheese stick with flour first. Next dip the floured stick in the egg mixture. Shake off excess liquid and roll each stick in the bread crumbs mix, pressing on the breading to make sure it adheres to each cheese stick. Place coated stick on a tray or baking sheet covered with wax paper or parchment paper. Repeat with all sticks. Cover with plastic wrap and freeze the cheese sticks at least 2 hours, but no more than 48 hours.

Step 3 — Fry and feast: Heat the vegetable oil in a large frying pan over medium heat. Working in small batches so they don't bump or bunch together, fry the frozen mozzarella sticks until they are golden brown, about 1 minute per side. Remove sticks using a *slotted spoon*. (If using tongs be careful not to crush the fragile, hot cheese.) Drain on paper towels and serve warm with a dipping bowl of Clare's 1, 2, 3 Magic Meatless Spaghetti Sauce (recipe follows).

1, 2, 3 MAGIC MEATLESS SPAGHETTI SAUCE FROM CANNED TOMATOES

Short on time? Use this quick and easy recipe to make an outstanding fresh-tasting sauce for your pasta or casseroles, one that's far better than jarred sauce from grocery store shelves. This is Clare Cosi's adaptation of the famous Marcella Hazan recipe. (*See page 573 on how Clare adapted the original.) To a can of whole tomatoes, Clare adds 1 medium white onion, 2 cloves of garlic, and 3 tablespoons of butter. This 1, 2, 3 method produces a meatless sauce with sweet tomato flavor, making it a wonderful backdrop for pasta, lasagna, eggplant (or chicken) Parmesan, as well as meatballs and meat loaf. Great spooned on vegetables, too. Try it on: steamed green beans; spaghetti squash; diced and sautéed eggplant; even cooked green peas.

Clare's buying tip: Use San Marzano whole canned tomatoes. These imported

Italian plum tomatoes are the finest in the world, largely for the same reasons that make great wines and coffees (the *terroir*). San Marzano tomatoes are grown in the volcanic ash of Italy's Mount Vesuvius, making them sweeter and more delicious than any other canned tomato you will find!

Makes 2 cups of tomato sauce, enough for one 16-ounce package of pasta.

If doubling sauce, add 15 minutes to cooking time.

1 (28-ounce) can *whole* imported Italian plum tomatoes (for very best results use San Marzano tomatoes!)
1 medium white onion
2 cloves garlic
3 tablespoons butter
Optional additions (not needed, but if you like, you may add): 1/4 cup red wine, 1/8 teaspoon coarse sea salt, 1 teaspoon dried Italian spice mix

Open the can and pour the entire contents — whole tomatoes and all of the liquid — into a saucepan. (If using any of the optional ingredients — red wine, salt, or dried Italian spice mix — stir in now.) Peel the onion, cut it in half, and place it *cut-side down* into the saucepan. (Cut-side down will better release the onion flavors.) Peel the garlic cloves, cut each clove in half, and toss in the pieces. Add the butter and heat the pan's contents until just simmering (*do not boil*). Cook *uncovered,* keeping the pot at a *low but steady simmer* for about 45 minutes. Stir every so often, but be careful not to break up the onion — do your best to keep it whole. The sauce will reduce and thicken while cooking. When finished, remove from heat. Remove the onions and garlic pieces and serve. (Clare suggests eating the onion layers separately as a side dish. They're delicious!) Finally, if the finished sauce appears chunky, use an immersion blender to smooth it out.

Sauce troubleshooting: This sauce should *simmer* and not boil. You must also *stir it.* If those things didn't happen and you boiled your sauce down to an amount below 2 cups, you will need to correct the thickness. This is easily done. Measure the finished amount of sauce. If it's 2 cups, you're good. If it's less than that, add water (or red wine) until the amount reaches 2 cups. Heat the sauce through for 5 to 8 minutes and stir in one more tablespoon of butter. This will correct the error of overreducing the sauce.

Canned tomato tips: As mentioned above, for best results use San Marzano whole canned tomatoes. If you cannot find these, look for canned whole plum tomatoes. *Do not use crushed.* Crushed tomatoes may contain bruised fruit and/or pieces that are not of the best quality. *Also note:* Check the ingredient labels on the cans that you buy: "tomato juice" is okay as an added ingredient, but *not* "tomato puree."

***Note on adaptation:** Clare credits the late Marcella Hazan for this recipe's inspiration. (Marcella calls hers "Tomato Sauce with Onion and Butter.") Ms. Hazan's version starts with less tomato (2 cups fresh or 2 cups of the canned with juices). She also adds more butter (5 tablespoons). When Clare first tried it, she felt the sauce tasted a bit too cloying and unctuous, so she adjusted the recipe to her taste by reducing the butter and increasing the tomato to the entire contents of a 28-ounce can, which is how you'll find most whole canned tomatoes (imported or domestic) sold in the United States. Clare also loves garlic, and she believes it makes the sauce even sweeter while adding a classic note of flavor.

CLARE COSI'S THREE-CHEESE (MEATLESS) BAKED ZITI

Baked Ziti is a well-known Italian American staple as universal as spaghetti and meatballs. Like spaghetti, baked ziti is a casserole dish made with a red tomato-based sauce, along with the pasta, and large amounts of rich (mozzarella), creamy (ricotta), and sharp (Pecorino Romano) cheeses. Many ziti casseroles contain meat — beef, pork, or pork sausage — but Clare prefers to make this meat-free version, and serve it with a side of her "Secret Ingredient" Meatballs (page 576).

Makes 8 servings

1 pound package ziti
1 1/2 pounds whole milk mozzarella, grated
1/2 cup Pecorino Romano, grated
15 ounce container whole milk ricotta
1 extra-large egg, lightly beaten
2 1/2 cups Clare's Magic Sauce (page 570) or your favorite tomato sauce
1 teaspoon olive oil

Step 1 — Prepare the ingredients: Cook the ziti al dente, per package instructions, strain, and rinse under cool water to stop the cooking process. Set aside and continue draining. (The pasta will cook a little longer in the sauce so don't fret if it's a bit chewy.) Now grate the whole milk mozzarella and set aside 1/2 cup. Grate the Pecorino Romano cheese. In a very large mixing bowl, stir together the whole milk ricotta with the lightly beaten egg. Mix in the Pecorino Romano and mozzarella (minus the reserved 1/2 cup).

Step 2 — Assemble the casserole: Add the cooled, cooked ziti into the bowl with the cheeses and toss to combine. There will be lumps of cheese, and that's fine. Now add about half the tomato sauce to the bowl and mix again. Grease a large casserole with the olive oil, and then add half the pasta-cheese mixture. Cover the mixture with half the remaining red sauce. Add another layer of cheesy pasta, and then the rest of the sauce. Top with the remaining 1/2 cup of mozzarella.

Step 3 — Bake and serve: Bake for 20 to 30 minutes in a preheated 375°F oven, until the cheese is melted and the sauce is bubbling. Remove from oven and let stand 10 minutes (to set) before serving.

CLARE COSI'S "SECRET INGREDIENT" MEATBALLS

Meatballs, that's Italian! And like many Italian recipes, there are hundreds (if not thousands) of variations on preparing them. Clare has her own unique take on this traditional dish, using the same secret ingredient and cooking method that her nonna *used when making the meatballs for the customers of her little Italian grocery in Western Pennsylvania. The result is a juicy, delicious meatball that is fluffy and light rather than heavy and dense.*

Like her grandmother, Clare layers the meat with many flavors, producing an aromatic meatball that is far from bland. The flavor and the lightness make them pure pleasure to eat — as Mike Quinn discovered when Clare lovingly made them for him, attempting to provide comfort with this classic comfort food after Quinn's very tough day on the Job.

To get this recipe with a free PDF download and step-by-step photos, visit Cleo Coyle's online coffeehouse at coffeehousemystery.com.

CLARE COSI'S AMERICAN FETTUCCINE ALFREDO

Fettuccine Alfredo was created by Alfredo di Lelio at a humble restaurant in Rome. The original, authentic Italian version contained no cream, just butter and cheese. Di Lelio didn't need cream. Italian butter has a higher butterfat content than its American counterpart. That's why Clare adds heavy cream to her American-style Alfredo, which helps reproduce the rich texture and flavor of the original. The results delighted her good friend, NYPD sergeant Emmanuel Franco, who gave Clare a ride home the night of that fireworks display — literal and figurative, if you count Lieutenant McNulty's temper. Clare cooked up some for Mike Quinn, too, although on that particular night, he was interested in something much hotter . . . and sweeter.

Makes 4 servings

1 pound fettuccine
4 ounces (1 stick) butter
4 cloves garlic, whole
2 cups heavy cream
1/4 teaspoon white pepper
1/4 teaspoon sea salt
1 1/2 cups grated Parmesan cheese

Step 1 — Boil the water: "The sauce waits for the pasta" is a good rule of thumb. So boil the water as you begin preparing the sauce below. Then make the fettuccine according to package directions. Strain the pasta and mix it with your finished sauce.

Step 2 — Make the sauce: Melt the butter in a saucepan over medium heat. Add the whole garlic, cream, pepper, and salt. Bring to a low boil and reduce heat. Gently simmer for 8 minutes. Remove from heat, discard the whole garlic cloves, and slowly add the cheese. Return to the stove over low heat and cook for an additional 2 or 3 minutes, stirring constantly to melt and blend the cheese.

Step 3 — Serve: Add the freshly cooked and drained fettuccine to the pan of sauce and toss gently but well, making sure to coat the pasta well. Heat for 1 or 2 minutes to blend the flavors and give the fettuccine a chance to soak up much of that delicious, creamy sauce! Serve immediately.

Garnishing tip: This dish is delicious as is or try finishing with freshly ground black pepper. For zing, grate on a little lemon zest. For color and flavor, sprinkle on a bit of finely chopped fresh Italian parsley or basil.

CLARE COSI'S SKINNY PUMPKIN ALFREDO

This beautiful pastel orange fettuccine has all the buttery fall flavor of pumpkin ravioli, and the rich and decadent creaminess of regular Alfredo, but with less fat and calories! The pumpkin brings more fiber and vitamins to the pasta party, too.

Clare's culinary tip: When making this recipe, you can use Parmesan, Pecorino Romano, aged Asiago cheese, or a combination of all three. But avoid preshredded cheeses! They contain "nonclumping" agents (e.g., potato starch) that retard the melting process. Buy cheese fresh and shred it yourself. You will be much happier with the results!

Makes 2 servings

8 ounces fresh cooked fettuccine (half of a 1 pound box)
1 tablespoon butter
1/4 teaspoon garlic powder (or 1 clove fresh garlic, minced)
1/2 cup milk
1/2 cup pumpkin puree (use real pumpkin, not pumpkin pie filling)
1/4 teaspoon kosher salt (or 1/8 teaspoon

table salt)

2 ounces Neufchâtel cheese (or low-fat cream cheese)

3/4 cup freshly shredded Parmesan or Pecorino Romano or aged (hard) Asiago cheese (or a combination of all three)

Step 1 — Boil the water: "The sauce waits for the pasta" is a good rule of thumb. So boil the water as you begin preparing the sauce below. Then make the fettuccine according to package directions. Strain the pasta and mix it with your finished sauce.

Step 2 — Make the sauce: Melt the butter in a medium-sized saucepan over medium heat. Add the garlic powder (or minced garlic) and cook and stir for about a minute. Stir in the milk, pumpkin, salt, Neufchâtel or low-fat cream cheese, and *freshly shredded* hard cheese (Parmesan, Pecorino Romano, or aged Asiago or a combo of all three). Stir continually for roughly 3 to 5 minutes, until cheese completely melts and the sauce thickens. Keeping the sauce nice and hot, fold in the drained fettuccine, and coat the noodles well. Serve immediately.

Garnishing tip: This dish is delicious as is

or try finishing with freshly ground black pepper. For zing, grate on a bit of lemon zest. For color and flavor, sprinkle on finely chopped fresh Italian parsley.

MATT'S 21 CLUB–STYLE STEAK WITH CREAMY PEPPERCORN SAUCE

When Matt Allegro realized he and Sophia had inherited a priceless jewel believed lost for sixty years, he speculated there would be a flurry of folks who'd claim ownership. Facing a legal feeding frenzy, Matt went on a foodie one. Going "full carnivore" at the 21 Club, he ordered and devoured this classic steak. This is Matt's version of the recipe.

Makes 2 servings

2 8-to-10-ounce strip steaks, about 1 inch thick
1 teaspoon pink salt or sea salt, coarsely ground
4 teaspoons black peppercorns, coarsely crushed
1 teaspoon ground white pepper, divided
3 tablespoons unsalted butter
3/4 cup beef stock
2 to 3 tablespoons brandy (or cognac)
3/4 cup heavy cream

Step 1 — Prepare the steak: Preheat oven to 200°F. Season the steaks on both sides with the coarse salt, crushed black peppercorns, and half the ground white pepper (1/2 teaspoon). Melt butter in a large sauté pan and add the steaks. Cook over medium heat, 2 to 3 minutes on each side for rare, 3 to 4 minutes per side for medium. Remove steaks and place on a rack over a sheet pan in the preheated oven to keep warm.

Step 2 — Prepare the sauce: Add beef stock to deglaze the sauté pan, scraping all the flavor bits off the bottom of the pan. Reduce the liquid for 4 to 5 minutes over medium-high heat. Add the brandy (or cognac), the heavy cream, and the rest of the white pepper (1/2 teaspoon). Increase heat to high, whisking continually, and cook until sauce thickens enough to coat the back of a spoon, about 5 to 7 minutes. Plate the steaks and top with your peppercorn sauce.

CLARE'S 21 CLUB–STYLE CHICKEN HASH

After finding treasure in an underground vault and a near-dead body in a hidden West Village courtyard, Clare Cosi needed some foodie comfort. She got it at the legendary 21 Club, where she ordered this famous entrée.

In the 1940s and '50s Chicken Hash was the most popular dish at the restaurant, especially with the after-Broadway, late-night crowd. The original recipe was prepared in a heavy béchamel sauce with finely chopped chicken. The modern incarnation has a Mornay (French cheese) sauce and larger chunks of chicken, and it is just as popular as ever. Clare enjoyed the dish so much she came up with her own adaptation. This silky cheese sauce is excellent and delicious over vegetables. Try it over cooked broccoli, cauliflower, or asparagus.

Makes 4 to 6 servings

3 cups chicken stock (fresh or good quality premade)
2 pounds skinless, boneless chicken breasts
1/2 teaspoon coarsely ground sea salt, divided (if using fine or table salt, reduce to 1/4 teaspoon)
1/2 teaspoon white pepper, divided
1 stick (8 tablespoons) high-fat unsalted butter, softened
1/2 cup all-purpose flour
1/3 cup heavy cream
1/4 cup dry sherry (drinking sherry, not cooking sherry)
1/4 cup Gruyère cheese, freshly grated

Step 1 — Prepare the chicken: Bring the chicken stock to boil. Season the breasts with half the salt and pepper and add to the boiling stock. Lower the heat and simmer the chicken breasts for 20 to 25 minutes. Remove the poached chicken and cool. Reserve the stock. Dice the cooked chicken breast into 1-inch pieces.

Step 2 — Prepare sauce: Combine soft butter with the flour, mixing them until you have a soft paste. Return the chicken stock to boil. Whisk in the butter-flour combination 1 tablespoon at a time. Cook for 5 minutes, then add the cream and sherry. Add the rest of the sea salt and white pepper and gently simmer on low heat for 8 more minutes. *Off the heat,* add the cheese and blend well.

Step 3 — Finish the dish: Return pan to heat and add the diced chicken. Cook gently for 5 more minutes or until chicken is hot. Serve over white rice, brown rice, or wild rice. The modern 21 Club serves it over a bed of sautéed spinach. Years ago, patrons enjoyed it over pureed peas. It's also delicious poured over broccoli or cauliflower. Or simply serve it in a rustic fashion — in a shallow bowl with crusty slices of baguettes to sop up the rich cheese sauce. May you eat with joy!

CLARE'S CHICKEN CACCIATORE "HUNTER'S CHICKEN," RED OR WHITE

Historically, chicken cacciatore was a meal prepared by hunters and trackers in the forest from ingredients found in the wild. Rabbit was used as often as poultry. Over the years, cacciatore has become a highly popular Italian (and Italian American) meal. It was even served aboard the original SS Andrea Doria *luxury ocean liner.*

Different regions of Italy prepare cacciatore their own way, with Northern Italians preferring white wine, and Southern Italians Chianti or red wine. The addition of flour and tomatoes is not traditional, but it's become a common way to make it — and it's delicious, so why quibble? Mushrooms are traditional, but are often absent in the Italian American version. Clare's recipe below gives you the option of making red or white cacciatore.

Makes 6 servings

3 chicken breasts, bone in, skin on
4 chicken thighs, bone in, skin on
3 teaspoons coarsely ground sea salt or

kosher salt, divided (if using fine or table salt, reduce by half)

3 teaspoons freshly ground black pepper, divided

1/2 cup all-purpose flour

1/4 cup extra virgin olive oil

3 slices thick-cut bacon (or pancetta) chopped

6 cloves garlic, chopped finely

1 large white onion, chopped

1 red bell pepper, chopped (optional for red version)

3/4 cup dry white wine (or red wine if using tomatoes)

1 28-ounce can diced tomatoes, drained (optional for red version)

1 cup chicken broth

1 1/2 teaspoons dried oregano

1 teaspoon dried rosemary

1 teaspoon dried thyme

1/2 teaspoon sage

1 bay leaf

12 ounces *fresh* mushrooms, chopped

Step 1 — Prepare the chicken: Season chicken with half the salt and pepper and dredge in flour. Add the olive oil to a large skillet or sauté pan over a medium-high heat. When oil is hot, add the chicken to the pan and sauté until brown, about 5 minutes per side. Set chicken aside.

Step 2 — Prepare stock: Add the bacon or pancetta and brown in the oil for about 5 minutes. Add the garlic, onion, and (optional for red version) red bell pepper to the same pan and sauté over medium heat until the aromatics are tender, about 5 minutes. Add the rest of the salt and pepper, the wine (red if using tomatoes), and simmer until reduced by half, about 5 minutes. Add the (optional for red version) tomatoes, broth, oregano, rosemary, thyme, sage, bay leaf, and chopped fresh mushrooms. Return chicken to the pan and turn to coat in the sauce. Bring the sauce to a simmer.

Step 3 — Finish the dish: Continue to simmer over medium-low heat until the chicken is cooked through, about 30 minutes. Remove chicken and boil the sauce about 3 minutes or until thick. Drizzle the sauce over the chicken. You can enjoy this dish many ways. For a rustic version, simply serve it in a bowl with hunks of Italian bread to sop up the delicious sauce. Or you can serve it more formally over a bed of cooked and drained pasta or rice.

MATT'S SOUTHSIDE

Though the 21 Club restaurant menu is cele-
brated, the place began as a speakeasy
where drinks were the main attraction. Aficio-
nados agree that the cocktails are still the
reason to go there. Matt ordered a 21 "South-
side" for Clare on the night they dined to-
gether. A signature drink of the club, the
Southside is a delicious variation on a mint
julep, using gin instead of bourbon. A
"Southern-style" cocktail may seem odd at a
New York club until you consider the entrance,
which more resembles a New Orleans French
Quarter facade. And then, of course, there's
the line of donated iron jockeys that greet you
at the door, including a few wearing stable
colors that have competed in the Kentucky
Derby, where the classic mint julep reigns
supreme. This recipe is Matt's version.

Makes 1 serving

1 ounce simple syrup (or 2 teaspoons
   granulated sugar)
5 mint leaves
2 ounces of quality gin (Beefeater or Tan-
   queray)
1 lemon (juice)
4 to 8 ice cubes
6 to 8 ounces soda water

In a martini shaker, or container with a tight lid, add simple syrup (or sugar) and the mint leaves. Using a muddler (or the back of a spoon) bruise the mint leaves by pressing them to the bottom of the container and twisting. This releases more of the mint flavor. Add the gin, the fresh juice squeezed from 1 lemon, and the ice. Close the container and shake vigorously. Pour the contents, including the mint and ice, into a highball glass and finish by adding the soda water.

THE VILLAGE BLEND'S "SPEAKEASY" IRISH COFFEE

Sometimes you just have to break the law — or bend it a little, as so many elite New Yorkers did at the famous 21 Club during Prohibition. At the Village Blend, Clare's friend Sophia Campana was rocked by double tragedies. First her beloved father was stricken, and then her handsome Viking of a husband was hauled away by the NYPD for attempted murder. Needless to say, Sophia was in a state.

Unlike the new Washington, DC, branch of the Village Blend, Clare's flagship coffeehouse in New York has no license to sell liquor. But assistant manager Tucker is always ready to extend their "friends and family" exemption, and he happily serves Sophia and Clare the complementary ingredients for this warm and soothing Irish coffee.

Makes 2 servings

1 to 2 tablespoons light brown sugar
4 tablespoons Jameson (or your favorite
  Irish whiskey)
Strong, hot coffee (about 1 1/2 cups)
Whipped cream

Get out two large (at least 8-ounce) mugs. Into each mug, spoon 1 tablespoon of light brown sugar (or less, if you don't want that much sweetness). Next stir in 2 tablespoons of whiskey (or more, if you prefer a stronger drink). Now add about 3/4 cup of hot coffee, stirring to mix the flavors, while leaving plenty of space for the finish. Dollop generous layers of whipped cream into both mugs. Irish coffee is traditionally sipped through the cream, so expect a happy hard liquor mustache!

Baileys whipped cream fun: For a special treat, make your own sweet, spiked whipped cream by pouring 1 cup of heavy cream and 2 tablespoons of Baileys Irish Cream into a large metal mixing bowl that has been pre-chilled in the refrigerator. Using an electric mixer, whip the cream and Baileys until stiff peaks hold their shape. This cream can be kept in the refrigerator for 1 day. Be sure to cover the bowl with plastic wrap. (Makes 4 servings.)

BLUEBERRY MATE BAIT
(BLUEBERRY BUCKLE CAKE)

Back in 1954, just two years before the SS Andrea Doria *would sink to the bottom of the Atlantic, a fifteen-year-old Chicago teenager named Renny Powell submitted a blueberry buckle recipe to the "Pillsbury $100,000 Recipe & Baking Contest" (now known as the Pillsbury Bake-Off). Renny's tasty blueberry coffee cake only took second place in the youth division, but this sweet delight — named for its alleged powers in attracting the opposite sex — has been in circulation for over sixty years.*

First published as "Blueberry Boy-Bait" in an early edition of the Pillsbury's Bake-Off Dessert Cook Book, *this cake now has many variations, one of which was used by Clare Cosi's youngest barista, Nancy, to "bait" herself a Superman. The hooking of said man didn't work out as Nancy hoped — although her cake sure did!*

This recipe is slightly adapted from Renny's original with the new name a nod to barista

591

Esther Best, who felt "Mate Bait" was a more fitting title for the sensibilities of the twenty-first century.

1 cup white granulated sugar
1/2 cup light brown sugar
2 1/3 cups all-purpose flour
2 sticks (16 tablespoons) unsalted softened butter
1 cup whole milk
3 large eggs (divided into yolks and whites)
3 teaspoons baking powder
1 teaspoon table salt
1 cup fresh or (unthawed) frozen blueberries, tossed in a bit of all-purpose flour

Step 1 — Begin to create the batter: First preheat your oven to 350°F. Line a 13-by-9-inch baking pan with parchment paper. In a large bowl, whisk together the white and brown sugars with the all-purpose flour. Using a pastry blender or two knives, cut in the *softened* butter and knead the mixture with clean fingers until particles are the size of small peas. Measure out 1 cup of this "crumb" mixture and set it aside to use as the cake's topping.

Step 2 — Finish creating the batter: To the remaining flour, butter, and sugar mixture, measure in the milk, 3 egg yolks, baking powder, and salt. Using your electric mixer on low, beat for 3 minutes. Set aside. Finally, beat 3 egg whites until stiff but not glossy or dry. Fold them gently into the cake batter. (The whites should be fully blended in, but do not mix too much or you'll risk deflating the added lightness of the whipped whites.)

Step 3 — Pour and bake: Spread the batter evenly into the greased and floured pan. Toss the blueberries in a bit of flour (to absorb juice while baking). Spread the flour-coated blueberries on top of the batter and sprinkle the reserved 3/4 cup of the "crumb" mixture on top. Bake at 350°F for 40 to 50 minutes.

Serve squares of this delicious cake to "bait" the "mate" of your choice in one of two different ways: plain as a coffee cake, or topped with whipped cream or ice cream as a special dessert.

From Nancy, Esther, Tucker, Clare,
and everyone at the Village Blend,
we wish you . . .
Happy baiting . . . whoops . . . baking!

ABOUT THE AUTHOR

Cleo Coyle is a pseudonym for Alice Alfonsi, writing in collaboration with her husband, Marc Cerasini. Both are New York Times bestselling authors of the Coffeehouse Mysteries (*Dead to the Last Drop, Once Upon a Grind, Billionaire Blend*) — now celebrating more than ten years in print. As Alice Kimberly, they also write the nationally bestselling Haunted Bookshop Mysteries. Alice has worked as a journalist in Washington, D.C., and New York, and has written popular fiction for adults and children. A former magazine editor, Marc has authored espionage thrillers and nonfiction for adults and children. Alice and Marc are also bestselling media tie-in writers who have penned properties for Lucasfilm, NBC, Fox, Disney, Imagine, and MGM. They live and work in New York City, where they write independently and together.

The employees of Thorndike Press hope you have enjoyed this Large Print book. All our Thorndike, Wheeler, and Kennebec Large Print titles are designed for easy reading, and all our books are made to last. Other Thorndike Press Large Print books are available at your library, through selected bookstores, or directly from us.

For information about titles, please call:
  (800) 223-1244

or visit our Web site at:
  http://gale.cengage.com/thorndike

To share your comments, please write:
  Publisher
  Thorndike Press
  10 Water St., Suite 310
  Waterville, ME 04901